# CHANGEABLE WORLDS

# Deliverance

by Bart King

Published by Changeable Publishing
publishing@changeablepublishing.com
www.changeablepublishing.com

ISBN: 978-0-9571611-0-8 (Paperback)
ISBN: 978-0-9571611-1-5 (Digital)

Cover design by Alexis West

**www.changeableworlds.com**

4

*The author wishes to thank*

Those infernally downstairs
and those sometimes upstairs

His fantastic parents

Fellow software developers

&

Runemagick

Be sure to visit Changeable Worlds online!

# WWW.CHANGEABLEWORLDS.COM

Featuring The Compendium – a vast encyclopaedia to
accompany the series which goes into great detail about
the concepts, people and factions found in the story!

# Preface

What creatures on this planet — both human and otherwise — choose to do in life is something that will forever fascinate. The activities of what one person revels in would be seen as ridiculous to at least one other.

I am no scholar on psychological behaviour, nor am I a student of biology and I can't even begin to explain the intricacies of galaxies. But these sciences, and many others, are topics of great wonder for me. How do things become what they are? Why do they decide on doing so?

These are hard-hitting and complex questions, and the answers to these one will certainly not find among these pages. But I have always found the concepts to be fascinating.

The apple in this field of oranges is another subject that stems from these ideals, especially across history. Religion is a historic and important part of people's lives. It has gone to some length, in all the denominations, to try to explain questions such as before. No-one can really explain why certain events occur or why some choices are made.

It was this unknowing, a void between certain aspects of science, religion and reality that was the inspiration behind creating this story and beyond. The concepts that I have introduced, such as the star of Ramor and her Lightbearers, are my interpretations of those gaps.

Of course, I proudly declare that this is a work of fiction, but reading between the lines, perhaps clues to inspire the reader await.

*In sam kro fom,*
*Bart King*
*February 2012*

8

# Arena of Pri
# Historical Timeline

**First Era — the Shaler Classics period**
~50/1E: Founding of the city of Thoridon.
~55/1E: Creation of the People's Union.
~65-90/1E: Great conflict besieged the Shaler people.
~90/1E: A coordinated effort ended most of the civil war with a great discovery being made.

**Second Era — discovery of the Synth**
~10/2E: Foundation of the Synth Institute.
~15/2E: Construction of the Synth Institute completed. Temple of the Shaler became assembled.
~50/2E: Major discoveries to do with utilising the Synth create a rift between relationships.
~55/2E: Temple of the Shaler renamed to Temple of Ramor.
~80/2E: People's Union and Synth Institute conflict with each other on a larger scale.
~110/2E: Breakthrough in negotiations seeing peace between the two factions.

**Third Era — progression and serenity**
~40/3E: Grandfather to Serenus dies.
~90/3E: Mastery of the Synth is generally believed.
155/3E: Serenus is born.
174/3E: Serenus becomes emperor.
~185/3E: Political descent grows among the people.

11

# Part I: The Third Era
## Year 193/3E

12

# Chapter One

## Creation

Progression and advancement are two concepts that are frequently in the interest of those that wish to prosper. It only takes one person to change the world and there are many that dream to do so. However, perhaps such ideals are detrimental when the lands of Pri are practically idyllic.

People are easily corruptible, either directly or indirectly. There are those that have passion, those that lust for change and those that demand greater power. But in a civilised society, all of these motivations are difficult to attain, all requiring at least a great deal of time and effort.

One way to reach these goals is to do so through a strict routine of education — learn from the masters, adopt ideas to fuel the passion. Maybe one day, it will bloom into a person that can really make a difference, satisfying those requirements and sating the need.

The humanoid society that resides here on this relatively large continent is known as the Shaler. There is a common belief, an appreciation for what is believed to be the almighty provider for everything that is living and beyond — the star of Ramor: the sun central in the planetary system it occupies. Its light and its various energies provide for all, both on and off this world.

Situated in temperate lands, surrounded by rolling hillsides, green pastures and a backdrop of mountain ranges and rivers, the city of Thoridon is home to the centre of this single civilisation. It is a sprawling capital, divided into distinct districts, but central to it all are three major buildings. Built around a large, open cobbled area known as the Quadrangle, these recognisable buildings are central to the life of the Shaler.

# CHANGEABLE WORLDS: Deliverance

With Ramor rising in the east, the Temple of Ramor stands situated on the eastern side of the Quadrangle. It is an octagonal cathedral built from brilliant white stone, with huge arrays of windows adorning each side in order to catch as much light as possible. As the light of the sun is an endearing symbol of their belief, exploiting its potential is seen as critical in enforcing the symbolism.

In the west is the Senate House. The modest but important building is central to the Shaler's system of governance, providing for the people, by the people. The government is divided into two with each division representing distinct responsibilities: the People's Union and the Synth Fellowship. A single figurehead sits at the top to oversee the administration: Emperor Serenus has the ultimate decision.

To the north of the Quadrangle sits a grand university, central to the Shaler's desire for progression and advancement, known as the Synth Institute. It represents all that is wisdom in both the natural and existential — the expression of that knowledge and the empowerment to harness what is known as Synth: an additional energy being delivered by the star of Ramor that absorbs itself into life. Only through method, practise and ritual discovered, devised and implemented by students at the Synth Institute is one able to command this additional power.

One of these students has already passed all of his exams up until now, and is showing incredible aptitude in all the work he does. This student is named Kaidan and is in his final year at the university. His superiors are all delighted with his progress and he is set to head on to advanced study of Synth usage, where only a select few are invited to do so and even less complete the course.

Even though it is custom in Shaler society to perform and be the best with high intellect and respect, even Kaidan has experienced separation from his fellow students. He tends to spend most of his time alone in private study, spending many hours in the Institute's Library, researching from the many thousands of documents written by students over the years.

But he is one person that looks for progression. His final year's work is to complete a thesis about a subject that his peers are not entirely comfortable about him preparing. For a student that has shown so much potential, the topic of exploring opportunities to enhance the potency of Synth energy is an idea that has been attempted by students before him. None were able to provide a reasonable conclusion or any idea about how to do so. Kaidan's work into this field seems to be a waste, but he is not deterred. He knows that it is possible — why else would students in the past have suggested the same idea?

* * *

The Synth Institute extends behind its front entrance from the Quadrangle in the middle of Thoridon. Its campus consists of two buildings with a courtyard central — a carefully crafted stone statue stands there, depicting the magnificence of the Shaler emperor. To the right stands the vast Library, several floors high. It contains the complete history of works written by students and scholars of the past and present. As students are encouraged to perform their own studies, it is here where most spend their time. The other building is the Theatre, providing a small enclosed stage, surrounded by workbenches. It is the main focal point at the Institute for where lectures are held.

It is mid-morning and Kaidan is sat in the Theatre, along with other students sporadically dotted around the benches, each one with paper and pen, taking notes on what Master Conjurer Camaro is speaking about. Camaro is the most senior lecturer at the Institute — he has been a practising Synth user for over thirty years and is instrumental in the known advanced theories of harnessing its use.

His talk today is explaining the mechanics behind one of his personal discoveries in applying Synth energy. One of the main exploits of the Synth energy is its ability to change the natural course of a natural element — essentially, manipulation of fire, water and air, but crucially not the earth. No matter how many attempts the Shaler have made in trying to make this occur, the fixed manifestation of the ground has been unable to be changed — old-fashioned physical work is required instead.

Camaro's discovery was how to bend fire to his will — by his command, he can alter the direction in which fire is spread, entirely by focusing the Synth onto it. One other known property, but not fully understood is that the Synth energy can exist in another dimension, for what the Shaler have dubbed the Synthetic

Domain. Once the energy transmitted by Ramor has been absorbed through a process similar to photosynthesis, this chemical reaction converts it into its purist form and when released, alters the fabric of time and space at an extremely localised point, as commanded by the conjurer that wields it.

But despite what may seem as an extensive knowledge about the Synth, there are two aspects to it that the Shaler are yet to understand. The first is that while they have a name for the Synthetic Domain, they do not know anything more about it, other than being aware of it. The second problem is why the energy exists; why there needs to be an extension to the known natural world. They may have a significant grasp about Synth usage, but its true purpose remains a complete mystery. This question, though, is only a recent one — only the current generation are starting to ask why such a powerful energy can be utilised, answers even the Master Conjurer cannot provide.

Regardless, the older Camaro talks to the several younger students who sit attentively and includes Kaidan. They all thirst for the knowledge that the Master knows, wanting absolute control over their discovered power, even though they are unprepared for the years of study that await after their final year in their initial course.

'In conclusion,' booms Camaro. 'Fire is a natural disaster waiting to happen. But through practise and acute direction of the Synth, one can bend it to his own will. Do take note, however. I do not want to see any of you trying what I have said. You will fail. Fire is more powerful than you will ever be, it is not something trivial.'

The lecturer stands in the centre of the raised rectangular platform that is the stage for the lecture theatre and takes his time to look at the eyes of all the students that listen, a certain lack of trust in his expression, knowing the eagerness of the young. He does so in complete silence, but he stops when he sees someone in the audience that seems unfamiliar.

'You there,' he commands, pointing toward the figure, who sits in a row behind Kaidan. 'Stand up when I'm talking to you!'

The student does so, a little confused about why he is being singled out.

'Tell me: what is one of the most important details about controlling fire?'

Camaro waits for an answer for two reasons: as this is the final year in the course, he has grown to be familiar about the students that regularly attend his lectures, but this one appears to be new. He also wants to make sure that the other students have been paying attention, and asking a relatively intermediate question such as this allows him to gauge the reactions of the others.

Surprisingly, the student stands confident about giving an answer. He has a hood over his face, only revealing his mouth, the reduced light in the theatre casting a shadow over his other features. His name is Toraq and has come to the lecture not to hear what the Master Conjurer has to say — in fact, he is mildly disinterested in his theories — but is eager to speak to one of the students, specifically the one he sits near.

'In order for fire to be accurately controlled, it needs direction toward suitable fuel in order for it to burn and possibly increase its effectiveness.'

'A correct and detailed answer!' congratulates Camaro. He takes a moment to eye Toraq, raising an eyebrow, before telling him to sit down again. The other students have all focused their attention on him as well, slightly suspicious. No one has been able to give such a confident answer after being grilled by the lecturer.

'Tell me, where are your notes?' Camaro questions him, looking at the bench in front of him, seeing no papers.

'I forgot to bring them,' Toraq replies, making up a simple excuse, perhaps not as effective as the answer before. 'I will refer to what Kaidan has after the lecture,' he hesitates.

'Be sure that you do,' says Camaro before redirecting his thoughts back to concluding his discussion.

Kaidan still looks at the invading student. He has never seen him before, and is slightly alarmed by the fact that he knows his name. After Toraq sees he is no longer the centre of attention by anyone else, he subtly leans over his bench toward Kaidan.

'I have information you will want to know,' Toraq whispers to him. 'It is in regard to your thesis. Turn to face the speaker. We shall speak afterwards.'

With that, he reclines back and sits in silence pretending to listen to Camaro's conclusions. Kaidan is a little surprised, but he follows his instruction and turns around. Thoughts race through his mind, wondering if he has spoken to him before, but the face from what he can see seems so unfamiliar.

When the talk has concluded, and all the students leave the Theatre, the last one out is Kaidan, clutching his notes under his arm. This is not unusual: he generally is the last one to leave, spending most of his time alone out of personal choice. He is incredibly keen on learning from the Masters, such as Camaro, and will spend a little extra time editing his notes just to make sure what he has written is correct.

But this time he is a little anxious. There is no immediate sign of Toraq, but Kaidan is curious to learn more about him, especially about what he has to say in regard to his thesis. Should I wait, he thinks to himself. As he gazes at nothing in particular thinking about the situation, he is unaware of Toraq approaching him from behind, still with a hood draped over his face.

'So, you have waited,' he speaks, in a deep voice with a slightly slower than normal tempo. This startles Kaidan who turns around quickly to see the stranger.

'Yes, yes,' replies Kaidan in a fluster. 'What do you want? How do you know my name?'

'I have been watching you for quite some time,' smiles Toraq. 'You are showing great promise. I believe that you are someone who can make history for the people of the Shaler.'

'What? I'm just a loner student, writing about things they don't want me to write about. How can I possibly be of interest to someone?'

'Do you not see? It is because you are doing so means you have the potential to change everything.'

'I don't like what you're saying,' replies Kaidan, hesitantly. 'You speak as if I am Ramor herself. Are you crazy?'

He starts to move away, increasingly convinced that this seems like a bad idea. Making no reaction, Toraq raises his voice slightly.

'Then perhaps you are not interested in knowing the key to unlocking the true power of the Synth?'

A topic close to the heart of Kaidan, he stops, turns around and returns to stand in front of the strange student.

'What secret?'

'This is not the place to discuss such matters,' Toraq says, returning to his normal volume. 'But I am the wielder of certain information that you would be highly interested in.'

'I may be interested, but so far, it's all words. Where's your evidence? I still think you're crazy, and if you can't show me anything, I am walking away.'

Toraq nods. He lifts his arms up to his hood, and pulls it back revealing his entire face. Making no further comment or action, he simply stands there, looking at Kaidan.

At first glance, Kaidan wonders what this notion means — there doesn't seem to be anything out of the ordinary, he just looks like a normal student, appearing to be the same age as him. But just before he is ready to turn around and leave, he spots something that is unique.

Peering closer at the face, his attention is drawn to the eyes of Toraq. There is something entirely unnatural to them — the eyes are like voids, cold black clouds enclosed in the eye whites, swirling around like tornadoes. The swirling seems to intensify the deeper Kaidan looks into them and a shine of purist light becomes clearer.

Becoming shocked, he stands back and Toraq pulls the hood over his face again, seeing the surprise on Kaidan's face, a clear indication that he has seen what he wanted to show.

'What— what is wrong with your eyes?' he asks, stammering.

'There is nothing wrong,' Toraq replies, calmly. 'Perhaps this has shown to you that I may not be who I seem to be. Are you now interested in the information that I have?'

'What do you mean? Are my eyes deceiving me? Am I dreaming?'

'No, this is all very real, I can assure you. For you see, what you refer to as the Synth, its very existence is vital to mine. There are things that you have absolutely no idea about, what your people have discovered is only the start. I am willing to give you a boost, based on purely what I have witnessed from your achievements so far. This is your opportunity.'

Kaidan has heard enough, he wants to know everything now. The intrigue is so great.

'Come,' he says, not giving a second thought to the strangeness of the situation, leading Toraq out of the Institute courtyard.

✳ ✳ ✳ ✳

Where Kaidan leads Toraq is directly to his home, located in the eastern district of Thoridon. His own self-portrait of his independence from everyone is reinforced simply by its appearance. For Kaidan is a man that spends a lot of his time working, considering everything else as less important in his life. It is his single goal to become a highly powerful sorcerer, perhaps to the level of Camaro, and he certainly has the potential to do so.

As such, all of this time doesn't afford much for what he would consider more trivial matters. While the Shaler are people that don't pride themselves with their homestead — they see grand houses to be a waste, even at the high end of society — Kaidan's is still smaller than a home belonging to a typical Shaler family. He lives alone, and left his parents behind in a town west of Thoridon to pursue his dreams of fulfilling a life dedicated to the study of the Synth.

The owner of the modest house hurriedly motions for Toraq to enter, gently closing the wooden front door behind him. Inside, Toraq sees a single room — the windows covered in dust, obscuring the available light. He removes his hood so he can see better, and Kaidan watches as he does so, still not entirely sure about the eyes that he saw.

Toraq looks around and sees a big table central, surrounded by piles of papers and other written materials. Shelves adorn the walls, similarly stacked high with documents. On the table rests Kaidan's thesis, in process of being written as a first draft. Various trinkets are spread around the small area it occupies, along with small tools and dried flowers, all of which would have been used as some kind of basis for his current theories.

'Can I interest you in something to drink?' asks the host, as he watches Toraq glancing all around.

But this question brought on by a degree of nervousness does not entertain his guest. He is far more interested in the progress that Kaidan has been making, if any. Toraq moves up to Kaidan's table and picks up the papers containing the thesis, beginning to thumb through what is written, not making any comment.

Kaidan isn't really sure what to do. He has a relative amount of confidence in the strange student, but doesn't want to intervene in case something untoward occurs. He nervously rubs his hands.

Speed reading the document, Toraq sees that Kaidan is on the right track, but is definitely missing some key information.

Placing the thesis down on the table again, much to the quiet relief of its author, he looks at the objects instead and especially taking an interest in the dried flowers.

'How far have you understood these?' asks Toraq, picking one up.

'Er, they are just a common herb,' replies Kaidan, interrupting his own thoughts. 'They were suggested by a previous student that ingesting them dried was a possible link in providing some indication to the answers I seek.'

His voice trails off as he starts to think about what that student in the past wrote, and begins flicking through piles of papers, trying to find the source material, completely not realising that Toraq is in no way interested, who sighs as if to suggest he should stop and listen.

'It is not the flowers that you should be interested in for that purpose,' he says. 'It is the seeds.'

'Seeds? But those plants do not produce seeds.'

'Indeed, but they are seeds from a different plant — the Urtica plant. Are you familiar with this species?'

'I'm no expert in flora... but forgive me. I still don't know who you are, despite all these dramatic revelations.'

'Who I am is no real concern to you, but if you must know, my name is Toraq. Perhaps I will tell you more in due time and maybe it is time for more demonstration.'

Around his shoulder hangs a small black bag on a single strap, the colour contrasting his white robe. He opens the bag and empties its contents onto the table. Two additional bags fall out, each having a slight blackened sparkle to them, like glitter. Toraq takes one of these bags and undoes the cord holding it closed and pours out the contents; rolling over his thesis, these are pea-sized white balls.

'Urtica seeds which I collected in the forest to the east of Thoridon a few days ago,' explains Toraq. 'This plant is bountiful over there, and easy to find if you know what you are looking for. It is highly poisonous, but it is this toxicity — when extracted from these seeds — that you shall find to be important to your studies.'

'You expect me to believe that some mystical plant seeds are the answer to my questions?'

'You will have to trust me on this matter — I speak the truth.'

'I find this a little hard to believe,' considers Kaidan. 'First, you appear out of nowhere and act like I am the saviour of my people. Then, you suggest what I think is quite a ludicrous idea that pathetic seeds are what I need to see. Oh, and also the fact that they are toxic? Who do you think I am?'

'I think you are a rational person, ready to answer your challenges,' says Toraq, using the same confidence when confronted by Camaro earlier.

'Well, I think you are crazy,' replies Kaidan as he dashes over to the front door, opening it. 'Please leave, I have much work to do.'

Toraq smiles as he replaces his hood.

'Remember what I said,' he says, as he makes his way outside and Kaidan closes the door swiftly behind him. He pauses for a moment. While there is significant doubt in his mind about the proposal, other thoughts battle with his conclusion.

Perhaps he is being a little hasty to dismiss what Toraq was suggesting, even if he can't make any sense from what he said, or indeed, why it should change his original theories. But then, why is such a person so emphatically convinced that he was telling Kaidan the truth? Maybe there is some weight to his suggestions — but no, other students have written before about using particular plants to enhance the Synth potency. But those theories were based on exactly that: specific species of plants, which doesn't mean the answer isn't out there in all variety of plant life. Perhaps these strange Urtica seeds are that answer. It is, at least, a theory to work towards.

These thoughts are enough to convince Kaidan to spur into action. He moves over to his desk and sits down on top of a stool. Picking up one of the seeds, he looks at it intently, even though there is nothing remarkable about it — just a pure white sphere. It is slightly soft to touch, however, and he gently pinches his fingers, observing that the shell of the seed does take some pressure being careful not to apply enough so that the seed would break, just in case Toraq was speaking the truth about its toxicity.

In the corner of his eye, he sees a sparkle from the other glittered bag which Toraq didn't open. Returning the seed to the desk, he picks up the second bag which has a degree of weight to it. Undoing the cord and peering inside, all he can see is some powder. After apprehensively sniffing the contents he doesn't detect any noticeable smell.

Reaching over to the various tools on his desk, he picks up a small plate and empties out some of the powder. It is slightly yellowed and parts of it are clustered together to form small crystallisations, but other than that, like the seeds, seem to be unremarkable.

Kaidan has a brief moment wondering how these two possible items could be connected. He shakes his head — this is nonsense, there is nothing of interest here. Ready to dismiss the whole theory, he remembers what Toraq said as he was leaving and begins to replay in his mind the conversation.

With nothing to lose, he reaches for a mortar and pestle, placing a seed in the bowl and begins to roll it. Even though he was not expecting anything to happen, the core of the seed beneath its shell is finally crushed, and a green liquid starts to flow. An eyebrow raised, he crushes another seed and again more liquid oozes out. As he crushes all of the seeds, the liquid turns into thick oil, deeply green in colour and giving off a displeasing odour. Out of pure curiosity after a moment's hesitation, he takes some of the yellow powder and pours it over the oil. To his amazement, the liquid completely solidifies forming a green sponge-like lump with hints of yellow speckled all around.

While Kaidan is no expert on chemicals, he knows that it is rare for something to completely solidify instantly. Increasing his curiousness, he pokes the spongy lump. It feels soft to touch but solid enough to pick up. The unpleasant odour has also disappeared with the yellow powder acting like a neutraliser.

Recalling more of the conversation, he remembers what Toraq said about the flowers. He said that they were not "for that purpose" — the original idea being that they should be ingested. Was he suggesting now that these seeds were to be eaten? If they were toxic before — and the smell was certainly an indication of that — what if they are still toxic in this strange cake? But the yellow powder did remove the smell; maybe its reaction also changed its noxiousness.

By this stage, Kaidan doesn't know what to think. There are too many questions, too many uncertainties, and this is all happening too fast. He starts to think that this whole meeting with Toraq was a huge error. Then he remembers what his lecturers all say, that his thesis' subject has already been disproved so many times before in the past. They are all fully convinced that there is no way to enhance the potency of the Synth. All of his current efforts are going to be shown as futile and he will fail his final year and never progress into advanced study. He is wasting his life. It is all for nothing.

'Why do you torment me so?' he roars at the green sponge in an outburst.

His state of mind utterly spun out of control, on impulse he takes his chances and picks off a piece of the lump and stuffs it into his mouth as a final answer for its purpose. As he begins to chew, its taste starts off to be incredibly unpleasant, but as more saliva begins to react, the taste changes and he finds himself unable to stop chewing, increasingly enjoying whatever he is consuming.

With the taste wearing off after a while, he swallows and sits in silence for a moment. His eyes dart around in front of him erratically and a thousand thoughts still deafen him inside his mind. He takes another piece of the green, yellow-speckled cake, not experiencing the vileness of the first time but also less of an enjoyable flavour. Nevertheless, he still swallows and he finds himself taking a bigger piece, each mouthful having less of an interesting taste every time.

But there is something about the foodstuff — Kaidan isn't sure what it is, but the noises in his mind have quelled and all increasingly say that he should find more after eating it all. Whatever it was, he was now exhibiting signs of addiction even though he is unable to recognise it.

He stands up from the stool, slightly dizzy. His stomach feels like it is fighting against what he has eaten, his heart rate has accelerated and the movement from the stool has an effect of a blood rush. Entirely unsure about what has occurred, he opens the door to the outside with a lot of unnecessary force, causing it to slam into the wall with a crash. The noise jolts him as he wasn't expecting the door to open so violently.

'Where am I going?' he says to himself. 'I need to be working on... on... my work. Yes, but what was it all about?'

Confused, he steps outside into the evening, the brightness of Ramor pouring horizontally through the gaps of each of the houses on the other side of the path. Raising a hand and squinting to obscure the brilliant light, he staggers away from his home, leaving the door open, not really sure of his next intentions.

26

# Chapter Two

# Elixir

The city of Thoridon is generally peaceful. There are no known outside threats, the people are incandescent to each other with no sense of serious rivalry or warfare ever crossing their minds. For there is no reason for this attitude, as they live in idyllic lands with plentiful resources and only their own dreams and goals to keep them occupied.

But there are the doubters, the ones that aren't entirely sure. For them it is all too perfect — borderline artificial — and they have cause for concern that there is something else, but entirely unable to prove or even dare to suggest such radical ideas. One such secret doubter is the most senior person — Emperor Serenus.

He would never reveal his thoughts to anyone except himself. He doesn't really know why he has these thoughts, but every once in a while he has a moment of recall, dwelling on the possibility that everything has an ulterior motive.

It is now that Serenus has such a thought, sitting in the large throne that is central to the Senate House. The throne is lavish with a tall wooden back, gemmed and sequined with various colours, positioned on a raised platform. Surrounding this are benches aligned in rising tiers like a stadium, all filled with dignitaries, appointed officials and general members of each of the groups that they all belong.

The benches are divided into two, the division making a clear cut line between the separate organisations that have the right. To the left of Serenus sit the People's Union — a socialist group that represents their members who have no interest in learning about the Synth or its science. They are the builders, engineers, woodworkers, blacksmiths, architects and traders, central to everything in the daily life of the Shaler. It was the Union that constructed the Institute, the Temple of Ramor and the Senate House itself, all incredible demonstrations of their talents.

On the emperor's right is the second dominant Shaler organisation — the Synth Fellowship. This is the embodiment of graduated students and lecturers which seek to give advice to government about anything relating to the education of the people, especially when it comes to dealing with Synth energy. They are more liberal than the Union, and will approach matters from the perspective of all, instead of only caring for their own interests.

Serenus is oblivious to the current debate as he daydreams about the possibility that everything is a fraud. He has no reason to his thinking and he stares out into the many windows that adorn the walls, east and west, gazing into the sky. A certain thought about whether the world as he knows it is all entirely make-believe, looking into the clouds wondering if they are behind everything. Perhaps there is something behind the clouds themselves that he cannot see, maybe a sophisticated being in control of everything.

'Are you even listening to my plea, Emperor?'

These words are spoken by the most senior representative of the People's Union, President Ikis. He is quite a forceful speaker; the way he delivers his speeches is with incredible volume — almost dramatic or righteous — but are generally rather long and it can be easy for someone like Serenus to drift away.

'Just give me the brief version,' Serenus replies, mentally coming back down to his throne. It is as almost as if he doesn't really care for what is being said anyway.

'This is exactly what I'm trying to say. No-one outside of the Union takes any interest in our own personal endeavours, but when we work towards making others interests reality they are more likely to respond! It is double-standards — and even our own Emperor seems to exhibit precisely the same attitude!'

Applause rises from his own benches with definitive nodding in agreement. Serenus is less than impressed and just sighs deeply when the encouragement dies down.

'But I thought we had already agreed to your plans to expand the construction of the Union Hall. There is plenty of land on the western side of the city. I don't see why we have to sit here when there is no cause for disagreement.'

The Union Hall has been a great source of contention in the Senate ever since the suggestion was put forward a few years ago. Due to their own political stance and secretive nature, having a self-contained building for the Union troubles those who are not involved. A certain amount of distrust has always existed towards the Union, mostly because of its size, with the member count being in the thousands. Compared to the Synth Fellowship – whose numbers are less than two-hundred – scepticism is rife about their ultimate intentions.

With this new proposal of an additional building, the Union Hall would become twice the size of the Synth Institute in area and there are fears that such a project would divide the Shaler into two, with such an organisation obtaining incredible control and influence. But the Union itself doesn't see this argument, for they are only interested in what is best for their members and in providing the tools, such as a grand venue, for those members to flourish.

'What do you make of all this, Nazar?' asks the emperor, directing to the right-hand benches.

Conjurer Nazar is the current representative for the Fellowship. The group switches who speaks in any Senate session for they don't believe in having a single person directing their organisation. It is only the various lecturers at the Institute that have the honour of representing the Synth at governmental level.

'It really isn't any of our concern,' Nazar says. 'The Union can do whatever it wants as far as I see it.'

'Thank you, Nazar,' says Ikis. 'What an unusually direct answer for a change. Is that the matter settled then, Emperor?'

'I presume so, unless you have plans to change whatever you are doing next time we convene?'

'What do you mean by that?' asks Ikis.

'Nothing,' replies the emperor, mincing his words. 'Forget I said anything. Is there any other business before I end this session?'

He looks in the direction of the People's Union and their president sits down. Finally looking over towards the Synth Fellowship, raising an eyebrow, he pauses momentarily. Satisfied that there is nothing, he starts formally dismissing the Senate.

'Well, there is one matter,' stands Nazar, interrupting the emperor before he finishes the formality, met with grumbles from the Union benches. 'Although, I don't know if it is any interest to the Senate.'

'The fact that you have stood suggests otherwise,' replies Serenus.

'Perhaps... Master Conjurer Camaro spoke of a stranger in lectures today. He apparently was able to express great knowledge about the use of the Synth, yet no-one knew who he was. I was wondering if the Union knew anything.'

'What are you implying, Nazar?' shouts Ikis, clearly angry about being accused of something.

'Nothing, but do you not agree that it is a little bizarre?'

'It seems to me, emperor, that the Fellowship has no idea about its own members!'

'Silence!' booms Serenus as more grumbles make themselves heard from the Union benches. 'What sort of stranger, Nazar?'

'I don't know, emperor. You would have to speak with Camaro since it was during his lecture.'

Serenus takes great interest in this development, mostly because it is something different for a change – something so radical that it may support his thoughts about there being something else.

'I may do that after we have adjourned. Now, can I finally close this session?'

He rises from his throne and resumes dismissing the Senate. Nazar and Ikis make eye contact across the room, with the Union president not entirely happy about such a public accusation from the other side.

* * * *

Slumped in an alleyway still in the eastern residential area of Thoridon, Kaidan groans after his experience with the strange green and yellow cake that he ingested. While he has all the symptoms of being ill, it is a curious state that he feels. He is no physician and has no real idea of his condition, but the cake did seem to be poisonous.

His mind is a jumble of questions still. The experience seems to be fruitless — promised to him by that stranger calling himself Toraq that it would enhance his perception towards utilising the Synth. But he feels no different in that regard, especially since he is unable to concentrate, let alone able to specifically manipulate the power.

'What am I doing? This is crazy,' he says to himself, alone in the alleyway as the setting of Ramor completes and darkness begins to encroach. He tries to stand up but his body disagrees and feeling nauseous he returns to the floor.

A figure turns the corner at the nearest end to the alley. Kaidan blinks erratically, trying to focus on whoever comes closer towards him.

'There you are,' says the deep, unwelcome voice of Toraq. 'I was wondering where you had gone.'

Kaidan recognises the voice, despite not being able to see the detail of the stranger and starts to reel back in fear.

'You!' he grunts. 'You stay away from me.'

'Why would I do that?' Toraq questions, maliciously. 'You seem to be excelling quite well.'

Kaidan starts to take offence to what he suggests.

'What do you mean by that? Is this all some kind of wicked trick to you?'

'Not at all, but you could see this as an experiment. So far, this is working out as expected.'

'An experiment? You've drugged me into this... this...'

His voice trails off as the anger boils up inside him, but in doing so just makes him feel even more unwell.

'I have done no such thing,' iterates Toraq, who extends a hand towards Kaidan looking to make him stand. 'I merely provided the materials, and you acted upon your own volition.'

Grunting, Kaidan sees the outstretched hand, grabs it and is pulled up onto his own two feet once again.

'But I am pleased that you did,' smiles Toraq, his eyes still hidden behind a cowl. 'For you see, this is only the beginning. There is much work to be done and great benefits wait for you.'

He removes his cowl so he can get a better look at his experiment. Nodding to himself with a sly chuckle, he is satisfied with the results so far.

'What is the yellow powder?' asks Kaidan, still groggy.

'Ah, the mysterious ingredient? That is something I had to obtain from lands far down to the south that your kind have yet to explore in detail.'

He stops himself from saying any more, revealing slightly more information than he wanted to at the moment. Kaidan looks at him still trying to focus through a series of blinking.

'The south? The deserts? The Sulphur Deserts?'

'Indeed,' nods Toraq who reaches into a pocket and takes out a vial containing a clear liquid. Undoing the lid, he moves it in the direction of Kaidan, who is reluctant at first, but the sickness takes hold once again making him stop. Taking the chance, Toraq waves the vial underneath Kaidan's nose — smelling salts have an incredible reaction on him and his grogginess miraculously disappears. Now able to stand still and focus properly on the stranger, he gives Toraq a scalding look.

'What have you done to me?'

'You wanted to see if it was possible to enhance your control of the Synth. But what I have enabled you to do is enhance yourself. You do not need that energy. You have so much potential in yourself to be much better. You are the perfect candidate to receive my assistance.'

'That's not what I asked!' shouts Kaidan, becoming increasingly hostile. His voice is one that starts to threaten and this is entirely uncharacteristic of the quiet, gentle student usually left on his own.

'I shall tell you more in due time,' says Toraq. 'But this is only the beginning.'

'I feel as if I should hit you,' replies Kaidan and his fists start to clench.

'But you do not know who I am, and I would strongly advise against doing so. Come — we need to leave the city and gather more Urtica seeds to increase your capability.'

Toraq moves to the end of the alleyway, but turns around as he sees Kaidan standing there.

'Why?' grunts Kaidan back.

'Because you need more of the recipe do you not?'

Kaidan takes a moment. He realises he is starting to perspire and seems to have muscular spasms. Toraq is right — he needs, he craves, he wants more of what has transformed into a drug. The stranger smiles as he sees his subject move towards him and the two leave the city via the eastern road into the night.

* * * *

With twilight disappearing, this is the usual time when those that have strenuously dedicated themselves to the energies provided by Ramor turn to worship the almighty and infinitely powerful star. This incredible loyalty to it is represented fully in the enormity and grandeur provided by the Temple of Ramor.

The entire building is designed to exploit light, using white stone and countless windows, all perfectly aligned to capture as many sunbeams as possible throughout the day. The distinct use of white stone, the irregular octagonal ground floor and the conic roof are key design features. It is also a shining beacon central to the city; a symbol for all that the Shaler represent.

Inside, it has similar qualities to a cathedral. On the eastern and western walls are benches and pews; a lectern is positioned near the rear wall facing inward and a curious glass column stands central. From the floor up to the flat ceiling above, the square column glimmers. With a square hole in the roof above it, the hole tunnels all the way to the peak of the cone roof. A multi-sided crystal is affixed at the top, designed to capture the light from the sky, refracting it around the maze of prisms and mirrors inside the tunnel, leading down to the glass column.

The lectern is where the High Priest of the Temple delivers his sermon for the congregation, who the Temple refers to collectively as the Acolytes. It is decorated with a golden, perfect sphere at its front that symbolises Ramor. Behind the lectern is a sizable gap between itself and the wall, which has a large old door in the centre leading to stairs and up to the second floor above.

In the gap stands a row of white-cloaked priests with each robe having an insignia of the golden sphere neatly stitched in to the fabric. Each one either holds a set of chimes which create a soothing, high-pitched sound when they are waved, or a small bell with the intention of keeping a rhythmic tempo in accompaniment.

The organisation of the Temple itself is a mental refuge for those in Shaler society who cannot meet the rigid requirements of either the Synth Institute or the People's Union. If one cannot bring talent or have any interest in pursuing a career in Synth studies, or cannot demonstrate aptitude in engineering, commerce or labour, the Temple is their last chance at proving themselves. It takes a different class of person to become a member of the priesthood — they are the councillors of government and the general populous, the glue in-between holding the civilisation together, philosophers for a generation and the future.

As such it is one of their purposes to chronicle history with the second floor of the Temple a permanent archive of all of those records. Many thousands of hand-written parchments line the shelves, some hundreds of years old, recounting important — and not so important — events and advancements made by the Shaler. The masters of documentation; some of these writings are so greatly admired, they are chosen to be part of a special, holy book — The Twilight Compendium. It is this collection of passages and texts that sits open at a specific page on the lectern, where High Priest Rais stands, looking around at the congregation.

They all sit in the two sets of benches on both the eastern and western walls in silence, almost transfixed by the jingling soft tones created by the priests behind their superior. It is this moment where they can contemplate their accomplishments and desires in self-contained thought and near tranquillity.

Rais raises an eyebrow as he notices two unusual guests in the benches: that of Emperor Serenus in the west and Master Conjurer Camaro in the east. Regardless of affiliation or organisation, the Shaler know their place in the presence of the priesthood with the Temple becoming neutral ground for all. But to Rais, the presence of either someone who has no interest in respect for Ramor or another that is far more interested in exploiting the energies rather than worshipping them, it seems a little strange.

The priests ease their music as Rais wishes to deliver his sermon while twilight is beginning to fade. When silence descends, the congregation stand and face the central glass column, bowing their heads in unison as it sparkles from all angles in a ritualistic acknowledgement to Ramor and the infinite light.

'Acolytes of Ramor,' he announces, raising his arms aloft. 'For it is now that we celebrate the conclusion of the great Ramor's cycle; for it is her that provides all with the incredible gift of life. We are all in her infinite admiration and the demonstrations that she provides in front of us at this moment is testament to this appreciation.'

Lowering his arms, he directs the attention of the Acolytes towards the glass pillar. Recognising the conclusion of the opening dedication, the Acolytes raise their heads and watch as the lights and energies of the twilight, captured by the elaborate centrepiece, dance around inside the enclosure providing an entrancing display. The priesthood behind Rais play a short melody with an extremely slow tempo to emphasise the light show.

When the music stops, the audience sits down in the benches most feeling spiritually rejuvenated by the experience. But it is the non-believers that do not have the same attitude — those of Serenus and Camaro. Despite their elevated status among commoners, they are just like the rest in the environment of the Temple. As they sit down, they notice each other and make eye contact across the floor. Serenus gently nods towards the Master Conjurer; Camaro with a raised eyebrow upon recognising the gesture nods back to the Emperor.

'I would like to read a passage from the Twilight Compendium for today's conclusion,' Rais says. 'May it provide the Acolytes with wisdom and repose.'

Pausing for effect, he places both arms onto the top of the lectern and provides a dominating stance as he reads from the pages. The passage he has chosen was written more than one-hundred years ago, around the time when the Temple was formalising itself as the organisation it is now.

"The rise to power is important, where the one, the individual, makes the decisions to last a lifetime and beyond. It is this decision, this change in the way we live our lives; by dedicating ourselves tirelessly to the one true power that gives us the will to achieve our own personal goals and to aid others. It is Ramor, the ultimate power, embodied within the Temple and its priesthood that will light the way for the Shaler people."

"This incredible evolving life that we possess is paramount to our existence, but it can also be our undoing. Where advancement and progression are desired, it is change that provides the opportunity. But change is also incredible power. With the Temple as one that accommodates and encourages, we are proud to be representatives of Ramor, for all to enjoy."

Rais stands back after finishing reading.

'Ramor is with all of you. This is the message.'

Stepping down from the lectern, he retreats into the door behind him which leads to the stairs, as is ordinary procedure. The priesthood begin to walk forward and stand waiting in front of the central pillar ready to take questions from the Acolytes, provide advice or just converse with the people in an informal capacity.

Serenus approaches Camaro who waits at the exit, acknowledging those that recognise him either through his celebrity status or because they have been students at the Institute. The two powerful figures retreat away from the door, out of earshot from anyone else.

'I assume you wanted to speak to me, emperor,' Camaro begins, both of them speaking in low voices.

'I don't know, do I?' questions Serenus. 'In the Senate earlier it was mentioned that you may have something interesting to tell me, for a change.'

'Indeed I may. I had the most curious engagement inside the Theatre earlier. There was a student, who I had never seen before, yet he was seemingly proficient in the ways of the Synth.'

'So, someone took an interest in the Synth and learnt about it themselves? How does this interest me?'

Camaro sighs sharply.

'As stubborn as always, Serenus. I know all my students, past and present, yet this one... He was just a stranger to me and possessing knowledge about work I had done in the past. It was as if he didn't belong in the room.'

Serenus looks at him with a slight realisation on his face waiting for the words he wants to hear. It is almost a story that is fitting with his daydreams.

'I don't even think he was in the room,' Camaro hesitates. 'There was something about him. I just couldn't tell. What am I saying? This is all madness.'

'So who was he, then?'

'I have no idea, but he seemed to have an affiliation with that other student... what was his name? Oh yes, Kaidan. They were sitting together.'

'And this Kaidan knows the mysterious student, you say? Who is he?'

'I'm only telling you what I saw, emperor. I don't know what my students do outside of the Institute. But Kaidan is a loner; he has no family that I'm aware about, living alone and studying. He excels at his studies, but there is concern among the Conjurers that he is throwing it all away with his ridiculous thesis.'

'I'm unsure what you are suggesting, Camaro, but from what you describe, something seems a little suspicious.'

'Really?' startles the Master Conjurer. 'Suspicious? How so?'

'I intend to find out,' replies Serenus. 'Think of it as a personal interest.'

Not really sure why the emperor is jumping to strange conclusions, Camaro is not in a position to question. Without saying anything further, he bows his head and scurries out of the now emptied Temple leaving the emperor alone with his thoughts.

He turns and gazes at the glass column in the centre. With darkness fully encompassing the sky, it stands dulled, except for reflected orange glimmers from lit torches around the walls of the building. Wondering who this mysterious stranger could be, he has wild thoughts that entertain his dreams about a higher being; one that knows all the secrets to everything and ultimate power.

Leaving the Temple himself, he decides to observe the student referred to as Kaidan for he may know more than is led to be believed. Finally, something interesting, Serenus thinks.

✱ ✱ ✱ ✱

Out towards the eastern side of the city is a straight roadway that leads directly into an enormous forest. The journey to this forest is unencumbered, but the views to the north, across the Flatlands, provide breath-taking vistas of the jagged, snow-covered peaks interspersed with bright white plateaus. These mountain ranges, known as Iskap, stand tall and proud and provide a critical source to the entire world — it is the primary origin for fresh, pure water with vast waterfalls cascading down the ranges and leading to wide and plentiful rivers.

It is one river — the main artery known as Still travels north to south — that all life depends upon and an infinite source of uncontaminated vitality providing lush landscapes up and down its length, with a smaller tributary delivering its water to Thoridon itself. The river of Still leads directly through the western side of the forest called Mistwood.

The forest gets its name appropriately, as the spray generated by the animated river showers the forest repeatedly; gentle winds and the tall trees provide an enclosed environment, allowing for the water droplets to collect and create an eerie, misty area. As such, the forest is plentiful with all kinds of flora: not just wood. In parts there are even hidden repositories of crystallisations, formed by bonding elements in the earth, creating spectacular — and well sought after — treasures that some in Shaler society prize.

With a starlit sky above, it is other treasures that two unlikely companions seek inside the enormous forest. Toraq leads the way, and knows exactly where he is going and what he is looking for. Kaidan follows behind, but a few paces back, his walking more haggard and laboured. Even though he is a young man, he is not exercised and stamina is what he lacks. But despite this, he has made the journey following the stranger; not because he wants to, his drive is fuelled by the changes his body seems to be taking.

Trawling through Mistwood increases the clamminess he unconsciously notices, with the water droplets in the air merging with his increasing sweat as if his body is trying to resist the fever he has developed. Rippling of the river makes itself heard as the pair moves through the forest litter and around exposed tree roots and low shrubs.

'I need to drink,' Kaidan remarks. 'The river. It sounds so delicious.'

'But we have almost reached where we need to go,' Toraq replies.

Kaidan stops in his tracks as he realises that the stranger seems to have different priorities.

'I need to drink!' he shouts, almost in a tantrum.

The outburst makes Toraq reconsider — it is important to him that his test subject survives regardless of the exhibiting condition. Thinking to himself, it would be expected that there would be some increased hostility over time and he turns around to face Kaidan.

'Fine,' he retorts, and changes his direction towards the nearby river, disappearing behind a tall bush as he pushes his way through it.

Kaidan follows him arriving at the river's bank. He falls to his knees in great admiration at the water, cupping his hands, scooping up as much as he can hold and pours it into his mouth, water splashing over his face from the eagerness. The cool water has a refreshing feel against his skin.

After repeated gulps, he stands again and faces his guide.

'Can we continue?' questions Toraq, perturbed at the diversion and starts to move back to the original path.

'Wait,' says Kaidan with Toraq halting his movement. 'My stomach has settled. I feel a lot less burdened now. But, I have so many questions and you have refused to tell me what is going on and who you really are.'

'I would really like to continue before dawn,' Toraq replies. 'But I suppose now would be a time to afford you with some answers especially as we are all alone.'

'Tell me,' Kaidan starts, hardly giving Toraq time to finish speaking. 'Before, in the alleyway, you said something which struck me. Your exact words were "your kind". What did you mean by that?'

'Ah, so you were paying attention,' Toraq summarises, a grin on his face. He takes a step towards the river and stands at its edge, taking a moment to listen to the water rippling over the tree roots in the bed.

'I have always favoured practicalities. Words can only mean so much, but backing them up with action provides much more of a clearer message.'

Outstretching both arms in parallel, Toraq begins to speak under his breath. What he says is not of normal Shaler tongue, but in the language of his own kind. In appearance, he seems to be a Shaler, but the eyes which Kaidan witnessed before are the difference. For the swirling vortexes are Toraq's own life essence — a visible manifestation of his actual self; the body that he occupies was a Shaler student in the past, but whoever that student was no longer exists, at least in a mental state.

Toraq is an ethereal being, one of many that reside in the existential environment that is overlaid with the physical world — what the Shaler refer to as the Synthetic Domain, an invisible conduit that allows the power of the Synth itself to be utilised, altering localised time and space at the control of the user. But Toraq, and the rest of his kind, refer to themselves as something that would translate into the name of "Lightbearer". Ramor is the star central to the galaxy and also the creator of her children of the Synthetic: they bear a unique quality, derived from the energies of Ramor, manifesting itself as light as seen in the eyes of the mortal body they possess.

'What are you doing?' asks Kaidan as he watches Toraq.

As Toraq repeats the same words over and over, the water in the river begins to slow. As the speed reduces further, it starts to freeze with a thin layer of ice forming — but crucially the ice only forms over part of the river that is aligned between his arms; the water on either side appears to flow normally.

Kaidan watches with open mouth at the extremely unnatural occurrence that presents itself before him. Based on this demonstration, he is now entirely unsure what to make of the stranger. In all the years he has been studying at the Synth Institute such a conjuration has never been discussed, let alone demonstrated.

'Do you see?' questions Toraq. 'Have I shown you enough?'

After getting no response, he drops his arms down and the water that seems to rush through the ice breaks the frozen layer and it is carried down the river, melting back into the water itself.

'I don't know what I just witnessed,' Kaidan replies cautiously. 'The words you spoke... They sound familiar to me as a student of the Synth, but I couldn't make any sense of them.'

'You recognise my vocalised representation of the language that is native to me. It is the language of the Ethereal, and your kind — the Shaler, an Ethereal word — was given to you by parties I am not going to reveal.'

Kaidan just stands and stares at Toraq.

'Really, who are you?'

'I do not think you would understand. For you see as I explained before, there is much more at stake than what you think. More than your kind could ever attempt to comprehend.'

It all becomes too much for the Shaler student. He has been incredibly tolerant so far, but the riddles that Toraq keeps revealing boil up inside his mind, coupled with extraordinary experiences he seems to be manifesting with the eating of the green cake.

The quiet, self-contained Kaidan begins to explode in a fit of physical violence. He rushes towards Toraq without really knowing what he is doing or what he is going to do, propelled by anger. A wry smile on his face, Toraq moves out of the way and stands behind a tree. Its thick trunk, high branches and slightly silver bark provide enough to separate the two from contact.

But this is all part of the test by Toraq — he is growing Kaidan into someone else and blinding him with obscure details has provoked a reaction he was hoping to achieve. Still in a blind rage and under the darkness, Kaidan practically doesn't see the tree blocking his path and crashes into it. Dazed slightly, he bounces back a few steps — what would normally be enough to bring on a concussion seems to merely delay him. Shaking off the surprise, this time he outstretches his arms towards the trunk while Toraq takes a few steps back.

The force is so great, the tree uproots as Kaidan roars like a strong beast, and it falls to the ground with Kaidan losing his balance under shear disbelief, following the tree onto the forest litter. Breathing heavily, collapsed in a heap, his eyes are wide open as shock begins to set in.

'What an excellent display,' Toraq cheers, almost in applause. 'You are proving to be quite the excellent student.'

He waits for a moment, but sees that Kaidan doesn't move. Approaching him he outstretches a hand, a gesture to encourage him to stand.

'What's happening to me?' asks Kaidan, shuddering on the ground with eyes still wide open. He reaches for the hand and is pulled up onto his feet.

'Come,' assures Toraq, moving away to return to their original path.

After a short while, the two discover what Toraq was looking for. In a natural clearing inside the forest, a shallow trench naturally occurs in the ground created by engorging tree roots. But it is rich with a particular plant — the Urtica. Its leaves are long with sharp needles covering the edges, but they sag to the sides exposing the prize that Toraq seeks. A white stork grows vertically from the centre of the plant covered in massive clusters of round white seeds.

The Urtica only grows on slopes so when the seeds separate from the stork they roll down and away, creating curved lines of the species all around the clearing. Some have large red flowers all over in preparation for seed production, but most have already developed their seedlings — and are ripe for the taking for the intrepid travellers.

Toraq swings into action taking a large, folded bag from a pocket and starts collecting all the seeds. He pulls on the storks and the seeds effortlessly disconnect. In a short space of time, he collects hundreds of them as Kaidan looks on.

'These will be enough to continue,' Toraq says as he pulls a cord to close what is now a sizable sack, all the Urtica plants behind stripped bare of seeds. He retraces his steps and moves back in a direction towards the roadway, making a gesture encouraging the silent Kaidan to follow.

# Chapter Three

# Cult

With only a short time before dawn, Kaidan arrives back at his modest home in Thoridon. Extremely tired from the late night excursion into Mistwood with Toraq, he staggers up to the front door. Still open from when he left, he almost falls into it out of exhaustion, but manages to slam it closed behind him as he crashes onto the stone floor.

Clutching in his grasp is the sack of Urtica seeds given to him by Toraq as they approached the city. Toraq himself took the liberty to leave the young student, disappearing into the night in a northerly direction. He made no comment to Kaidan about his intentions, not giving any advice about how to proceed in his experiment.

Although, such advice would prove to be unnecessary: still surprised by what occurred in the forest — either Toraq's incredible command of the Synth, or his own improving physicality — it is this surprise that is changing his own perception of himself. At first, he was scared and concerned for his own well-being. All the craziness still didn't make any sense when he thought about the situation in a rational way, but the events in Mistwood have turned him. Rationality itself seems crazy now.

He picks himself off the floor as the mild craving for more of the Urtica cake advertises itself to him. Slumping on his stool, he reaches for the mortar and pestle, scoops out the shells of crushed seeds from before, takes a handful from the sack and repeats the procedure. With the mixture of the yellowed powder and the poisonous liquid forming more of the solidified foodstuff, he chews on it and swallows without any of the prior concern.

But then the stomach starts turning and he remembers how the water of the river quelled this sickly feeling. Leaving the stool, he moves to a sideboard and picks up a jug and eagerly consumes part of its contents. It has a repeated effect as in the forest, and he smiles, sating his lust for the curious compound. Tiredness now gets the better of him and he slumps down onto a makeshift bed, falling asleep as his muscles spasm, surrounded by towers of papers containing research notes and essays into the possible enhancement of the Synth.

Throughout the night, he tosses and turns in his sleep, going from cold sweats to completely drying out, and at times wakening for a short moment as if in pain before dozing off again. Dreams vary recalling previous times in his life: the high moments such as admiration and acclaim for excellent results in exams, the happy farewells from his parents as he left them to start at the Institute; the lower moments, including being taunted by the younger children in his home town for being intelligent; and the criticisms by Conjurers about his direction.

One dream makes itself prominent — a scene from when he was a young boy, neatly tucked up in bed with his loving mother at his side. She sits on a wooden chair clutching a single piece of paper and reads a bedtime story to her son. The story itself is titled "Beware the Daimons", and is a short, scary tale told to all Shaler children. It tells of a time when a group of Shaler came under attack from a strange beast, like a bear with rugged hair and walking on two feet, breathing fire from an enormous head, and commanding great winds from its humanoid hands. The villagers are terrorised by the Daimon day and night, and no-one can explain why it attacks or where it came from.

Eventually the villagers in the story trap the beast in a cave with a large boulder. The howls of the beast haunt the village for days until one day they fall silent. But the villagers all begin to start acting strange, driven mad by the nightmarish screams, eventually turning on themselves until there are only a few left. As the mutilated bodies litter the village, the beast returns and gorges on the rotting corpses — but the dead reawaken after being touched by the beast: a legion of risen returned to terrorise the remaining few.

It is after this recalling of the story that Kaidan awakens. He turns to look out the window and sees it is bright daylight outside.

Startled by this revelation, he realises he has overslept and has likely missed lectures at the Institute, something he doesn't normally do. But despite this, feels indifferent rather than anxious to return to school.

Standing, he takes off his cloth clothes, scrabbling around looking for slightly more presentable ones. In this frenzy of movement, he catches a glimpse of his naked body in a dusty mirror. His physique seems slightly different and he moves closer, fanning the dust away from the reflective surface. Upon closer inspection his skin is starting to pigment with the same colour yellow of the powder used in combination with the Urtica seeds.

Slightly shocked, he tries scratching at the spots on his chest but they do not redden or seem to want to be removed. As a last resort, he attempts to squeeze them but they remain — the yellow powder has fixated itself to his skin. Despite his initial desperation to remove these blotches his opinion changes erratically again, no longer caring and returns to finding some clothes.

Once he has dressed he immediately begins to create more of the green cake without even thinking about it, drinking more water after eating, deciding to make this his only source of nourishment from now on, convinced that the organic food is an excellent supplement based on his impressions in the mirror. He wants to be whatever he is becoming.

But then a moment – spotting his thesis on the desk, he sits down at the stool and picks it up, thumbing through the pages. Thoughts in his mind warp as he reads the countless sentences written down, skimming over specifics and eventually feigning an interest in his own hard work. His attitude to his long essay changes: he no longer cares about it.

In a burst of energy he throws the papers to the side, not bothered that they fall into an unordered mess on the floor. Taking new paper, Kaidan decides to write down his current thoughts, specifically recounting his encounters with Toraq. As he recalls, he thinks about various new ideas, drawing on inspiration from his newly claimed teacher and his own recent experiences.

"This is a new beginning," he begins to write. "These are the words of the revelation, the birth of true power. Everything that represents the known energies of the Synth is a falsity, and there is nothing more great than the observations and declarations that are to be presented on these pages."

"It has been shown that what is known to be is not the whole truth. There is a greater power among us, one that flirts with our own desires and toys with us constantly. This power, the domination, subverts us and everything known to all. This is what we should be putting our trust within, not the trivialities of the Synth."

He stops writing and re-reads his opening lines. In the forest, Toraq never entirely revealed everything to him so he needs to personify what he is writing about.

"The Daimon lives, even though he is dead and he walks with us, watching us every waking moment. It is impossible to resist him, for he knows the truth and who he chooses to share the knowledge with are the ones worthy to receive it."

Continuing to write for several more pages he documents his experiences with Toraq, including instructions about how to create the Urtica cake. Although he is unclear exactly what effects it has upon him, he is happy to write what he expects it to be — a gift of excellent physical power.

Coming to an end, he realises that what he is writing is extremely doctrinal. The more he thinks about his work, the more he is convinced. He must entrust himself to Toraq for greater things are bound to come to fruition. But a doctrine is useless without others to support it. Loosely binding his papers together, he writes a title upon it: The Book of the Daimons. He quickly stuffs his mortar and pestle, some Urtica seeds and the pouch of yellow sulphuric power into a shoulder bag and clutching his new book under arm, bursts outside and heads in the direction of the Institute.

However, he is not alone. As he moves towards the Quadrangle, several paces behind him, he is tailed by a shadowy figure, keen to keep a close eye on where Kaidan is going. It is not Toraq but someone working under the employ of Emperor Serenus, tasked with following the student and reporting to the emperor about his movements.

As Kaidan approaches the entrance to the Institute, the scout disappears into the crowds of shoppers at the afternoon market provided by the People's Union making himself invisible. A gut feeling makes Kaidan turn around just as he arrives at the main gate, but seeing nothing out of the ordinary he continues inside.

# CHANGEABLE WORLDS: Deliverance

* * * *

Milling around the outside of the Theatre inside the boundaries of the Institute, there are groups of students waiting for their next lectures. Under the warm sunlight, they discuss their studies, theories or just general social chatter to pass the time.

Looking slightly haggard, Kaidan observes the scene. With his doctrine under arm and keen interest to propagate his new master's gift, he starts to approach a group of students minding their own business.

'Hello,' he starts, interrupting their conversations.

'What do you want?' questions one of them, having no interest in him and certainly not recognising who he is.

'Have you ever considered the possibility that this is all a lie?'

His question is met with laughter.

'A lie?' replies another of the group. 'What do you mean by "all this"?'

'Everything,' Kaidan says sharply, waving his arms around to emphasise his point. 'Where we stand. What you are learning. Who we are!'

Receiving a severe frown from the group, one of them sniffs the air.

'And I suppose that awful smell coming from you is a lie as well?'

Seeing that his tactics aren't having the desired effect, Kaidan walks away from the laughing students and after trying with several other groups and getting scalding replies, he starts to get extremely agitated by all the negativity. Moving over to the central statue of the emperor in the courtyard, using his new found strength, he propels himself up by grabbing onto the statue and hangs off with one arm.

'How can you deny the truth that I speak?' he yells around the courtyard, his voice reverberating. 'For I have seen all that is responsible for everything and I am willing to introduce you all to the true wonders of the world.'

His plea is met with a cold silence. The students just stare back at him, with none wanting to make any kind of protest other than the silent despise.

Dropping down from the statue, now convinced that these so-called intelligent students are blinded from his suggestions, unable to change their perceptions he marches proudly out of the courtyard and returns to the Quadrangle. As he does so, the groups of students resume their previous conversations, thankful that the crazy has decided to leave.

With frustration written all over his face, he starts to doubt if the Institute is the idyllic haven of super intelligence that it promotes itself as. Turning around to look at the place where he once had his heart and mind set on as being the ultimate achievement, thoughts of content and ineptitude rebound.

'How was I even thinking that the Institute was the answer to everything?'

He speaks out loud to no-one in particular, just reinforcing his thoughts into a definitive statement. But even though the words were not directed at anyone, this doesn't mean that no-one was listening: he receives a tap on his shoulder from a person of no particular significance.

'How long did it take you to figure that out?' asks a slightly gruff female voice.

Spinning around suddenly to wonder who is questioning, Kaidan gives the woman a look up and down. She is dressed in dirty clothes, but has an unusual, orange-gemmed necklace. Her hair is dark brown, long and slightly curled and similar height to Kaidan whom she looks at straight in the eye.

'I suppose... about twenty years,' Kaidan cautiously replies.

'Come with me,' she says, smiling. 'You will probably want to meet my friends.'

With a playful giggle, the anonymous woman dashes off into the crowd in a westerly direction, through tall arches and into a wide street, the entry point to the commercial and production area of Thoridon; the home of the People's Union.

The Quadrangle is the central hub of the city, being the prime location for trade, surrounded by the buildings that are paramount to Shaler life; the manufacturing, engineering and food production vocations represent most of the people. The acts of commerce and the skilled workings are perhaps the real Shaler achievements, as demonstrated with the construction of the Temple, the Institute and the Senate House.

As Kaidan follows the woman, she leads him down streets with straight, perfectly constructed rows of buildings, most with opened fronts and awnings to allow for traders to hawk their wares. But going further down the street forks into two and central is a construction site, piled high with scaffold and various carved stones, sands and woods distributed around. This is the location of the Union Hall, the soon-to-be hub for everything related to the day-to-day business of the People's Union.

The woman stops in front of the site and turns to Kaidan who catches up, always being a few paces behind.

'This is my travesty compared to your Synth Institute,' she says to him, pointing. 'It represents everything that is wrong about the Union, everything that I disagree with.'

'I don't know anything about the Union,' replies Kaidan. 'Why are you talking to me? Why should I care?'

'It's not just me that shares the same view,' she says.

From behind her, a more dedicated member of the Union approaches. His facial expression suggests he has little respect for the woman.

'Come to convince others of your wrongdoing have you?' says the stern worker, who was ordering the gathered materials as part of the in-progress construction.

'My wrongdoing?' she snaps at the worker. 'You do realise what the Union is becoming?'

'Of course, why else do you think I'm building this glorious hall?'

'There is nothing glorious about what President Ikis has planned! He is going to be responsible for the failure of society as we know it.'

The worker gets increasingly more hostile towards the woman and before the clearly differing opinions begin to get out of hand, Kaidan interjects and suggests to the woman that they should move on. She agrees, but not before spitting in the worker's face, and marches away with Kaidan following on behind.

✽ ✽ ✽ ✽

Following a back alley, the two arrive at a blackened door which has no handle and is heavily painted. The area around is fairly untidy. A single illuminating torch is burning a dull orange next to the door, and it shimmers across the necklace of the woman.

She knocks six times and the door opens from behind. A man in his twenties pulls the door and is dressed in a black robe. Inside, the room is small and incredibly dusty with a single table in the centre and an assortment of chairs positioned around it. There are no windows and it is relatively dark compared to the bright sunlight of outside with a single candle burning on the table. Another robed man sits at the table, with the level of blackness on each robe varying due to their quality. He looks attentively as Kaidan and the woman enter.

'Come, sit down,' the woman says as the man closes the door. 'We have much to discuss.'

'Who are you?' asks Kaidan.

'Indeed, I am sure you are wondering by now. My name is Gregoria,' the woman says. 'As a group we are known as Dis, a small organisation that opposes everything that the Union has become.'

She points over towards the man who opened the door.

'This is Xarash, the original member of the group who first discovered his contempt for the Union after his opinions were always ignored.'

'Ikis never listens to anyone,' Xarash says. 'He is always thinking for himself, under the guise of the Union. He is tearing the organisation apart from the Shaler — as if he wants to be emperor himself.'

Kaidan isn't really sure what to make of the situation. The environment and the people that gaze at him with a hint of hope in their eyes clearly want something from him. His stomach starts to feel a little unsettled as the craving for the Urtica cake makes itself known, but this spurs on the suggestion that the assembled could be suitable targets for his doctrine. They do seem to be fairly suggestible, at least.

'I don't really care for your cause,' he replies after a short hesitation.

Gregoria moves over towards Kaidan and takes his free hand.

'But we are looking for a true leader,' she says, darting eyes between his doctrine and his own. 'You seem to have the qualities that we need to make our cause heard.'

'Oh, I see,' Kaidan replies. 'But how can I lead if I have no interest?'

'But from what you were saying before, you appear to have no interest in anything anymore. Why not help us and lead an uprising against the oppressive president?'

'Because you are not aware of the full situation,' says Kaidan as he moves towards the table in the centre of the room. He slams his doctrine — the Book of the Daimons — down along with the bag containing the mortar and pestle and the ingredients. Standing over the table, he turns to face Xarash and Gregoria who still stand at the door.

'My book is my purpose. For you see, the Union, the Institute and even the Senate are trivial compared to what I have witnessed. So far, I am entirely disinterested in your cause, but perhaps I can introduce you to ideals that are the real truth.'

Emptying the contents of the bag on the table, the man who sits at it — named Sagar — is a little surprised, but slightly impressed at the determination of the stranger.

'I am Kaidan, and I am aware of unnatural occurrences that have been present in this world for ages. I have been shown secrets that all would desire, but no-one at the Institute would acknowledge what I had to say. But in order for you to understand, I need you to take part in an experiment — a demonstration, a testament to my own cause.'

Placing some Urtica seeds into the bowl, he begins to crush them with the green poisonous liquid oozing out. As he mixes the two ingredients, the strange smell makes itself present and the three members of Dis revere at the odour, but their attention is restored as they see the liquid solidify when the powder is applied.

'This may not be all that appealing, but it is necessary to understand,' Kaidan summarises as he eats a piece of the cake and takes his time to chew before swallowing. He smiles at the assembled, as if to will them on to follow his lead, like the leader they crave.

'What is the meaning of all this?' questions Sagar, who is the oldest in the room.

'This will enhance your perceptions and yourself to truly understand,' says Kaidan to him, pointing at the green foodstuff.

Sagar stands up from his chair and chuckles to himself, looking Kaidan squarely in the eyes.

'What do you take me for?' Sagar protests. 'If I eat this... drug... I'm sure it will "enhance" me to the state of a vegetable!'

He turns to Xarash and Gregoria.

'You can't be taking this man seriously? I thought the purpose of this meeting was to recruit more to our real cause; to put an end to Ikis's tyrannical rule of the Union?'

Gregoria leafs though the Book of the Daimons, reading the hastily scribbled texts, but actually paying more attention to it than Sagar.

'That is our intention,' she says. 'But do you not see what Kaidan here is proposing?'

'Yes, I do,' replies Sagar. 'I fear it would put an end to everything because Ikis will become unopposed. You would be in a different place!'

'But based on what I'm reading here, we could physically stop the Union.'

'What? Just listen to yourself, Gregoria. The only way to stop the Union is to lobby them and protest. I thought that was what we were going to do?'

'Maybe,' she says. 'But if Kaidan here is to lead us, we should follow his suggestions.'

'Are you serious? I no longer want any part of this,' Sagar says, moving to the door. 'I will go find others that want to see real change.' He slams the door behind him disturbing the thick dust that covers the floor.

Xarash doesn't really care about what Sagar said and seems to be merely fascinated with Kaidan so far. Being the impressionable type, he has no qualm with the proposal and takes a piece of the Urtica cake, following the lead of Kaidan and begins to chew on it. However, unlike Kaidan's initial reaction, Xarash has no issue with the taste and does not have any complaint, almost enjoying it, even taking another piece to reinforce his commitment. Within moments, his muscles start to twinge and all the familiar effects start to take hold, without the suffering.

'How do you feel?' questions Kaidan, with Gregoria looking at Xarash.

'How am I supposed to feel? It feels like something inside me is rattling around. Is that right?'

'You are on your way to enlightenment,' confirms Kaidan. 'What about you, Gregoria?'

Slightly hesitant, she isn't entirely sure, taking in Sagar's comments. But based on what she has briefly read and also the simple fact that she is slightly attracted to Kaidan with his improving physique, she gives in and samples the cake as well. In almost a repeat performance of Xarash's reaction, she too suffers no ill effects.

Kaidan sits down at the table and the other two do the same and he begins to explain the encounter with Toraq, who Kaidan believes is the Daimon in the children's story, detailing his impressive power and control over the river. Also, how he believes the mutation effect created by the Urtica cake was the secret to understanding Toraq's abilities and eventually emulating them.

They talk throughout the night, discussing their own philosophies, struggles with the Union and even their childhood, all the while consuming more and more of the cake. Eventually tiredness gets the best of them and they collapse in their seats, falling asleep, and suffering the same reactions as Kaidan the night before as the mutations and drugged effect continue to manifest themselves.

54

# Chapter Four

# Birth

Two weeks pass and Dis has grown into something more popular. The original ideal of revolting against the totalitarian People's Union now taking a much lower priority to their cause; it is the discovery of the Urtica cake that has given a sense of purpose to the common Union member.

Gregoria lured more to the group with her charming smile and suggestive playfulness, with grand promises and almost devious methods, preying on any weakness she could find. Her efforts have paid off with the numbers recruited to the group increased to twenty, all addicted to the Urtica, some showing similar symptoms to Kaidan, others not.

Each of the new recruits have also been introduced to the Book of the Daimons and its theories, with Kaidan adding more to it over time, documenting the habits of the recruits against the Urtica. Xarash has also been inspired to write for the Book, but rather than taking a slightly scientific approach opted to flesh out the doctrine, playing to fantasies of being a little militaristic using strong language and rhetoric.

The small, dusty room has been transformed into something that resembles a drug den, with all of the recruits hardly stepping outside, but all talking with each other, developing the ideals and suggestions made in both the Book and by Kaidan and Xarash socially.

But to Gregoria, there is only so much that can be discussed. While the males are locked heavily into discussions about their own transformations and theories, she easily grows tired. As she is also going under the same mutations, her opinion is to just wait and see what happens rather than endlessly talking about it. The yellow spots have made themselves apparent to her, but most on her face are masked by her long hair, allowing her to frolic in the city without being negatively singled out.

Despite her best efforts, those movements have not gone unnoticed to a trained eye. Emperor Serenus' scout has been observing despite their original target of Kaidan not making much of an appearance in public lately. But the late nights, unusual disturbances down the narrow passageway and her apparent recruiting tactics around the city sparked suspicion, with Gregoria being blissfully unaware of the unwanted attention she receives.

Master Conjurer Camaro has also grown increasingly suspicious, noticing that Kaidan has not been to lectures since he brought up Toraq's appearance in the Theatre to the emperor. With no local family to liaise, while not concerning himself principally with the situation, he occasionally thinks about Kaidan's disappearance. It is not something that is publicly known, but his fellow students at the Institute have been starting to question his whereabouts with Camaro being reluctant to entertain them with answers.

Toraq himself has not been entirely absent wanting to keep a close eye on his experiment. He is pleased that Kaidan has resulted into someone that has blossomed, taking the affliction to heart and relishing the situation. The experiment, through indirect social engineering, has transferred itself to others and Toraq quietly waits for it to erupt into what he desires — destruction of the Shaler, at least partially. For this is Toraq's game as a Lightbearer — he needs to attain his result in order to succeed.

The living bomb in this experiment, Kaidan, has developed into a physically strong person; the constant muscular spasms resulting in dramatically increased strength and stamina. But he finds himself less desiring the Urtica — his body becoming immune to its effects. Despite this, it does not undo what he has become, retaining the mutations and other benefits. Even though Xarash and Gregoria started after Kaidan, they too are experiencing the same symptoms, no longer wanting to take in the Urtica.

During an afternoon, Gregoria decides to join Kaidan who sits in the corner of the darkened base of operations, trying to write more of his observations. His hands have inflated in size due to the muscular mutations, and he finds it increasingly more frustrating to hold the pen, making his handwriting deteriorate.

Amid a backdrop of muffled agonising groans from recruits, coupled with deep conversation and preparation of more Urtica, Gregoria looks around as she sits next to Kaidan, making sure that she isn't being watched. One of the reasons she approached Kaidan initially was his good looks, which were further enhanced from the early effects of the Urtica. She is an attention seeker and conspires against anyone so she can manipulate them to giving her the satisfaction she craves, especially from the opposite sex. Kaidan has certain qualities above the good looks — despite the blotches created by the mutations — such as leadership skills and enjoying control of a situation. But Xarash is also a man that stands out to her as he displays similar traits. Kaidan is a little taller, however, and she prefers this over Xarash: but it is purely a sexual attraction.

Watching Kaidan scribble away, crossing out words as he makes mistakes through his fumbling hands, Gregoria finally cannot contain herself any longer. With the Urtica flowing through her veins, her strength increased and her intelligence slightly diminished, almost giddy in euphoria she places her similarly inflated hand on Kaidan's leg and rubs up towards his groin.

'I want to fuck you raw,' she whispers in his ear, drawing out the final words with a smile on her face, followed by her characteristic and slightly cheeky chuckle. The use of harsh language has become another quirk in normal speech, something members of the Dis organisation would use sparingly before.

For Kaidan has also changed via the use of Urtica — before, he was quiet, kept himself to himself, hardly acknowledging anyone else around him, continuously focused on his studies. But it is not just physicality that changes via its use — mentally it returns the person to a more primal instinct, with dreams and desires reverting from knowledge to natural compulsion.

The pen falters in his hand, falling to the table and he turns to look at Gregoria; her orange necklace catching the reduced light as he moves. Since the changes, he finds himself also becoming attracted to her and feels emotions he has never experienced before. The two subtly embrace in the darkness initially before pausing and the full desire makes itself apparent. Becoming locked in each other's arms, passionate kissing takes over, with Gregoria starting to grope at Kaidan more aggressively.

A quality that is entirely missing from this encounter is love. Gregoria is not interested in love, she only wants power and sex, and the Urtica has accelerated these urges heavily. With Kaidan's emotions running wild, he also starts to become more physical. Passions rise to boiling point and the pair collapse off their chairs onto the dirty floor and items of clothing start to be shed.

All of this action suddenly makes itself apparent to the rest of the enclosed room and conversations start to fade. In among the recruits is Xarash, discussing his war-like proposals. His ideals are driven from a hatred of the People's Union and all that it stands for, and the Urtica has turned him into someone who would prefer all out violence against them, instead of lobbying and protests, perhaps inspiring something more primal inside of him.

Unlike Kaidan, Xarash does have genuine affection for Gregoria. It was Xarash that fell in love with her the moment they teamed up to form Dis. But, trying to be more of a gentleman (and maybe being a little foolish) decided to keep these feelings from her, realising that she may not necessarily share the same view — until now. Seeing the two partially naked on the floor, and Gregoria trying extremely hard to encourage Kaidan to copulate, Xarash's love decides to make itself burst into a fit of rage. It would seem the full effect of the Urtica has made itself apparent.

Xarash dashes up to Kaidan and utilising his new found strength, lifts him off Gregoria by his arm which pulls Kaidan on to his feet. Gregoria, who was starting to approach climax, becomes shocked by Xarash's actions and she retreats back to her seat, retrieving pieces of clothing to cover herself. But this initial reaction wanes as she sees the undressed Kaidan — his skin covered in yellow dots — dropping any gathered clothing to the floor once again, and smiles at both of them.

'What the fuck do you think you are doing?' Xarash yells at Kaidan, who moves to retrieve undergarments to cover him.

'I could ask you the same thing,' Kaidan replies, forcefully. 'What I do is entirely my own business! How dare you interrupt!'

Xarash laughs, as the entire room is focused on the two.

'You expect me to take orders from you?'

'Well, I came here to lead originally.'

'Lead? You haven't led us anywhere yet. The only thing you have taken charge of so far is Gregoria!'

Kaidan narrows his brow as he starts to see what this is all about.

'So what if that's the case?' he questions. 'We are merely waiting for everyone to be as developed as us in the stages of Urtica ingestion. When that is done — and only then — we will make ourselves known.'

'I am done waiting!' Xarash booms. 'And it seems you can't wait to get your hands all over her!'

He points towards Gregoria who smiles and claps excitedly, enjoying this little battle of words, with Xarash looking over the shoulder of Kaidan to see the delight on her face. It is Xarash that really wants her, and he will not let anyone stand in his way. She looks so happy, so pleased that the two men are fighting over her — at least that is what Xarash thinks. The rage starts to boil in him once again and he returns his attention to Kaidan. Looking at his eyes, he starts to shake. His fists start to clench.

'I am sorry,' he says to him almost in a whisper, crippled by a wave of emotions. 'My blood... It is in a rage. I cannot fight it anymore!'

He then grabs Kaidan by the shoulders and propels him around, pushing him back into the blackened door with such a force, Kaidan crashes through the woodwork into the outside. In doing so, the room is flooded with daylight — the silhouette of Xarash disappearing through the bright light.

* * * *

Bleeding slightly on his back from the force of the impact on the wooden door, Kaidan sees what Xarash has become. Even though he is wounded, his large frame and strength prevent it from being an issue. Instead, Kaidan can feel his own blood pumping heavily. It is an unusual sensation, feeling like tiny splinters flowing freely around his body — just being conscious to it increases his anger, knowing he can't do anything about it.

This anger is fully directed at Xarash who stands watching him pick himself up from the ground. The pair stand hunched with large shoulders, breathing heavily, and lock eye contact for a moment. The true power of the Urtica-induced affliction makes itself known to them — it is to fight that they now strive.

Kaidan and Xarash exchange smiles as they realise this and laugh at each other.

'Do you feel that?' asks Kaidan, seeming to relish the moment.

'Yes,' nods Xarash. 'I feel exhilarated! I feel the blood and rage coursing through my veins.'

'The Bloodrage...'

With the effect officially named, Kaidan makes the first push to settle the conflict. Charging forward towards Xarash, the two wrestle, thundering around the narrow alleyway and crashing into buildings alongside – rolling between the walls, they eventually spill out onto the main trading road and the site of the Union Hall, still under construction.

This would be the first time that they have been seen in public, especially during normal trading hours. The great hulking towers of brawn are a huge surprise to the Shaler people, and upon seeing the tussling start to panic, some fleeing the streets.

Eventually the two unlock from each other's grip and stand opposed with more people retreating. Serenus' scout recognises the facial likeness of Kaidan and is aghast to see what he has become. Panicking himself, but curious as to where they came from, he retreats towards the alleyway and disappears down it, without being noticed.

As the two Dis members look at each other, still breathing heavily, Kaidan starts to scratch himself frantically as the unusual sensation in his veins makes itself apparent again.

'I can't fight it,' he says, becoming increasingly frustrated.

'I don't want to fight it,' Xarash replies, threateningly.

'What are we fighting about, anyway?' asks Kaidan, losing grip on reality, still scratching all over.

'You were trying to fuck my woman! Are you losing your mind?'

With the Bloodrage still running through his veins, Xarash moves over to the construction site of the Union Hall. The workers have all fled in terror — the building itself has its outside walls erected and a partial roof. Quite tall and occupying a lot of space, once finished, it would be a spectacle of a building.

Its interior, with its open space and little in the way of obstacle makes for a perfect arena. The recruits of Dis have all followed their leaders to the Union Hall to watch along with

Gregoria who has replaced some clothing for the venture outside. She makes her presence unquestionably known, cheering at the sight of the two.

Xarash has already restarted the fight by throwing small chunks of brick at Kaidan, which simply bounce off his chunky frame, acting as a way to provoke a reaction. But Kaidan seems to be more and more confused the longer the effects of the Bloodrage last. His vision seems to cloud over and he stumbles over his own feet, losing balance as he tries to focus.

'What's the matter, Kaidan?' shouts Xarash, his wicked voice echoing around the hollow building. 'Are you too fucking weak? Can you not bear any more torment?'

In a random burst of energy Kaidan roars loudly, and despite his adverse reactions charges head first into Xarash, both flying across the floor. The collision results into a large force, a testament to Kaidan's developed strength and Xarash is dazed by it. Shaking the blow to the chest off, he rises to his feet once again.

'Come on Kaidan!' cheers Gregoria. 'Kill him! Rip his fucking limbs off!'

Her extravagant cries have her desired, manipulative effect. While Kaidan to her was merely a bit of fun, she does actually have real feelings for Xarash. This display of grotesque combat is proof that Xarash's affection is genuine, and if she seemingly supports Kaidan, she hopes to confirm this based on Xarash's reaction.

He doesn't disappoint — hearing her encouragement, he turns to face her for a brief moment, narrowing his eyes. She smiles back at him, her orange necklace sparkling and she nods to him. Xarash returns the smile, and returns his attention to Kaidan, who clambers to his feet once again unaware.

Before Kaidan recovers fully, Xarash spots the ultimate weapon to end the fight – shimmering in the daylight and resting on a work surface, an in-progress metal cutting: the insignia of the People's Union. It has not been painted, but it would become the centrepiece of the interior. He takes it from the bench without a second thought and rallies towards Kaidan.

Always dreaming to exhibit a warmongering role, but never having either the opportunity — because the Shaler have no reason to be at war with each other — or the capacity to be a warrior, the power given to him by the Urtica has unlocked this potential.

Talking about his ideas with the Dis recruits, seeing the support that he was attaining, it seems that being a warrior was his calling — especially one that could lead.

'You call yourself a leader,' yells Xarash as he rushes towards the stumbling Kaidan, who cannot stabilise himself. The perfectly cut shape of a metallic hexagram, with its flat edges coupled with the pointed angles, would seem to make it the perfect weapon. Xarash thrusts the jagged metal insignia towards the muscled neck of Kaidan — the force is so great, it cuts right through his flesh. His body crashes to the floor, bouncing on the recently laid stone floor with a dull thud; slightly yellowed blood oozes out of the corpse, landing on its back.

Instead of being repulsed, the members of Dis applaud and roar in gratification at the macabre scene — both because it symbolises blood spilt over the People's Union itself, and the elimination of what could have been a pathetic leader, even if he didn't get a complete chance to prove himself.

Xarash roars in celebration with his brethren and thrusts the insignia into Kaidan's body, blood erupting out of his pierced chest — the hexagram standing upright, its polished metal shining in the daylight. Still charged from the battle, he moves over towards Gregoria who stands smiling and applauding. Unexpectedly, Xarash outstretches a hand and slaps her right across the face, scolding as he does so. He hits her with some force and knocks her back slightly and she is surprised at the reaction. Despite her face being visibly sore from the attack, she raises her head after recovering and smiles back at him as if to suggest she enjoyed it.

Locking her arms around his shoulders, they embrace extremely passionately — all the tension between them relieves itself, as well as her sexual lust for Xarash. After a few moments, he suddenly releases himself from her grasp before they get too involved, smiling at Gregoria with a wicked grin.

'Will you be my queen?' he says to her.

Gregoria isn't entirely sure what to make of the suggestion — there is no royalty in Shaler society, and such a concept is initially foreign to her. But, everything seems to have been a dream lately.

'I will,' she smiles, her cheek now visibly reddened. 'King Xarash...'

Embracing once more, this time both of them being more engaged with each other, they are unaware of what approaches. The

Dis recruits turn around to look past the shell that is the walls of the Union Hall to watch the arrivals.

* * * *

Emperor Serenus, led by his scout, accompanied by President Ikis, Master Conjurer Camaro and a dozen post-graduate students from the Institute wait at the front of the building. A crowd of normal Shaler, from the Union, the Institute and the Temple surround them.

'What is going on in there?' queries Ikis after hearing suggestive, reverberated noises coming from inside, concerned that his precious building has been damaged.

'I don't know, but I intend to find out,' says Serenus as he starts to move towards its entrance. As he enters, he sees Xarash, Gregoria and the recruits.

'In the name of Ramor!' he exclaims, horrified to see the muscular, mutated Shaler and also at the pool of blood surrounding the Union's fabricated mantle. 'I have never seen such barbarity!'

Ikis and Camaro follow behind him; both are equally shocked and disturbed by what they see. Once the recruits see the Union president, they take a step back riled by his presence.

But Xarash and Gregoria — now in a state of undress — are blissfully unaware of the presence of the top-end of society. It is only by chance that Xarash looks up, and in the corner of his eye sees the most important Shaler standing aghast.

To Gregoria's disappointment — denied what she desires once again — Xarash stands up and moves towards the Emperor, recognising Ikis at his side and sneers at him as he approaches. Serenus isn't sure what to make of the situation as he looks from toe to head of the approaching partially naked hulk.

The emperor starts to speak, ready to question what is going on, but before he can finish uttering the first word Xarash stands in front of him. His heavily mutated and yellow-spotted body becomes focal to Serenus and he simply becomes lost for words.

'Do not try to understand,' Xarash says in a low voice. 'You have been blissfully unaware of the situation the whole time in this cesspit that you call a city.'

Ikis barges up in front of the emperor and Xarash growls as he does so.

'You have soiled my Union!' he outbursts. 'This is utterly disgusting!'

'Disgusting?' chuckles Xarash. 'Your organisation is what is "disgusting". You are the sole reason for its corrupt, underhanded and deceitful practises. It should be your blood on the floor.'

'How dare you speak to me like that!' Ikis protests. 'Do you know how much power I have in this city?'

'Of course I do, you fucking pathetic worm! We are only a few of those that despise the Union, your direction and what you are planning. This building you are constructing — well, others are constructing for you — represents everything that you stand for. It is now officially defiled.'

Gregoria approaches from behind as a feeble Ikis lashes out at Xarash in contempt, but his weak blows provoke no reaction and cause no damage. He may have the speech, but he doesn't have the strength to back it up.

'Is the worm bothering you, my king?' she playfully questions, stroking at his chest.

'King?' says Serenus. 'Who are you?'

Before Xarash can answer, a shrill wail rises from behind as Camaro discovers that the body on the floor is Kaidan.

'One of my finest students!' Camaro cries.

'Kaidan was one of your finest?' asks Xarash, surprised. 'He was a student at the Institute?'

Kaidan never really discussed what he did before the discovery of the Urtica and Xarash didn't care to find out. He smirks as he hears this news.

'Well, that explains a few things,' Xarash comments and Gregoria giggles.

'Answer me!' shouts Serenus, getting more frustrated at the situation with not enough fact being presented.

'We are the Kaidis,' reveals Xarash directly to the emperor. 'We once called this place home, but it seems we have outlived our stay.'

He turns to the recruits.

'Come, it is time to leave Thoridon,' he commands. 'There is nothing for us here anymore.'

With that, and with no chance for further discussion, Xarash walks forward directly into Ikis who is knocked onto his back. The recruits take the opportunity to walk over him, and he yells out as various feet trample him. As the Kaidis walk outside, they are greeted by gasps of surprise from the various crowds, with many moving out of their way as they move towards the Quadrangle.

They quicken their pace the closer they reach the centre of Thoridon; many burst into wicked laughter as they do so, becoming anarchists and terrorising the streets and stalls in the Quadrangle, ransacking goods and destroying anything that might be related to the Union. With the Quadrangle left in nearly complete disarray, they depart south and march towards the southern perimeter.

'You just let them go?' Camaro questions to the emperor, anger in his voice.

But Serenus is in one of his daydreams. He is quietly fascinated by Xarash and his subordinates — just where did they come from? How did they achieve such power and physical size? What else lurks in the streets of Thoridon and beyond?

These questions just excite him — he has been craving for something interesting to happen his entire reign as leader of the Shaler, but the constant politics and trivialities have made him become tired. Now with the discovery of these new destructive people, he finally has something to keep him entertained.

'Yes, I did,' he replies, after some delay. 'Did you want to try and stop those monsters, Camaro?'

The Master Conjurer pauses for a moment — no matter how powerful he considers himself to be in the art of the Synth; tested against such juggernauts may not be enough. In a brief moment, he reconsiders his priorities.

'Perhaps not,' Camaro answers in defeat.

The emperor's scout approaches Serenus and hands him something that he might find interesting — the Book of the Daimons, recovered from the alleyway. Leafing through the first pages, his eyes light up at the words he reads.

'Confiscate everything that you find,' he orders the scout. 'Do not destroy any of it. This may come in useful.'

'What is it?' asks Camaro.

'It seems our visitors left something behind,' he replies as he moves back towards the Senate House, clutching the handwritten notes.

# Changeable Worlds: De|iverance

* * * *

Following the southern road out of Thoridon, the newly formed Kaidis descend a ridge and the city disappears behind them, leading into much flatter ground known as the Flatlands. Lines of trees occupy the way, but their numbers are reduced as the People's Union harvest them for their wood with the area becoming visibly barren.

Disowning their home and breaking any ties with the Shaler, it is a liberating experience. While their numbers are small, the group of twenty — all in varying states of mutation, some stronger than others — think nothing of their past and revel in what may await them. But this uncertainty also presents new problems. Free from the Union and from Shaler society as a whole, in the back of their minds they wonder what the future holds for them. A small, strong force of brutally transformed machines suddenly have an entire world to explore — that being a concern as well as an intriguing adventure.

Approaching the tree line, the sound of the rushing water by the river Still behind presents itself to the group.

'The sound of freedom,' says Xarash, calmly. 'Today, we are reborn and have removed all our concerns. This gift that has been given to us makes us unstoppable and we can achieve anything that we desire.'

He stops and takes a moment to take in a deep breath of the fresh, energised air.

'We are at peace,' he says, turning to the group, with almost a smile on his face.

For Xarash is delighted to be released from the Union — he never found place or purpose in it, his wild and damaging views conflicted with the organisation the moment he was forced into it. The Institute wouldn't take him since he had no desire or will to learn about the Synth and he has no enthusiasm to help others with the Temple. This is the break he was looking for.

However, he hasn't really had any idea about what to do if his dreams of liberation came true. His rough plan was to disappear into the woods and beyond, discovering the world, especially the places never travelled to before. The situation is now further complicated by the fact he now has people of his own to lead. He doesn't know what their aspirations are, but he doesn't really care.

What about Gregoria? Getting involved emotionally with someone else absolutely wasn't in those dreams, more of a love with the exploration than a person.

'What do we do now, my king?' she playfully asks, similarly enjoying no reservation about leaving everything behind.

'We cannot go back; the Shaler and Serenus are weak compared to what we can do. We have a whole world at our disposal now. What would you prefer to do?'

She giggles and smiles at Xarash, moving closer to him.

'You know what I want...'

Before they can kiss, a rustling noise makes itself known to him from behind in the trees. Changing from a passive attitude to being on the defence, Xarash drops all thought and homes in on the sound of a twig snapping.

'Who's there?' he barks in its direction.

'Do not fear,' responds a deepened voice. 'I pose no threat to you. In fact, I have a proposal.'

Making himself known, Toraq emerges from the trees. Still in the same appearance as he was known to Kaidan, he clutches another of his small, black pouches, contrasting his near-brilliant white robe.

'A proposal? Who the fuck are you, Shaler filth?'

'Ah, that is where you are entirely incorrect,' responds Toraq, unperturbed by the threats. 'I am neither Shaler, nor filth. Who I really am is no concern to you, but what I am to suggest will benefit you and your people greatly for the future and beyond.'

'I say we kill him,' shouts Gregoria. 'We have no interest in whatever games he's trying to play. Look at him — he is clearly Shaler, one of the Union's pawns, I assume?'

'No,' responds Xarash, actually listening to what Toraq is saying. 'He recognises us as our own. We are not Shaler to him.'

'It's a trick, Xarash! Can't you see that?'

'You would be wise to listen to your leader,' Toraq nods, as he places a hand inside his bag and retrieves a single Urtica seed, clearly displaying it to the Kaidis. This indication is proof enough to silence Gregoria and the rest of the group. They all recognise its distinctive spherical appearance and to the best of their knowledge know that the Shaler have no idea what it is and what it would be used for.

'I can see from your reaction that you understand that I pose no threat,' says Toraq.

'Fuck,' yells Xarash suddenly as he realises a complication in his previously simple future. 'You must be the Daimon spoken about in the Book... and I left it behind!'

'Perhaps,' says Toraq, who is unaware of such a name and the book Xarash refers to. 'But perhaps you would be more interested in your future?'

'Speak now, stranger,' says Xarash, angry that he left all evidence about Dis's activities and rhetoric in Thoridon, and also that it would have been discovered by now.

Toraq approaches Gregoria, who becomes anxious as he does so. His eye is caught by her distinctive and reflective orange necklace. It is not a gem, but looks like polished amber.

'Tell me, how did you obtain such a fascinating necklace?'

'What business is that of yours?'

'Your reaction suggests that you may not know,' Toraq says with a smile and he backs away, refocusing his attention on all of the Kaidis.

'The critical ingredient to your transformation was a yellowed powder, similar in colour to your shining necklace. It would be in your best interests to go to its source and revel in the vast resources that exist in the same place.'

'And what is this place, Daimon?' asks Xarash.

'The Sulphur Deserts, of course. They are far to the south, in much harsher conditions — the Shaler themselves would easily perish in such an environment, but all of you with your enhanced physique and high tolerance to heat — given to you by the sulphur in your skin — will be able to conquer these lands for your own.'

'How do you know all this?' questions Gregoria.

'Because,' hesitates Toraq. 'I engineered it all. I am responsible for your affliction.'

Pausing for a moment, Xarash can now fully believe what Kaidan was writing about in the Book of the Daimons. While it seems strange to him that the apparent engineer of everything related to this uprising would be so direct, it is at least reasonable.

'But what of Kaidan?' he asks. 'He introduced it to us, even if he turned out to be pathetic.'

'His vulnerability and independence was the reason — but while he initially showed promise, he did successfully transfer its knowledge to people of more... capability.'

Suddenly, Toraq seems to freeze. He begins to vacantly stare at nothing in particular. Xarash starts to look at the other Kaidis with questioning eyes as if to ask what happened. But within seconds, he awakes again and breathes a deep sigh.

'Now you must travel south,' he says, without making any reference to the unusual phenomena that occurred. 'Proceed past the canyon once you reach it into the Deserts. Do as I suggest and you will be greatly rewarded.'

Before the Kaidis have any opportunity to question him, he raises his hands to the sky, closing his eyes and speaks in the Ethereal language. In a brief moment, the air surrounding his Shaler body seems to shimmer and this sudden apparition of light travels directly up into the atmosphere, acting like a funnel taking Toraq with it and disappearing without a trace. The black pouch containing Urtica seeds falls to the ground.

'What the fuck just happened?' says Xarash in disbelief.

'He spoke in the language of the Synth,' speaks up a voice from the group. Xarash turns to look at him as if to question his loyalty.

'How would you know that?'

'Forgive me, my king,' says the less-developed Kaidis. 'I was once a student at the Institute. I recognised a few of the words.'

'I see,' says Xarash wearily. 'You're not going to do that as well, are you?'

Shaking his head, Xarash retrieves the bag from the ground and returns his attention to Gregoria.

'What are we supposed to do with these seeds without the other ingredient? We left everything behind.'

'The stranger mentioned the Sulphur Deserts,' she replies, touching her necklace as she remembers what Toraq said.

'I suppose we should find out what awaits us to the south at this canyon,' says Xarash. 'I don't really know why we should follow his suggestions, but there was something about the way he was talking.'

'As long as we can take a few stops along the way,' she says suggestively with a smile.

Taking the lead, he chuckles to himself and proceeds to walk along the river's edge with his band of miscreants following.

# Chapter Five

## Destruction

Infinite near nothingness is the abode of the Lightbearers — what the Shaler refer to as the Synthetic Domain. It is there in an ethereal realm that is overlaid with reality, where the source of change, influence and effect manifests itself. Only energy can exist inside this realm — it is impossible for physical objects and matter to belong there, even at an atomic level. For the ethereal transcend all of this to be as pure as possible.

The only object that is able to exist directly inside the Synthetic Domain and in the mortal universe is Ramor — the sentient star of the galaxy, the source of all energy and light, and her power is so great that she is able to cross the boundary of both the Synthetic and mortal. But Ramor's role in both differs — inside the mortal universe she is the sun, the provider of heat and light. In the Synthetic Domain, she is Mother to her Children of the Ethereal — the individual Lightbearers themselves.

In order to enact the change and influence that the mortal worlds that orbit her require, this is fulfilled by what is known informally among the Children of the Ethereal as the Tournament of the Lightbearers. The Children serve one purpose in their individual, sentient existence — to play games inside the Tournament, and thus resulting in the desired cause and effect in worlds. These acts would be considered by some as what would make life worth living.

Each game itself is devised entirely by the Child — the planets in the mortal realm are Arenas; the people are the weapons or tools in the challenge and the Child fights or uses the people in a manner created by the Child. How these puzzles of wit or brawn are won is decided by a higher hierarchy of Children, known as Ascended Lightbearers, or simply the Ascended. Above them is their Mother — Ramor — who has absolute say over matters relating to the Tournament. She promotes individual Children to the status of Ascended based on their performance in the Tournament as a whole.

This performance is gauged on how successful the games that they play are. In order for a game to be won, the Child must exert as much change over the Arena as possible, and that is the only required criteria — how they achieve this depends entirely on the Arena: the planet and its civilisations. What the change could be varies — it may be social change, by encouraging populations to run their day-to-day lives differently; it may be environmental change, altering how the planet operates to inflict indirect differences upon the world; it may be something else entirely, it all depends on what the Child considers a winning strategy, given the parameters provided.

One Child has been excelling in his games — this is Toraq, and his indirect creation of the Kaidis is a defining moment upon the Arena of Pri. By sowing the seeds — almost literally — of a new civilisation that has their own agenda different from the Shaler, this is enough to satisfy the completion of his game.

Toraq has been summoned by an Ascended — this was what occurred during his recent conversation with Xarash. When he appeared to freeze, he momentarily returned to the Synthetic Domain after receiving a signal — Children can communicate between each other via low-frequency, electromagnetic radio which transmits itself via the Synth energy projected by Ramor. These messages can also be spoken — that is the language of Ethereal, what the Shaler have learnt to utilise in order to manipulate the Synth.

The Ascended, named Uriro, stands in front of Toraq in the mortal Arena of Pri at the foot of the Iskap mountain ranges. Once a Lightbearer becomes Ascended, their duty to the Tournament changes — they are no longer players in the game and instead they become adjudicators of a single Arena, watching the progress of the non-Ascended that may be present at any one time, reporting their observations to Mother. Not only do they have this direct link with her, they also exhibit an additional quality — a highly prized gift.

A cold chill blows around the two Lightbearers from the mountains above and Toraq's possessed mortal body shivers. The area is very exposed, with dirt mounds having little grass and hardy shrubs are sparse around; snowflakes dance carried on the wind. Uriro is unconcerned and unaffected by the environs. Standing tall in a black cloak, covering all features including the head, Uriro is much taller than Toraq and casts an ominous shadow over him. In Uriro's right hand is a wooden staff, carved in an irregular style as if it wasn't quite finished with an unusually coloured gem on its top.

'What is it you want?' asks Toraq, speaking in a transmitted message over the Synth.

'I have called you to discuss your position,' Uriro replies, choosing to speak vocally with a female voice.

She removes her cowl, exposing her possessed Shaler body. There is no hair, completely bald and no eyebrows or eyelashes, but the skin is as pure and smooth as a young child. Her perfect eyes swirl around much more visibly than Toraq's with a bright shade of green.

'My position? Have I received judgement from Mother?' Toraq questions frantically, eager to know.

'You are quick to jump to a conclusion, Toraq. But you are correct in your analysis. Mother has spoken and has judged you accordingly.'

'Tell me, then. Am I to receive the gift? Am I to be one of Mother's chosen?'

'I cannot tell you this,' Uriro smiles. 'She has requested to speak with you directly.'

Toraq has no knowledge about the procedures of the Tournament — players such as he are not told anything. Becoming excited, which is out of character for one that takes pleasure out of manipulating others, he no longer notices the cold conditions.

'Let us visit Mother then,' he demands. 'I must know!'

'You do not have to go now,' Uriro replies. 'Are you sure? There may be no return to this Arena — I do not know what she requests from you.'

Echoing down from the mountains above, a strange bestial roar is heard. It is an entirely unfamiliar sound to Toraq. Despite being resident on Pri for many years, he couldn't venture towards Iskap because of its intolerable cold. The roar, akin to a lion, distracts him from what seems to be his destiny — he is intrigued to discover what it is.

'Well?' asks an impatient Uriro, who knows the sound but will not reveal it.

'Yes,' says Toraq, refocusing his attention upon her.

'Very well.'

She replaces her hood and then repositions the staff in front of her and grasps it with both hands. The green eyes stare directly at Toraq.

'Take hold of the staff with both hands,' she commands as Toraq gingerly obeys, not knowing what will happen next and still slightly distracted by the primal scream. As he does, Uriro refocuses her gaze at the gem on the staff and it begins to increase in brightness. With the light increasing, the snowflakes that fall around begin to slow their movement and ultimately freezing in time. As Toraq realises this, a blinding flash of white takes command of his vision as they return to the Synthetic Domain.

✳ ✳ ✳ ✳

'Collect everything, even the furniture! I don't want anything left behind here!'

Emperor Serenus orders the Union members at the birthplace of the Kaidis, who dash around the dim building picking up every last object inside that Xarash and his followers carelessly forgot. Bags of evenly distributed Urtica seeds, tables, rugs, clothing, even plates and cutlery are all gathered, sorted and placed in large wooden chests.

The emperor wants everything to be stored securely, amid protests from President Ikis who really detests Serenus' handling of the situation. Ikis has absolutely no desire to let the Kaidis roam freely doing whatever they please, especially after they defiled his own Union Hall and smeared his entire operation. But no matter how he would prefer to be in Serenus' position, he is not, and has to stand by and watch.

Serenus has his own motives. His dreams call out for change and even if it has been a long wait — seeing as Serenus is in his senior years — this is the opportunity he has been waiting for. Shaler society to him has become incredibly boring; everything has pretty much a perfect existence. Sometimes, he questioned his own position: what is the need for an emperor — there is nothing to rule. This silent harbouring of something to oppose, perhaps forcefully, has awoken his yearning. He was entirely unaware that the questionable practises of a single student would erupt into its own movement complete with disfigured creatures. A truly joyous occasion!

Standing outside in the alleyway with the sun beginning to set, Serenus starts to squint at the Book of the Daimons that he holds. The reducing light coupled with sometimes illegible scribbles across the pages makes the writing harder to read. From what he has been able to understand, Serenus is both concerned and delighted by its contents. On one side, the writings are diabolical, completely abhorring Shaler life; but also an insightful commentary as well. Blind to the opposition that seemed to fester at the lower end of society, Serenus takes great notice of what is being said between the lines.

A crash is heard from inside the building as one of the Union drops some plates in his haste. Serenus looks up from the papers, tuts and shakes his head and moves back towards the main street. He approaches a frantic Ikis who seems entirely preoccupied with making sure his building work is still going to plan, despite the bloodied floor.

'Come on, come on,' he clamours to the workers, who repulse at the mutilated corpse of Kaidan being removed by others. 'Haven't you seen a dead body before?'

Serenus clears his throat in an attempt to attract the attention of the Union president.

'What is it, Serenus?' Ikis questions, without stopping or turning to face the emperor. 'Can't you see I have work to do?'

'Clearly you do,' replies Serenus, arching his brow. 'But I wonder if I could have a word.'

'I don't think we have anything to discuss, emperor. Not right now.'

'You haven't told me what your people are going to do with the artefacts collected from the Kaidis.'

'Oh, I see,' hesitates Ikis, slightly disconcerted. He finally turns to face Serenus.

'I had my own plans for those things. I was considering a bonfire outside the city — is that to your pleasing? Maybe the wind direction would steer the flames towards wherever those creatures have gone, because all that junk would surely burn quite well!'

He starts to laugh, but this merely angers Serenus.

'You will do no such thing!' Serenus shouts at him, who cowers slightly at the volume.

Ikis' face lightens up slightly as takes a step back.

'You are just like those savages,' he suggests. 'You want to keep it all? What is that under your arm, anyway?'

'I want you and your people to store all of this "junk" in the basement of the Institute's Library,' Serenus threatens. 'Or I will cease your leadership of this despicable organisation you call a union.'

'My dear emperor,' Ikis chuckles. 'Even if you did such a thing, there are more just like me waiting in the wings. But there is no need to make hollow threats — I will command my people to do as you suggest.'

He starts to walk away towards the alleyway.

'I won't forget this little chat, Serenus,' he says as he leaves the emperor.

By nightfall, the former headquarters of Dis stands empty with the front door boarded up. The alleyway itself is also cordoned off since news of the activities that took place there becomes more common knowledge and interested people try to get a glimpse of the scene.

In the Quadrangle, all of the traders have cleared out, some nursing the wounds to their saleable goods as the Kaidis trashed anything they could see on their way. Even the Temple is quiet, doors firmly shut as the nerve centre of the Shaler is definitely disturbed by recent events.

Shattering the peace, there is a jangling with an iron handle to the door of the Senate House. As the wooden door creaks open, Serenus steps out into the dimly lit Quadrangle. With a mischievous expression on his face, making sure the way is clear he briskly crosses the Quadrangle towards the archway leading into the Institute's courtyard.

Almost having a permanent fixture under his arm is the Book of the Daimons; not wanting anyone else to see what the document contains, or even be wise to its existence. Serenus doesn't want it to get into anyone else's hands but he considers it too important to destroy. Being a smart man, he recognises the fact that the Kaidis may actually want their sacred book back — the ultimate bargaining chip.

Luck on his side, the courtyard is also quiet, adding to the success of his covert operation so far. Heading to the right, he approaches the tall Library. Steps lead up to its entrance — pillars support an overhanging wooden canopy. A blazing torch illuminates the area and Serenus pensively wonders inside.

The ground floor of the Library is known as the Hall of Legends, where pictures and posters hang on the walls of admired students and lecturers at the Institute. A column of stairs in the centre climbs high up to four stories above — but Serenus is only interested in one location. Again, there is no sign of anyone and he quickly makes his way towards the stairs — but goes around them to be greeted with a single wooden door. He tries to open it but it is locked and he quietly curses to himself as he remembers. Fumbling around his pockets in a mild panic, he finds a key and undoes the lock. The door makes a slight creaking sound as he pushes it open and the light from the Hall reveals a series of stairs leading down into darkness. Taking a nearby torch from a wall, being careful not to set light to the Book of the Daimons, Serenus descends into the shadow.

Inside the basement of the Library are many oddities — it extends for some distance, purposely being constructed to take up more space underground to allow for centuries of expansion as required. The latest additions are the boxes containing the Kaidis property, haphazardly placed around the vast open vault with no real care to their order. But Serenus wouldn't expect anything less — at least they are here.

Placing the torch on a hanger, he moves down as far as he can see. Without paying close attention to anything in particular as he progresses into the darkness, a shelf advertises itself as the ideal location to store the papers and he places the manuscript on it with a smile. Serenus has added a more robust cover to the book, made from leather; its natural colour blends in well with the wooden shelf — perfectly unable to draw unwanted attention.

Satisfied that no-one will find it, retrieving the torch he hurriedly climbs the stairs and locks the door behind him. Hotfooting towards the Library exit, he turns around just to see if he was spotted and seeing no-one returns to the Quadrangle. Despite his best attempts, Serenus' subtle noises had not gone unnoticed as a shadowy figure watches him leave the Library, peering around the corner of the flight of stairs.

* * * *

In the following morning, Serenus arrives at the Senate House after a short nap. Throughout the night he has been concerning himself about how to deal with the politics surrounding the Kaidis. Entering inside, moving towards his throne, he is very surprised to hear loud discussions already taking place. A throng of conversations all going at once as he sits, with everyone knowing Serenus is there but refusing to acknowledge his presence.

Taken back by this apparent rudeness, he stands and appeals for quiet. The benches are full of representatives of both the People's Union and the Synth Fellowship, with some standing at the sides as there isn't enough room. While there are many conversations in progress, some louder than others, there is only one theme — the appearance of the Kaidis and the emperor's handling of the situation. On both sides of the political spectrum, there is clear indifference with many unsure about how to proceed; such fear stokes a fire of uncertainty only adding to the tone.

Serenus attempts to call for calm again, but nobody wishes to hear his pleas. Becoming increasingly frustrated, he decides to settle his request for attention once and for all. Behind his throne stands a large bronze gong — striking it hard with its hammer, the metallic reverberating crash echoes around the entire Hall. It comes as a surprise to most and instantly become startled by the distinctive noise. All turn to the throne to see Serenus return into view.

'That's better,' he says, smiling. 'Now that I have your attention, would someone please brief me on the discussion?'

His question remains unanswered for a few moments as he looks around the room at the assembled. Ikis and — to his surprise — Camaro are featured in the audience: surprising because Camaro rarely deals with political matters, preferring others to sit in for him.

'So no-one is going to speak?' Serenus questions again and after a pause views start to make themselves known.

'You don't seem to realise what you have done!' comes a disguised shout from the back of the benches.

'Those monsters are running rife and it's all your doing!' protests another.

'How could you have let this happen?'

With the final protest, shouts of agreement rise from both Segments as these complaints chime loud and clear. But while Serenus is surprised by the numbers protesting, he is ready to accept these challenges. He waves his arms up and down to try and appease the crowd.

'Silence!' he booms and the jeers gradually die down. When calmness descends, the assembled are ready to pounce on his first words. But they are disappointed in that they have to wait. Biding his time, in a rare move, Serenus walks up to the front of the arced benches, pacing up and down, looking pensive and building tension before delivering a speech.

'How long have I been emperor now?' he asks generally, pausing afterwards.

'Too long,' whispers a comment in the silence, which is met with murmurings, even though the question was rhetorical.

'I am past just over forty years in this position,' Serenus continues, brushing aside the remark. 'I have to be entirely honest with everyone — it has been the most uninteresting and depressing time we, as the Shaler, have truly experienced. My reign has had to sit through days of conjecture, insults and mindless bickering from all of you — some more than others — and it has become tiresome in recent days. Politics may be what we involve ourselves with, but what do we actually achieve? Where is our progression, our advancement? How much of the very little that has been accomplished recently we can actually feel proud about? From the look on some of your faces: nothing. As a people, we have lost our way.'

He moves to stand in front of the throne and throws his arms up to the roof to direct the vision of the audience.

'This great building itself was built as a testament to ourselves being a strong civilisation. With our ambitions firmly at the forefront, it is a symbol for us to become what we were. But what happened? I believe we have forgotten our traditional goals and we are sending ourselves into oblivion, destroying the very fabric that we once were. I have sat on this very throne and watched each one of you systematically break down our foundations with corruption, deceit and behaviour comparable to animals.'

Sitting down on the throne, he looks around and sees stunned faces. It is clear that they were not expecting such a damning speech, with some rethinking their position.

He continues: 'But what does my assessment have to do with the Kaidis, for that is what they call themselves? While you can label them as you wish, the "monsters" and "savages" have made a definitive point which demonstrates exactly what I am saying now — they sought change in Shaler society and the extremes they went to find that resulted in their mutations. Do not forget that I did not banish them, nor did I request for their demise — no, that would be counter-productive and as most of you seem to howl for their blood, they simply wanted to start anew, escape what we have become. They left on their own free will. They have sacrificed their own identity to support this. That, my consul, is truly remarkable.'

His words have definitely struck a chord as a smattering of applause rises up. But not everyone is impressed with his speech, most notably President Ikis. Standing to make himself heard, as he does so, he is met with grumblings as opinions in the room are now more divided, with Ikis being the driver behind the original dismay for the emperor.

'Thank you for that rousing speech,' Ikis starts. 'While parts of what you say have some weight, I think you are forgetting the seriousness of the situation. Was free will responsible for the murder of that Institute student? How is that justified? What does that say to the people, whom we represent? You question terms like "savage" being applied to these Kaidis, but despite what you say, we would never turn on our own, regardless of opinion — that is "counter-productive" as you suggest. What is to stop them from coming back and repeating this savagery on a larger scale, simply because they don't agree with what "we have become"?'

'I understand your point, Ikis,' replies Serenus. 'I do not support what happened to that Kaidan boy — that is a tragedy in itself. But I am not blind to what the Kaidis are — they are strong, they are warriors: we are none of those things, and have no desire to be. You suggest that they could return — this is what I would consider an opportunity.'

'An opportunity? You would want them to come back and reek complete chaos and destruction upon all of us? Have you gone mad, Serenus?'

The murmurings return as reality seems to hit.

'You are aware yourself that I specifically asked for their possessions to be stored,' he says, before being interrupted.

'Indeed, and I was going to set fire to it all, but you stopped me!'

'Yes, but the reason for that is because they will come back, and they will want what they came for. If we destroyed it all, that in itself would more than likely start a rampage.'

Ikis seems to agree as he returns to his seat — Serenus has clearly done his research and was ready for this line of questioning. The emperor stands from the throne once again to present his opportunity.

'I propose that we need to be ready for their return. While we have seen their barbaric capabilities, we don't know what they would do and what they would seek. This is our opportunity to return to our past and honour our ancestors by continuing what they started.'

What he proposes would be a monumental task, but he has the confidence that each Segment is up to the challenge. Because there are too many unknowns about what the Kaidis' intentions actually are, Serenus feels that they should cover all eventualities. Controversially, he wishes to cancel the Union Hall building project, denying the People's Union for their own headquarters for two reasons: fear of cementing segregation inside Shaler society and also that the area is to have a new purpose.

The Synth Institute has been able to produce excellent students in the teachings and utilisation of the Synth energy, but they are yet to have a real test for their abilities — it is mostly hypothetical. Serenus proposes that the very best graduates head up a new, neutral Segment charged with the defence of the city and the Shaler as a whole, using the partially constructed Union Hall as their base. All materials and workers would be transferred into creating a walled boundary to surround the whole of Thoridon, essentially fortifying the city from outsiders.

Surprise is the general reaction as he finishes outlining his proposals. It all provides the Institute and the Union something to achieve and the rewards would be great, redefining the Shaler as the power that they strive to be, rather than the sorry state of what it has become. The plan is ingenious and well-thought, but wise Camaro has one question.

'You wish to start a war?' Camaro asks, rising from his seat.

'It is my duty to protect the city from both inside — and now — outside influences. The war, as you so definitively put it, has already begun.'

'I can only hope you know what you are doing, Serenus,' replies the Master Conjurer. 'I feel this is a dark day for the Shaler.'

Before the emperor has a chance to respond, Camaro has already made up his mind and walks out of the Senate House, amid a backdrop of silence. While Serenus seems confident about his plans, he is aware that it could go either way — protection or destruction.

President Ikis is ready for the challenge, having been won over and realising the opportunity — for both glory and profit — that arises from the prospect of a war. Someone is going to need to build, design and construct.

'The Union is with you, emperor,' he smiles, watching Camaro leave.

* * * *

With a blinding flash lasting no longer than a blink of an eye, the frozen in time mortal body occupied by Toraq returns to life. He takes a sharp breath from his reawakening with the oxygen filling his lungs, releasing the air with a long sigh. The atmosphere around him is still freezing cold, a biting chill blown down from the mountains of Iskap above with snow carried on the wind, lashing against his face in the frequent gusts. Before his encounter with Uriro the conditions were fierce, but since his return to the mortal world from the Synthetic he doesn't notice the harshness.

On his return his hands are still grasping the irregular staff with its curious gem. As the feeling of holding the staff registers itself with him, he looks at it for a moment and across to see that Uriro is no longer there. Tracking his vision to the snow-covered ground, a black robe has a barely visible outline from the drifting snow that has begun to cover it.

For this is a brief moment of celebration to Toraq — Mother officially granted him Ascended Lightbearer status: the game for him is over. But, since he has been present on the Arena of Pri for a considerable time, biding over it, waiting to make his mark, he was also judged to have developed a great affinity for the people and the Arena itself. Therefore, in his capacity as new Ascended Lightbearer, Ramor assigned him permanently as the adjudicator of Pri to replace Uriro.

But since he is no longer a player in the Tournament he is not permitted to influence the Arena. In due time, as is determined by Mother, another Lightbearer will be sent to Pri with Toraq having his watchful eye over the proceedings. This in itself will become a problem for him — he is specifically unaware of the Book of the Daimons and what Kaidan wrote about his experiences with Toraq in the forest of Mistwood.

Regardless of what the future holds, Toraq takes a moment to study the staff in his hands. The gem is a dulled colour but it is hollow and inside its imperfect shell swirls a gas-like vapour, similar to Toraq's own eyes. He nods as he recognises what it represents and smiles; happy to be in the possession of an intriguing idol.

His interest is suddenly broken as he hears the primeval roaring he heard before. Turning, he looks around erratically trying to see what is making the noise. There is something about the sound that is distinctive to him — he doesn't know what precisely. But there is nothing — the echoing beast could be a great distance away. Not believing this conclusion to be finite, he decides to move in its direction closer towards the foot of the mountain ranges. On doing so, Toraq soon discovers that the journey becomes arduous — the levels of snow and ice increase the closer he gets making physical movement a lot slower. Even though the temperature plunges well below zero, dressed in a thin white robe his mortal Shaler body would have succumbed to the elements by now — however, he still strides along in the snow, oblivious to the arctic climate.

Reaching the mountain bottom, the landscape is now extremely jagged — the volcanic architecture of the ground now defiantly impassable. Toraq looks up through the blowing snow at the height of the mountains, climbing for tens of thousands of metres, covered in ice and snow, interspersed with various plateaus — flat islands between the ragged terrain. As he marvels at the wonderful views, he hears the roar once again and this time it is much closer, being able to see where it came from.

On the plateaus are borne holes — caves — which lead into the mountainsides. Created when the lava spewed forth during the birth of the planet, these vast ice caverns provide a connected network of shelter from the harsh weather. Something must be living inside these caves, Toraq considers.

The route towards them seems to be impassable. There is no way at all that Toraq has the strength or agility to climb the landscape, and Shaler adventures before him would have drawn the same conclusion. The winds are too strong to control via the Synth — gale force, gusting to severe; as they are central to the ecology of the mountains and the world as a whole, even attempting to alter their natural path could have repercussions on a global scale.

Determination gets the best of him — there must be a way, and he begins to scout along the edges of the mountain looking for even the slightest path leading up. But with the winds and snow drifting around him, visibility varies between narrow to nothing. Becoming unsure of what he is seeing, this confusion just adds to the complications — Toraq knows when he is beaten and the mountains have won.

He travels the short distance back, retracing his rapidly receding footprints left in the snow, and the same cave makes itself visible once again. Just as he is ready to admit complete defeat and return south towards Thoridon, the distinctive roar projects itself in his direction, the volume much louder. Looking in its direction, he sees an outline of something through the gusting blizzard, charging towards his position.

One's normal reaction by this point would be to at least run — but Toraq stands defiant, perhaps a suicidal notion. He is emphatically interested in what beast could make such a distinctive calling, even if his own mortal existence would depend on it. His curiosity is satisfied as a beast of considerable mass approaches. Covered in long, white hair, the blades thick to protect against the snow; a large snout for a face, black beady eyes and a jaw full of razor sharp teeth; running on fours, two black spots are present on its strong shoulders. The male beast charges straight into Toraq with considerable speed and power, and he is knocked back a good distance landing on the soft snow. As if to threaten Toraq, a roar is directed at him as he lands — the impact being a warning shot.

Despite this throw, Toraq struggles in the snow, eventually finding a foothold and pushes himself up onto his feet, not wounded or otherwise incapacitated. The furry beast stands there, breathing deeply, his warm breath blowing into the snow melting it slightly — strangely compelled at the unnatural defiance that Toraq is exhibiting.

He moves closer to the animal who snorts in surprise. Now standing in front of the bear-like creature, he notices the frontal limbs are much smaller than the hind legs with the paws more closely resembling humanoid hands. But before Toraq can get a closer look, the creature pushes back and rises to stand on his back legs, his height now almost twice the size of Toraq. With the snow lashing behind him and the wind howling, it is truly a menacing vision.

Unperturbed, the Lightbearer is completely calm — in fact, he is entirely impressed with this display despite the initial reaction which should have been life-threatening. Toraq smiles at the towering animal — for this is an absolute opportunity to him. If he is to be the Ascended Lightbearer upon Pri, he needs a mortal life that commands and demonstrates that position. What could be better than a fearsome creature such as what stands in front of him? It is a proverbial powerhouse of strength and agility, disguised in a fluffy, distinctive shell.

The threat isn't the creature — it is absolutely Toraq himself.

Toraq slowly walks closer to the animal, which now senses the fact that he is not the danger, but the humanoid that moves towards him. Still standing on his back feet, he takes a few steps back trying to avoid Toraq and his threatening roar changes to almost a whimper. There is definite emotion being displayed by the creature as he lets out a wolf-like howl attempting to signal others. But this just makes Toraq hurry his pace towards him.

Stumbling over the snow, the beast falls to its back. Struggling in a similar fashion to Toraq before, he attempts to right himself. This delay is enough to allow the Lightbearer to catch up. He places his left hand directly on the furry hand of the creature, closes his eyes and starts to speak.

In what seems like a microsecond, there is a definitive flash, followed by the immediate freezing of Toraq's Shaler body; it collapses to the snow with a dull thud, lifeless. What occurred is Toraq utilising a specific ability that the Children of the Ethereal can use — it is a procedure known as Ethereal Transference, and this allows the Lightbearer to possess a different mortal body, taking over its brain, replacing whatever personality that was there before. Once this has occurred, the mind which owned the body prior no longer exists.

Now in his new animal body, Toraq takes a moment to figure out the basics, such as breathing, motor skills and identifying the needs and wants of the functionality of the creature. Starting in an almost robotic nature, eventually he grasps how to control the formidable mass and he is able to right the body and return to a standing position. The beast also possesses improved vision and sense of hearing. He can see through the snow and focus on objects that might have been previously obscured by the blizzard. In the distance he can see the caverns high up on the plateaus much clearer. Looking at his hands, they are a combination of animal paw and humanoid hand — there are no claws, but separate fingers and can be used for traversing.

Toraq decides to drop to all-fours and return in the direction that the creature initially came. He realises that the strength of the animal allows it to reach fast speeds, even across the snow. Over the relatively short distance he travels, he meets the walls of the mountain — and instinctively seems to know that his frontal limbs can also be used for climbing. Being able to grab onto the harsh surfaces with considerable ease, he is able to scale the mountainside and reach the first plateau and the entrance to the cave. Impressed with himself for finding the perfect host body, he turns into the cave — the walls lined with ice but it is sheltered from the harsh winds. Inside there are variably sized hollows where the lava flowed to form the great caverns. Also, to the surprise of Toraq, are other similar creatures to him who watch as he enters. Unfortunately for Toraq, he has possessed what was the father of a small family of these bear-like creatures. There are two much younger children, an older child and a mother, the size determining their apparent status. Not entirely sure what to do next, Toraq stands there looking around — his eyes, even though already black, swirl around with his ethereal visible essence.

The mother is the first to react, as if to question what her partner saw outside. Not really understanding the signals or series of grunts, Toraq pauses. In the period of silence, one of the younger cubs approaches him and rubs his face against Toraq's fur in a playful manner. Rather than trying to risk confrontation, Toraq simply turns around and leaves the cave. The mother and the older child begin to roar in desperation — what was a close family now being split by the Lightbearer without any cause for concern. Toraq starts to climb down the mountainside with thoughts of returning to Thoridon, but as he does, the young cub attempts to follow him. But being much smaller and not having the strength to grapple onto the terrain, with Toraq near the bottom, the cub — with much protesting from his mother — loses his grip and falls down the mountainside.

As Toraq reaches the bottom, he hears the primeval wailing from above, seeing the snowball-alike cub heading straight for the ground. Making an impassive judgement, Toraq decides to leap over to where the cub will land and catches him. Heavier than anticipated, the two bound over into the snow but the cub is uninjured. The pair reorients themselves and Toraq returns to the position of where he originally took control over the cub's father. With a little bit of digging, he recovers the snow-covered staff, grips it between his strong teeth, returning to all-fours and charges off south in the direction of the Shaler capital. Turning to the side, he sees the cub follows him — it would seem Toraq now has a child to look after of his own, and he slows allowing the cub to catch up.

In the background, the echoing howls of the mother carry over the wind. While Toraq really doesn't understand what all the fuss is about, he has clearly separated the family — what that will do in the future, the cause and effect, will likely make itself known eventually. But for now, he has new strategies to devise, catch up on what the Shaler and the Kaidis are doing and also prepare for a new arrival in the Tournament of the Lightbearers.

# Part II: The Fourth Era
## Year 137/4E

# Chapter Six

# Broken

Despite the cause and effect played out by the Lightbearers, there is one additional constant that also fulfils a role in change — time. This brings its own opportunity to those that desire, and time alone breeds variance to the mortal.

Since Toraq's Ascendancy, opinions have been cast and revoked, actions made and undone, leaders come and gone. Generations have risen, then fallen and then remembered. A great deal of time has been responsible for this. But the Lightbearers have been absent. Toraq is unsure when the next Lightbearer will make itself present on the Arena of Pri. Most are preoccupied with other Arenas throughout the galaxy, and Ramor is reluctant to even give Toraq an idea.

Thoridon itself has doubled in size since the reign of Serenus. His wishes for construction of a great wall on the city perimeter were granted but what remains now is more of a crumbling ruin; a new wall has been emulated to cover the expanded area. For the Shaler are under relentless assault. The Kaidis have grown to an almost unstoppable force, vast armies of Kaidis under the command of a single, prospective king — and time has seen that these two communities have declared and remained at war. The incredible might of the Kaidis has seen them become the dominant power, with strong leadership, excellent engineering and a fearsome attitude that is winning them the war.

Despite this, the Synth itself has become a priority for the Shaler. Through unusual and, perhaps, underhanded tactics, they have discovered greater opportunity for its utilisation. These new skills have allowed them to fend off the Kaidis in the recent past, but for how long remains to be seen.

* * * *

Under the cover of midnight, a mysterious man dressed in darkened cloths, keen to disguise himself from anyone, hurriedly weaves his way through the stone-paved streets of Thoridon. His movements sway slightly around the paths, diving between dimmed corners, but he knows where he is going. As he moves along he sobs quietly to himself, eventually approaching a tall stone wall with a large archway — cloaked figures stand guarding it, muttering in disgust as they see the fumbling figure go past them into the Quadrangle. He scrabbles with a degree of urgency up the brilliantly white stone stairs of the Temple of Ramor.

'For the love of Ramor, let me in!' he yells, as he bangs the palm of his right hand against the door. His voice echoes around the empty Quadrangle, deserted of anyone but himself. Some hounds bark in the distance as the man's distinctive voice is heard from afar, shattering the silence of the calm city.

'This was not how it was meant to be,' he sobs to himself with his face pressed against the wood, tears streaming down his face.

He feels as if people are watching him, but does not want to gratify them with a reaction, even though the Quadrangle itself is devoid of life. He continues sobbing as footsteps begin to approach from behind the door, followed by a rattling of the door's iron handle. As the door is pulled away from the man, he falls in to the floor, whimpering. The priest who opened the door turns the man over onto his back and seems to recognise the eyes behind the disguised face.

He pulls the man into the Temple, closes the door and removes the scarf obscuring his face. The initial curiosity becomes reality as the priest identifies the man as the leader of the people – Emperor Solus. He exclaims his name and title in shock, the name echoing around the cathedral-alike building.

Solus grabs the robe of the priest with both hands lifting himself from the floor up into his face; straining, he instructs him to fetch the High Priest. The footsteps disappear into the distance and Solus lies with his back on the stone floor. He catches his breath and dries his eyes and face to look up to the ceiling, to the painted murals depicting emperors of the past. As he gazes above, he begins to talk to himself.

'Oh, how proud they look. You have so much dignity, so much respect. Why am I reduced to this – here, on the floor of the holiest ground in the land?'

He raises his arms upward in frustration, clenches his fists as he brings his arms down again, angry with himself. Entirely lost in his own thoughts, he doesn't realise the two figures that approach him and pull him up from the ground and into a pew. The two hands of the High Priest grab onto Solus' cheeks to focus his view directly into his face – a face showing mixed emotions.

'I can't possibly understand what has reduced you to this state,' exclaims the High Priest. 'What has gotten into you, child?'

'I cannot do this, Rogaro,' replies Solus, looking into the eyes of the priest. 'I am not fit to be emperor.'

'Is this about what happened in the Senate earlier?' asks Rogaro, who releases his grip on the emperor's face and takes a step back. 'The Union's representatives were quite forceful with their words, but they are always talking rot. You should not let them get to you so easily.'

He briefly raises a wry smile before it wavers.

'But, this is something bigger, isn't it?'

The other figure – one of Rogaro's assistants – starts brushing down the clothes of the emperor, trying to remove the dirt collected from the floor. She is obviously impressed to be in such close quarters with the leader of the Shaler people, such a rare opportunity, but her hurried actions suggest that her peer does not want her ears to hear what is being said.

Solus appears to relax upon seeing the calming face of the High Priest. He raises a right hand to signal the assistant to stop – she dutifully does so and briefly looks at Rogaro, who nods at her to leave. There is an echoing knock as the door she exits closes and then all is quiet.

The emperor looks around the nave, seeing that the two men are alone and Rogaro patiently waits for an answer to his question.

'I am not my father, Rogaro. I have lost all hope in myself to lead. My father before me was strong, resilient, but I am not. I feel like a burden on the people, I have failed the Senate in leadership; I have lost faith in Ramor. What is there left for me?'

Rogaro moves to sit down beside him and holds his hand.

'Every time you come up against an obstacle you let yourself down. You have never come running here before, and if you say you have lost faith in Ramor... How can I help you?'

'I just need guidance. I don't know what I'm saying. It's all such a mess – what am I doing wrong?'

'You are doing nothing wrong! Can't you see? You can't win every race.'

'But my father—'

Rogaro interrupts.

'What has suddenly brought all this on? You are not thinking clearly, my child. Are you alright?'

'I have lost all confidence in myself as a leader. I just wish my father was still here,' Solus sighs.

'Emperor Vimlor passed on into the spirits over 20 years ago. He was a great man and brought great prosperity to our people, but he is gone. Your mother spent these years raising you to follow in his footsteps, and she is a great teacher – she is very bright and you have benefited greatly from listening to her.'

'It isn't what you think, Rogaro. You were never there all the time.'

'But that's because I cannot be a father figure to you. I have Ramor to watch over along with my devoted Acolytes.'

Something doesn't quite agree with Solus as he stands up in a fit of rage, moving into the aisle.

'My mother was not truthful, Rogaro,' he yells, his voice echoing around the nave. 'She was hiding things from me, things which cause me great pain – I hate her for all this deception!'

'What do you mean by pain and deception?' Rogaro asks with a shocked expression on his face.

'It took her ten years to tell me that my father was murdered. She has been deceiving me and feeding me lies that I can be a great emperor, that I can be my father. I don't know what to believe anymore.'

Solus slumps back onto the pew with his head in his hands, closing his eyes. All the tension and anxiety of hating his mother for not telling him straight while she raised him was all out in the open now. Deep down, he doesn't want to disappoint the family – he knew his father died when he was an infant, but he didn't know of the murder.

On his tenth birthday, his mother – Avornia – looked him in the eye and told him that a Kaidis scouting party had entered into Thoridon. They used furtive tactics to avoid the guards – something the Kaidis were not previously known for. Previous attacks by the Kaidis would see them preferring to run in, with swords and axes waving, enjoying the blood of the fallen splattering across their armour and yellow-pigmented faces. But the murder was different – it was as if the Kaidis had inside knowledge, as if it were arranged.

They quietly broke into the private residence of the Emperor, and as all lay asleep, they entered into Vimlor's bedroom. They were quick and merciless — a single poisoned dagger with a blade crafted from the darkest ores of the southern Sulphur Deserts, pierced his father's side. Avornia, awoken by the disturbance, could only look on as the blood reddened the bedclothes. The wielder of the dagger looked at her, smiling with his bloodied teeth showing.

With the alarm raised, it was too late for the Warlocks that arrived as the Kaidis had slipped away without resistance into the shadows — the dark corners of the streets of Thoridon providing the perfect cover. Their family distraught and torn apart, Avornia cradled her infant son, crying out to Ramor for help. But not even Ramor's infinite light could remove the darkness that beset their family.

'You need to be strong, Solus,' says Rogaro softly, as he squeezes on his shoulder. 'That day was a terrible setback for our people, not just you and your mother.'

'But you don't understand. My mother lied to me, Rogaro. When I was young, she said my father died in a terrible accident, it was never murder.'

'We had to tell you that. We had to tell the people as well.'

'You lied to the people?' gasps Solus.

'We had to. I didn't like the idea more than you from what I can tell in your tone. But if we told the people that Emperor Vimlor – our great emperor – was murdered by the Kaidis, we would have an unstoppable civil war on our hands. There would be riots, militants, and whatever else looking to seek revenge. We are not like that, Solus.'

'So, we just let it pass? We let the Kaidis get away with it?'

'We are not savages! Do you think that we should degrade ourselves to their level? They were once like us, but their crimes of the past committed them for their ways.'

'I just want vengeance for what happened...'

The High Priest stands up and sighs.

'Your mother wasn't lying to you – she was protecting you from yourself. I can see it in your eyes. You want blood but it is not as simple as that.'

Solus starts to feel a sense of despair waving over him. His fledgling diplomatic mind is agreeing with Rogaro, but his personal feelings are calling for revenge.

'Have I forgotten my purpose? Have I completely lost my sense of direction?'

'You are the emperor now, my child. You cannot let the past and your father's death haunt you for the rest of your life. That is no good for anyone.' Rogaro says this with a much defined tone.

'I just wish I knew what my father would do,' laments the young emperor.

Solus takes a breath before continuing and turns to look the High Priest directly in his eyes.

'I need to know. I don't know if I can lead without knowing.'

As the pair stare at each other, as if the eyes themselves were having a conversation, Solus notices a glint in Rogaro's eye, and in turn the eyes of the priest begin to look right through Solus. A strange thought enters into the mind of Rogaro. It begins to bother him – the more he thinks about it, the more stressed he becomes. Solus stands up and walks over to him, and as he does so, Rogaro starts to backtrack. After a moment, he refocuses his attention on the emperor.

'There is something. But, it is too dangerous. I don't know why I'm even thinking about it.'

He starts to stutter his words and it looks like he is losing colour in his face. He moves to sit down in a varnished oak chair, near the Shrine of Ramor — its glass pillar shimmering in the low ambient light. Rogaro gazes into the shining symbol of all that he entrusts, but is very disturbed by what he is thinking.

'What if I were to tell you that it may be possible to find out what your father would do?'

He starts muttering under his breath.

'Speak sense: what do you mean?' Solus raises his voice, struggling to control his anger. 'Is my father still alive, somehow? Am I being lied to again?'

'Necromancy!' screams Rogaro, stuttering as he does so in an outburst. He jumps out of the chair, turning his back to the emperor, head in hand.

Solus stands there, replaying the last few seconds in his mind: did he just suggest necromancy? This is not what the Institute teaches — something parents told their children about as stories. The High Priest starts speaking after the silence.

'I know what you're thinking; you don't believe it is possible. But I believe it is. Many years ago, even before Emperor Vimlor's father, the Institute was under the impression that necromancy – the act of communicating with the dead – could be researched. Out of pure fear for the encroaching Kaidis, the scholars of the time decided to put resources into the emerging theories of these dark arts. However, there was an incident — historical documents we keep here in the Temple have never detailed exactly what happened, with some parts of history seemingly disappearing from written record. All that we know is the Institute destroyed all their research when this happened.'

He sighs, takes a pause and then turns to Solus with the unease on his face being quite apparent.

'I have told you this because I believe in you, Solus. You need to be strong, and if you need to hear the words of your father, this is the only course of action possible.'

Solus doesn't really know what to make of what has been suggested – excited by the possibility that he could be able to speak with his deceased father, but from what tales he has heard about necromancy as a child, he is unsure.

'But if, as you say, all the research has been destroyed, how is this even possible?'

'Master Conjurer Ferlor knows more about this than me, my child. I believe in you as much as I believe in Ramor to guide and protect us. If the stability of the emperor, his Senate and his people demands it, I am sure Ferlor will know what to do, even if he is initially hostile to the idea.'

'I don't know, Rogaro. Why can't I just resign my position? I am not fit to lead.'

'You really think that would work? We cannot be without an emperor, and there is no one to replace you immediately. You are forever an emperor in the minds of the people, and they will always look to you to provide. You cannot undo that. Emperors before you have done extraordinary feats to demonstrate to the people they are of full mettle. The people need a strong leader, and while you have their heart, you need the confidence to have their minds as well. I believe the spirit of your father will have great things to say.'

'You seem to be pretty set on the idea, and it would appear I have no choice.'

'You do have a choice. But if you want a chance at knowing the great leadership that Emperor Vimlor provided...'

His voice trails off as if to imply that Solus would be foolish not to persevere. The emperor looks back at him with unsure eyes, but being in such a vulnerable and suggestive state of mind, he warms to the idea and accepts the proposal without a second thought.

'If the spirit of my father can give me that guidance I deserve, as you suggest, I am sure I can lead the people.'

'So be it,' concludes Rogaro. 'I advise you to go home, rest a little. We shall meet again in the Senate in the morning.'

He turns and hurriedly leaves the nave by the same door as the assistant earlier, closing it behind him. Listening to the silence for a brief moment, Solus moves towards a corridor leading out of the nave to a graveyard.

The graveyard is an extension to the octagonal Temple, without a roof, serving as a home for the bones and spirits of past emperors, including Serenus. He walks around, reading the plaques of his peers, knowing that someday he will end up here himself. He finds his father's tomb, near the centre of the hall, with a cenotaph, surrounded in tributes, flowers and other small trinkets of appreciation. Avornia used to bring him here as a small boy – it has a certain atmosphere, like being in a room of the best people.

A tear falls from his eye onto Vimlor's grave.

'Maybe I'll speak to you soon, father,' he says under his breath, even though not fully understanding how that would be possible.

* * * *

As Ramor rises in the east, the infinite light is projected across the Quadrangle, illuminating the dusty and well used corrugated stone. It is still used as the daily market place, where traders from the People's Union, surrounding Shaler towns and the occasional exceptional visitor come to hawk their wares to the population. This early in the day sees various traders arriving and beginning to configure stalls and displays.

Inside the Senate House, change has taken hold. With the Kaidis threat being a constant, a new Segment was introduced fairly recently. On the left-side remain the People's Union, on the right the Synth Fellowship — but in the middle is the new Segment, the Warlock Council: an arm of government in charge of civil defence, staffed by the many black-robed graduates from the Institute and responsible for the protection of the city.

Each of the platforms all face the focal point of the room – the Seat of Power, the lavish, wide throne reserved for the emperor of the Shaler. Behind this is another introduced group, but they are merely present in an advisory role, reporting directly to the emperor. The Branch of Ramor, a wooden bench, carved with symbols of the star, reserved for members of the Temple.

Despite it being early morning, the Senate is usually devoid of people; instead, Emperor Solus sits slumped in his throne, still dressed in the same awkward clothes from earlier, quietly snoozing. He didn't follow Rogaro's advice to return home.

Below the windows on the walls of the Senate House are proudly displayed works of art – pictures that document various moments in the history of both the Senate and the Shaler as a whole. Each one of the artworks is elaborately detailed, painted with great care and each individual scene is perfectly captured. One of the largest portraits depicts an exaggerated artist's impression of the birth of the Kaidis — a monstrous image of Xarash, smashing his way through crowds of innocent Shaler, his face full of rage and Serenus cowering in fear.

Solus fidgets in his throne still bemused and emotionally drained from his diminishing grip on his own situation. An echoing crash brings him to a surprised attention as the large oak doors of the Senate House open wide. The loud noise makes him realise where he is and his realisation of his location combined with an uncomfortable sleepless night comes to a head. The usual civil servants – known as Canons – begin to arrive, charged with dealing with trivial administrative affairs and also wait to receive the actual members of the Senate.

As they arrive, they are startled to see the emperor already sitting in his throne, dressed in unkempt clothing. It is an unusual sight, one that Solus becomes acutely aware to, and he barks at them, questioning what they are looking at, dismissing their reactions, and clearly wanting to be ignored.

It is not long until the first more important person arrives – the familiar face of High Priest Rogaro hurries inside. As he does so, a Canon standing at the door announces his name and full title in a formal tone, echoing around the building, once again acting as an alarm call to the dozy emperor.

'What is this?' questions Rogaro as he approaches Solus, still slumped over in his throne. 'Have you lost your mind entirely?'

'Leave me be,' mumbles Solus back, like a grumpy teenager not wanting to be bothered.

'This is no way for an emperor to behave!'

The High Priest claps his hands and begins to shake the emperor to bring him back to reality. Solus moans and whimpers as he does so, the scarf he used to obscure his face in the night wriggles free and falls to the floor.

'Is this how you want your father to see you?'

These words eventually resonate with the emperor as he remembers the conversation in the night. If the necromantic can offer an audience with the respected Emperor Vimlor, being coy and careless in both his physical and mental presentation is absolutely not the correct approach. Even though Solus is not drunk, the realisation has a sobering effect upon him.

'I apologise,' says Solus to Rogaro, in a much more authoritative voice: the voice of how an emperor should speak.

'You do realise the Senate is due to convene at any moment?'

As he finishes speaking, a bell sounds outside, signifying the arrival of the dignitaries into the Quadrangle, with rows of Warlocks providing a corridor leading from the southern archway up to the open doors of the Senate House.

Rogaro gives the emperor a disapproving look as he moves to sit down in the Branch of Ramor. Solus straightens his darkened robe, collects the scarf from the floor and hides it behind his back. Formality dictates that the emperor is the last to arrive when the Senate starts a new day, so Solus being present when everyone else arrives is going to be a surprise.

The first names of the various senators begin to be read aloud by the Canon at the door and as each one enters, before moving to find their designated seats, they all take a moment to glance at the throne, where Solus sits straight in his chair, a plain expression on his face, his eyes making contact with each that dares to look in his direction.

One of the last dignitaries to enter is the one Rogaro warned Solus about – the flamboyant but intelligent Master Conjurer Ferlor. He is a middle-aged man who, unlike Camaro, prefers to lead the Institute's representation in the Senate. One of the most powerful people in the current Shaler climate, he is highly respected in not just Synth usage but as an individual as well. His point of view is valued and as such is influential in the past, present and future. With an acute mastery of known Synth usage he has a track record of excellence, reaching his current position in a short space of time. Despite all of this, he has a darker side — he doesn't actually value his knowledge or his position.

As his name, title and responsibilities are announced by the Canon, he notices the emperor in the chair, but does not make a reaction, unlike others. Solus has always been suspect of him, and the attitude he takes does not surprise. Ferlor takes to his seat – almost swaying as he does so, like everything is amusing to him – and attentively puts eyes forward ready for the day's business to start, even though it would appear to have done so already.

With all the senators seated in their respective Segments, idle murmurings resonate around about the emperor's apparent break of tradition. Solus looks around, knowing they are all talking about him, but is holding back, fearful of blow back that he might not be able to handle, making his personal situation much worse.

Breaking the uncomfortable situation, one of the senators from the People's Union stands and begins talking about normal business. As he does so, the rest of the senators slowly fall back to silence and focus on the speaker, while Solus slowly sinks back into his throne, knowing that he is no longer the centre of attention.

* * * *

Midday approaches and with a full morning of discussion and decisions being made inside the Senate House, the senators begin to file out and return to where they came. However, Rogaro approaches Ferlor as he stands to leave and invites him over to Solus for a private word. Solus wants to make sure that the last of the remaining senators have left before he starts speaking to Ferlor, as he doesn't want anyone else to hear what he has to say.

'What do you want from me?' asks Ferlor, an impatient tone to his voice, who uncomfortably looks around.

'I need your help in a personal matter, Ferlor,' replies Solus.

Ferlor raises his eyebrows and smirks a little.

'A personal matter, eh? What can I possibly do for you, his noble majesty of the highest regard?'

'Lose the attitude, Ferlor,' says Rogaro, who stands at the side of Solus' throne.

'Oh, so the priest is in on this as well, is he? Well, this has got my attention fully now!'

Ferlor claps and rubs his hands in anticipation eagerly waiting for what bombshell is going to be dropped upon him. Solus turns in his throne towards Rogaro.

'Are you sure about this?' says Solus, in a lowered whisper, to which Rogaro puts out a hand to silence the emperor and takes a step forward towards Ferlor.

'Tell me what you know of necromancy,' asks Rogaro, without hesitating, stroking his chin.

This wasn't the bombshell that Ferlor was expecting and his demeanour changes from being playful to serious. The smile on his face is removed and he becomes a little suspicious.

'What makes you think I know anything about that?'

'Come now – the greatest Synth user we have ever known, the leader of the Institute, and you don't know anything about necromancy? I find this hard to believe.'

'Well... I may have seen or heard one or two things, but—'

He takes a moment to consider what he says next.

'Why? What's so interesting about necromancy all of a sudden?'

'You sound a little defensive, Ferlor,' says Solus, still having his suspicions about him.

'No, not at all. But, forgive me; it is not every day someone asks me about necromancy.'

'It has been brought to my attention that you have been covertly speaking with my priesthood,' reveals Rogaro. 'You were very interested in the Compendium, particularly about the time when the so called "beast" ran wild.'

For Ferlor would be highly interested in referring to the Twilight Compendium — the compilation of important observations has been greatly expanded over time, featuring writings about the early days of the conflict between the Shaler and the Kaidis, breakthroughs in Synthetic studies and prior events from the founding of the Temple. There are also fragments of detail alluding to a catastrophic event sometime in the Second Era, which has not been fully documented because either sections of the Compendium that relate to it are missing or leave more questions than answers.

One thing that is clear in the Compendium is that an entity of some kind was systematically able to fragment the Shaler people, perhaps to the point of complete domination. Some of the texts suggest that many buildings were destroyed by the unknown "beast" and the evolution of the Shaler was considerably set back. But it has never been clear what, or who, that entity was.

This event is what interests Ferlor. Despite being a genius when it comes to anything with the Synth, even pioneering his own discoveries, he doesn't really have any interest in it. What he seeks are answers to a question that have still eluded the Shaler for many years — what is the Synthetic Domain? Ever since he realised that the Synth itself was artificial, and an extension to the natural world early on in his career at the Institute, he has constantly believed that there must be a way to discover its shady, inaccessible dimension.

But this question about necromancy makes him think. He doesn't believe for a moment that the practice is possible, merely folklore, but he is not adverse to the fiction and even learning from past mistakes — the suggestion sparks a degree of inspiration in his mind, but chooses to keep this quiet.

Solus looks at Rogaro, entirely unaware of Ferlor's poking around and just adds to his suspicions about him even more. Ferlor's usually animated body language wanes and he stands more rigid as the discussion progresses.

'So, what? I was interested in our past – what's wrong with that?'

'Nothing, but my priests claimed that you were overly interested in details that they could not provide. You were keen to know more specifically about the "beast" – and what we do know about it is that it was not of these lands.'

'Fine,' booms Ferlor with a sigh. 'I can see I am being persecuted here, and I suppose I had better square with you.'

'You damn well better!' yells Solus, who is deeply shocked and angry by what he has heard.

'I have been secretly trying to understand what this beast was, for I have read from the Compendium that it had incredible control over the natural elements – it could give us clues to further our development of the Synth.'

He says this with a degree of confidence, even though he really lacks any interest in actually believing the proposal.

'But that is nothing we don't already know – common knowledge,' says Rogaro.

'Yes, but I was given additional information from an anonymous source – a parchment that included extra detail.'

'Anonymous source? Another parchment? I don't believe this – the papers we hold in the Temple's archives are extremely old! They don't just turn up!'

'Don't you think I know that as well, Rogaro? I say it as anonymous because I just arrived at my home one day and it was waiting outside my front door. There was no note, no details about where it came from: untraceable.'

'I've had enough of this ridiculous story,' says Solus, starting to lose his temper. 'Just answer the question: what do you know about necromancy?'

'That is what I'm trying to get to,' replies Ferlor. 'This extra parchment is an account made by an Institute student of the Second Era, talking about a strange book that was responsible for the "beast", saying it was the dead causing the tragedy to unfold.'

Rogaro takes a step back as the three men pause looking at each other. The High Priest is still entirely sceptical about a missing page from the Compendium suddenly transpiring from thin air; the emperor, who is not a man who cares for the Synth, doesn't really understand what is being said, but warms to the fact that at least Ferlor is making some interesting suggestions.

'What sort of strange book?' asks Rogaro, eventually.

'I don't know,' replies Ferlor. 'That is where my trail has gone cold. Now are you going to tell me about the interest in necromancy?'

'I would rather not go into details,' says Solus. 'But, I would like to know if it is possible to communicate with my father.'

'I was not expecting that! I suppose that book could help there, if the parchment is anything to go by,' theorises Ferlor.

'Perhaps I could see this mythical writing?'

'Of course, Rogaro – I shall bring it to the Temple right away. I haven't been able to understand its entirety, maybe you could help there.'

Without further hesitation, Ferlor hurriedly turns to leave and dashes out of the Senate House.

'I still don't trust him,' says Solus.

'I would rather pass judgement when he shows his proof.'

Solus and Rogaro and any remaining Canons also leave the Senate House, with the last closing the heavy oak doors behind them. The darkened scarf remains on the throne of the emperor, its colour of black eclipsing the bright blue furnishing of the Seat of Power, potentially symbolising change to come.

106

# Chapter Seven

# Invocation

Inside the grounds of the Institute, the courtyard between each building is busy with academics and others moving around. A great bronze statue of Emperor Solus stands central, slightly gleaming in the sunlight. It has several benches surrounding it, allowing for people to relax and admire the statue. Master Conjurer Ferlor approaches an empty bench underneath a shady tree, clutching a slightly yellowed parchment – the untraceable and anonymous document that Ferlor received. He sits down on the bench, taking a moment to familiarise himself with its text once again.

What he reads appears to be a genuine missing piece of the Twilight Compendium. Parts of the parchment are torn, either over time or deliberately disfigured. But the most readable part is what Ferlor is interested in:

*The Beast has arrived. I write this with haste.*

*As it is written in the Book, its destruction is unparalleled.*

*I am plagued – the dead are alive, under the control of the Beast. They are doing its bidding.*

*But I cannot see the Beast. The Book is in control. Blinded by the Bloodrage!*

*Ramor has no presence here.*

Throughout his career, small hints or clues have become apparent as he progressed with his training. Spurred on by the war imposed upon the Shaler by the Kaidis, the Institute has progressed in its Synthetic manipulation. New theories and ideas have allowed conjurers to have near complete control over the three elements – fire, wind and water, with Ferlor being well versed in these new discoveries.

Death has always been defined as the absolute end, but Ferlor has decided to draw his own conclusions. He believes that nothing ever dies, but merely recycled instead. Necromancy is the supposed ability to communicate with those that are deceased. But with Ferlor constantly thinking and always fascinated by the concept, he asks radical questions. After inspiration with his conversations with Solus and Rogaro earlier, he wonders if necromancy would be merely a form of recovery — a way to restart the metaphorical wheel of life.

As he sits on the bench, almost in a daydream continuously thinking about the words on the page, his train of thought is interrupted by a tap on his shoulder. He becomes startled, almost dropping the parchment onto the ground.

'I'm sorry, I didn't mean to disturb you,' says a female voice. 'I don't know where you were, but it wasn't here.'

Ferlor looks up at the middle-aged face, surrounded by long, auburn hair – she looks as if she were much younger than she is. It is the relaxed and soothing voice of Avornia that looks down upon him, mother to Solus, but also the Shaler's second most competent student of the Synth. She wears a green dress that stretches down almost touching the floor, with her soft hair gently playing in a light spring-like breeze. It is as if she has a glowing aura surrounding her.

'I was deep in thought,' Ferlor says.

'Thoughts about what you are reading?' she asks.

He passes her the parchment and her eyes widen as she recognises what the page represents.

'Why are you reading a page from the Twilight Compendium?'

'It isn't just any ordinary page – it was given to me from someone I have no idea.'

'But I have never seen this page before,' she says, scanning over what she can read.

He begins to explain to her how he came across it, but then he stands up from the bench and ushers Avornia from the open courtyard, away from any potentially listening ears. Ferlor has a dilemma – he doesn't want to reveal his own goals and certainly doesn't want to tell Solus' mother that her son wants to talk to her dead husband.

'That is quite surprising,' she says, as they move out of the Institute's grounds and cross the bustling Quadrangle towards the Temple of Ramor. 'Why haven't you mentioned this before?'

'I didn't want to cause a fuss. I don't even know if it is genuine. I mean, how can the dead be alive? Ridiculous.'

'You have a point, but the Compendium is one of our most sacred documents. I don't believe anyone would write untruths about it.'

They ascend the stairs to the Temple and walk in to find Rogaro and Solus waiting in the nave, ready to see if Ferlor's claims about a missing page are true. With them, behind a table, sits the curator of the Temple's archive, clutching a magnifying glass and has some fluids arranged on the table. None of them expected Avornia to be accompanying the Master Conjurer.

'Mother!' startles Solus, hurriedly greeting Avornia as soon as he identifies her. 'What are you doing here?'

'What an odd question,' she replies, looking toward the others as she realises that more knew about this discovery than she was led to believe. Solus lowers his head slightly as he notices Avornia looking at him with a puzzled face.

'I couldn't pass on the opportunity to witness the discovery of a missing piece of the Compendium,' Avornia enthuses.

'Indeed, you are right,' he says, relieved that she doesn't know his true intent.

As he and Ferlor exchange eye contact to acknowledge that this is the case, Ferlor moves up to the curator who patiently waits to examine the parchment. Handing it over, he picks up a bottle of a blue liquid and a fine brush, wets the end and over a corner of the parchment draws a thin line. Giving a blow to dry the liquid, he then holds the parchment up to the light, using the magnifying glass to peer at the painted section.

After a moment, his face lights up.

'This is genuinely a page of the Compendium! The paper construction is a perfect match for the rest.'

Excited by the discovery, he lowers the parchment and begins to read its text, but is interrupted by Rogaro who takes it from him to read. Avornia and Solus patiently wait the brief moment for the High Priest to make sense from the text, with Solus asking him to read it aloud. Ferlor is relieved that Rogaro quotes exactly what he read himself, confirming that he wasn't imagining what it says out of disbelief.

'So there is a strange book,' concludes Solus.

'It would appear to be the case,' agrees Rogaro.

'But why does it mention Bloodrage?'

It is a good question — the Bloodrage has never been documented prior to the Third Era. This doesn't mean it couldn't have been existed before the birth of the Kaidis, but as it appears to be a real page from the Compendium, this detail seems questionable.

'I don't know the answer to that,' says Ferlor. 'I may be able to find out, however. If Bloodrage is part of this, then that suggests this "beast" was more recent than we thought.'

Solus becomes shocked.

'Are you suggesting that the Kaidis are involved?'

'It's possible. Perhaps I should investigate.'

'I would love to spend some time trying to make more sense over what this new discovery says,' perks Avornia. 'Would you mind if I worked with your priests, Rogaro?'

'Not at all, we need to understand this as quickly as possible.'

Avornia is a little surprised by Rogaro's choice of words.

'Why? What's the hurry?'

'Think of it as a tribute to me, as emperor,' Solus suggests, slightly stuttering, thinking on the fly. 'Imagine what the people would think of me as a discoverer of a lost page of the Twilight Compendium!'

'But I still don't see why there seems to be so much urgency.'

'We must proceed now!' Rogaro says with some force. 'Please, trust us on this matter, Avornia.'

Meanwhile, Ferlor doesn't care for the emperor's glory-taking and uses this as an excuse to disappear, leaving via the door without making comment and scurries away towards the Synth Institute once again.

With Avornia's suspicions raised much higher, she faces a dilemma – one to press her son for more reasoning behind these courses of action, the other to follow her desire to learn by pursuing whatever theories Ferlor has. As the Master Conjurer leaves suddenly, this makes her decision much easier: she cannot give in to learning, even at the stubborn sacrifice of her family. She gives Solus a look as if to say she knows something is amiss – as a mother – but her thirst of understanding makes her follow after Ferlor as he descends the outside stairs.

'What are you hoping to find?' she says to Ferlor, excited as she catches up to him.

'I hope I don't find anything,' he replies, a little surprised to be followed by an almost schoolgirl-like adult.

'Don't you think my son was acting a little odd?'

'Can't say I noticed,' he exclaims as he accelerates his pace into the bustling marketplace.

As the pair become further apart from each other, separated by the waves of Shaler eager to purchase their various goods from inside the Quadrangle, Avornia concedes and turns around to return to the Temple to follow up on her son instead.

*** * * ***

Ferlor arrives at the Library inside the Synth Institute and walks into the Hall of Legends. The Hall is still a growing museum to those dedicated to the Synth with practitioners being honoured for making ground-breaking discoveries. As much has been discovered since the reign of Serenus, the walls are adorned with many plaques, busts and sculptures of the honoured faces. Some of these have dedications from students over time admiring their work. It is a large shrine to those that develop and create. It is also well guarded, with several Warlocks either patrolling or stationary, watching anyone that comes in and out — since the war with the Kaidis, they cannot take any chances with one of their most prized assets.

Ferlor has, naturally, free access of the entire facility. The first and second floors are home to the vast archive, where people such as himself and Avornia have spent many months and years studying – and even contributing to – its catalogue. But this is not where he is heading — he knows about the locked door behind the stairs, and has a key to access it.

Having similar traits to Serenus, he rummages through pockets in his cloak and shirt, trying to find the key to open the door. Gibbering as he does so, these meaningless noises break the tranquil silence of the Hall, prompting a patrolling Warlock to raise his suspicions. Turning the corner around the staircase, he approaches Ferlor dressed in a typical uniform of the Warlock Council: black robes with a hooded cowl, lined with golden seams. Ready to scald a lost student for trying to go where he shouldn't, he is surprised to see Ferlor.

The Master Conjurer turns his head to look at the Warlock, narrows his brow and without actually saying anything, questions what the Warlock is so interested in. Realising whatever the leader of the Institute is doing is none of his business, the Warlock just nods and returns to his duties — Ferlor tuts and sighs as he does so, agitated by the disturbance.

Finding the small key eventually, it rattles in the lock — the door has not been opened for some considerable time and it creaks as the hinges strain. Descending the stairs, closing and locking the door behind him, he feels his way along the wall as he carefully steps down into the darkness.

Reaching the bottom, he begins to speak in Ethereal to utilise the Synth. Between his hands, the air that occupies the space starts to become increasingly dense as the passage of time is slowed inside the area. As more dust particles move into the area, the air solidifies, creating a mass of suspended debris. Changing his incantation, the debris heats up and catches fire. A push with his hands against the irregular ball of flame, he projects the fire into a receptacle on the wall and immediately the basement illuminates.

What becomes visible is a treasure trove of forgotten memories and documents. The various scrolls, parchments, idols and other devices that litter the shelves, containers and floor are not just the relics of the Kaidis' beginnings with the Bloodrage – there are also details about failed experiments practised by the Institute itself. Virtually everything that exists in the basement are memories that the Shaler wish to forget, yet, it may be useful in the future, hence the hording of all that is scorn.

Ferlor, however, in his journey to find answers has been a frequent visitor to the lost archive, but has only managed to brush the surface of the potential horrors that lurk on written page. The scale of material here would take one person many years to discover, and many more to understand. He realises that learning about the Bloodrage could ultimately corrupt him, but he believes it to be a necessary evil in order to find what he eventually seeks — he even secretly admires Kaidan and Xarash for writing what they did.

He moves further down the hall, its seemingly infinite length disappearing into the reduced light, retracing to where he had previously interrupted his own research. One detail that is plaguing him from the anonymously received page of the Twilight Compendium was a keyword: "control". He has not read about anyone (or anything) being able to control others directly, as if to have some kind of deliberate influence.

Up until now, his research has led him to the details that are well known about the Kaidis: their yellow, pigmented skin which is much tougher than typical flesh and resilient against heat; their increased physique and dominating, hulking presence; their anger and intense hatred for anyone, even themselves. But any sense of third-party control has been absent — other than their military training — with each Kaidis being fully conscience of their own actions.

Curiosity gets the better of Ferlor and he moves even further into the archive, beyond where he has ventured before. As the shelves come into focus, a larger cabinet stands central, one that has not really grabbed the attention of a casual observer before. It is an old, wooden cabinet, many times the age of the Master Conjurer that stands before it. He brushes off the caked-in dust that covers an operable panel and the wood appears to be entirely rotten, covered in blackness.

He places a finger into a slight notch to the top-left of the cabinet's front panel and pulls forward to open it. However instead of doing so, it splinters into tiny pieces falling to the floor. Inside appears to be nothing but more rotten wood – a definite continuation of the blackness on the outside. Slightly disappointed, he takes a step back after expecting something to be there. He grunts in disapproval and not really able to fix the cabinet turns his back to it and moves down to the next shelf.

The disturbance in the heavy, underground air caused by Ferlor's sudden movement does cause an effect. Something becomes slightly disjointed inside the rotten cabinet, revealing a lighter patch behind the object that has moved. The sound of it scraping against the decomposed wood alerts him to look again into the cabinet. He sees a rectangular object, as black as the rotten wood surrounding it, and reaches to touch it and eventually picking it up.

It is a book, but an unusual book, looking exactly like the rotten wood, yet it does not splinter or fragment – it is very solid. He turns it around to have the front facing him and in amongst the rotten, dried leather is a tiny handwritten white label that looks as if it has merged with the hardened cover: "Do not read".

He stares at the book, continuously rereading the label, knowing what it says, but replaying in his mind about what led to this – the strange materialisation of a missing page of the Compendium; the emperor's bizarre suggestion of necromancy; the references to an unusual book; his own dreams of knowing about the dark arts.

The temptation of it all is too much. He opens the Book of the Daimons and begins leafing through its crinkled pages.

* * * *

Outside, loud cheers and general jubilation reverberate around the Quadrangle. In the centre is a raised platform, circled by the trading bazaar, used by anyone who wishes to perform a song or other exhibitionism. However, the on-going performance isn't the usual attempts at entertainment, but men using wooden swords, light armour and shields – sword-fighting.

The event is further raising interest by onlookers because one of the men inside the mock arena is no less than Emperor Solus. A raucous cheer is raised as Solus' opponent – a challenger from the amassed crowd – admits defeat as Solus imitates slicing his leg and therefore would have severely crippled him, if this were a real fight. He seems to revel in the loud reception he receives, touring around the stage to the onlookers, encouraging them to cheer more.

As his dejected opponent climbs off the stage, playfully jeered at by the spectators, a new challenger rises up. Solus has never followed in his mother's footsteps, not taking interest to her fascination with the Synth and the Institute's teachings. Instead, he takes after his father who was much more of a physical fighter, expertly wielding a fantastic blade that personally saw use against an encounter with the Kaidis.

The two faux-fighters circle each other on stage, Solus with eyes of daggers, taunting his opponent, waiting for him to make the first move. His stance is near perfect and arches over with his wooden sword pointing down from shoulder height. As they circle, Solus is charged, but ready for the challenge, he parries and flicks him back as the two pieces of wood collide. The crowd laughs and applauds.

Meanwhile, Ferlor returns from the Institute, clutching the book he found inside the Library basement and sees the ensuing display in progress on his way towards the Temple of Ramor. Bemused by what is transpiring, he hurries through the crowd up to the stage and tries to get eye contact with the emperor. Calling his name, Solus fails to hear as he concentrates on the fight, the voice of Ferlor drowned by the varying roars and cheers from the crowd, reacting to his movements.

There is a loud clatter as the two wooden swords collide once again, but this time Solus disarms with his deflection and causes his opponent to spin around. Before he knows it, Solus moves to stab the wooden sword into the back of him, but protected by his armour is spared what might have been a fatal injury. Conceding, the emperor is victorious in the fight once again, lapping up the noise from the now frenzied crowd, all behind their leader, all unaware of his own personal problems which seem trivialised by his current limelight.

Touring around his amassed audience, he finally notices Ferlor watching him.

'This reminds me of the call of leadership,' exclaims the emperor as he jumps down from the arena, meeting the Master Conjurer.

'Why is that?' questions Ferlor. 'Surely you know you are the emperor of the Shaler?'

'Of course I know that. But combat is what I live for. This is what it feels like to be a leader.'

He starts receiving congratulatory slaps on his back and shoulders from the people, loving his performance on the stage. If anything, he certainly has their full support. Solus smiles and thanks all of the well-wishers before returning to face Ferlor who isn't quite as impressed.

'What's with the glum attitude, Ferlor? You have your Institute, your Synth, whatever all that is. Surely you should be proud of your achievements? I am proud to be a skilled swordsman, and I'm sure my father would appreciate that.'

But Ferlor just shakes his head. How little the emperor realises that he does not care for the things he states, and how he is only interested in a glimpse at the Synthetic Domain and the great untold powers that remain to be discovered inside. No, this prancing around with swords, endless discussions about theories behind the Synth; everything is sub-par compared to what awaits.

He just sighs at the emperor and turns to resume towards the Temple.

'What?' Solus yells after him, behind a backdrop of cheering. Shrugging his shoulders, he returns to his adoring crowd and jumps back up onto the arena.

'Who is next to face the might of your emperor?' he announces, his voice echoing around the Quadrangle. Ferlor from the top of the Temple stairs turns around to see him lapping up the encouragements. He shakes his head again in disbelief before entering inside — such a waste.

With a new challenger stepping up to take on Solus, they continue to duel. The crowd swells and recedes on every blow and contact, but Solus seems to be less focused as before. In his mind he can just see an image of a disapproving Ferlor, standing there.

As he thinks more about the image, he sees the black rectangle of the Book of the Daimons under his arm — how did he not notice this before? Lost in a thought, his challenger smashes his wooden sword against his, this time knocking back Solus and he staggers to regain his balance as his opponent comes back into view. The crowd becomes pensive, unsure if they want their beloved emperor to actually lose.

There is a lull in the fight as Solus holds out a hand to ask for a moment. He recalls what Ferlor was trying to do before, and realises that the book that he clutches could be instrumental in his desire to communicate with his father.

Roaring, he charges his opponent and knocks him back onto the arena's floor and lunges his sword as if to stab him in the heart. Breathing heavily, he stops himself as he sees the eyes of the defenceless man on the ground, almost pleading for the emperor to stop. Realising the situation, Solus relaxes and with a deep sigh, offers to help the man up — and cheers and applause return to the crowd as do the smiles.

Solus jumps down from the arena without saying another word and pushes his way through the crowd trying to catch up with Ferlor at the Temple.

* * * *

'Look at what I have found,' boldly states Ferlor towards Rogaro, busying himself inside the Temple. He holds the book aloft.

'I don't believe it,' says the High Priest who is alone in the nave, moving closer to inspect the book. 'Is this the book the Compendium page mentioned?'

'See for yourself,' smiles Ferlor.

Rogaro takes the book and is immediately taken aback by the unusual texture of the books cover; the blackened, seemingly torched roughness would cause anyone to question its presentation. He notices the strange denying label on the front and arches his brow, looking at Ferlor but does not speak. Naturally ignoring the labels advice, he refocuses his attention on the book and opens the cover.

Inside, the pages are extremely tarnished as if weathered for many years, yet the writings contained on the paper are as clear as if they were written yesterday. Rogaro flicks through the thick pages — he sees handwritten scribbles, occasionally diagrams and strange symbols. It is only fifty or so pages long, but the text is so small, each page contains a lot of information.

After his initial inspection he turns to a random page. Some pages appear to have been more read than others as it has a habit of opening at certain sheets. Rogaro narrows his brow, peering at the words on his selected page. As the eyes move left to right, trying to make sense, he stops after a few lines.

'I can't understand what this says.'

'That is because some of it is written in Ethereal,' replies Ferlor.

'I see. Does that mean you can understand it?'

'I have a rough idea.'

Ferlor trails off as he speaks. The leather binding on Book of the Daimons, added by Serenus, hidden in the Library basement and never touched since has rotted giving it the unusual texture, but since the basement is extremely dry, it has otherwise preserved itself for generations.

The page that Rogaro is failing to read is a piece written by Kaidan, explaining the technical details used by Toraq out in Mistwood during their encounter and recited to him on their return to Thoridon. But what Ferlor doesn't want to reveal — for reasons of pride — is that there are words he does not recognise, even being an outstanding scholar of all things to do with the Synth. He takes the book from Rogaro and reads the first sentence from the open pages.

'This particular page seems to talk about something to do with a river, trees and plant life. I don't know much about that,' he says, purposely skipping over the details that he does recognise.

Rogaro nods, blissfully unaware, putting his full trust inside the Master Conjurer as Ferlor opens a different page. His eyes widen a bit as he reads what is contained.

'Have you found something?' questions Rogaro as he sees the reaction.

Ferlor simply coughs. The page he reads has a definite crease in the books binding. It contains diagrams that illustrate a large circle with a smaller circle inside and measurements between the two circumferences. The accompanying text describes something that Ferlor would be extremely interested in – the ability to communicate with outside forces. But there are many words he does not understand, let alone what an "outside force" could actually be. It is more information revealed to Kaidan by Toraq.

'I don't know what I've found,' he eventually replies. 'But it could be the answer we are looking for.'

'You mean for necromancy?'

Ferlor is genuinely surprised by what he has found. He has no actual idea what it is from the brief look, but some select words jump out at him on the page, striking a resonating chord with the language on the Compendium parchment. Possibly jumping to conclusions, he looks up at the High Priest and sees that Rogaro waits for an answer.

'Yes,' Ferlor affirms, knowing full well that it isn't anything to do with the preposterous notion of necromancy.

At that moment, Solus finally arrives after being hounded by his adoring public outside. He staggers up to the two men slightly out of breath, catching a glimpse of the book once again.

'So, I assume this is what we are looking for?' he says eventually.

'Well, without the proper study, and indeed time, I cannot fully say,' Ferlor replies. 'But I believe it is.'

'What a stroke of luck,' Solus excites. 'Does my mother know?'

'She is busy with my priests studying the Compendium and related works,' Rogaro answers.

'Excellent – what are we standing around for, then? What do you need me to do?'

'You can do nothing, emperor,' says Ferlor, almost laughing at the idea that Solus could actually assist. 'This is a delicate Synthetic matter – you seem to be, well, in a bit of a fury at the moment.'

'A "fury"? What do you mean by that?' barks Solus, moving a little closer towards the Master Conjurer as if to threaten him.

'This ritual I have identified in the book is a very careful and coordinated endeavour, and you have just been playing outside with stupid sticks! That is not the right state of mind.'

Solus looks at Ferlor, anger boiling up inside him – how dare he suggest such things to the emperor! But before he does something he might regret, and indeed, may even prevent the chance to speak to his father, he stands down.

'Fine,' he snaps. 'You do whatever you want – just get this underway immediately.'

With that, he returns outside in disgust. Rogaro looks disapprovingly at Ferlor.

'That might not have been the most tactful way to handle him,' comments the High Priest.

'I don't have time for his games,' Ferlor retorts. 'We could be on the brink of a major discovery here — such barbarity is inappropriate.'

'While I agree, he is not himself.'

'Do you think I care about that? Sometimes it is clear to me why we are losing the war against the Kaidis with these stupid attitudes. If he wants to be a warrior, he has to learn a few things first.'

'Enough,' Rogaro says. 'You have clearly made your opinions known Ferlor, but I do not share them. We need to be ready for this attempt at the necromantic; I suggest you get to it.'

'You seem to the one pushing for this,' chuckles Ferlor. 'Weren't you the one who suggested necromancy in the first place? Just think of the damage you would have done if this turns out to be a false hope.'

'I am just doing what I think is in the best interests of the emperor,' thunders Rogaro. 'I suggest you do the same.'

'I do not take orders from you — if anything, you should be taking them from me. But, you are right for once. I am as eager to understand what this discovery means.'

'Eager to see the well-being of our emperor, I assume?'

'You can believe what you want, Rogaro. Perhaps this experience might teach you something as well.'

Ferlor storms out of the Temple and descends the stairs to see the emperor is once again fighting in the arena. He hurries towards the Institute and prepares himself to read what he has discovered.

✻ ✻ ✻ ✻

Throughout the evening, Ferlor has been studying the pages of the book. He has so many questions about the book itself, and doesn't see any connection between the detailed Synth usage and the draconian doctrine once penned by a young Xarash. The frequent references to the Dis organisation, a rebellion against the People's Union, talk about a fascination of fighting. He doesn't realise the document is the beginnings of the Kaidis itself.

Nevertheless, his attention has been primarily around the pages with the circle diagrams. They demonstrate a practice which Ferlor has titled himself as a ritual called the Necrocircle. Although he doesn't completely understand the text, he has decided to use the necromantic as an excuse for filling in the gaps. Based on this, he reckons the ritual allows for the communication with the dead and the circle acts as a device to focus on the spirit from their resting place. Also contained in the text are passages that supposedly invoke the ritual and allow for the contact with the "outside forces": he assumes these to be the spirit of the dead, even though he doesn't believe his own conclusions. It isn't really necromantic in any way — but it provides an excellent cover. The circle is a very real symbolic device for use in the ritual. Based on Ferlor's instructions, Rogaro has retrieved corpse dust left behind when the deceased are incinerated in Thoridon's crematorium. Aside from this disturbing item, nothing else is required to complete the ritual.

In the meantime, Solus has been anxiously waiting for something to happen. As the preparations for the ritual are readied, Solus is told to wait in the nave of the Temple. The reasons for this are two-fold: firstly, because the Necrocircle needs to be supposedly positioned at the location of the dead, Ferlor will perform the ritual in the Emperor's graveyard annex to the side of the Temple; secondly, Ferlor simply doesn't trust someone who is not versed in the ways of the Synth, nor has any interest in it.

Ferlor and an apprehensive Rogaro enter into the graveyard, closing a full-size wooden gate behind them, giving explicit instructions to Solus to only enter when Rogaro calls for him. He takes some persuading but eventually bows to the resistance given by his father-like mentor, with assurances guaranteed.

The High Priest and the Master Conjurer prepare for the ritual. Ferlor takes the corpse dust provided and following the instructions carefully places it onto the stone ground, circling Emperor Vimlor's tomb. It is an ornate tomb, with carvings and symbols relating to his time as emperor – a picture of his immortalised sword, used in the battle against the Kaidis, etched into the stone.

Ferlor stands inside the circle and looks at Rogaro, telling him to stand at the gate, ready to let Solus know when to come inside. Closing his eyes, a wave of wonder falls over him as he realises this is the moment he has been waiting for all these years.

'This is the time of miracles, Rogaro,' he says. 'We are going to make history.'

'I just hope you know what you are doing,' whispers Rogaro.

He reopens his eyes and holds the book with arms outstretched, ready to quote an incantation from it. Excited by the possibility of what could transpire, all the anxiety he had before about reading words in Ethereal that he didn't understand has seemingly vanished. Nothing matters to him anymore for this is it.

The incantation, pronounced in Ethereal, starts.

"Awaken lost essence: Barel calls. Leave the dream: Gadno calls. Stir into life: Uriro calls."

With the first incantation complete, nothing seems to happen. Ferlor repeats the verse again and still nothing happens. Deciding that he needs to concentrate more, or perhaps, change his pronunciation of the names in the verse, he closes his eyes again.

From memory he repeats the incantation over and over – still nothing. Eventually, his arms become tired and he closes the book and drops it onto the floor: it lands with some force, but does not bounce to the surprise of Rogaro who watches.

At the moment it hits the stonework, the air becomes heavy. Any notion of a light breeze in the external graveyard dissipates. Ferlor still with eyes closed feels the hairs on the back of his neck rise. He repeats the incantation several times once again. Eventually, he feels a strong jolt run down the back of his spine, flowing out into his arms and down to the tips of his fingers. He can no longer hear anything else, except his own voice, repeating the incantation over and over. As he does, the jolt becomes more frequent and he starts to struggle reciting as if he were experiencing an electric shock.

A strange smell becomes more noticeable as Ferlor breathes in more air and his heart rate accelerates. The smell becomes a stink, smelling like rotting flesh combined with expired eggs – almost sulphurous. He gives one last incantation before he opens his eyes.

His senses become awash with differing feelings. The circle of corpse dust has caught alight, surrounding him in a ring of fire. Thick smoke blows around in a cyclone, outside of the Necrocircle, and Rogaro is nowhere to be seen. There is no sound. Ferlor tries to tilt his head, but the pulsing energy running through his body is preventing him from moving. He tries to cry out for help, but the paralysis becomes too much. He feels an even more strange sensation, like a fiery brush is scraping at his insides. The pain becomes unbearable – his vision starts to cloud, the colour fades. He can no longer recite or even speak. Before he seems to disappear, he thinks to himself: 'Who are you?'

As the smoke starts to swell, Rogaro decides that something is not what it should be. He takes a moment to look at the rapidly eclipsing figure of Ferlor, pain and torment evident on his face. It is as if he is becoming a shell of a man, everything except the mind is present — the High Priest terrorised what he is witnessing, fumbles with the gate, eventually bursting it open and dashes through into the main Temple. The gate slams itself shut as it rebounds back.

Solus watches as Rogaro rushes past him, flailing and mumbling, and disappears outside. His mind was full of thoughts about what to ask his father, wondering if the questions are too silly or too obvious. But all of this is instantly forgotten by the bizarre behaviour of Rogaro and also of an ear-piercing scream that echoes around the whole Temple, followed immediately with a loud electrical explosion. A pure white second-long flash filters through the cracks in the closed gate.

Not really too sure what to make of the situation, he moves up to the gate and can feel heat emitting from its wood and ironworks. Touching the handle proves too much as the emperor singes his hand on it. Looking around in the nave, he finds some white cloth and uses it to shield his hand. Pulling on the gate, it opens, but the frame surrounding it is in flames.

To his horror the graveyard is filled with thick blue smoke, blotting out the sky above. The air smells acidic, but the arid smoke and inducing stink is not his concern. In the middle, where his father's grave once was, a small crater exists, but he sees Ferlor crouched down on the floor with his back towards him.

Approaching, Solus is unsure whether or not the ritual is a success. The tomb where Ferlor crouches is blown apart with little trace of the original monument. The ground where Emperor Vimlor's bones once laid is absent. Looking more closely at Ferlor, he sees his clothes are burnt and his previously thinning hair has all gone.

'Is that you, father?' asks the emperor, quivering as he speaks. After a short pause, and a series of hacking coughs, he gets an unusual response.

'Father?' replies Ferlor, followed by hysterical laughter.

Turning around, a startled Solus sees that his eyes are a strange blue and appear to glow, and takes a few steps back.

'Do not look so surprised,' Ferlor chuckles. 'We are all friends here.'

He smiles and holds out a hand for a shake. His hands are scarred with blackness with the skin almost peeling off. Reluctantly, Solus limply shakes the outstretched hand before quickly retracting.

'Now, that was not so bad was it?' he says in a calm voice, still smiling.

'What has happened to you, Ferlor?' asks Solus, clearly shocked.

'Ferlor? What a puzzling name, I presume. Who or what is this Ferlor you speak? No matter – I suppose this body was he.'

It dawns on the emperor that who he is talking to is not Ferlor at all, and going by what he said before, it may not be his father either.

'I can see the confusion on your face. I suppose I would be so as well, wondering who I was looking at, wondering about many things. I too am wondering right now. There is a great deal I need to discover it seems. But, instead of referring to me as some stranger, you can address me as Barel.'

Solus looks into the deep blue swirling vortexes for eyes – whoever this is now, it is not Ferlor or his father.

'You are inquisitive,' smiles Barel, followed by a playful chuckle.

The emperor snaps out of his confused trance and remembers who he is.

'I am Emperor Solus, leader of the people of the Shaler, state your business,' he says defiantly.

'Such an authoritative voice, and well-spoken too! Emperor, you say? Ah yes, it is coming to me now. The Shaler — this name seems very familiar,' ponders Barel.

'You talk as if you are a stranger to all that is known! Explain yourself,' demands Solus.

'Dearest emperor,' he replies in a soft condescending voice. 'There is so much you cannot see.'

At this point, Solus is going through mixed emotions of anger, disappointment and sorrow, accumulating in a state of confusion. He reaches over to a ceremonial sword hanging on the nearest wall and grips it tightly.

'This is your last chance, Barel, father, Ferlor or whoever you are!'

Barel gives a wicked grin and chuckles again.

'That will not do you any favours,' he says confidently.

Overcome with ire, Solus swings back the sword and makes a forward push. As he approaches his target, Barel narrows his brow, outstretches his arms and speaks in Ethereal which is entirely unfamiliar to Solus. Immediately, lightning emits from his hands which sends Solus flying backwards and releasing his grip on the sword. He lands on his back with a thud, but aside from being shocked he is uninjured.

'That was just a warning, emperor, you cannot defeat me. No-one can defeat me, not this time,' he yells. 'For I am the Warmonger of the Elements, and you are powerless to stop me!'

He cackles loudly and the sound carries around the graveyard.

Several lower priests charge in via the open gate and see Solus struggling to come to his feet. They ignore Barel and rush to the emperor and lift him up while the Lightbearer looks on.

'Yes, come to the aid of your emperor. He is the reason why I am here, for what end I do not yet know, but you will all regret your actions. It is great to be here once again,' announces Barel, who turns around, raises his arms to the sky and speaks again in Ethereal. A tornado appears around him and is launched high into the air and disappears, the swirling vortex following.

The priests look at the scruffy emperor who answers their questioning eyes: 'I do not know.'

Smoke filling the graveyard has dissipated via the open roof. The emperor sees the scorched marks where the circle was drawn with the ash – despite the electrical explosion, the circle remains fully intact. Solus cries out, sobbing uncontrollably, kneeling on his legs, feeling a deflated and defeated man. Any hope of getting the answers from his father are now truly lost.

A thousand thoughts, questions and scenarios fly through Solus' mind all with no answers and leaving more questions. He idly scans around the ground where he kneels and something catches his eye. Resting perfectly on the edge of the blackened circle lays the Book of the Daimons, closed and completely untouched by what just occurred. Picking it up, Solus rises to his feet, clearing tears from his face. He opens the book and starts to flick through the pages, hopelessly looking for clues, but none of it makes any sense to him.

Avornia arrives at the graveyard, taken aback by the whimpering and lingering smell of burnt flesh. She sees the emperor desperately trying to find answers in the dark book. The expression on his face is that of despair – not really attempting to read the pages, more looking through them in a hope that something will make sense.

'What are you doing, Solus?' she asks. 'What is going on?'

The emperor is startled and he snaps the book firmly closed, before turning to look with wide eyes at his mother. Avornia looks down and sees the blackened circle and the destroyed grave of her husband.

'What have you done?' she barks, turning towards Solus.

'I have done nothing, mother! I am as shocked as you.'

Avornia then strides up to her son and snatches the book from his grasp. She opens it at a random page and instantly recognising the language, closes the book, looking at Solus.

'How did you find this?' she asks surprised, almost entirely forgetting the scene of destruction surrounding her.

'It was lying on the floor just there,' he replies, pointing. 'It was Ferlor that found it.'

'That clever old fool,' Avornia nods. 'He was always the smart one, if a little deceptive.'

Solus becomes curious with his mother. Her original scorching tone when she entered has changed to almost one of delight.

'It would appear you know something I don't,' he says. 'Something else that you haven't told me, perhaps?'

She gasps at his insinuation, referring to her husband's murder.

'I know what this book is. It is the Book of the Daimons — the creation of the Kaidis and all its secrets. A missing piece of the puzzle we have been searching for!'

Solus cannot believe what he is hearing; his jaw drops as she speaks.

'What I have done?' he blurts out. 'I was a fool – why didn't Ferlor tell me about any of this?'

'I don't know – I can't speak for him. You should probably start from the beginning.'

Moving into the nave, Solus goes on to explain to his mother — who listens intently — about his desperation to find his father, the suggestions made by the High Priest about necromancy, the discovery of the book by Ferlor, the ritual that followed and Ferlor's disappearance.

'That is quite the tale. And you kept all this from me?'

'Ferlor told me so, he told everyone. He didn't want anyone to interfere. I trusted him, like I trusted him for some foolish reason, blinded by my own desires,' Solus sighs.

'You couldn't have possibly known,' Avornia says, comforting her son. 'But necromancy as you say is really just myth. There is no such thing. You have been misled in more ways than one. We shall never know the truth if Ferlor is gone.'

The emperor's initial grief turns to anger learning about the incredible deception led by his former associate. He cannot believe he was so blind – have they been manipulating him for his entire life? How is that even possible? To what end?

Avornia flicks through the book until she finds the ritual for the Necrocircle. She scoffs as she reads the instructions.

'Solus, this is all about calling into the Synthetic Domain — we have had many theories about how to do this at the Institute, but have had never found conclusive instruction about how to do so. This is quite the discovery, but if it has actually happened, I don't know any more without reading further.'

'It isn't anything to do with necromancy?' he asks, not really understanding what his mother is saying.

'You must stop thinking about those ridiculous children's stories,' she smiles. 'These texts are revolutionary and must be studied immediately.'

'But what about the "beast" the Compendium page mentioned?'

'I have no idea,' she replies. 'But with this book in our hands, it should provide us with some insight.'

'And Ferlor?'

'There are so many questions that need answering, Solus. We can only hope that Ramor will guide us and the book reveals more.'

128

# Chapter Eight

# Heretics

Over towards the great forest of Mistwood to the east of Thoridon, afternoon sunlight shimmers through the branches of tall pine trees, the green needles bobbing around in a light breeze. The forest covers a long distance where many varieties of tree, plant life and insect exist. Also, the river Still runs through the area and splits into smaller tributaries making the entire forest rich with life — a self-contained macrocosm which nurtures itself.

To the north-west of the forest is an area that the Shaler uses for forestry. Having harvested all the wood to the south of the city, they expanded to the east to recover more of the desired resource. With the receding trees opening up the area, the light breeze blows directly across the plains, strewn with tree stumps.

Breaking the serenity, the winds begin to rapidly increase in speed, creating a cyclone as clouds start to form in the sky. In almost an instant, a swirling mass of air and debris extends down, surrounded by bolts of lightning. It touches the open glade with a loud thunderous crash and a brilliant flash, only to dissipate as fast as it appeared.

The winds recede and upon the ground which is now scorched by the electrical blasts, the unkempt and possessed figure of Ferlor stands, with singed blades of grass surrounding. Still dressed in a charred robe with eyes of swirling seas, he brushes himself down undaunted by his dramatic entrance and looks around to try and restore his bearings.

'I am sure this was not like this before,' speaks Barel the Lightbearer, talking in Ethereal to no-one but himself. 'It has been too long.'

Because the People's Union are very well organised, they created a series of small paths and roadways up and down the river and around the harvested forest, all eventually leading to Thoridon with the intention to make transporting the wood and gathered materials much easier. But to Barel, who has visited the Arena of Pri before, it was most certainly an untouched forest last time.

After looking around briefly, in the near distance he hears the sound of rushing water and decides to follow one of the many paths leading east. Being not entirely familiar with the situation, he cautiously looks around as he moves along. Arriving at the riverbank, the water rushes past at a fast pace. It is pure, as if it melted off the mountains just recently. He kneels down and cups his scorched hands in the water, the singed skin washing under its force and removing the blackness. He looks at his own reflection in the water.

'Do I really look like that?'

He picks up some more water and drinks it, letting out a sigh of relief. Despite Barel being a Lightbearer, he still needs to keep his mortal body alive. Rising to his feet, he surveys the area once again. Across the river lies a lonely beech tree, providing ample shade from the warm sunlight of his mother.

With a smile on his face, he outstretches a hand towards the river. The flow of water starts to arc into the air, looking like a liquid bridge. Jumping down onto the exposed river bed, he proceeds to walk underneath the wall of water. Some of the water drips onto his head as he moves towards the other side and then climbs up. He turns to face the water, outstretches the same hand and moves his arm down – the water splashes back into the river bed restoring its natural flow.

Sitting down underneath the tree, resting his back against the bark, he sighs looking out over to the west. There are plenty of old remnants where the Shaler used this part of the forest for wood. There are many tops of exposed tree trunks with their roots scattered around and the odd random bush or tree still stands. It appears the immediate area is deserted, with just the sound of rushing water from the river in front and the periodic rustling of a gentle breeze in the treetop above.

He ponders about how he came to be inside the body of Ferlor. With the mind of Ferlor replaced by that of Barel, it would be impossible to determine what his motivations were. When he was last here, things were very different – he recalls his last confrontation with the Shaler, long before the reign of Serenus at the end of the First Era. He smiles as various memories of that time are reminded to him. Such memories include when he would unleash a wave of destruction upon the people, when they were much less technologically advanced than they are now.

These memories lead on to others which are more troubling. One of these is being overpowered by the Shaler – his acts of pure destruction, merely for his amusement, turned against him. The people rose up and plotted against what they believed to be a monster in fear for their own lives. Completely taken by surprise, Barel was lured into a trap, resulting in him falling down into a chasm – while he is a master of elements, moving of the earth is an ability he does not control. Despite many howls from inside, his pleas became unanswered, left to rot in the hole, his possessed host eventually succumbing to starvation. This was the end of his game upon this Arena, and it is this event that formed the basis for the Daimon tale, revealing the Synth to the Shaler.

But this is not Barel's time, a fact that he becomes conscience to. When a Lightbearer is deployed to an Arena, the Lightbearer is typically greeted by the occupying Ascended — a formal introduction to the game field. However, this has not been the case so far: Toraq is nowhere to be seen. There are no Ethereal thoughts in his mind being broadcast by the Ascended. It is all too quiet.

Regardless of this strange situation, his thoughts return to his past. Barel sees this return to the Arena of Pri as a personal opportunity and coming to the conclusion that there seems to have been some kind of mistake, decides what to do next. That memory of the dank chasm, the darkness inside — it is time for revenge against those who denied his chance at Ascendancy. His course of action would be to continue where he left off – restart his fun against the Shaler. Barel was not expecting the grand buildings and seeming advancements that the Shaler has made, since they were so unorganised and barbaric the last time he saw them. The notion of an emperor is also completely astounding.

His thoughts of the past are broken when from the peaceful serenity of the shady tree and rushing water comes a muffled scrape on a muddy path along the edge of the river, followed by what seems to be laughter and clattering of metal. Rising to his feet and moving out of view behind the tree, he awaits to see what arrives.

* * * *

The path leads along the river in a southern direction and is heavily trodden. Further down is a branch off the main river that leads east into the forest. It is quite deep, with steep banks on either side from many years of erosion by the water. A wooden bridge has been constructed over, built by the Shaler in the past. The wood of the bridge is fairly rotten and it is not very stable from neglected maintenance.

Peering around the tree trunk to get a view of what approaches with the bridge in line-of-sight, Barel sees four burly folk dressed in heavy blackened armour, with helmets, encrusted shields and sheathed short swords. All approximately the same height, slightly arching themselves toward their fronts, with pigmented yellow skin and beady little eyes barely visible inside the strapped-on helmets, these warriors laugh and tease each other, blissfully unaware that they are being watched. They also speak the language of the Shaler, but with deep, gruff voices and hearty laughter, these are no Shaler.

This Kaidis scouting party is a prime example of the development of the break-away Shaler. As time has progressed, the beginnings of the Kaidis followed the instruction of Toraq at the start of the Fourth Era. They sought what was suggested and discovered the great riches that the landscape had to offer.

It was not just the resources that projected the Kaidis into the powerhouse of muscle and brawn that they are now. What Xarash and Gregoria created was a new civilisation, an alternative might to the Shaler without the need for the Synth. Their Bloodrage genetic mutation is passed on to new generations of Kaidis, each time the potency of the affliction increasing, creating tougher and much more menacing revisions of what was the beginning. Their numbers have swelled into the thousands — and with Xarash's original dream of being a warrior resulting in an army, he might have been proud of what the Kaidis have become. But perhaps, the challenges of creating, maintaining and running an army are more complicated than was originally thought.

'What are we looking for again?' asks one of the scouts behind a more senior looking one.

'For the love of the Bloodrage! How many more times do I have to remind that thick-fucking-skull of yours? The captain told us to look for signs of that spinning tornado that appeared around here,' replies the stern sergeant.

'But it's gone now,' comments the scout, looking straight ahead and not really listening to his superior.

Reaching breaking point, the sergeant stops abruptly, making the scout crash into his back, not realising.

'Look where you're fucking going!' he yells, turning around. 'Why did I have to get grouped with you idiots?'

'Sorry,' the scout whimpers.

'Sorry?' barks the sergeant. 'What sort of a soldier are you supposed to be? I should kill you right now! Would do us all a great favour.'

He hits the scout around the head a few times, almost knocking his helmet off.

Barel thinks this would be a good time to introduce himself. He sweeps around the tree and approaches the bridge, waiting for the sergeant to turn around.

'You seem to have a bit of a problem,' Barel says sarcastically.

To this, the sergeant turns around hearing a much softer voice of what appears to be a Shaler and starts to draw his sword. The rest of his squad wises up and unsheathe their own short swords, readying shields, going into a defensive formation and standing in a line in front of the sergeant. Barel stands directly in front of the meat wall, blocking their path off the bridge, with enough distance to react should the situation change.

As the sergeant peers over the wall, he starts to recognise the face of Ferlor without noticing the swirling deep blue eyes. He changes to a more relaxed stance, concluding that the leader of the Synth Institute could easily outmanoeuvre his small squad.

'What the fuck are you doing out here?' he boldly questions.

'And what, may I ask, are some comically dressed Shaler doing out here as well?' chuckles Barel.

The sergeant rallies himself, pushing through the scouts up to the front and readies his own sword.

'We are not some fucking Shaler filth! You, of all those scum, should fucking know that.'

'Oh, really? Tell me who you are then, if you are not Shaler.'

The sergeant turns to his squad, a confused look on his face to which triggers muted giggles from the lower ranks.

'Have you lost your fucking mind?' he says again, turning back around. 'We are Scouting Party 246, Attachment D4, and Second Division of the Kaidis! Forward march for glory!'

With this final order, the Kaidis charge toward the Lightbearer, swords drawn and shields up, making loud roars as they advance over the bridge. Not wanting his fragile host to become skewered on the end of a sharp bit of steel, he whispers and sweeps his arms towards the rushing party. As he does this, a great wind blows in their direction and all four of the Kaidis are knocked back three times the distance, putting them back on the other side of the bridge. A loud crash of metal shatters the calmness of the forest. Groans are heard for a brief moment as they wonder what just happened but their sheer strength gets them back on their feet.

As the sergeant calls to regroup, the shield wall reforms and they recover their exact same stance as before with efficiency and speed all within a few seconds. Before the sergeant could give the next order, Barel focuses his attention onto the bridge. Continuing to manipulate the Synth via his more natural electromagnetic communication, he charges up the air and forms a ball of fire, directing it to the bridge. The rotten wood is easily set alight and the bridge becomes engulfed in flames.

'Are you afraid to die, you disgusting piece of shit?' yells the sergeant over the flames, politeness not being his distinguishing feature. He orders one of his men to walk into the burning bridge to see if their strong armour can withstand the path of flames. Gingerly following his superiors order, he tip-toes onto the flames, gets about a third of the way in and has to retreat back as the fire burns so hot it penetrates his armoured boots. While the Kaidis have inherited the ability to be more resistant to heat due to the Bloodrage, they are not impervious to fire.

Barel smiles as he watches, bending down and etches a rudimentary circle in the damp, muddied ground. Beginning to quietly chant in Ethereal, the trapped Kaidis become more agitated as they cannot understand what he says. The sergeant commands his scouts to lay their shields upon the fire, forming a protective path over the bridge which starts to collapse.

With the plan successful as he and the three scouts make it to the other side, the sergeant lets out a satisfying chuckle and regroups without shields as they are too hot to hold. Barel, meanwhile, stands in a trance in the middle of the circle and looking like a prime target.

'Too fucking easy this – forward!' he yells to his men, and they charge ahead as before.

The sergeant stands back as the other three Kaidis run forward and move to enclose Barel, circling his position. After making sure that nothing else seems to be out of the ordinary, the sergeant commands his group to attack. As soon as they storm into the circle they become paralysed and drop to the floor, letting go of their swords and thrashing around in agony, screaming, holding their heads. It is as if they were overcome with a disabling headache; an electrical field surrounding Barel, electrocuting their brains. They eventually come to a rest, lifeless.

Barel comes out of his trance unharmed and walks out of the circle, stepping over the bodies on the floor and approaching the sergeant who has a degree of fear across his face. However, the Kaidis are not known for their cowardice, and he roars, raising his sword high and advances. The Lightbearer smirks and uses the same trick of a strong gust of wind to force him onto his back, once again with a crash.

As the sergeant picks himself up, now with less enthusiasm, he looks to see Barel grinning with pleasure as he stands in an unusual stance, as if he were trying to pick up the ground. The water in the river alongside them begins to churn more erratically.

'What is it you want, Shaler?' he questions, slightly out of breath.

'Well, your first mistake was calling me a Shaler,' Barel smiles. 'For you see, I am not who you think I am. Your second mistake was immediately suggesting I was some kind of threat.'

'Aren't you?'

'Who is to say? You appear to be the threat right now along with whoever the Kaidis are.'

'Your words are confusing to me!' roars the sergeant.

'I suppose they might be, but it seems you have learnt not to come running towards me.'

'I don't have time for your fucking games, whoever you are.'

'Fine,' says Barel, defiantly. 'Tell me where you came from and perhaps we can come to some kind of arrangement.'

The sergeant looks over at the river as it seems to swell further. He grunts as he sees what appears to be happening and he looks back at Barel.

'I think I already know the arrangement,' he replies. 'But you want to continue down that path and find the captain.'

'Excellent,' concludes Barel as he finally lifts his arms. The water in the river makes a leap directly on top of the sergeant and carries him away into the torrent, without a scream.

Quietly impressed by the Kaidis display of military precision, Barel considers the possibility that they could become allies in assisting with his task of toying with the Shaler, but he needs to be entirely sure first. When the sergeant first recognised Barel as Ferlor, he became instantly hostile — vigorously so. This was a clear indication of their intentions but not entirely proof.

Choosing to follow the direction of the sergeant, he calls upon the winds and the fires are blown out on the now extremely fragile bridge with the Kaidis shields still tentatively resting on top of the disappearing wooden frame. Tip-toeing over, he crosses the bridge successfully like a child on stepping stones and continues down the southern path.

* * * *

Strolling down the well-trodden path from where the Kaidis scouting party came, Barel looks at the river of Still. It rushes past vigorously as he moves in a southerly direction, with a sound of constant trickling as the water cascades over stones that litter its path. This peaceful noise returns the Lightbearer to a state of calmness and his thoughts return to his rediscovered objective.

As he progresses, the forest builds up again as the Shaler haven't pillaged the resources this far. The pathway starts to move away from the river and enters into a much more enclosed landscape, with overhanging trees and obscured light. Birds call from the treetops and around, all while Barel continues to travel. To him, this is how he remembers his last visit to this Arena — the lush vegetation and with a fledgling people trying to make sense of their existence. But the game of change that he plays has progressed well beyond his previous experiences.

Thinking about his encounter with the Kaidis earlier, he hopes that they can best that performance and actually stand up and make a presentable challenge. Even though he knows nothing about them, a first impression is hard to reverse — an impression they certainly made; far more interesting than those pathetic Synth addicts.

Barel's footsteps and gentle merry chuckling have not gone unnoticed — as he wonders through the forest, he is not alone. A twig forcefully snaps to his left and he turns to look immediately in its direction. There is nothing there. He stops and narrows his brow, peering into the shadowy wood. The wind rustles in the trees as he looks around.

His attention is finally grabbed as a stone is thrown from behind him. It lands on the muddy ground with a thud at his feet, and he turns at the noise. Peering at the rock, it providing an excellent distraction, a figure stands up from behind a bush, wearing nothing but painted camouflage and disappears into the deeper forest. The Lightbearer gets a brief glimpse of the figure.

'It would seem the forest has eyes. How things have progressed!' he exclaims to himself, but loud enough just in case someone else is watching.

Continuing south, the wood thins and the vegetation becomes increasingly sparse, turning to green fields and rolling, unbroken landscapes. This sparseness has a reason: Barel eventually arrives at what is simply known as the Crossroads, where four well-trodden paths spiral off into their directions.

Central to this arrangement of roadways is an obscure object. These roads have been used for many years, carrying carts or thundering troops from Kaidis invasions into Shaler territory. But the Crossroads represents a special kind of symbolism to all, with the towering pile of metals and other materials standing as a makeshift cenotaph, surrounded by silence. From its base and rising to the sky is a memorial to fallen Kaidis and Shaler — pieces of well-weathered Kaidis armour, rusted weaponry and various trinkets are piled high. Hundreds of necklaces adorn the various metals, either left by passing Kaidis warriors or even Shaler well-wishers. Dusts and sands cover the entire structure.

Barel observes curiously at what it is; such an unusual display of compassion between two supposedly warring factions. Not one for compassion himself, he quickly dismisses any attraction to the sentiment and brings himself to the more immediate concern about where to go next.

He looks down the connected roads. To the west, the green fields turn into bog — an area referred to as the Flatlands. The river Still forks into two through the Flatlands, providing water to Thoridon as well as continuing south — the Flatlands itself is simply the partially waterlogged land in-between. Mistwood used to extend through here, but since the Shaler's forestry, boggy land remains. There is a striking image of the Temple of Ramor visible in the distance, past the river, as the road almost directly leads to the south-side of the Shaler city.

The road to the east, from the perspective of Barel, seems more greener with trees bordering the road but it disappears to a more south-easterly direction and he cannot see where it leads.

Along the southern road, the path is much more punctured with heavy boot prints. It is certainly an extremely straight road with no concern for anything getting in its way. As Barel peers down into the distance, he sees the river snake around to become parallel with the road and it seems to increase in width further down.

'Follow the river, he said,' mutters Barel to himself in Ethereal, remembering what the sergeant told him. Before moving off, he looks at the strange cenotaph for a final time and shakes his head, not understanding its significance.

* * * *

Against a backdrop of warm, orange sunlight, the path that Barel travels is destined to a collection of outbuildings situated at a unique landmark. This is at the edge of Shaler territory and a deep canyon acts as a definitive divide between the two factions.

The canyon is known as Wodar Drop, aptly named as the distance to the bottom is considerable. Carved from a combination of volcanic eruption and subsequent shifting of the earth, the enormous crack in the landscape is the end point for the river Still. As it flows off down into the dark canyon below, the water creates an almighty waterfall where torrents of water cascade down into the Drop. At the bottom in the darkness, the water itself continues to the right in an eastern direction — but not to the west as the rocks below are elevated as this is the tail end of the crevice.

But what occupies the area is not the Shaler — the Kaidis have claimed it and do not expect the Shaler to question this. They are not concerned with such land grabbing, largely because it is not a considerable threat to them and even though they are at war, they have no desire to fight in complete contrast to the Kaidis.

Warm winds constantly blow over the canyon from the south, the heart of Kaidis territory. Wodar Drop is vitally important to the existence of the Kaidis — not just strategically, but very much for survival as well. Because the river flows into the canyon, this is the last point at which the Kaidis have a reasonable chance of utilising it.

Across the canyon is simply desert — hot, sandy and notoriously bleak, coupled with the strong, stormy winds, it is not a land where mere mortals can survive for too long. But despite this, it is where the prized resources that the Kaidis initially sought originate. Central — disguised by the blowing sands — stands a tall volcano. The Sulphur Deserts are rich with ores and minerals, and the volcano is largely responsible for these prized materials. Mount Sindre is also the home for the Kaidis Kingdom.

As the deserts are obviously dry, it is Wodar Drop that provides the last chance to bring home the required water supply. When the Kaidis were formed, the auxiliary Shaler that became the backbone for the new civilisation was either skilled engineers from the People's Union or intelligent students defected from the Synth Institute. These skills have been paramount in their adaption of the landscape, coupled with the minerals from the volcano, the Kaidis have been able to construct and develop new tools, weapons and resources that define them as the leading power.

Such prudence has been detrimental to their conquering of the Drop. Where the waterfall is situated, suspended from either side of the canyon by strong chains spins an elaborate waterwheel, crafted from metals forged from the volcanic ores. It is durable and able to withstand the pressures provided by the falling water. On its wings, the wheel collects the water as it spins around and this harvested water is deposited into large troughs at the bottom.

Again, as a true testament to the engineering ingenuity that the Kaidis are able to demonstrate, a steel platform also extends the width of the canyon. It is upon this suspended walkway that a team of Kaidis workers shuffle the vats of water as they fill to the other side, and attach them to hooks that extend down from an overhead pulley system. Through manual pulling, the water is carried through the air and up, where they are collected by more workers on the Kaidis side of the canyon.

This is non-stop work, day and night, with teams of Kaidis working in shifts to serve themselves and also the Kaidis Kingdom housed inside Mount Sindre. Despite their incredible, genetic resistance to heat, they still need to drink to survive; the function of the water collection facility crucial to this.

On the Shaler side of the canyon is where Barel approaches from. Here, the engineering and purpose of the operation is not entirely obvious. A tall, solid parameter fence extends all around with no noticeable gaps or windows to see through inside, but there is a large gate central. There are no patrolling guards around the complex and aside from the loud rushing of water, no sounds give any clues.

Lurking in the shadows, a curious Barel surveys the parameter. The river is moving too fast to try and sneak around that way, so without really knowing what to expect — but conscience to the fact that this will be what the sergeant he encountered earlier was most likely referring to — he takes his chances and edges along in a westerly direction.

The rising heat becomes a noticeable feature as he gradually makes his way around. With the sunset, long shadows are cast by the fence and behind the parameter is a long, wooden building. Meeting the end of the fence, he sees the canyon below and the jagged rocks, with the river flowing away in the distance. But luck is on his side as there is a small gap between the end of the fence and the edge of the canyon. Ferlor's body is slim and nimble despite his age which allows Barel to slowly teeter on the edge of the canyon, gingerly shimmying along the edge of the parameter. Not wanting to look down, he makes it around the fence and swings himself around the steel post at the end, slightly relieved — if he fell, his unscheduled game on the Arena would have been ended abruptly.

Turning around, he finally gets to see what is on the other side of the fence. The long building is a barracks, providing accommodation for the workers and engineers. There are no windows so Barel is unable to see inside and determine what is going on. He peers around the corner of the building and sees where the gate is and what is before it — a courtyard with nothing out of the ordinary. Storage huts are dotted around and a forge glows orange in the middle. There are distinctively no signs of anyone, however.

On the far side of the courtyard is a smaller wooden hut, but larger than one used for storage. It is built with a little more care and attention with a single closed door on its front. This belongs to the captain of the operation who is in charge of running the facility and delivering orders to the workers. It also stands quiet.

Barel is increasingly more anxious to find out some clues as to what is going on and also where anyone is. He should have been tearing up the place, throwing his weight around and causing general chaos by now. But without anyone to inflict this upon makes the whole idea worthless. Not defeated, he returns to behind the barracks and runs along the back, in full view of the other side of the canyon, his appearance only diminished by the shadows.

As he moves along, the waterwheel and the platform below makes itself apparent. Finally, there are signs of life as the workers heave the collected water. Reaching the end of the barracks is a path leading to a ladder which goes down onto the platform. He bends down and looks over the edge to see what the Kaidis are up to.

'What do you think you're fucking looking at?' comes a gruff voice from behind as Barel peers over, freezing as he realises he has been caught.

It is a Kaidis sergeant: the single warrior at Wodar Drop who mans the gate at the front just in case the Shaler decides to try something. Before Barel has a chance to turn around, the sergeant grabs him by the back and forces him down onto the ground. The pain of doing so makes itself known to Barel.

'Why don't you have a closer look,' suggests the sergeant, pressing his boot on Barel's back. 'See? It's amazing, isn't it? Isn't it!' he yells.

'Indeed, very much,' whimpers Barel back.

'Before I press harder on this foot, care to tell me what you are doing?'

'I am looking for someone.'

'Oh, really? What sort of "someone"?'

Barel isn't really sure if the question is genuine. Giving the situation, it is unlikely, but he tries his chances.

'The captain, I need to speak to the captain.'

Grunting, the sergeant pauses for a moment. He thinks it is clearly a Shaler who has lost his way, but he also considers that Barel has given a correct response. He could just press harder and push him off the edge without any further trouble. Although the singed robes along with the burnt hair on his head are signs that something may not be all it appears.

Releasing his boot from Barel's back, he disapprovingly picks him off the floor and carries him towards the captain's hut in the courtyard.

'You are lucky,' says the sergeant, a grin on his face. 'I'm sure the captain will do much worse to you.'

* * * *

The door on the captain's hut crashes open as the sergeant throws Barel into it with a smile, like a tossed rag. Landing on the hard wooden floor face down, he groans after the ordeal. The situation isn't exactly going how he thought it would, but then he has clearly understated how the Kaidis actually work. Looking up, the door is closed by the sergeant not before coming inside and standing in front of it.

Picking himself off the floor — albeit a little cautiously — he brushes himself down nonchalantly before turning his attention to a large desk that is central to the single roomed, wooden hut.

At the rear is a curtained area, sleeping quarters for the captain. The desk faces the door with the captain himself sitting behind it, entirely unperturbed by the thunderous noise of the arrival of an unwelcome visitor. With a pen in hand, he scribbles away on papers strewn across the desk, and stacks of paper pile up around his immediate area. A single burning torch illuminates the room and it crackles as the embers project into the air.

The three men are silent, with Barel looking curiously at the most senior Kaidis at the water facility. His name is Karzol and always referred to as "the captain". He has a long history, even if the Kaidis' overall history is much shorter than their rivals. The rank of captain attained through his service and dedication in the earlier years has seen him reduced to a desk job, even if he is in charge of the most vital operation to the Kaidis as a whole.

'What is it you want, Ferlor?' says Karzol, not looking up from his papers.

The sergeant then suddenly marches across the room to a small chair in front of the captain's desk.

'Sit!' he yells at Barel, who cautiously moves over and does as he says. He then returns to the door, his metal armour and sword clanking as he does and folds his arms.

'Well, out with it Shaler. I haven't got all day.'

'But I am not "Ferlor",' replies Barel.

The unusual response is enough for Karzol to stop what he is doing. Dropping the pen on the desk, he runs his hands down his yellow-pigmented face and looks directly at Barel.

'You look like Ferlor to me,' sighs Karzol, who is very well spoken in contrast to Barel's previous encounters with the Kaidis. 'Clearly, you have lost your mind, especially since you seem to be a long way from home.'

'What you say does have some truth to it,' smiles Barel. 'But I do not expect you to understand that.'

'I don't have time for this nonsense. This is your last chance, Ferlor.'

'The threats that you speak are meaningless, but I have a proposal for you and your Kaidis.'

'A proposal? You mean surrender?'

'Captain, you seem to be really unaware of the situation. I shall repeat: I am not Ferlor. He has long since been removed from this mortal existence. The people that he represented, the Shaler I understand, are in much torment since certain developments have taken place. I am the reason for these changes.'

Karzol raises an eyebrow.

'Either you have completely gone delusional or you speak the truth,' he replies. 'While it is true that we don't hear news from the Kingdom unless the workers are told, I think we would be aware of the situation you describe. But I will give you the benefit of the doubt, if you can demonstrate to me this is the case.'

'Agreed,' states Barel, who immediately moves to stand from the chair. The sudden reaction startles the sergeant and is ready to move in to apprehend Barel, but Karzol raises a hand to signal him to stop. The sergeant returns to the door with folded arms, and watches as Barel moves over towards him.

The sergeant is brutish, with strong, overly-developed muscles and the yellow pigments of sulphur in his skin are prolific. An adapt example of the kind of machine that the Kaidis warriors have become since their beginning, he growls as Barel smiles at him. His superior is clearly interested in seeing what Barel is going to do.

'Stand still,' Barel advises the sergeant as he outstretches a hand.

'Get away from me you fucking pest!' he booms and flinches away from being touched. But in his anger, he notices Barel's eyes, the subtle blue voids swirling around. Becoming mesmerised, wondering what is going on, it is enough for Barel to strike. This time, successfully placing a hand on the exposed arm of the sergeant and grabbing on to it, in a low voice speaks in Ethereal and begins the execution of the Ethereal Transference ritual. With a bright white flash, the ritual is complete in a matter of moments and Barel successfully possesses the brutish body of the now former sergeant.

The body of Ferlor is now entirely lifeless and collapses to the wooden floor with a thud. Completely unsure of the situation, Karzol stands up from the desk as Barel coughs and stumbles around momentarily; what is normally the case with the Transference ritual while he discovers how to control the hulking body.

'Sergeant!' shouts the captain.

But as Barel manages to stand still and impressed with the abilities that his new host can provide, he looks at Karzol.

'I am no longer your sergeant,' Barel says. 'Do you not see? The corpse of your apparent enemy lies on the floor. I am not Ferlor — I am Barel, Warmonger of the Elements! Now, will you hear my proposal?'

'What is this trickery? Sergeant, stand in line!' yells Karzol, entirely not listening to what Barel is saying.

This is the final straw for the Lightbearer — his patience is running thin and the captain has little scope for imagination. He shouts in Ethereal to emphasise his next action, raising his arms. The door his stands in front blows open as a strong gust of wind commanded by Barel knocks over the piles of papers.

'Is this not enough to demonstrate that your sergeant and the Shaler you keep referring to are no longer alive?'

Karzol returns to his chair and nods to affirm the question. He is slightly concerned about what has occurred but fear is a reaction that he lost many years ago. Seeing that he has finally made his point to the stubborn captain, Barel calmly closes the door and moves towards the desk.

Picking up a sheet of paper that remained on the desk, Barel looks at it, wondering what it is. Despite their warrior instinct, the Kaidis are also very administrative — it is an itinerary cataloguing how much water needs to be collected. After taking a glimpse at the waterwheel before, he connects the dots to understand what they are doing here.

'What is your proposal, then?' questions Karzol, who would be angry at anyone else reading the papers.

'I would like to speak with the leader of your people. I think we have a mutual concern.'

'Forgive me, Barel, was it? But, no-one just asks to see the King. What do you mean by a mutual concern?'

'You dislike the Shaler? So do I. The details I will not go into, but before, they made a mockery of me and I seek revenge.'

The captain strokes his chin.

'You're asking for our help?' he chuckles.

'I suppose,' nods Barel. 'As much as I would like to take them on myself, I feel that if we worked together, we could achieve our desired goals much more efficiently. But why am I telling you this? A king, you say?'

Karzol grunts, realising that he might have suggested too much.

'Yes, our King resides in the Stronghold, out in the Deserts. You should probably take your proposal to him. If you make it that far.'

He goes on to explain how he should get to the Stronghold. The steel platform across the canyon has ladders on both sides, acting as a bridge across the gap. Karzol advises Barel to take this route and speak to the workers on the Kaidis side who will give him transport on their next shipment to Mount Sindre. Normally they don't take passengers, but in matters of utmost importance they can do so. With Barel's appearance being that of the stern sergeant, he shouldn't meet too much resistance.

Taking the advice, Barel leaves the captain's hut and proceeds towards the first ladder. It is now dark outside, but the steel walkway is illuminated by torchlight. Meanwhile, Karzol looks at the corpse of Ferlor and realises that this is of great significance and that it was Barel who was responsible. The leader of the Synth Institute, one of the best brains in Shaler society, deceased. He recovers a blank parchment from the wind-swept chaos and proceeds to write a message. Rolling it up and burning a seal onto the paper, he calls for a worker from the barracks and one dutifully arrives.

The instructions: to take the message to the Stronghold, before the "sergeant" arrives. Knowing exactly how to do that, he leaves by the gate and runs in an easterly direction. He also has plans for Ferlor's corpse, one that he sees as an excellent bargaining chip with the Shaler.

# Chapter Nine

## Confession

In the early morning, Avornia and her son Emperor Solus sit around a long table on the second floor of the octagonal Temple of Ramor. Here, the Temple keeps its own archive of observations, musings and logs of important events that have been notable ever since the Temple was founded.

Because of the symbolic conic roof that the Temple has, this floor has less area than in the nave below. Projecting up through the centre is the glass column with a prism at the roof, used to collect the light from the sky, central to the representation of Ramor during Temple meetings. As the Temple has been around since the Second Era, the archive itself is enormous. On each of the walls are rows of shelving with millions of varied papers neatly stacked in chronological order.

Upon the table is a large book referred to as the Register — a catalogue that the curator of the archive maintains. It contains an inexhaustible list of everything that is written on page, with any titles or brief synopsis coupled with its location upon the indexed shelves. With each paper containing a subject about pretty much anything to do with Shaler life, past and present, it is an invaluable reference to learn from past mistakes or decide the future, containing a rich social commentary. Unlike the Library in the Institute, only journals and observations are here, with little technological or scientific conclusions being drawn. The air in the room is heavy and many of the papers are covered in dust, without being touched for hundreds of years.

Ferlor's disappearance has been more of a wake-up call to Solus than anything before. The transformation of Ferlor is something he could never have prepared for; his emotions changed from sorrow to remorse as he realises that he was the catalyst for recent developments. He is a young emperor, in his early twenties, and he has never had to deal with a tragedy so close to his own life.

His mother is much more prepared, having to come to terms with the murder of her husband while Solus was an infant. Nothing could now be more damaging to her other than the loss of her only son. Despite not having her priorities right in the past, the recent experience has changed her attitude as well. Avornia sees that she never spent enough time with Solus, always preferring to study the Synth or the archives in the Temple, reading about her culture, and indirectly letting others — such as Rogaro — to do the upbringing of the heir to the empire.

But her private research over the years has allowed Avornia to get a grasp of the seriousness of the disappearance of Ferlor and what he did before becoming possessed by Barel the Lightbearer. As the two family members sit across from each other, surrounded by various papers that Avornia is familiar with, the Book of the Daimons is one key component to unlocking the mysteries of the situation and it is positioned at an open page. Solus has neither the intelligence nor will to even attempt to understand what the book contains and is putting full confidence in Avornia in order to translate it into something he can follow.

What she has been able to conclude is that the Necrocircle ritual that Ferlor conducted was a method to communicate directly into the Synthetic Domain. But her knowledge of Ethereal is far from perfect, and similar to what Ferlor knew, can only recognise a few choice phrases from the ritual's incantation. She also has no idea what could have happened to Ferlor, with the story told to her by Solus about a giant cyclone carrying him up into the air being incredibly baffling.

'I just want to go over this once more,' says Solus, standing from his chair. 'What do we know about Ferlor, personally?'

'He was always a bit of a loner,' Avornia says, recalling the conversations of the past few hours. 'He never seemed to be all that bothered about the Institute, as if to be preoccupied with something else.'

'So do we think he performed this ritual because he was a traitor?' questions Solus, facing his mother. 'Was he working for the Kaidis? A spy, perhaps?'

'I think that's a little extreme — I have known him for years and he has never wanted to do any harm.'

'But how do you know that, mother?'

She sighs at Solus.

'I know you and he never really saw eye to eye,' she says. 'You were always suspicious of his intentions. But I didn't see anything wrong with him. He was just a little vacant at times.'

'I have to present something to the Senate shortly,' says Solus sternly. 'They will be demanding answers to what happened last night, and I can't simply say anything.'

'I agree Solus, but we can't simply jump to conclusions without knowing the facts.'

Solus scoffs as he still scorns his mother for never revealing the truth about his father. It is interesting that she should be so interested in getting fact when she can't even give them to her own son.

'What's so funny?' she questions.

'Nothing, but as far as I see it, Ferlor had malicious intentions. What's more, that Barel character is no doubt on the loose somewhere and we have absolutely no idea of what he — I assume — is capable of doing.'

He moves towards the stairs, leading down to the ground floor.

'Where are you going now?' Avornia raises her voice, now quite angry that her son is acting on impulse.

'I have to address the Senate and inform them of the situation. You keep trying to understand that book. It is time for action.'

His mind is entirely made up, regardless of what conclusion Avornia eventually devises.

* * * *

Arriving at the Senate House, Solus rushes in through the open door.

'Emperor Solus, leader of the Shaler, ruler of all in the name of Ramor,' the Canon at the door announces. Despite his loud voice, he still struggles for himself to be heard over the hubbub inside. With Solus approaching the Seat of Power, he sees that the benches of all the Segments are in full attendance. The rich discussion continues as Solus takes his seat. He is relieved to see High Priest Rogaro is also here, quietly sitting on the Branch of Ramor and vacantly staring into nothingness.

As Solus attempts to listen to what is being said, he finds it increasingly difficult to do so with everyone talking over each other. No one wants to hear his pleas for quiet, either because he is merely a boy to some or that he simply cannot make himself heard. Standing up, he walks over to the gong behind the throne and gives it an almighty smash.

He returns to his seat in silence. The leaders of the appropriate organisations and its representatives all diligently return to their own benches and recognising that the emperor is in session. But there is one that does not sit. This single man dwarfs all in the room with a dominating presence and he is fully aware of this fact. Dressed in thick black robes with a purple lining and a long cowl bathing his head in an almost permanent shadow aside from his mouth, this is the leader of the recently created Warlock Council. He is known as Levak, and he refuses to talk about anything to do with his past. He doesn't want anyone to know about him, not even what he looks like.

His reasoning for this is good — Ferlor was responsible for his presence and subsequent creation of the Council. For Ferlor was tasked to defend the Shaler from the constant assaults of the Kaidis upon Thoridon, but he was never really up to the task of training up a group of fighters, empowered by the knowledge of the Synth. As Ferlor was a man for theory and not necessarily practice, he needed someone to take charge while he attended to his duties at the Institute.

The Kaidis have become more sophisticated in their attacks against the Shaler over time; they now also opt to utilise the Synth as well. For the Kaidis are not all sword-wielding, bloodthirsty maniacs — they have their own core collection of former Institute students, quietly nurtured over time by Xarash and his successors, working closely with the Kaidis Kingdom. This section of Synth users are known as the Doctors Division. They do their own private research into the Synth, inspired with the old teachings of the Institute, and also more inclined to use less ethical means in order to achieve desired results.

Levak was a member of this elite Synthetic group inside the Kaidis. But during an assault against Thoridon, he became tired of the constant failures of the military might and a Doctor's role of providing backup to the warriors, deciding to surrender and defecting to the Shaler. Among his reasons were one of pride — he never really had any appreciation for his contributions in the Doctors Division. Also quietly admiring the Shaler for their much greater understanding of the Synth, he seized his chance and managed to convince the Shaler and ultimately Ferlor that he could work for them, against his own kind.

In what was more of a back alley dealing, Ferlor was looking for a quick solution to his defence problem and enthused by the suggestion that a Kaidis wanted to assist the enemy, he agreed with the proposals. The Master Conjurer announced the creation of the Warlock Council and that it was to be headed by a mysterious stranger to mute applause from the Senate. Levak and Ferlor agreed that if anyone discovered that he was formally an operating Kaidis it could be seen as double-standards and decided to keep his identity a complete secret — this secret now further reinforced with the death of Ferlor. In public, Levak will never reveal who he is, as demonstrated with his thick clothing.

The leader of the Council stands in front of his modest benches, with a few of his trained Shaler students behind. Despite being a Kaidis, like all members of the Doctors Division, their mutations caused by the Bloodrage are less prevalent. They have not developed the massive size that a regular Kaidis warrior would attain, much wimpier in comparison. In the silence of the Senate House, Levak's slightly laboured breathing echoes around as Solus just looks straight at him, even though he cannot see his eyes underneath the deep hood.

Being eternally suspicious about Ferlor before, anything that Ferlor was directly involved with inherits the same suspicion. But despite this, he recognises that the Warlock Council have been delivering with results and have proved that they are a vital asset to the security of the Shaler. He can still doubt the ability of their leader, however.

'I suppose you are all wondering what occurred last night,' begins Solus, standing from his chair. 'While I cannot give you complete answers, simply because I do not know the full facts, our inspirational and charismatic leader of the Institute — Ferlor — was responsible for the phenomena that you all witnessed.'

Gasps are expressed from the Institute's benches, as they fear for the worst.

'My problem is that I have no knowledge as to where Ferlor has disappeared. For what seems like something that isn't known to be possible, he spoke with different words, called himself a different name and spirited himself away into the sky above, leaving no trace to his whereabouts. His intentions remain unknown and what he plans to do next is unfounded.'

'Are you suggesting that Ferlor is now a threat to our society?' heckles an observer from the benches of the Union.

'Based on what I have witnessed, I believe this to be the case.'

'What do you mean? You were there with Ferlor at the time?' asks a representative of the Institute.

Solus takes a pause for moment and such an action is enough to confirm to his audience who engage in mumbled conversation around the benches. He doesn't want to reveal to the Senate that he was partially responsible for the actions of Ferlor, chasing dreams of speaking to his father, even if he didn't realise that Ferlor was communicating with the Synthetic Domain.

To the rescue of the emperor, High Priest Rogaro stands from his bench. His face is stricken with fear and most of his colour has been drained, scared of what he saw the night before — the pain and suffering that Ferlor was obviously going through, burnt into his mind. He takes a step forward to make his presence known, and the murmurings trail off as they see that Rogaro is not entirely all there.

'You should all be proud of Emperor Solus,' he says, pointing around at all the benches. 'He was there to protect us all from the horrors that Ferlor has unleashed onto this world. Accept that Ferlor is no longer with us. We should be mourning his passing into the spirits and hailing Solus for his heroic deeds that have allowed us to see another day.'

He raises his arms and his voice.

'To the powers of Ramor, we are forever grateful for your grace and I honour our great Emperor that you have blessed on us. Ramor is with all of you!'

As he completes his dedication, he returns to his bench in appreciative silence, followed by an intensifying applause. Solus smiles as he realises it is for him, and his focus is returned to a resigned Levak who just stands motionless.

'What seems to be on your mind, Levak?' questions Solus from the Seat of Power as the applause dies down.

'This ridiculous pageantry is pathetic compared to the threat that has been introduced,' he replies in a deep gravelled voice. 'You speak of a flying man! We all saw the lightning and heard the explosions from the Temple. If this is the work of a powerful individual, on the loose, this is a serious situation. Your Ramor or whatever will not save you.'

Solus chuckles.

'I agree that this is serious, and this is why I have already taken action. With the Institute without a leader, I shall be appointing my mother, Avornia, to take the role. Her great knowledge of the Synth has already come into use as she is analysing an important document left behind by Ferlor. We shall be able to find answers from this in due time.'

'But how long will that take?' questions Levak, forever the sceptic. 'What if the threat returns and we are defenceless?'

'I would not bother yourself with such matters,' replies Solus. 'Your primary concern is to be aware of any Kaidis situation. Surely I don't need to remind you this?'

Grumbling, Levak sighs and concludes that he isn't going to get any more information from the emperor. Solus, now satisfied that Levak won't query the matter anymore, returns his attention to the rest of the Senate.

'To conclude the session, I know many of you doubt my capacity as leader of the Shaler,' he remarks. 'But I believe this is my test and I will prove to you all that I shall lead us through whatever threats are imposed on us. Ramor will guide us and we shall be victorious for the future. We shall rise again.'

Standing without saying another word, he leaves the Senate House and returns to the upstairs of the Temple to meet his mother. He knows that there are great challenges that await him — realising that this experience has awoken the emperor within him. Even if he didn't speak with his father, Emperor Vimlor is definitely inside.

* * * *

With recommendations directed by Levak taken firmly into action, the city of Thoridon swiftly becomes fortified. The outer walls that surround the city all have their gated entry points firmly closed and an increased number of darkly-cloaked Warlocks stand guard or patrol them. Nothing will get in or out without a reason.

At the various wall towers that puncture the tall defences, further guards stand inside as lookouts. From the western side of the city, a lookout notices a large dust cloud being kicked up along the approaching roadway. A large object travels along at more than normal walking pace. The late-afternoon sunlight silhouettes the approaching threat, making it difficult for the lookout to identify.

The lookout signals down to the guards outside the gate, warning them of what appears to be a moving vehicle. The guards move closer to see if they can get a clearer look at what approaches. As it moves nearer, the guards hear clattering of metal and the wheels of a waggon as they grind deep into the ground. Rhythmic shouting can be heard by a single deep voice, counting in steps of one and two.

Large layers of tarpaulin cover its contents with one figure sitting forward-facing, bouncing up and down as the waggon travels over the bumpy road. To the watching guards, it seems as if the vehicle is being pulled along by a similar figure as the one above. The jangling and clanking becomes louder on approach and the shouting begins to ease. With what seems like incredible speed compared to the weight of the vehicle, it clearly comes into view of the guards that moved forward to inspect the threat.

'Halt!' shouts one of the guards, raising a hand as he does so, and the vehicle encased in a dust cloud comes to a stop with some heavy breathing being heard. As the dust settles, the figures become much clearer to the guards and the visual identification based on what their initial thoughts were are satisfied. They knew what approached was not Kaidis since they simply don't move that fast.

The person sitting on top dismounts, jumping down with a large thud as what seems like a pair of elephant-sized feet hit the ground. The large figure with massively broad shoulders approaches one of the guards.

'Is there some kind of problem here?' Toraq asks. He removes a white shawl that covers his shoulders and head to protect his fur from the dust.

The guard stands dwarfed by the Ascended Lightbearer. Still in possession of the same bear-like creature from the mountains, covered in a thick white fur with two black spots on top of his shoulders. Various trinkets hang from a necklace which jingles as he moves around.

'Yes, Toraq, we are under strict orders to secure the city,' the guard replies, recognising who stands in front of him.

Toraq stands back, surprised. He moves a paw-like hand — with well-defined fingers — to his chin and rubs it in thought.

'What is going on?' he questions.

'We don't really know. We were told to be on the lookout for anything suspicious and be ready for an attack,' replies the guard.

'An attack? Are the Kaidis up to no good that I should be aware about?'

'They won't tell us anything, but who else would attack Thoridon?'

'Well, not I,' chuckles Toraq. 'I mean no-one harm, and you should know that by now. Will you allow me into the city to trade my wares?'

The guard turns around to the lookout, signals that there is no threat and the gates open. Toraq smiles and pats the guard on the head as if he were a small dog. He then climbs back onto the waggon behind him, and he commands Eko — the smaller creature who he has looked after all this time — to start moving forward. After some straining, Eko with a similar frame to his master pulls on two handles that extend from the front of the waggon and it starts moving towards the gate. As they speed through the gates, they are firmly closed behind and the guards return to their duties.

As the cart moves forward, Toraq smiles and waves at various young and old Shaler coming outside of their homes to see what all the noise is about. They are excited to see the furry humanoids with their large waggon full of goods and interesting items heading toward the Quadrangle market.

Ever since Toraq's Ascendancy, his time upon the Arena of Pri has been largely uneventful. Having received no word from his mother about any introduction of a player over the years, he decided to create an affinity with the people. Adhering to the rules of the Tournament — even if there are no recent challengers — he has become a travelling salesman. Going between the Shaler towns that litter their entire territory and even down to the outposts of the Kaidis in the south, he provides a service of transporting goods and passes any profit onto the people. Carrying a vast array of strange and normal items, he is met with a degree of friendship regardless of where he goes — Shaler or Kaidis, purposely staying neutral and not wanting to get involved with the warring factions.

His choice of profession is deliberate, however — it allows him to keep an ear to the ground and see what happens on both sides of the fence. He has developed a trust between the Kaidis and the Shaler, and his presence is tolerated — he rarely talks politics, generally not revealing anything too important to the opposing side as this would be seen as interference, something as both a neutral party and in his capacity as an Ascended he should avoid.

Toraq and his fellow companion pulling the waggon along have become known as the Matoh, a name given to these rare breed of humanoids by the Shaler meaning "the long walkers". An expedition of Shaler tried to investigate the mountains of Iskap before Toraq appeared in this guise, but only a few returned from their journey, with stories of huge, white fur-covered beasts dominating the landscape. One characteristic that was observed was the need to explore and forage, with their powerful physique and ability to carry, pull and travel over very long distances across the mountains, earning their name. Toraq has a reputation in being able to uncover great rewards in terms of food and other fascinating creations, such as minerals and gems, during his travels.

If his appearance isn't strange enough to the Shaler or the Kaidis, another oddity is that he is the only Matoh known to anyone that can actually speak. His companion Eko never does and is more of a wild animal, but he is completely loyal to Toraq, as if there is a definite connection between the two. The age of the pair is also an unknown, with Toraq and Eko both outliving generations.

Both approach the inner wall of the city, remnants of the original wall that encompassed Thoridon around the reign of Emperor Serenus in the Third Era. The distance between the outer and inner walls is fairly substantial, a testament to the increase of population and size that the Shaler have endured since the earlier days. Guards nod their approval at the Matoh and open the gate into the Quadrangle allowing them inside. Their arrival instantly seems to provide a carnival-like atmosphere to the Shaler.

Alerted by the tremendous noise and subsequent celebration that the waggon and the Matoh have provided to the Quadrangle, Emperor Solus descends the white steps of the Temple with a smile on his face and warmly welcomes Toraq.

'Good day Solus, it is great to see you once again,' acknowledges Toraq, again dwarfing his receiver, speaking in his naturally slow and deep voice.

'I must apologise profusely for the unwelcoming defence the city has in place, but we are under threat,' explains Solus, not hesitating.

'Threat, you say? But the days seem so quiet. I do not see any reason for alarm.'

'It would appear you are not aware of the recent turn of events,' says the emperor with a surprised tone.

Toraq queries as to whether the Kaidis were involved in the unknown threat, suggesting that they didn't have any suspicion for a future assault by them. Not really wanting to go into great detail out in the open, Solus considers his options.

'Come,' he says. 'You and your assistant must be tired after an arduous journey. Please, make use of what we have available, food and shelter, perhaps?'

Becoming curious, Toraq accepts his offer, telling Eko to rest, who diligently lies down next to the waggon and gently snoozes. The emperor invites Toraq to his personal residence and proceeds to lead him away towards it.

✳ ✳ ✳ ✳

The Shaler are individually humble and do not live in large palaces or have grand estates, even at the top end of society, as is demonstrated with the emperor's own home. Situated in the eastern area of Thoridon, it is also where most of the senators and other dignitaries generally reside.

The emperor's residence is, however, one of the few homes in the city that has two stories. The building itself is fairly old, located inside the original walls; the stone used to construct it has blackened slightly. But that is not to say the building is unattractive: surrounding it is a beautiful garden laid out with many ornate hedges and various exotic floras providing an immense variation of colour and design – a great example of the countryside that flourishes in Shaler lands. There are great perfumes that swell around the garden, with either Solus' mother finding solace in its upkeep, or local neighbours who take pride in their emperor.

As Solus hurries up the short path between the hedgerows leading to the front door of the house, Toraq behind him takes a moment to appreciate the snapshot of nature. He breathes in the smells that emit and a sense of relaxation flows over him. One blotch in the landscape makes itself apparent to him — a decaying tree stands to the right of the path. The trunk and branches withered with blight and there are no leaves. The Matoh ponders about why a dead tree would be almost central in an otherwise perfect locale, but his thoughts are interrupted as the front door opens with a creak.

'Come, friend,' announces Solus, waiting at the door before disappearing inside.

Approaching, Toraq ducks his head slightly to fit through the door of the old building closing it behind him. Entering into a hallway, it is the first time he has seen the home of the emperor. At the rear are small stairs that lead up to the bedrooms of Solus and his mother, with a door at the side leading into the kitchen. The walls of the hall are filled with paintings, some more colourful than others, but in the reduced light are difficult to see. To his immediate right, Toraq enters into the reception of the house.

More paintings adorn the walls, but they are much larger — portraits of previous family members. Over a roaring fire at the back wall, a single portrait of Emperor Vimlor stands proud in chained armour with a white colour to its shining finish, holding an extremely distinctive sword. There are also various shelves around, all containing papers written by Avornia during her time studying the Synth. But one item hangs freely from another wall — the distinctive sword featured in the portrait.

This sword is ornate, featuring a hilt styled in the shape of talons. In the centre of the motif is a small emerald which catches the light beautifully and cut in the shape of an eye. The blade is polished but punctured with various notches where it had been used in combat. Nonetheless, it is still extremely sturdy and takes pride and place hanging central to the room.

A collection of chairs and lounges with associated tables stand in the middle of the cosy room with the roaring fire producing quite a heat. It is this feature that troubles Toraq, and Solus notices him being a little uneasy as he looks at the flames with disdain.

'Oh, I apologise,' Solus says and extinguishes the flames, realising that Toraq is not all that comfortable around searing heat with his thick, hairy coat.

'No matter, I cannot say that I was expecting this hospitality,' replies Toraq as he sits down on one of the chairs.

Solus walks up to a dresser with various bottles of elixirs and alcohols adorning its shelves. Each of the bottles has a generally distinctive colour, ranging from greens to blues and reds to yellows. Reaching for two tumblers, he pours a whisky-alike drink into one tumbler, but pours fresh water into the second. He hands this to Toraq who refuses to drink alcohol.

'Tell me now, Solus, what is this threat you speak?' questions Toraq, feeling refreshed after taking water.

'If I may be brutally honest with you,' Solus replies, sitting down. 'I don't know what the threat is. Everything has happened so fast and there are many questions that I have no idea how to answer. It's as if there is something I am completely unfamiliar with.'

'There must be something to cause so much alarm in Thoridon,' ponders Toraq.

The emperor goes on to explain some of the detail as Toraq sits and listens attentively. He briefly details the perceived lies and deceit plotted against him, how Ferlor mysteriously disappeared into the sky with an existence of a strange book and the miraculous appearance of a lost page of the Twilight Compendium. As he tells the stories, he recounts the events with a dramatic tone, adding unnecessary emphasis on some detail, but not outright lying to make sure Toraq was on his side. He does, however, neglect to tell him about his prior emotional turmoil, not wanting to sound weak in front of outsiders, respected as they may be. Most of this becomes a complete surprise to Toraq.

'How have I managed to miss all of this? I have only been away for several days, touring the Shaler towns. But I have not heard of this news until now.'

'That's because it has only been a day,' says Solus, finishing his drink and returning to the dresser to refresh his glass.

It dawns on Toraq that not everything is what it seems. There are two things that trouble him: the page of the Compendium he was fully aware about, although is curious about what happened to it. The talk of Ferlor vanishing in such an elaborate manner concerns him the most. Such ability is not something the Shaler themselves possess.

'Tell me more of Ferlor,' he asks, to which Solus sighs upon hearing the name.

'He was stubborn, never wanted to let anyone else know what his true plans were. I'm still not sure about Levak who he introduced as leader of the Warlock Council.'

'I mean, tell me more about how he disappeared.'

'Ah.'

Solus turns to look at the portrait of his father hanging above the fireplace. He wonders what he would think about the desecration of his tomb at the Temple, all because of Ferlor. Toraq looks at him as he stares into the picture in complete silence.

'He called himself Barel,' Solus eventually says, still looking at the painting. 'I don't know who or what that means.'

Upon hearing the name, Toraq reels back in his chair in shock, but the emperor doesn't notice, entirely lost in depressive thoughts. Barel the Lightbearer is someone that he is completely aware, but not aware of his apparent presence on the Arena of Pri. How is this even possible, he thinks to himself. Why did Mother not communicate this to him?

There is sudden shouting from outside — the sound of a Warlock booming the infernal words: 'Kaidis inbound!'

Solus bursts out the front door to see what is happening. The emperor turns around to look at Toraq who stands from his chair hiding his thoughts, as Solus asks him to follow. At the end of the garden the Warlock stands waiting.

'A Kaidis scouting party has been spotted from the south, emperor,' he diligently informs Solus.

'Are you sure about this?' queries the emperor. 'They don't usually attack when it is still light.'

'We are, sir. Their volcanic emblems were confirmed positive, they are moving up the road to the gate.'

'How many are there?'

'Two, sir.'

Slightly perplexed by this, the emperor commands the Warlock to rally the defence and prepare, even if the reported number seems to be a little small.

'You do not seem so convinced, Solus,' says Toraq.

'Even though the sun is setting, it is still too light for them to launch an attack by themselves. And a scouting party would not just run up to the gate.'

'I see what you mean. It is suspicious.'

The two follow close behind a group of Warlocks heading in a southern direction to see what is coming.

✻ ✻ ✻ ✻

From the external southern gate, the road leading from Thoridon is straight with the city itself positioned in a grassy basin: this being the scene for Kaidis-lead assaults in the past. The road rises up a fairly steep incline disappearing down the other side into the Flatlands. Approaching the peak are the two Kaidis which the Shaler lookouts reported.

Peering over the top, this pair is very different from each other. On the left is a seasoned warrior, dressed in hulking blackened armour with a large helmet — an outlined painted symbol of Mount Sindre on its top — and also carrying a twin-bladed axe on his back. His counterpart is a much less Bloodrage-developed individual, with much lighter armour, no helmet and no weapon of any kind.

'Do you think they've seen us?' questions Dorek, one of the Doctors Division.

'Of course they've fucking seen us,' booms Goroc back, who has a definitive slashed scar across his face. 'I've been here enough times to know that they are always ready!'

'There's no need to be so crass. I think this is whole idea is ridiculous.'

Goroc laughs back at his unwanted companion.

'And I think you are ridiculous!' angers the warrior. 'Come, let's get this over with.'

Just as he is ready to leap over the other side and charge towards the city, Dorek grabs him by the arm making him stop.

'What is it, pathetic worm?'

'I'm having second thoughts,' responds a dejected Dorek. 'This is suicide. I've got much work to complete back at the Stronghold. I don't have time for this.'

Before he can share any more pleas, Goroc roars in defiance and drops a large white sack from his shoulder. He picks up the Doctor, who almost squeals as he does so.

'Enough of your shit! You Doctors are all the same. Whining and moaning.'

Throwing him down the other side of the peak, Dorek slides down the dusty track a little way as Goroc retrieves the sack with a smile on his face, marching past the struggling Doctor. Picking himself up off the ground, brushing himself down, it suddenly dawns on him that he is within full view of the watching Shaler. Standing alone, with Goroc more of a distance away, he panics and dashes to catch up with his burly protector, even if he may not actually provide any protection.

As they proceed down the road towards the gate, the numbers of Shaler awaiting their arrival become apparent. Lining the walls from above, it is as if the entire Warlock Council is ready to greet them. There is one dominating figure that stands in front of them all, directly above the gate. Goroc is unperturbed by the immense threat that awaits him, striding along following his military training to the letter, with the curious white sack over his shoulder. Dorek, on the other hand, gasps as they move closer.

'Are you crazy?' he whispers to Goroc. 'We're not leaving this place!'

Again, his pleas are ignored, with the warrior fully focused on the task at hand. Following specific orders from Captain Karzol at Wodar Drop, the two are to deliver this single sack to the Shaler, regardless of cost. It contains an extremely important message.

Stopping fifty paces from the gate, the dust kicked up from the road blows around in silence. Dorek's eyes dart around in fear at the Synthetic might that stands before him, but Goroc just stands there, contempt in his eyes for all that wait.

Levak looks down upon the two Kaidis, still shrouded in clothing to hide his identity as best as possible. There seems to be something familiar to one of them and he pauses for a moment. As the numbers in the Doctors Division are small compared to the rest of the Kaidis' military might, being a close community of thinkers, they all have an inherent affinity for each other, even if the larger warriors have complete disdain for them all. Despite Levak's defection, he cannot betray his own upbringing.

'What is it you want?' he yells. As soon as he speaks, Dorek stops fretting and his attention is drawn to Levak as the voice sounds distinctive to him.

'We have a present for you!' laughs Goroc back, making light of the situation and dropping the sack from his shoulder into his arms. With a grunt, he throws the weighty sack in front of the closed gate, but not before it bounces off the wood and hitting the floor.

He turns to the Doctor at his side.

'Your turn,' he growls.

Realising his cue, Dorek fumbles around on his person and finds a folded piece of paper, sealed by hot wax. Gingerly looking around at the Shaler who all seem ready to pounce the moment anything untoward occurs, he begins to step forward moving to the gate. Levak gestures to his awaiting Warlocks telling them to hold. Dorek can't keep his eyes off the leader of the Council as he makes his way to the gate. There is something about him that he can't place, but nonetheless he bends down to the sack and places the paper on top before scurrying back to Goroc.

A single guard opens the gate and takes the note — the seal carrying the volcanic symbol of the Kaidis. The sack has a rope holding the end closed and the guard pulls on this to bring inside the heavy package. Even though the sack is white coloured, blotches of red can be seen through the cloth material. The gate is pushed and bolted closed once it is in.

'Run, you idiot!' screams the Doctor as he quickens his pace, passing Goroc, not being able to take the unbearable situation any longer. But the warrior just chuckles and refuses to follow his advice. Despite his stubborn military mind, he knew that there would be nothing to back him up as he is seasoned on this grassy plain outside of Thoridon, fighting in previous lost battles and always recognising when to retreat in those times. But today is different for him.

With Dorek now a considerable distance away, Goroc pulls his axe from his back and decides to end it all with a blaze of glory. With this aggressive action a clear signal, Levak starts chanting in Ethereal. The warrior roars with axe held high and charges straight towards the gate, knowing that it is entirely futile.

Manipulating the Synth energy directly onto the enraged Kaidis, Levak's choice of action is a signature move that he pioneered with his time at the Doctors Division. As Goroc charges forward, the effect of the Synth upon him makes him rot from the inside — the very atoms and molecules that make up his body ripped apart. His armour and axe fall to the ground, with nothing left inside other than bloodied goo.

Now standing at the peak, Dorek sees that his foolhardy companion has been unsurprisingly defeated and tuts to himself, shaking his head, before having one last thought about the mysterious Council leader and returning back to Wodar Drop.

With no further sign of any Kaidis advancing, attention turns to the bag. The guard that pulled in the sack cautiously undoes the rope. With no initial surprise, he opens the bag further and repulses at the smell that follows and also what he sees inside. He then pulls on the rope to close it again.

Just at that moment, Toraq appears on the scene, dropped to all-fours with Solus riding on his white furry back. A crowd of general people has assembled, wondering what the situation is. Toraq stands up as Solus dismounts from him, with the emperor approaching the sack with the guard alongside.

'This was delivered by the Kaidis,' he says to Solus authoritatively, handing him the note.

Tentatively approaching the bag, Solus crouches down next to it and identifies the sack to have a definite body shape. He prepares himself for the worst and pulls on the rope to look inside. The tattered and disfigured corpse of Master Conjurer Ferlor is stripped naked; beaten and bruised but not enough so he would become unidentifiable.

'Such a lack of respect,' sighs Solus, holding his head in shame. 'You silly old fool.'

In silence, he rips the seal from the note in disgust and unfolds it to read what is written. It only contains a few simple words — "Barel is with us now" — but this is enough to come as surprise to the emperor. His last memory of Ferlor was referring to himself as Barel the Lightbearer. If the note is correct, and the body of Ferlor lies before him, how can Barel still exist? How come the Kaidis are involved? These questions that arise in his mind trouble Solus.

He stands, revealing to all that it is the body of Ferlor and orders for it to be removed and buried at the Temple. Gasps rise from the crowd on hearing the news – the first proof to everyone that what the emperor referred to was real.

Toraq approaches Solus who hands him the note. Now entirely believing that Barel is really present on the Arena, he now has to make sure he tracks him down before whatever he has planned goes out of control.

'This is not the end of Barel,' Toraq tells him, keeping his thoughts to himself. 'I fear that this may only be the beginning.'

'Beginning of what?' Solus questions.

'I wish I knew the answer to that. In time, it will reveal itself to us.'

'I must speak with my mother. Clearly we have much more work to do.'

166

# Chapter Ten

# Kingdom

Out in the Sulphur Deserts, an almost momentary darkness turns to sunrise as the nights are much shorter in the lands south of the canyon. With the sunlight of Ramor peaking over the horizon, the incredible heat of this barren landscape emphasises itself as a feature to Barel as he travels across the sandy plains. It is obvious to him how the land is so barren: with heat like this, nothing could survive without some degree of precaution. Alongside the road various bones and other signs of decay are littered, succumbing to the harsh conditions, with dust and sand blown across in turbulent winds.

How Barel traverses the landscape is not by foot — the early People's Union engineers at the birth of the Kaidis recognised that the ever-present winds could be harnessed as energy for transportation. Resembling a sailed boat in rudimentary design with an array of wheels, the device is known as a Knoria, and is operated by a single driver that sits on top with a series of pulleys to control the sails and direction. Without much protection from the winds and heat, it is a perilous task but an important role in the Kaidis military machine.

With the Knoria now approaching the volcano, Barel can now see evidence of life. Various structures seem to adorn the foot of the volcano, but from this distance — and with the reduced visibility — it is hard to see anything specific. His driver makes a shout through the orange sand being blown into his face down to Barel that they are approaching "home" – the Kaidis Stronghold.

The Stronghold itself is almost completely contained inside the volcano. There is a large cavern at the front, covered by a series of gates, serving as the main entry point leading down and deep within. The cavern was carved out over time by the thriving engineering community of the Kaidis — known as the Engineers Division — to allow for an entrance to the many naturally occurring tunnels inside the volcano. As such, the layout of the Stronghold turns into a complicated rabbit warren of tunnels and passages. Every so often, symbols and the occasional sign are the only clues as to which tunnel goes where – one would need to be born here to understand how to get somewhere.

The Kaidis are devoted to their military way of life. Most of the time, they work, live and die as small units of functionality, with each unit having their speciality. There are no comforts; the entire Stronghold has a rushed and unpolished air with natural caverns inside serving as random places for unrelated events. However, in amongst all the chaos one area stands out – almost central to the entire labyrinth lies an impressive spectacle: the Royal Seat.

A large open area, the Royal Seat contains many spoils and lavish ornaments dotted around its walls. Polished and clean rugs, skulls of victims and heroes, skins of both animal and otherwise adorn the floor. A mosaic of portraits of previous kings is painted on the ceiling with an enormous symbol central of the volcano itself – their military insignia.

In the centre, a raised platform and a huge throne sits facing the entrance. The throne itself is constructed from various bone matter and skins, with large animal tusks and horns rising up at the back. It is also positioned on top of a rotating pad that allows its occupier to swing around to see the whole room. Away from the throne area, various desks and large maps adorn the rear of the room, with captains and lieutenants working on battle plans and intelligence reports handed down from scouting parties.

Sitting on the throne is a formidable figure – bulky, muscled but still appearing incredibly agile, garnished in lavish red and gold body armour, the volcanic emblem emblazoned on the right breast. Epaulettes hang from the shoulders, symbolising that of the highest ranking person within the Kaidis organisation – King General Xarash IV.

The fourth in the current lineage, a direct descendant from the founder of the Kaidis, Xarash IV has proved himself as a strong leader and fierce opponent. Dedicated to the sole mission of the Kaidis – the complete annihilation of the Shaler for their banishment, due to their association with the Bloodrage – Xarash is stubborn to the cause. Fathers before him have shown the same resilience, either dying on the battlefield or succumbing to a late life, wishing to see destruction of their former people. The King has no time for anything else, seeing diplomacy and mundane activities such as survival of his own people as unimportant and just excuses to get in the way of the war.

Xarash stretches in his imposing throne. He is becoming weary that nothing particularly special has happened in the war with the Shaler lately. For him, everything has been too quiet and something needs to be done. He rises from his chair, takes a step around, and observes the lesser ranking officers in the back pushing papers and updating placements on a war table. Not entirely impressed with the lack of a frenzy of activity, he has an explosive moment of anger.

'What the fuck are we doing sitting here, doing nothing?' he questions, in a gruff and constantly threatening voice. His beady eyes and strong brow peer down on his subjects as he surveys the room.

'Why aren't I hearing news of glorious victories out in the field?'

A bead of sweat drips from his forehead as the constant heat from the volcano would be generally intolerable if it wasn't for the incredible resistance the Kaidis have been afforded from the Bloodrage.

'My lord, we just aren't having any success with recent orders. We send out parties and they never come back. We need a new strategy,' sounds a reply from the back.

'Are you questioning my authority?' Xarash growls.

'Not at all, my lord. But the enemy are constantly bettering our efforts,' he replies, not perturbed.

Xarash spits on the floor in disgust.

'Those worthless animals couldn't kill a Shaler if it walked up to them! Do I have to do everything around here?'

He spins around on the spot, like a child having a tantrum.

'You there!' he yells angrily, but not necessarily directing his voice to any one in particular. 'Why haven't we fucking killed anything lately?'

'The troops are under resourced and not well prepared to fight against—', comes a meek voice before being interrupted by Xarash's condescending laughter.

'"Troops" he says! Oh, that's fucking hilarious. Maggots are what they are! Not worthy to fight in the armour of our colours. We're supposed to be fighting a fucking war here, and winning! We are supposed to be fierce, merciless. I want to see axes in the skulls of the Shaler. I want to see Thoridon burn! But none of these so called "troops" have made it happen yet.'

As he finishes speaking, a soldier stumbles into the Royal Seat. On hearing the clattering of him entering, Xarash roars.

'What idiocy just fell in now?'

Catching his breath, the soldier manages to exhale his purpose.

'I have a message from Captain Karzol, my lord.' He clutches a sealed paper.

'Karzol, you say? Let me guess, some mundane problem with the water supply,' Xarash chuckles.

He approaches the soldier and snatches the paper from his grasp. Ripping the seal clean off, he proceeds to unravel its contents and starts to read attentively, pulling the paper up close to his eyes as if he were short-sighted. As he reaches the end of the message, he lowers the paper and looks at the soldier straight in the eyes, lost in thought for a brief moment.

'Is this true?' he asks sternly. The eyes of the soldier start to dart around uneasily; he doesn't know what the message says – he's just the delivery boy. Realising the solider knows nothing, he narrows his brow. Changing his stance to a defiant position, an eager grin ripples across his face, showing a series of missing teeth.

'This is just the sort of news I wanted to hear,' he shouts, so the whole room can hear. 'Let me read this to you.'

Almost the actor, he clears his throat in a theatrical style and starts to stride around the throne.

'Ferlor is dead,' he booms, adding emphasis on the adjective. 'Let me read that again – Ferlor is dead!'

He bursts into raucous laughter. The lieutenants and captains stop what they're doing and turn to face the king, watching as he cracks up, bending over and slapping his armour-encrusted thighs in hilarity. Jolting back into an upright position, a tear of happiness falls from his eye and he moves to wipe it away.

'Fuck, I don't know what to say,' he giggles. '"Was possessed by some creature; look at the eyes." This is unbelievable!'

He takes a moment to recover, sitting down in his throne. He spots the messenger still standing at the door and yells at him to leave. Lieutenants at the back of the room look at each other as Xarash restores his composure – it seems highly implausible to them.

'"Possessed", my lord?' asks one of the lieutenants.

'Sounds like Synthetic crap if you ask me. But Ferlor is dead? That must mean that they are weak! We must strike now!'

'I wouldn't be so hasty,' speaks a wispy, almost fragile voice. From the back of the room, a smaller and thin Kaidis approaches the throne of the king. Dressed in a slightly tatty white robe, with long grey hair and a wrinkly face, wielding a short cane with a large dulled green gem at its top, he looks at Xarash. The king grimaces at the sight of the older one.

'What now, Samal?'

'You say the message mentioned possession.'

'And what of it, you snivelling creature? I have no idea what it is!'

'Well, in the past, there were tales of a strange beast roaming the lands and causing havoc to our distant relations.'

'I have no time for pathetic stories!' laughs the king, directing his attention to the war room behind and ignoring Doctor Samal. 'Send out some better defended scouting parties towards Thoridon. I need to know what they're up to. Send the First Division – they don't fuck up.'

Various affirmatives are directed back at the General, who swivels back around in his throne to be surprised that Samal is still standing there.

'There are rumours that a powerful book exists,' he begins before Xarash can yell at him. 'This book contains details about how to call upon these beasts.'

'You seem really keen about this, Doctor. I don't care what you are saying and yet you bombard me with these rumours and stories! Did you not hear? Ferlor is dead,' energises the king.

'Well, yes, while that is tremendous news that the enemy may be weakened by this setback,' Samal replies sarcastically. 'I fear it is all too much of a coincidence.'

'I don't like your tone, Doctor.'

Doctor Samal sighs, clearly having a difference of opinion and proceeds to slope back to his corner of the room. In this corner sits a small chair and a desk with a solitary candle, illuminating the darkened area – the desk obscured with various documents in a chaotic fashion. To the immediate right are closed double doors, both of which are covered in further documents pinned to the wood. Samal sits down in the chair and sighs once again, attempting to busy himself with more papers, curiously studying them as if trying to make some sense from the bizarre diagrams and wording.

He is the head of the Doctors Division. Each one of its members reports directly to Samal, who in turn reports to Xarash, allowing each Doctor to work within their own defined methods. Their attitude to war is much closer to that of the Shaler than the Kaidis and would prefer discussion over destruction, and will sometimes go out of their way to change the course of events. The relationship between the king and this Division has always been one of suspicion, even though they are on the same side.

Xarash stands up from his throne and sees a series of couriers arrive through a door at the back of the room. Lieutenants hand them papers containing orders and they leave in the direction of their recipients. The king smiles as he thinks that having Ferlor dead, Emperor Solus will be weakened further and it makes for a fantastic opportunity.

✳ ✳ ✳ ✳

Barel's transporting Knoria arrives at its destination, allowing for the Lightbearer to see what the Kaidis call their home. The shear enormity and raw power of Mount Sindre becomes first hand; it rising high into the sky with an extremely blackened and charred coating. As it is still an active — but subdued — volcano, being close to it instils the kind of terror that such an awesome natural spectacle can produce. An ever-present low vibration is constantly in the background as the magma and lava at the core churns around. At the very peak of the volcano is an opened top, where solid white fire bubbles inside the crown, but it is not active enough to erupt.

Despite this seemingly impossible home, the Kaidis are completely oblivious to any chance of the volcano suddenly bursting into seas of destruction. It does not concern them in the

172

slightest. Such a hostile locale is beneficial to the Kaidis in two ways: it provides many valuable resources to them and has absolutely zero chance of the Shaler ever making an appearance, even if they wanted to.

The driver of Barel's Knoria pulls into an enclosed courtyard that is positioned directly outside of the front of the volcano. Its boundary is made from wood transported down from the forest of Mistwood via a military station on the border between Shaler territory and the Sulphur Deserts, known as Outpost Ora, north-west from the Stronghold. The boundary, constructed in a semi-circle, serves as a shelter from the continuous blown sands.

As Barel looks around, he realises that his vehicle is not stopping — in fact, it begins to accelerate as the driver steers it around, returning to the direction of Wodar Drop. He angrily yells down to Barel something unintelligible through the winds and Barel decides to jump off the back, rolling onto the ground, only to come to an abrupt stop as the armour on his possessed Kaidis body prevents him from going too far.

Picking himself up off the ground, he has a look around the courtyard. A great forge stands towards the rear and several Kaidis who were working with it have stopped to watch Barel, scoffing and laughing with each other as they see him rise to his feet, before returning to work. There are also shouts being made by superior officers to rows of warriors at opposing sides of the courtyard, with demonstrations being shown about how to use a weapon.

To the side of the volcano is a large outbuilding, positioned close to the mountainside. There are no windows and there is no obvious indication as to its purpose, but it is where the Doctors Division reside and a large door into the courtyard remains firmly shut.

Finally, Barel's attention is drawn to the front of the mountain itself. There are several gates at ground level that lead inside — six normal sized and two much wider gates central. Members of the Divisions move in and out of each of the smaller gates in single file as Barel observes, concluding that it is most likely where to find King Xarash whom he seeks.

On approach, the gates are more like full-height turnstiles, but wide enough to allow for bulky soldiers to pass through. A gate operator sits to the right of it, hidden inside a well-defended black box, with nothing but a grate to allow for speech to be heard. Barel stands at the gate and tries pushing on the turnstile, but it doesn't move. There is no obvious way to open it as there are no controls. After some infuriated rattling of the gate, a voice can be heard from inside.

'What are you trying to do, idiot?' comes the muffled voice from the other side.

'I am trying to get in, idiot,' replies Barel.

A metal bar that prevents the gate from rotating moves into the box and Barel pushes. It rotates around for a quarter of the way before hitting a buffer, trapping Barel inside. The metal bar extends back out behind him. A shutter on the side of the black box gets pulled down, allowing the gate operator and Barel to exchange looks.

'What do you want, sergeant?' asks the operator, identifying the insignia on Barel's armour.

'I have orders from Captain Karzol to see the King,' Barel replies.

'Really?' replies the operator sarcastically, turning into a chuckle. 'Yeah, everyone gets to see him. What are you, some kind of joker?'

'No,' answers Barel who lowers his brow, his swirling blue eyes becoming more noticeable in the light.

'Well, no-one just walks up to the King without some kind of authority. You are a no-one and I don't have any authorisation to allow nobodies to see him.'

As he finishes, a line of armoured guards assemble in front of Barel, still trapped inside the turnstile, after being alerted to the disturbance by the gate operator.

'But, I really must see the King,' insists Barel.

'Oh, I think you're past that now,' replies the operator, who closes the shutter, and sounds of latches click on the other side.

Barel starts to get annoyed and bangs on the hatch in an attempt to get the attention of the operator. The armoured guards start to smirk and begin to ready their axes, swords and maces. Not even the sergeant's body with its hulking strength and tough armour would get through this line without some kind of support.

The metal bar that prevents further rotation of the turnstile is retracted once again, allowing for it to be rotated into the

Stronghold and into the awaiting line of death. Barel stops for a moment to think about his options.

'Come on, you worthless grunt,' taunts one of the guards.

To the left of Barel is a similar turnstile with a similar black box to its left housing another gate operator. A wall separates the two entry points so the advancing guards can't see what approaches on the other side – the messenger that Xarash dismissed earlier. This messenger was present when Xarash read out the note he was carrying and therefore was aware that a stranger would be on his way.

As he shouts to the operator to open his turnstile, he sees Barel trapped inside the other one, and the impending fight that seems to be almost ready to start. The messenger and Barel make eye contact, with the soldier being surprised by the swirling blue voids that masquerade instead. As the bars retract from his turnstile, he thinks that the sergeant trapped inside could be this strange creature the note mentioned, with his unnatural eyes and unusual circumstance for a sergeant to be in.

'You're not a sergeant!' shouts the messenger so all can hear, looking into the eyes of Barel.

The operator's hatch lowers again and he looks across at the messenger.

'What of it, soldier?' he asks, wondering why such a lowly maggot would involve himself of the impending death of the out-of-line sergeant who clearly has no understanding of protocol.

'I think this is the possessed creature that I was sent to inform the King about,' he replies, pointing to Barel.

'What are you talking about?' scoffs the operator.

'Allow me to demonstrate,' smiles Barel, thinking it is time to drop the disguise.

He faces the operator and begins to chant in Ethereal under his breath. He outstretches his right arm and a bolt of lightning extends from the hand directed at the operator, who lets out a blood-curdling scream, becoming immediately paralysed and then falling to the floor, lifeless. Barel turns to the flabbergasted line of guards.

'He's a Shaler! Attack!' yells one of the guards, completely unaware of the situation, hastily jumping to conclusions, and they rally towards Barel standing behind the closed turnstile. The messenger stands and watches, shaking his head in disbelief.

As the guards advance further, they stupidly clatter into the turnstile and get knocked back, dazed, with Barel pinning himself to the back of the turnstile to avoid any kind of blade that was heading in his direction. Of the guards that remain focused, Barel takes the opportunity to utilise the Synth and blows a controlled gust of wind in their direction, propelling them up and then falling to the ground – a couple becoming impaled on the weapons of their associates.

The messenger chuckles at the fate of his fellow soldiers and the ones that survive wriggle around disorientated. Barel pushes the released turnstile open and walks through stepping over the guards. Alerted to the situation, some warriors from the outside notice the gate operator to be dead and yells resonate around, informing each other of a possible security breach.

Despite the chaos, Barel brushes himself down at the other side and begins to look around at the inside of the Stronghold. He sees the several tunnels that lead off into various directions with some symbols and colours marking each for identification purposes. Not knowing what the symbolism represents, he tries his hand at luck, moving towards a random tunnel in a vain attempt to try and locate the Royal Seat himself. The messenger hurries over from the gate to approach Barel, making him stop for a moment. Looking at Barel as if to give himself justification about the decision he then makes, tells him to follow, leading him down a red-coloured entrance.

Each of these tunnels is actually a lava tube — natural conduits formed by the volcano during previous eruptions, now adopted by the Kaidis as a way to navigate around the inside. Additional paths leaf off into other tunnels and the occasional open area where molten lava pooled before continuing to reach the surface. Along the way, various Kaidis from all of the Divisions pass by, with no recognition or reaction to each other — everyone is in a hurry to get to where they are going, no stopping, no distractions, no conversation, only the sound of heavy boots or clanking armour against a backdrop of low rumbles caused by the moving lava, deep inside the volcano's core.

✱ ✱ ✱ ✱

It is a fair distance to the location of the Royal Seat, allowing for Barel to experience more of Kaidis life, guided by the messenger he met at the Stronghold's entrance gate. With the flow of Kaidis rushing past him, the various associations that form the collective Kaidis are introduced for the first time.

As well as the Doctors Division, there are also the Engineers Division, the Production Division and three military Divisions — the First, Second and Third. Each one has a very distinctive role to play inside the Kaidis machine. The military divisions are the most familiar to Barel, having direct confrontation with members of the Second Division on his journey to Wodar Drop. Making up the bulk of the military, the Second are the general fighters, while the First Division are veterans but not necessarily officers.

All of the construction of buildings and transportation, creation and design of armour, and what would be considered more "civilian" duties are handled by the Engineers Division. Founded by former members of the People's Union, a lot of the skills and experience were transferred from the Shaler and helped begin the Kaidis. But the environment of the Sulphur Deserts required drastic thinking and new developments to survive and subsequently expand.

One other duty for the Engineers Division becomes apparent as Barel travels through. Sounds of hammering — axes chinking against stone, and much grunting from the physical force required to do so. The volcano itself provides a vital element known as Luvolite, almost black in appearance, and can be turned into a strong metal which is used to forge most of the armour and weaponry used by the military Divisions — mining this resource is also the task of the engineers.

Weaving through what seems like an endless maze of tunnels, the messenger that guides him keeps telling Barel that it's not far to go.

'You do not need to keep repeating yourself,' says Barel, becoming increasingly annoyed, but restraining himself as he realises he is mostly at the mercy of his guide.

'I wasn't aware that I was,' he replies, a short memory being his problem.

The numbers of Kaidis going the other way begins to thin as Barel moves closer to the Royal Seat. There is less of a presence and the sounds of mining have dissipated, only to be replaced by sounds the Lightbearer seems unfamiliar with. His guide slows his pace as they approach a large, echoing cavern home to the Production Division.

'Try not to stare as we pass the "Fuck Factory",' advises the messenger.

Inside this wide, underground chamber echoes passionate sounds of orgasm, rattling and masculine growling. For the Production Division isn't anything mechanical, it is very literal in terms of the Kaidis existence. Females are very important to the growth of the population — for obvious reasons — but while they have a choice at pursuing a career in other Divisions, few make the cut, and those that don't often find themselves relegated to positions more horizontal than normal. Males from any Division are encouraged to visit on a regular basis.

There is also a different aspect to this Division — occasionally, the Kaidis have Shaler sympathisers, displeased with the Shaler community for whatever their own reasons are and keen to join the Kaidis. What starts off as a dream quickly becomes a nightmare. They are not treated well and are subjected to torture amongst other activities. If they survive and can prove themselves worthy, they are introduced to the Urtica, becoming addicted to its effects and eventually see acceptance as one of their own. Their original dreams generally die shortly after, for life as a Kaidis is extremely harsh, compared to the quiet and simple Shaler.

Children produced in the Division inherit the Bloodrage affliction at birth and through fostering and simple education at an early age; they are eventually taken away and introduced to the Third Division. Effectively a school, it is overseen by the Doctors Division where classes are held to teach the young from all of the Divisions. During this period, they are continuously assessed, and as they grow older are assigned to their best Division based on their development and ability — most destined to the Second Division and only a handful to the Doctor's.

The messenger leads Barel into a smaller tunnel which leads to closed double doors. Both doors have the symbol of the volcano painted on them and a torch crackles at its side, flickering as they approach. Behind these doors lies the Royal Seat and shouting can be heard – the voice of Xarash barking at his subordinates, still displeased with the situation.

'I suppose it's up to you now,' replies Barel's guide, as he runs back down the tunnel leaving the Lightbearer alone.

* * * *

'I haven't got the time to run your errands, Samal,' Xarash yells from his throne, with Samal standing at his side.

'But I feel this has great importance for the good of the war effort, my lord.'

'What possibly can some hero do for me to serve the war effort?'

'Oh come now, you've seen how the Shaler defend themselves.'

'Yes, like the cowards that they are! They don't even pretend to fight.'

'But you see, they are fighting — just not with blades.'

'And how exactly is that fighting? They always stand up on those walls!'

'Well, we always attack first, that's why.'

'Enough!' roars Xarash, standing up from his throne, throwing fists aloft. 'Why are you always poking your nose into matters that don't fucking concern you?'

'But if we had the Book of the Daimons, we could use it against the Shaler!'

'I said enough! Your pathetic stories about these strangers are ridiculous! Sometimes I wonder if you are the enemy!'

Taking his cue, Barel crashes open both doors and strides into the Royal Seat.

'For fuck's sake, what now?' howls Xarash, turning around ready to give an earful to the soldier who he thinks just walked in.

Samal also turns to look. He is much more experienced in subjects that Barel is more accustomed to. Always the observant one, Samal is immediately attracted to the swirling blue eyes, a detail that he seems to be familiar with and he simply stands there muttering to himself, gazing at the strange masquerading Kaidis that has just walked in. As Xarash gets a glimpse of what enters his domain, instead of hurling a stream of abuse, something makes him stand there in silence and watch as Barel approaches. He comes up to the foot of the platform where the throne stands and stops.

'You must be the king, I assume,' states the Lightbearer, no longer pretending to be who he appears.

Xarash, for once, isn't quite sure what to say. Before him stands a Kaidis sergeant, but there is something of a theoretical aura surrounding him which Xarash cannot understand.

'You don't seem to be what I am seeing,' Xarash finally replies in an unnaturally calm voice.

'Ah, please forgive my appearance, this is merely a disguise,' Barel says.

At this point, the king is mostly dumbfounded. He is a person of strong mind but has no time for anything related to the Synth, preferring everything to be real without tricks. But when presented with such a quandary as Barel, he finds it hard to understand. It shouldn't be. It cannot be. It mustn't be. To Xarash's rescue, Doctor Samal steps in who is clearly in awe.

'Welcome, welcome! I hope my associates didn't give you too much of a hard time finding us?' Samal chirps.

'Nothing I could not handle,' Barel replies. 'Your messenger seemed to be more than willing to assist. Who might you be?'

'Oh, forgive me. I am Doctor Samal, Head of the Doctors Division of the Kaidis Kingdom. Excuse my King, he has difficulty with such issues as this,' he smirks, looking at Xarash who stands aghast with a puzzled look on his face.

'I see.'

'That messenger provided us with the detail that you were on your way.'

'Yes, I found that out when I got here. The reception was entertaining to say the least.'

'Ah. Well, I am certainly very pleased to see you. I never thought such a beast existed,' says Samal, with a wide-eyed grin on his face.

At that moment, Xarash comes out of his trance with a scream.

'Quiet, you fucking traitor!' he booms at Samal almost striking him but stopping himself. 'This beast came to see me, not some dim-witted moron who thinks he runs everything around here!'

He turns his attention to Barel as Samal cowers from the abuse.

'Forgive me, sir, but who the fuck are you?'

'I am Barel, Warmonger of the Elements. I would prefer that you stopped referring to me as a "beast". You are the king, I have heard about?'

'King General Xarash IV, ruler of Kaidis Kingdom, destroyer of the Shaler. Everybody knows who I am! Your question confuses me.'

'That is because I am entirely unfamiliar with your people, general. When I was here before, I was not aware of anyone known as the Kaidis.'

'What?' yells the King, completely astounded by what he is being said.

He steps down from his throne and right into the face of Barel. At this short distance, he finally notices the deep blue swirling vortexes that replace the eyes of the sergeant before him. This makes him take a step back in surprise.

'What happened to your eyes?' he questions, almost with the sound of fear in his voice.

'I assume you are referring to my visible essence,' Barel replies. 'What you see is a projection of me while I control this body.'

'Fascinating,' exclaims Samal, clapping excitedly. 'So, you are able to change your host controller at will? To completely change your appearance yet still retain full motor and physical domination of what you occupy?'

'You seem to be quite aware of my abilities,' says Barel, becoming interested in how Samal has such an understanding for a people he has never encountered before.

'We in the Doctors Division like to keep abreast of certain developments that have come to light recently,' replies Samal, coyly. 'There were rumours that powerful beings existed, but I never saw any proof.'

This surprises Barel, as this would be the first time that someone has talked to him about the fact that there is at least some common knowledge about the Lightbearers. But before they can continue into the realms of this conversation, the general snaps once again.

'I can't take this shit anymore!' Xarash roars. 'I just hear words that make no sense. I see something I cannot understand.

You are not of these lands, stranger. Your words do not mean anything to me.'

As he finishes speaking, he moves and grabs an enormous double-headed axe off the wall. It was the axe of his father and had been used to maim Shaler previously. His father, Xarash III, died on the battlefield but while he was alive, his wielded axe spun around in a frenzy, expertly controlled, crippling and severely hurting those that surrounded him. The blades have various chinks removed and other dents where they collided with bone. It takes pride and place on the wall, but Xarash IV takes up arms with it against Barel.

'Why shouldn't I just kill you right now?' he asks.

'Perhaps I should state my intention,' Barel replies calmly. 'For you see, you and I, despite our clear differences, have a common enemy.'

'The Shaler?'

Xarash lowers his axe.

'Indeed so.'

'Tell me, what makes them your enemy, stranger?' enquires Xarash.

'To put it simply, they imprisoned me and left me to rot,' he replies, not revealing exactly what happened.

'So, you want revenge for what they did to you?'

'Indeed. I heard about your plight and I wanted to assist in your battle against them.'

'Prove yourself, then. This is all talk. Right now, before I change my mind.'

Recognising the military rank and file within the Kaidis organisation, this would be a great time to get an upgrade to his disguise – something with a bit more power. While he could choose to target Xarash, he has demonstrated to Barel that he could be a formidable ally to have. Losing that would create more chaos than necessary and be detrimental to his cause.

Barel notices the war room located at the rear of the Royal Seat. He approaches the area, with Xarash and the rest watching intently and apprehensively. Without having any real knowledge about how the military machine works, he recognises the same insignia on his armour that is similar to the captains working in the war room. But he sees the lieutenants who have more pips on their armour – these must be higher up the hierarchy.

He taps one on the shoulder and Barel motions for him to follow. The lieutenant, surprised to see a strange sergeant in his face, becomes momentarily mesmerised by the swirling blue voids before eyeing the king looking for approval. The two of them take a step back from the war room as the captains and other lieutenants pause what they're doing to see what happens next.

'Close your eyes,' whispers Barel.

Placing his hand on the shoulder of the lieutenant, he begins chanting in Ethereal. As in the exact same circumstance when Barel possessed his current host back at Wodar Drop, the process of Ethereal Transference is complete as he takes control over the body of the lieutenant. The sergeant's body falls to ground with a loud crunch, and the eyes of the lieutenant change to the projection of Barel's ethereal spirit.

While this act may have been largely unnecessary, if anything, it was more of a demonstration to his Kaidis onlookers that he is what he says he is. But Xarash is still yet to be impressed.

'Incredible! A full demonstration of transference,' wows Samal, applauding the performance.

'Thank you, Doctor,' replies Barel, in his new host.

'Nothing but trickery, stranger. Now prove to me that you are a real fighter,' booms Xarash.

With that, Barel moves over to the throne in the centre of the room. The body of the lieutenant is lighter than his previous host but is less agile and has less physical strength. In order to finally prove himself, Barel has a problem – being entirely underground and buried deep inside a volcano, there is little of the elements that he can manipulate via the Synth. An outbreak of fire could prove to be an unnecessary death trap; water is practically non-existent.

He stands on top of the throne, raises his arms up to form the shape of a 'Y'. Calling in Ethereal, the air in the Royal Seat starts to accelerate, creating a whirlwind which circles him. The winds blow papers around in the war room and various clothing ripples in the direction of the breeze.

'For you see, general, I am a controller of the elements,' yells Barel, still maintaining the whirlwind rushing around for a few moments longer before slowly lowering his arms and the winds subside. He then steps off the throne and randomly targets a captain in the war room, firing off a bolt of lightning towards him, knocking the captain back, electrocuted.

This display certainly has the attention of everyone. Two corpses now littering the Royal Seat in a manner of seconds, Xarash has seen enough. He replaces the axe into the display hooks on the wall, no longer requiring it.

'Finally, you killed something,' he says. 'I just hope you don't take that long on the battlefield.'

'This was a mere demonstration,' smiles Barel. 'My powers are formidable, but I do not wish to quell our relationship.'

'If that is the case, why do you want my help?' queries Xarash.

'I am just one, general. If we join forces, we can move on the Shaler and that pathetic emperor with a definitive strike, and I know a way to rip right through their defences.'

'Perhaps we can have an agreement.'

With a smirk, Xarash directs to his war room to assign Barel some fighters to assist in his goal. Xarash is not really sure what Barel intends to do, but if it gives him the advantage over the Shaler, it could be worth his while. Before Barel departs from the king, he has one final request to speak with Samal in private. Xarash becomes a little suspicious, but gives him the benefit of the doubt and Samal brings Barel over to his corner of the room.

'Now, Samal, when I arrived, I heard you and the general talking about a book,' asks Barel.

'Ah, you mean the Book of the Daimons? I had a feeling this would interest you,' he smiles.

He starts to scrabble around on his desk trying to find something, but eventually only finds disappointment as what he seeks doesn't seem to be there. Tutting, he motions for Barel to follow him and opens the double doors next to his desk and disappears inside. Xarash notices that the two of them are leaving.

'Do not fail me, stranger!' he yells from his magnificent throne. 'Those that fail me never get a second chance. I shall be watching.'

Samal closes the doors behind the both of them, giving the king a glance as he does so.

* * * *

Where Samal and Barel are destined is the large barn-like outbuilding positioned in the courtyard outside the volcano — the headquarters of the Doctors Division. There are no windows and it has a flat roof with no invitation for outsiders of the Division to visit and built to be as secure as possible. A member of the Third Division reluctantly stands outside whose role is to simply not let anyone outside of the Division enter inside if a rogue Kaidis should become curious, even if such inspiration is rare.

Behind the firmly closed doors at the front is an environment similar to an open-plan office. There is a lot of space at the front with one large rectangular table occupying most — but not all — of the available frontal area. Behind this are rows of free-standing shelves containing papers, stacked high in almost a similar configuration to the Synth Institute's library. Further back at the wall is a Luvolic cabinet similar to a safe; it is strong and could withstand almost any eventuality with a single door on the front.

In amongst the shelves, the papers on which they lie are disturbed. Browsing the contents is a short and young member of the Kaidis — his name is Rakos, son of Xarash IV and heir to the throne. He is a teenager, and because he is the only child of his father, he has the freedom to do as he pleases. After being raised in the Production Division as all children are, he wasn't taken into the Third Division with Xarash instead taking his own son under his wing and providing him with the education and spirit to develop himself.

Xarash had dreamed for him to take after his own footsteps, following the rigorous demands of the military Divisions, but Rakos does not take much interest in commanding the armies as yet. Instead, he spends more time with the Doctors Division, reading and yearning for information about the past, present and future. A bright and intelligent boy, he shows great prospect for the future of the Kaidis, but seemingly has different priorities than his father.

Rakos, like all Kaidis, exhibits the affliction of the Bloodrage. Despite being a young teenager, his muscles have accelerated development and his skin is covered in the distinctive yellow spots. Wearing cloth instead of armour — perhaps as a symbol of defiance against his father — his head is also covered with a mantle as if to be uncomfortable with whom he is.

Browsing the shelves, he doesn't really have any idea what he is looking for. His mind is a jumble of thoughts, theories and concepts, having wild ideas but not really sure how to narrow them down into something to find on a shelf. The result of this impulsive behaviour is making the ordered papers as jumbled as his mind. He also knows that Samal does not like him poking around without supervision — with this in the back of his mind, he startles as the front doors burst open, the sound of the desert winds and shouting from outside making themselves known in the otherwise tranquil home of Kaidis research and development.

With a reverberating crash of the doors closing, Samal is followed by Barel as they enter inside. The Doctor walks further into the room, his gemmed cane tapping on the floor, approaching the long table covered in papers, containers and growing plants. He rummages around in an attempt to find what he was originally looking for down at the Royal Seat. Barel stands at the door taking a moment to familiarise himself with what he sees.

'What is all this?' asks Barel, who is entirely clueless to where he is.

Samal stops shuffling around the table and looks at Barel, an expression on his face suggesting that the question was a bit stupid.

'"This"?' he pauses with an arm outstretched, pointing around. 'This is where we do our own research into our affliction and into other matters which we have an interest. Surely you are aware of the Bloodrage from that body you command?'

Unfortunately for Barel, it would be the first time he had heard the term and remains silent at Samal's question. Realising that the Lightbearer has no idea, he gasps.

'You really have no idea who we are, do you? Fascinating!'

'All I seek is revenge,' Barel states. 'I do not care for anyone else, for I have my own motivations.'

Samal raises an eyebrow.

'Xarash wants the annihilation of the Shaler, but perhaps you really do have different reasons,' ponders the Doctor. 'No matter, what your business is has nothing to do with me.'

He resumes rummaging around on the table, but he hears a disturbance from behind.

'Are you there, Rakos?' Samal questions, without interrupting himself.

The cloaked child makes himself known and approaches the table. Barel looks curiously at the boy — the very concept of the young is unfamiliar.

'What is that?' he questions in surprise.

Samal laughs.

'This is Xarash's son,' replies the Doctor, who turns to face him with an expression on his face as if to query what he was doing. 'Introduce yourself to our guest.'

'Why should I have to do that to a meaningless grunt?' says Rakos. 'He asks strange questions.'

Approaching Barel, with similar stride to his father but without the dominating presence, Rakos looks up at him. Slightly more observant than Xarash however, as he makes eye contact, he sees the blue ethereal essence of the Lightbearer. Not really sure what to do next, almost the coward, he retreats back to Samal.

'I am Prince Rakos, son of King Xarash IV, ruler of the Kaidis Kingdom,' he boldly states from a distance, but with a tone that suggests he has been programmed to quote his title.

Barel is less than impressed and concludes he is not worth his time. Samal tuts as he knows that it wasn't the best introduction and sees Barel move over to the plants on the table, while Rakos stands in silence.

'Don't touch those!' exclaims Samal as he notices Barel. 'I'd hate to think where those hands of the lieutenant have been. That valuable plant is something we are researching to improve the potency of the Bloodrage — the disease that allows the Kaidis to be strong and the dominating force.'

The plant is a synthesised breed of Urtica that the Doctors Division have created. With all of the original Urtica plants made extinct by aggressive collection efforts by the Kaidis in the past, it is their only option at recreating the species. Stocks of original Urtica seeds have reduced to near nothing, and this attempt is seen as the last chance to enhance their affliction. Barel notices something that catches his eye as he moves to the rear of the building.

'Especially don't touch that,' Samal says behind him, holding a sheet of paper.

'What is in there?' looking at the sealed Luvolic cabinet.

'That is our secure holding for anything to do with Bloodrage. The king wants any artefacts or documentation relating to it to be kept, as it is part of our heritage as Kaidis.'

He sighs a bit, not comfortable talking about this subject.

'Xarash, like his father before is a bit of a hoarder. He likes to collect trinkets and spoils, anything he can get his hands on. The Shaler are keen to hold onto what is rightfully ours, so Xarash will use force to try and get our history back. Not that I necessarily agree with his way of doing things.'

'What do you mean by that?' questions Barel, returning to the table.

'You ask a lot of questions. Anyway, my fellow Doctors prefer to preserve life, yet the king is incredibly barbaric and – dare I say it – old-fashioned in his thinking and practises. We don't always see eye to eye, as I'm sure you are already aware. Maybe young Rakos will prove to be different,' he says with a smile in the child's direction.

He then holds the paper up to Barel. The text upon it is written in archaic Shaler language, detailing unremarkable observations of the time, but on the reverse is a strange note. Written in different handwriting, in a hurry and in Ethereal, it reads:

*The black book was stolen.*
*The thief called a destructive force.*
*Tell no-one.*

A signature of the unknown writer follows. After Samal reads out what it says, he is surprised by Barel's lack of knowledge about such a book and looks at the Lightbearer curiously.

'Are you saying you had no idea about there being a book like this?'

'No, but it might explain something,' he says, realising that the book was the probable reason for why he was called into the Arena. 'Perhaps the Shaler found the book.'

'Maybe they did, but I don't know what the book contains or what this "destructive force" is.'

'That could be me,' Barel smiles.

'I would say that could be a logical conclusion, but if you have no knowledge of the book, I don't see how it fits with this written account.'

This discovery makes Barel uneasy. If such a book exists containing information about how to call into the Synthetic Domain, and if the Shaler have possession of it and they used it to recall him, this may mean that they have the ability to reverse his existence. He wonders what else the mysterious book contains. Is this part of the Tournament? Perhaps his objective has just changed – his success of the Tournament depends on preventing the Shaler from doing anything with this book.

'But,' says Samal, looking at Barel who appears a little astonished. 'I can't understand how you wouldn't know about such an incredible tome.'

'I do not expect you to understand a lot of things, Doctor,' he replies. 'There are a great number of subjects that you do not know.'

'Really? Like what? What actually are you? Where did you come from?'

'Now you are asking a lot of questions. Answers I do not have to provide.'

Samal smirks at the Lightbearer.

'I see how it is. Fine, you don't have to tell me anything, but I will know. And you will help me.'

'I have already said I will not answer your questions,' Barel threatens. 'Do not push yourself too far, Doctor.'

'Yes, yes, very well, there is no need to get offensive. All that I ask is that you bring me the book, if it exists. I'm sure Xarash will find it very interesting as well.'

'Why? What value does this book have?'

'The very secrets of life itself could be inside!' yells Samal, becoming fairly emotive about the subject. 'It could be one of the greatest discoveries ever, and we cannot let the Shaler learn anything from it!'

'I see your point,' Barel replies, making his way to the doors and opens them. 'I make no promises!' he yells back over the noise from outside. 'Maybe we shall see each other again, Doctor.'

For this would be beneficial to the Lightbearer, as if the Shaler discover more of the secrets from the Book of the Daimons, they may become harder to stop and Barel doesn't want them to have the advantage. But then, he is not a slave of the Kaidis, perhaps the book would be best destroyed. As he moves around the courtyard in thought, it dawns on him that if the book contained the instructions to communicate with the Synthetic Domain, it must also contain more detail about the Domain itself and maybe even something relating to the Tournament — such details hidden from players such as him.

Before he can concern himself with the possibilities, his train of thought is interrupted by a member of the Second Division.

'You must be Barel,' states the warrior. 'Your support army is ready for your command.'

True to the word of Xarash, a group of fighters await his order and Barel smiles, making his way over to plan his assault upon the Shaler.

# Chapter Eleven

## Dawn

Three days pass. Back at Thoridon, Toraq and his companion Eko are preparing to leave the city having sold or exchanged most of their stock. Around them in the city the Shaler have been on edge the whole time, expecting something to charge towards them and fearing for the worst. Yet so far, nothing has come to pass.

In the meantime, Emperor Solus, his mother Avornia, members of the Senate and other miscellaneous well-wishers held an official funeral for Ferlor. A day of mourning was declared, since students past and present at the Institute had lost one of their great teachers despite any disagreements that some may have had. Solus delivered a sympathetic speech to the assembled and thoughts turned to his replacement, crowning his mother as Master Conjurer Avornia. Solus also took the opportunity to make clear that despite his past weakness, he has promised to lead his people through these uncertain times.

A memorial was added to the Hall of Legends — a chiselled stone monument in the likeness of Ferlor. Tributes from the people were donated and positioned around it as a mark of respect. However, the one single item that proved to be responsible for his demise was given a centrepiece. This item, the Book of the Daimons, was under great scrutiny prior to the funeral by students from the Institute along with Avornia. Solus ordered them to try and make sense of the passages, accounts and rituals described in the book to find a way to best understand the abilities of Barel and prevent the potential reign of terror against his people. Unfortunately, their work was hampered by the fact that the book is written in such a way that understanding its use of the Synth and Ethereal terms associated with its descriptions were not immediately clear, generally relying on sometimes sketchy translations provided by Avornia.

Of what progress they made is patchy at best. Ferlor was able to understand the ritual that called Barel into existence largely because much of the work has been already documented at the Institute, but it was the sequences and missing phrases in Ethereal that were pivotal – these being accurately described in the book. The students, with Avornia, had great difficulty in trying to understand other sections of the book, especially in such a limited timescale. Deflated by their inability to comprehend any further detail from it, the book has been positioned central to the memorial inside the Hall of Legends, its ultimate secrets remaining hidden to the Shaler, and the unknown knowledge pieced together by Ferlor dying with him.

Meanwhile, Toraq has kept away from what the Shaler are doing and is instead concentrating on his efforts of providing a trade service. The presence of Barel has not been without thought however, with Toraq becoming more and more curious about what the Lightbearer is planning – hour by hour, he grows increasingly concerned.

As he begins to prepare to dismantle his displays from inside the Quadrangle's market, this attracts the attention of Emperor Solus who had been completely caught up with the Senate and the funeral, not paying any attention to his guests. In the afternoon daylight, Solus breaks from hammering out a defensive plan inside the Senate House and approaches Toraq who is finalising his packing. On sight of the emperor approaching, he turns to greet his host.

'Ah, Solus,' he says, outstretching a white fur-covered hand for a shake. 'I have not seen you since we arrived, but I can understand your urgency.'

'I must apologise,' Solus replies, shaking hands. 'But I am curious – are you leaving the city?'

'Yes, it is time we moved on and we need to replenish our own supplies.'

'I see. You are aware of the impending threat?'

'I am, but you must remember that this campaign you are leading does not involve us. We are not fighters and I must remain impartial; my trade depends on it.'

Solus takes issue with this attitude. He had hoped that the Matoh would be able to provide support to their cause, but it would appear that they are not interested in defending the Shaler. Opting to take a more stern approach, he motions for Toraq to follow.

'I have something to show you,' says Solus, moving in the direction of the Institute. He leads Toraq into the Hall of Legends.

'Tell me, Toraq,' he says, as they continue further into the Hall. 'When your people are in desperate times, what do you do?'

'We are resilient, you know that,' Toraq replies.

'Just answer the question!' exclaims Solus suddenly. This makes Toraq think for a moment – it's not like Solus to be so demanding. But Toraq has a problem when it comes to answering.

'I do not know,' he replies. 'We have never come under direct threat from anyone.'

'Exactly – you are left alone as you are not seen as a danger. We are constantly under attack — or at least threat — by the Kaidis. They are relentless in their cause; they just want to make our lives full of terror while we want to be left in peace. I need those that I can trust to be at my side. People like you, Toraq.'

They approach the most recent memorial, with its many flowers, ornaments and trinkets adorning it and a great plaque with the name of Ferlor inscribed in the stone. The Book of the Daimons rests underneath on a plinth, its black and tarnished cover shimmering. Torches illuminate the entire memorial in respect for Ramor herself. This is the first time Toraq has seen anything of the activity that the Shaler have involved themselves with over the last few days.

'Ferlor died because of a desire to make me stronger – resilient as you say – against our continuing threat,' says Solus, gazing at the memorial with a tone of passion in his voice. 'But in great sacrifice, it became his undoing and unleashed a terrible malevolence to these lands. I have to repay his enormous debt to me and I cannot do that alone.'

With Toraq feeling slightly guilty by his selfishness, he starts to reconsider his immediate plan. Perhaps leaving the city would leave the Shaler vulnerable, but also it may reduce his chance to see

Barel. He looks over at the memorial, kneeling at its edge, admiring the items and symbols. His attention is eventually drawn to the diabolical book.

'You are right, Solus,' he says, returning to his feet and redirecting his attention to the leader of the Shaler. 'We shall stay and assist in any way we can.'

'Thank you,' replies the emperor, smiling.

'But tell me – what is the significance of this book?' asks Toraq, pointing at the memorial.

'That was what caused the destruction – it was the instrument that allowed such a travesty to occur.'

'I see,' says Toraq, raising an eyebrow. 'What does the book contain?'

'I'd rather not talk about it,' concludes Solus, turning away in disgust.

This sudden denial makes Toraq increasingly curious. As Solus looks towards the entrance to the Library lost in thought, Toraq picks up the book and is surprised at its cover. Opening the pages, he carefully flicks through its contents — the thick pages crinkle as each one is turned, and Solus bites his bottom lip as the sound causes him to remember the events back at the graveyard. The Lightbearer's eyes widen as he begins to recognise the writing. In the later pages, a great deal of the text is written in Ethereal with diagrams and drawings. Toraq quickly reads the words and is able to identify the meanings, especially the account of the Necrocircle which Ferlor took great interest in. Turning to the start, Toraq sees the writings by Xarash and Kaidan, and even though his name is absent, he sees a lengthy description of his endeavours with Kaidan in the forests of Mistwood.

Despite his shock, he closes the book and replaces it on the plinth. He realises that if Ferlor used this book to call into the Synthetic Domain, as would be fitting with the events described by Solus, it would seem the Tournament is truly under way. Ever the master of bluff, he doesn't want Solus to know what the contents of the book actually contains and chooses to hide his surprise.

'How can I assist you, Solus?' he asks, as the emperor turns around to face him.

'As it stands, dear friend, I do not know at the moment,' replies Solus despondently, having no idea about the real situation.

They both leave the Hall of Legends returning to Toraq's cart in the Quadrangle. Solus bids farewell to Toraq for now, thanking him for his support and disappears back into the Senate House to continue his discussions. With the Matoh confirmed to be at his side, this changes the plans of the Shaler for their defence.

But Toraq has issue with this book. His companion Eko noses around his feet, sniffing, trying to get his masters attention. He looks at Eko and decides he needs to act. It would be against the rules of the Tournament for Toraq to get too involved with political matters, but he thinks that this book could potentially be his downfall. Having built great relationships with the Shaler now, if they were able to fully understand the book, those relationships would disappear instantly, especially if the Tournament itself was revealed.

'There is a great prize located in there,' he whispers in Ethereal to Eko, who sits attentively, seeming to understand exactly what his master is saying. 'It is a book that must be destroyed. When the time is right, I believe our latest visitor can assist with its destruction.'

Eko snorts in acknowledgement and gets ready to move towards the Institute, but Toraq whistles and his companion stops, turning to face him.

'Not now,' continues Toraq. 'Only when the time is right — we do not want to draw unnecessary attention to ourselves.'

He moves towards the Senate House, feeling compelled to introduce himself to the other senators, personally declaring his loyalty to their cause. As he enters inside, the heated debates about the current situation are instantly interrupted as Toraq strides into the Senate, his hulking appearance and glistening white fur impossible to notice. Solus stands up to greet him.

'Senators of the Shaler,' speaks Toraq in his dominating deep voice before Solus can begin introductions. 'I am Toraq and I come to support your people in defence for this great city. I understand you expect an attack at any time from a forceful being. I have devised a strategy that should help when it strikes. I plan to create a significant distraction — one that will give you time. And time, senators, is all you need to win. Time is the ultimate restorer.'

Solus looks a little surprised. This is a completely different Toraq — one that has not shown its face to him before. Over the years of previous engagements with him, his demeanour has always been one of peacefulness, politeness and, of course, excellent salesmanship. Suddenly suggesting plans that involve distractions and defence seems a little shocking to him.

'You seem troubled by this suggestion, emperor,' says Toraq, noticing the uncertainty in his eyes.

'I cannot say I was expecting this.'

'Please – do not concern yourself. I believe it is time that I paid my debt back for your hospitality after all these years.'

One representative from the People's Union stands, clearly stunned by what Toraq has said.

'Forgive my surprise, but, to our eyes, you are nothing but a humble merchant, providing a great service to this city. What can you possibly provide to us in this time of – dare I say – war?'

'Senator! What you say surprises me,' barks Solus, who can clearly see Toraq being uncomfortable about such an accusation.

'I mean no disrespect,' he replies, speaking directly to the emperor. 'This seems a little out of character, shall we say. How do we know that what he proposes does buy us this "time" he speaks about? He is not known for compassion in such matters.'

The emperor twitches in both his face and in his hands, clearly taking what the senator is saying personally. How dare he suggest that the greatest ally of the Shaler cannot be trusted? But before Solus can explode into a fit of rage, Toraq places a furry hand upon his shoulder.

'I can understand your concerns, young senator,' answers Toraq in a calm soothing voice. 'You are quite right to be surprised by what I propose, even if I have neglected to detail specifically how I plan to create this distraction. I am not a fighter, I am most certainly a neutral party, but perhaps you underestimate the seriousness of the situation. Your own great city is under threat of attack from a superior foe – I believe you will need all the help you can get.'

The senator returns to his seat. Solus looks around the benches waiting for another to question the judgement of Toraq, but none is forthcoming.

'With that matter resolved, I believe you should tell us more about your "distraction",' says Solus, directing his attention to Toraq.

'Thank you, emperor. There are many secrets that I am aware, for I have seen much in my existence, but these secrets will remain so. I will perform a ritual that I shall not explain, but has a tremendous display associated with it. I believe it will create enough of a distraction for your people to ready themselves for the impending assault. There is a small hill to the north-east of the city – I shall be there.'

Without speaking further, Toraq turns around and leaves the Senate House. He does not listen to the unavoidable murmuring behind his back as he makes his way back to the Quadrangle. Solus tries to speak above the senators in an attempt to get his attention but he is entirely ignored. He returns his interest towards the benches.

'His mind is clearly made up, senators,' Solus booms over the noise, which quickly subsides into echoes. 'We will have to back up his plan.'

'And just how do you propose we do that?' shouts a senator, following by cheers of agreement by others. 'Why hasn't he come to help us before?'

'He is not one of us,' suggests Solus. 'I have full trust in Toraq. It is up to him how he proceeds with his plan. We can only wait.'

* * * *

In the barren and stifling south lands of the Sulphur Deserts, Barel is preparing to assault the Shaler city of Thoridon. King General Xarash is keen to have him – through their special relationship – lead a successful campaign against them, in order to finally have a victory worth remembering in his name. While the general trusts he will do so, he is not entirely sure about his strange ally – success will be the deciding factor.

The lieutenants responsible for controlling the armies of the Kaidis assigned Barel with two units – one from the Second Division, one from the First Division. Alongside each of these units come members of the Doctors Division, providing vital tactical support. The general fighters of the vast armies of the Kaidis are always a little apprehensive about the Doctors, for they are the ones with the smarts and lack general fighting skill. However, they are tolerated because they help keep them informed on the battlefield. The strength, power and fortitude of the Kaidis warriors are great, but without support, sustaining that proves a challenge when faced with opponents almost exclusively dealing with the Synth, and a

Doctor is seen as a useful asset in keeping the fight going. They don't have to be liked, though.

The Lightbearer himself has used Ethereal Transference to possess a body of a Doctor assigned to his army. This body is a much lighter and a more fragile creature in comparison to his previous host, but it is agile and more fitting for taking charge. It has not won him friends with the Doctors that remain.

Daylight starts to dwindle as the sun begins to set behind the horizon; the fierce prevailing winds still blowing all across the parched landscape. Barel and his unit of one hundred-strong warriors have their mission ahead of them, using a fleet of Knoria vehicles to transport them to the north. Spirits are high – the soldiers are keen to see active combat and there is an air of celebration amongst them, their mood bolstered by the fact that a strange, powerful being is on their side.

Barel sits on the back of the leading Knoria with members from the First Division and their attached Doctor. In among the eager rabble, he does not share their same enthusiasm for the impending fight, choosing to stare out over the sandy landscape being spun around across the flat nothingness; his deep blue swirling eyes reflecting nothing and showing no emotion. Boisterous laughter resonates around the vehicle as the sail above rattles in the strong wind. A solider nudges Barel in the arm.

'You may not be one of those Doctors, but, shit – why do you have to be as damn gloomy as them?' chuckles one soldier to Barel and pointing over towards the real Doctor on the other side of the Knoria. Roars of agreement follow from the other soldiers, as if it were a drunken party. Barel makes no reaction and ignores.

'Well, you would be too if you could see the futility to this whole endeavour,' replies the Doctor, clearly not wanting to be there.

'Oh, really?' questions the solider, glaring at the Doctor. 'What makes you so sure about that?'

'Do I have to spell it out? Our previous attacks on Thoridon have been in vain, and even with some strange presence on our side, I don't see what difference it'll make. We are all going to die, anyway.'

At this point, the soldiers burst out laughing.

'You really don't get it, do you?' roars the solider to the Doctor. 'This is a glorious day! For blood of the cursed Shaler and honour of the mighty Kaidis, we shall be victorious regardless!'

'I don't see how being dead is a victory.'

'And that is why you are not a solider, but some pathetic little thinker. This is why you have no respect,' replies the solider to cheers from his peers.

The fleet of Knorias arrive at a place known as Outpost Ora, tactfully positioned just on the edge of the harsh landscape, meeting with the more temperate lands home to the Shaler. Over time, the winds have collected great mounds of sand and other material from the south, forming an enormously tall rock face – a gap between serves as an ideal location for such an outpost.

As the winds are much less stronger, the sails fall empty on the Knorias and Barel comes out of his thought-provoking trance, jumping off the back of the vehicle, followed by the rest of the soldiers who begin to rally into formation. Waiting for their arrival, the captain of the outpost stands at large gates, similar to what Barel discovered at the entrance to Wodar Drop – emblazoned with the symbol of the volcano. Barel moves to greet the captain as his army stands behind, quiet and tall.

'You must be the one they referred to as Barel,' says Captain Selak, noticing the eyes.

'Indeed I am,' replies Barel. 'Do you have something to tell me?'

'King General Xarash has already sent a scouting party on ahead to gather intelligence about the situation with the Shaler. I have not heard anything back so far, though.'

'I am sure we will see for ourselves.'

The captain smiles and turns to tell his soldiers to open the barricade. The large, strong gates open wide with a great amount of straining from both the Kaidis pulling and the craftsmanship of the gate itself. Barel nods at Selak and proceeds to move forward through the opening. The various commanding soldiers yell to move their units, keeping a strict formation behind their assumed leader.

With all the troops behind him, all geared up in their sturdy armour, carrying an array of different types of swords, axes, shields and poles, the noise from a hundred moving machines resounds around the pastures of the Shaler. Their destination is the south of Thoridon — as they move north from Ora, the grass becomes greener and the trees of Mistwood make themselves known. With the sunlight of Ramor disappeared behind the horizon, lights from fireflies hover around random trees and puncture the void of darkness as they march up to the Crossroads.

*  *  *  *

Past the Crossroads and up through Mistwood, the scouting party sent ahead of Barel to perform reconnaissance on the Shaler arrives at the eastern outskirts of Thoridon. These scouts are similar to what Barel encountered near the forest when he retreated from Solus – made up of four Kaidis, a sergeant and three grunts from the Second Division. In the darkness of night, the sergeant whispers to his team about what he plans to do next.

'The general tasked us with finding out what the Shaler are planning, so my plan is to sneak in undetected and see for ourselves.'

'What if we get caught?'

'Then that will be our downfall, most likely. These bastards have become a lot more aware lately. There's a first time for everything, right? Follow my lead.'

What is distinctive about these scouts is that they are trained to operate at night. They don't wear heavy armour like normal warriors — much lighter leather-like material woven with Luvolite to give their clothing a pitch black finish, sporting small sheathed daggers tucked into their belts just in case.

On approach to the eastern wall, they keep to the side of the road and slowly make their way directly up to the wall, to the left of the closed – and heavily guarded – east-side gate. Light from the torches burning does not illuminate to the sides and the Kaidis are able to quietly shimmy along the wall remaining in the darkness. Continuing around, the sergeant identifies a possible weakness in the wall.

He gestures to his party to a small crack in the stonework. On top of the wall is a continuous path that snakes around the entirety of the city, allowing for the defending Warlocks to have a view of the surroundings. The sergeant takes a foothold into the crack and lifts himself, scaling the wall and climbing up on top of it. Looking around the dimly lit path, he sees no patrols coming in either direction, and peers over the edge, waving for the rest to do the same.

As the last of the party is pulled up and lying on the path flat to reduce visibility as much as possible, the sergeant crawls over to the other side looking for a suitable place to drop down. Slightly further around, he sees a flat-roof house close to the edge of the wall. The four of them gingerly tiptoe around the path towards the house and with no guards nearby dropping down onto it. Dull thuds are made as their well-trodden feet hit the wooden roof, but such a sound could be easily dismissed. Still in near total darkness, the Kaidis climb down the side of the house facing the perimeter wall, made from a flint-like stone, providing easy grips and natural footholds to descend quietly onto the ground.

With a successful breach of the city's defences made, the sergeant gives a wry smile to his colleagues – adrenaline pumps as they know there is no turning back. Still keeping to the shadows, weaving between various houses and other buildings they make their way west, moving closer to the centre of power to get a glimpse of what the Shaler are planning.

The layout of the city is very much consistent, with the Temple of Ramor and the Synth Institute providing a central focal point to how the city is constructed, with many residential areas surrounding the centre growing outward. To the Kaidis, these structures work like a pin on a map, broadcasting exactly where they need to head.

With a new defensive tactic in place, advised by Levak, even the gates at the inner walls of the city are now closed and guarded as much as the outside walls. But as the internal walls are much older than the externals, time has ravaged their capabilities and more significant cracks and other breaks are prevalent, allowing once again for the Kaidis to scale and climb down without detection in the shadows.

Their eventual traversal of the walls, shadows and building landscape comes to a head as the second wall drops them down directly into the Quadrangle, their intended destination. The sergeant and his minions are met with one enormous surprise they didn't foresee – the two Matoh, attending to their waggon. Making sure they are out of sight and earshot behind the Temple of Ramor, this provides a dilemma for the Kaidis.

'Why is that travelling merchant here? He should have fucked off a long time ago,' whispers one of the soldiers, angrily to his sergeant.

'We didn't really know what to expect,' he replies. 'Keep it down, I see movement.'

The sergeant peers around the corner of the Temple to get a better view. It is Emperor Solus moving towards Toraq and entering into conversation. From their distance, the Kaidis can't hear what is being said. Intrigue gets the better of the sergeant and he decides to moves closer, weaving through the shadows of the darkened Quadrangle, and crouching behind Toraq's cart. The other three stay in their position, astounded that their sergeant hasn't been spotted.

Solus and Toraq stand around small torches, illuminating their faces, but not enough to creep into the shadows behind the waggon. The pair is already in mid-discussion.

'I had no idea you were such a swordsman,' remarks Toraq to Solus with surprise on his face.

'Well, I can't give the impression of weakness to the people, can I, Toraq? As a leader of your own, you should appreciate that,' replies Solus, who proudly displays the finely crafted sword that was wielded by Emperor Vimlor, the hilt in the shape of talons and an emerald central.

'So tell me, what took you to swordsmanship?'

'My father used to collect various swords and always had wild ideas for forging his own blades – members of the People's Union flocked to craft them, according to my mother. Prized possessions, each having a unique theme, many of them hang at my home in remembrance of a great leader. This one I wield was inspired by the birds that fly high over the city. I was always fascinated by the power that such a blade commands, and I wanted to taste it, hence my interest.'

This conversation troubles the lurking sergeant – with the emperor claiming to be a powerful sword wielder, this narrows the Kaidis' chance of escaping should they be noticed. As Solus moves the blade around in the torchlight, the three others notice the metal sparkling, its sharp edges glimmering, each one starting to have similar thoughts as their sergeant.

Solus rests the sword against the cart and he outstretches a hand towards Toraq.

'It is good to have you here, aiding us in our plans,' says Solus, warmly.

'Think nothing of it, emperor,' replies Toraq, accepting a handshake with his furry hand, not making any suggestion about his own concerns.

This compassion and alliance between the Shaler and Toraq is serious news for the sergeant. He can't believe what he is hearing — the Matoh is supposed to be neutral and impartial, yet it seems to him that this is no longer the case. They are now both the enemy! How long has this been going on? Fury flows through his body – an uncontrollable urge to end the agreement ripples through his veins, empowered by the pulsating Bloodrage.

The adrenaline is all too much for him and he jolts up into an upright position from behind the cart, the back of Toraq facing him and becomes fully visible in the night air. He unsheathes his short dagger and begins to rally towards both of them. The three lurking soldiers see what their sergeant is doing and entirely bemused by his actions see no option to join in and assist.

'You will die for your betrayal!' yells the sergeant.

In the corner of his eye, Solus sees the charging Kaidis, daggers in his eyes as well as in his hand. He yells out to attract the attention of not only the Matoh, but also the Warlocks standing guard around the Quadrangle. Seeing the sergeant lunging towards Toraq, Solus intervenes between them with sword in hand and successfully manages to intercept the incoming dagger, causing the sergeant to lose his grip with the weapon falling to the floor. Knocked back by the strike, the sergeant recovers his balance.

Toraq realises that they are coming under attack and sees all the guards leaving their posts around the gated doors to come and assist with the intruders. This is the moment he was waiting for — with all the distraction going on, he attracts the attention of Eko and points towards the Institute. His companion knows exactly what to do and dashes over in amongst the increasing chaos.

When Toraq sees that his assistant is through, he begins to speak in Ethereal. With a simple command, all of a sudden he begins to emit a bright light around him. The Quadrangle becomes fully lit as if it were midday and the other three Kaidis, positioning themselves behind their disarmed sergeant become fully visible to all.

With no time to be surprised by what appears to be the first time Toraq has demonstrated usage of the Synth, Solus walks forward towards the heavily outnumbered group of Kaidis, his sword outstretched pointing directly at the sergeant.

'So, we have a full scouting party here, do we?' asks Solus, as the Kaidis shuffle backwards in parallel to the emperor's advance.

'Kill us now. You are a fucking disgrace,' shouts the sergeant.

'Why am I such a disgrace to your kind? The Kaidis always say that about me,' Solus replies.

The sergeant laughs.

'You call yourself a leader, but you are nothing except a dishonoured worm. Just like your father.'

Without further cause for conversation, such words cause hurt in the mind of Solus, reminding him of the earlier times. He loses his grasp on the situation for a brief moment, remembering his desperation suffered with Rogaro. But before slipping away entirely, he remembers that a scouting party killed his father and this is exactly the sort of revenge he was looking for. With a fierce yell, he accelerates his pace to a run; with a tight grip on his sword he pierces the skull of the Kaidis sergeant using the full force of his forward momentum.

A blood-curdling scream of pain emits from the mouth of the sergeant as the blade slices through his tainted flesh and into his left cheek and through to the other side. An explosion of blood runs out of both the entry and exit wounds, covering the blade of the sword, dripping and rushing down over the lifeless body. Solus pulls on his sword and removes the blade, it making a haunting slicing sound as it is fully retracted; the emperor stands there, breathing heavily as the body falls to the floor with a thud, blood pouring over the ground and trickling through the gaps in the cobbles.

The emperor looks up at the remaining three, looking to retreat.

'You think this is the action of a worm?'

Before they get a chance to respond, the Warlocks begin to invoke Synth-controlled fire directed toward the invaders – their screams resonate around the Quadrangle as their flesh and bones are reduced to ash from the intense heat.

As the fight ends, Eko returns with the Book of the Daimons held in his mouth just before the fight concludes. He tosses the book underneath the cart and makes himself visible to his master who takes his presence as a signal of success.

'It would appear things are happening, Solus,' speaks Toraq, who's self-light dissipates as the last of the Kaidis falls.

'Yes,' he replies, still catching his breath. 'They are coming.'

The guards return to their positions and a sense of normality returns to the Quadrangle. Solus takes a moment to glance at Toraq, realising that there is something special about him. He then retreats to the Senate House to speak with Levak and anyone else that may want to know what happened.

Seizing the opportunity under the darkness, Toraq moves over to the corpses of the Kaidis. Retrieving a small bottle from a pocket he carefully siphons some of the ash into the container.

'This is our only chance,' he says in Ethereal to Eko. 'I shall go prepare and perform the ritual that our incoming guest will be attracted to. Assist our friends of the Shaler in the meantime.'

With his final words, he returns to his waggon and pulls on a hidden compartment underneath the back. Inside is the wooden staff that Uriro left behind when Toraq received Ascendancy; the gem on top matching the colour of Toraq's own visible essence. After finally retrieving the stolen Book of the Daimons from underneath the cart, he moves – utilising his natural fast pace – towards the eastern gate of Thoridon, asking the guards to allow him passage. Climbing a small hill as dawn breaks to the north-east of the city, he stands at its peak and prepares to perform a similar ritual to what Ferlor performed as the Necrocircle. Now, he has to wait for the right moment.

❋ ❋ ❋ ❋

Marching through the night and crossing the flooded plains of the Flatlands, Barel and his army approach their intended destination – the south road leading directly up to the gate of Thoridon. It is a relatively steep climb over a ridge before the descent into full view of what ultimately awaits them; a perfect preparation point to lead an assault.

The legion comes to a halt before they can be seen. Always following protocol, the warriors stand without exhaustion, with an air of anticipation as they psyche themselves up ready to launch a storm of blades upon the disagreeable Shaler, bolstered by their secret weapon – Barel. Each unit of armed-to-the-teeth fighters, all with various experience but all with the same passion for a result, stand ready in their formations – in squares of four-by-four with a sergeant or commander depending on their Division taking the lead and a Doctor at the rear.

Barel stands at the front, still occupying a Doctor's host body and turns to face his army. He calls forward the unit leaders to discuss the plan who leave their positions and stand in a straight line in front of him. Despite the need for a result, the Doctors that make up the minority never have shared the enthusiasm. But their descent is never recognised and they all know that this will be their demise. No matter how hard the Kaidis try, whatever small gains they make during an encounter, such progress is undone as quick as it came.

'This is your chance to prove yourself,' Barel begins, his voice resonating to his group leaders, but loud enough for the fighters behind to hear. 'While you may have your own goals, the Kaidis and I share one: to destroy the Shaler for what they are. You may not know who I am. Allow me to introduce myself officially — I am Barel, Warmonger of the Elements. I am more powerful than the Shaler's most prepared scholars. I will take charge in causing the utmost destruction to their existence! It is my destiny to see that this happens.'

He makes clear reference in his closing statement to the game he is playing – he longs for the chance of Ascendancy, and his decree to wipe out the Shaler would certainly define his cause and effect.

A muted cheer rises up from the army behind with some battering their swords or axes against shields as to encourage applause, even though they are entirely unaware of Barel's greater challenge. The Kaidis commanders are not as impressed, turning to the horde and yelling for them to quiet – such a noise may undo their chance of surprise. After the rabble calms down, the commanders refocus their attention on Barel.

'I appreciate your support,' Barel continues. 'But let us wait until victory. The plan is simple yet effective. Because I command unlimited power with the elements, I shall unleash a torrent of winds and waves of fire will rise from the ground, burning and crushing anything in the way. Their defences will be defeated and this will be your chance to strike hard and destroy the enemy. This will be your proving grounds and it is your calling.'

As he finishes speaking, the commanders and sergeants immediately break into issuing orders. They devise a plan to try and outsmart the defence with units advancing from the left, middle and right of Thoridon's south gate. Barel will lead the middle group since he will need to focus directly on the point of entry before the Kaidis will have a chance.

With dawn breaking, Barel issues the order to advance. As they cross the apex of the ridge, the three groups branch out as the plan dictates, amid a backdrop of thundering feet and clattering armours. It doesn't take long for this to become apparent to the Shaler who have been waiting for this moment — the lookouts yell around the city defences, reporting the gross sight advancing on their position. Swarms of Warlocks begin to line the walls ready to command their second-rate knowledge of the Synth when compared to the Lightbearer that goes unnoticed, appearing to be just a regular member of the Doctors Division from afar.

But the Kaidis' plan forgoes one detail. To the east, Toraq also observes the advancing army and begins to prepare himself to utilise the Necrocircle ritual. Finding his bottle of collected ash from the fallen Kaidis scouting party, he begins to outline a circle with the peak of the hill he stands on central to his crude outline of decay. No prevailing winds help keep the ash from blowing away and Toraq moves to stand central to his circle. He begins to chant similar — but crucially not identical — phrases from the Book of the Daimons like when Ferlor attempted the ritual.

Meanwhile, the Kaidis armies move closer to the gate. On the left and right sides of the advancement, they continue to move in, but Barel's unit comes to a halt some distance away from it under his order. He takes a sword from one of the Kaidis behind and takes several steps in front. Digging the sword into the grass, he carves a makeshift hexagram into the ground. After discarding the weapon, he stands central inside his markings, facing the direction of the wall surrounding the city, raising his arms skyward and clenching his fists.

Looking up, he begins chanting phrases in Ethereal over and over. The Kaidis behind him become uneasy as his pointless muttering appears to make them vulnerable in the middle of the battleground.

'What are we waiting for now?' whispers one of the warriors standing in their box formation.

'I don't know, but he's a fucking loony,' whispers back another.

'Silence!' hisses the Doctor behind. 'He is talking to the elements, you idiots.'

No sooner as the Doctor finishes, dust starts rising from the carved hexagram in the ground. The fists of the Kaidis Doctor that Barel possesses begin to emit steam. Aghast by what they are witnessing, the Kaidis behind stand there dumbfounded by what happens next. Barel struggles under the power being wielded to move his arms so that they are parallel to each other, still with his smouldering fists clenched. Ultimately, the forces being applied to him as he utilises the Synth become too much to hold and Barel lets out a loud roar, releasing his fists. A wall of fire rises from the carved outline on the ground and projects itself across the air at an incredible pace in the direction of the Shaler's defences. Upon seeing this huge flame, the Warlocks above begin to yell in a panic, not really sure how the Kaidis are able to command such ferociously.

Running, trying to escape from the impending collision of conflagration hurtling towards them, their attempts are futile and they are either blown off the wall and fall to their deaths as they hit the ground from the drop or are lacerated by the shrapnel of exploded debris. A hole is ripped right through the south wall and it continues to crumble.

With smoke rising and small fires burning on rubble, the left and right side Kaidis units charge through the wide opening and disappear past the smoke into the outer city. Behind the smokescreen, the sound of metallic clattering from weapons and armour complemented with roars of enjoyment as blade meets Shaler flesh resonates down to the middle unit, still standing at their position. Barel has collapsed to his knees due to the required power to obliterate the wall, catching his breath, his hands scorched from the fire.

The sound of battle is too much for the waiting Kaidis behind and they decide to break from the Lightbearer and charge ahead towards the fight. However, the Doctor associated with the unit decides to stay with Barel. He walks up to him and crouches down, showing the same level of disdain for the situation as he did back on the Knoria.

'I know what you are going to ask,' says Barel, in a laboured breath. 'I just need a moment to regain my strength.'

The light of Barel's mother beams down on the pair, the energising properties allowing for Barel to recover. Commanding such an inferno required immense power.

'You must be in great pain,' says the Doctor, as he looks down at the scorched hands.

'These are not my hands,' Barel replies. 'It is nothing.'

Not convinced, the Doctor retrieves a bottle from a small knapsack he carries, pouring some green coloured water over the hands. The washing effect combined with the unusual formulated chemicals created by the Doctor back at the Stronghold appears to have a restorative effect, quelling the burns. He smiles at Barel, a sign of admiration in his eyes. But before he can get recognition from the Lightbearer, something stands out in the corner of the Doctor's eye. He rises to his feet, peering in a north-easterly direction in an attempt to focus on the unusual occurrence in the distance.

What he sees is a tall figure, grasping some kind of thin object. With the rising sunlight obscuring his view, it seems that there are electrical pulses and orange glows surrounding the creature. Toraq is in deep concentration and focus.

'So you can see it,' states Barel as he rises to his feet as well.

'I can, you know about this?'

'I can feel it and hear it, trying to pull me in. It calls to me. I must go to it.'

'But what about the city? The assault is counting on you!'

'This seems to be more important.'

Not entirely sure how Barel came to this conclusion, the Doctor becomes bemused as the Lightbearer starts to move towards the hill. The Doctor's admiration quickly changes to one of condemnation seeing as he appears to be deviating from the plan — without his support, the army of Kaidis will most likely be defeated in the city. As Barel approaches the hill, the Doctor decides that Xarash will need to hear about this and retreats south.

* * * *

Barel arrives at the small hill and is fascinated by what he sees. As he approaches the circle of ash, he can hear Toraq chanting in Ethereal. Intrigued by what is both occurring and the strange creature controlling it, he stares intently at the Ascended Lightbearer, who's white fur stands straight, statically charged; his eyes seem to flash periodically. The grass inside the circle has turned black and withered as if anything within the boundary has succumbed to death.

'Stand in the circle, Lightbearer,' speaks Toraq in Ethereal through clenched teeth.

Barel stands aghast as the circle of ash begins to smoulder. Who is this creature and how does he know him? As an entity that has great command over the elements, the combination of the electrically charged air and the rapidly igniting ash creates a connection in the mind of him, as if they are speaking directly to him, yet he cannot decide on what they are saying. Any previous thoughts about the destruction of the Shaler or his responsibility towards the Kaidis have all temporarily diminished. He does not know who this strange character is, or why he is speaking in his language, or how he is performing this ritual.

Choosing to follow the advice, he moves into the circle with his blue swirling eyes firmly fixed on the unusual black eyes of Toraq. As he steps inside, the ash catches fire and circles the pair. Barel then feels a strange sensation, his mind a jumble of thoughts. As if to approach some kind of ecstasy, he is unsure whether to enjoy or fear the moment. But before he has a chance to draw any kind of conclusion, Toraq commands him to grasp onto the staff with both hands. Without hesitation, he obeys the instruction.

The attention of Barel is diverted to the strange gem on top of the staff. On closer inspection, it isn't actually a gem and more of an optical illusion. It matches the colour of Toraq's visible essence, but it can only be seen from one direction — as one's vision moves around, this colouring looks exactly the same as it exists only in two-dimensional space.

In only a moment, Toraq utters a single Ethereal word: 'Dom!'

Everything immediately freezes in time to both Toraq and Barel. Any sound that was present before cut off, and there is complete silence. Visibly, in a microsecond flash, there was nothing — the known world of Pri completely disappearing from view; absolute zero.

Just as quick as the Arena vanished, a different view appears to Barel as he regains an orientation on wherever he is now. The background is a dull grey, as if one looked through closed eyes, and there is no sense of distance with visibility being infinite. But there is one large, white sphere that remains in a fixed position.

One other detail becomes apparent to the Lightbearer — he has lost control over the body of the Doctor that he was in possession. He has no hands and no head — in fact, he has entirely reverted to his natural state of being: a ghostly blue cloud of gas that swirls around with a light blue outline, what would be the edges of his essence.

To his right he can see that he is attached to a white outline which matches the dimensions of the staff Toraq was holding. Even though he has no hands, he is still grasping the curious staff. He also looks up to see a black cloud with a defined outline is also attached to the staff.

'Do not look so confused, you know where you are,' utters a voice inside Barel's mind. It is Toraq speaking directly to Barel in Ethereal, but through the normal radio communication method that the Lightbearer's utilise.

'Is this the Synthetic Domain? How can this be? Who are you?' replies Barel.

'I am not surprised that you do not recognise me, but I am here to ask the questions.'

'Questions? You are in no position to be making demands!'

'You are mistaken, Barel. Your threats are meaningless. I am charged with making sure you adhere to the Tournament correctly. You have already caused too many problems.'

This makes Barel silence himself, thinking that this stranger knows a great deal more than he.

'I take from your silence that you are ready to listen. I am Toraq the Ascended. You are an unfortunate mistake in this; you were not the player that was to be expected.'

'Toraq the Ascended? You have excelled yourself after all this time. It has been too long. But this is not the time for celebration. You are querying my presence in the Arena?'

'Your calling was a mistake,' replies Toraq.

'A mistake? How is that even possible?'

'It would seem the mortals in the Arena possessed knowledge that should not have been made available to him.'

Toraq refers to the Book of the Daimons. The calling of Barel via the Necrocircle ritual was what Ferlor knew to be diabolical information, and he simply wanted the power for himself. But Toraq's problem is that he has no idea how the ritual became to be so vividly documented — especially as it is up to the Ascended to facilitate the arrival of a Lightbearer into an Arena. Barel's untimely entrance into Pri was in error, in terms of both what he has achieved thus far and his ranking in the Tournament.

A dark green gas cloud appears from the direction of the white sphere in the background. This is a different Lightbearer who goes by the name of Gadno and is angry with Barel.

'You are playing my Arena!' he immediately informs Barel.

'Gadno? I thought you had already Ascended.'

'This was my final test to become Ascended! You have seen to destroy my chances!'

'How could I have possibly been aware of the situation? You know that they never tell us anything,' replies Barel, speaking about the secrecy between the Ascended and non-Ascended.

'Enough of this,' Toraq interrupts. 'I had planned to settle this rationally. Mother will not be impressed.'

Before the two Lightbearers can continue their argument, Toraq's ghostly outline becomes separated from the white staff. As soon as this happens, there is another microsecond white flash, forcing Barel and Toraq out of the Synthetic Domain and returning to the Arena of Pri. Their host bodies become unfrozen in time and both stagger back as they realise this, the staff falling to the floor.

The circle of ash is no longer lit and a breeze has blown parts of it from the hill, but the grass is still blackened and dead. While the Lightbearers were in the Synthetic Domain, time itself continued even if their bodies were stone-like.

'This is the reason for your entry into the Arena,' says Toraq in Ethereal, returning to a speaking voice and shows Barel the Book of the Daimons.

'So this is what Samal was looking for,' replies Barel. 'I can understand why now.'

'Doctor Samal is asking for this book? Interesting,' ponders Toraq. 'I am prepared to allow you to have this, but I require something from you first.'

'You want to strike a deal with me? That is rich!'

'I propose nothing – I wish for you to take the book and give it to Samal. Perhaps it will be a way to resolve your erroneous presence here.'

Barel is surprised. The Ascended are the adjudicators of Tournament games, they are not supposed to be directly involved with how a Lightbearer plays, especially if one offers what seems to be a cheat.

'Why am I here?'

'It would seem the mortals did some of their own research,' explains Toraq. 'But this is your game now, you had better complete it. I suppose we will meet again.'

With that he collects his staff from the ground and using his superior speed empowered to him by the creature he possesses, Toraq dashes back to Thoridon. Various thoughts race through the mind of Barel – perhaps he is not as powerful as he once considered himself to be. What about Gadno, the other Lightbearer? Perhaps answers wait within the book he now holds.

He opens the cover and begins to turn through its thick pages. But he realises he has a problem – he cannot understand the Shaler handwriting, making parts of the book unreadable. Becoming frustrated with himself about the whole situation — he was sure he was going to win this Arena, but is now aware that it wasn't his Arena to begin with. Such a waste of time and energy! He throws the book on the parched ground in anger, howling up to the sky. After regaining some composure, he has a thought – if Doctor Samal knew about the book, perhaps he could assist in making sense from it.

And Xarash — Barel had completely forgotten about the assault led onto Thoridon. He retrieves the book from the ground and turns around to observe the scene from the hillside. The burning southern wall obliterated and the smoke cleared, he sees that the city still stands and that there is no roar of battle. It would appear that the Kaidis were defeated which would make having the audience with Xarash complicated.

But if Barel wishes to seek his answers and at least attempt to salvage something from this mistake, it is a chance he has to take. With a call to the sky in Ethereal, a great tornado-like cone erupts from above enveloping him in an identical effect as when he disappeared from Solus before — his intended destination: the Kaidis Stronghold.

# Chapter Twelve

## Liberation

On his return to Thoridon, Toraq is met with cheers and congratulations from all the people in the city as he makes his way west towards the Quadrangle to reunite himself with his companion. With the Kaidis invasion thwarted, there are no sounds of battle or conflict resonating around, meaning that there was some success in his distraction. If Barel had become more involved in the assault, there most certainly wouldn't have been much of a city to return to.

But Toraq doesn't consider the situation as a victory; with the many things that have come to light, he will now have to explain some details to the Shaler and he is unsure whether or not Emperor Solus will be able to understand.

On approach to the Quadrangle, he looks down in a southerly direction and sees the destruction and suffering that both the Kaidis and the Shaler took from the attack. While the powerful assaulting army made a significant gain in becoming so close to their prize, it is now reduced to rotting corpses with blood lining the ground. Toraq laments over the loss of so much life – all of which instigated by Barel. Damage to property and the city itself will last for many years to come in both the physical and mental state of the Shaler.

He enters the Quadrangle with a nod from the guarding Warlocks and sees a sense of normality inside. With no sign of a breach, Toraq has a sense of relief that no-one else succumbed to the assault. He is welcomed by applause and Eko sits nearby their waggon and howls pleasingly at the sight of his master returning as Toraq returns the staff to the compartment.

Surprised by the commotion arising from outside the Senate House, Solus comes outside to see what requires such jubilation. He sees Toraq and his surprise changes to delight at the sight of such an accomplishing victor.

'You have returned!' greets Solus, with arms outstretched. Toraq focuses his attention on the emperor with a look of seriousness on his face.

'Now is not the time for celebration, Solus,' he states. 'I must speak with you in private.'

Solus' smile wilts and slightly taken back by the harshness of his tone, he nonetheless escorts Toraq in the direction of his private residence. Toraq refuses to answer questions on their way about the current state of affairs and also the simple matter of whether everything is all right.

As they arrive, Toraq stops in the path leading to the front of the house and surveys the gardens of the emperor's home. Around he sees flourishing beds of white, yellow and pink flowers, bushes blooming with leaves and lush grass in a brilliant green. But not all is well in this near-perfect example of horticulture – the decaying tree that Toraq previously observed stands central to the garden, surrounded by the other vibrant plants. It has no leaves, the branches are thin and the bark is diseased.

He steps into the garden off the path, focused on the tree. Toraq places a furry paw against the trunk and closes his eyes, as if trying to communicate with the tree. Surprised by the sudden lack of urgency by the Matoh, Solus approaches.

'What are you doing, Toraq?'

'I feel you have questions to ask me,' he says, in a low voice with eyes still closed. 'I could sense your surprise during our earlier encounter with the Kaidis.'

'I don't know what you mean.'

'You were hesitant to fend off the attackers – you were watching me.'

Solus recalls the moment, even though it felt like a second. He refers to the sudden explosion of light that seemed to be projected by Toraq himself, illuminating the Quadrangle exposing the Kaidis scouts. It took that moment to realise what had happened and that it was most unexpected.

'How did you want me to react?' he exclaims. 'It's not every day I see anyone suddenly become as bright as the sun itself!'

He listens to his own words. All the time he's spent around Synth users of his own kind, he didn't consider that someone — or something — else could command it as well. Thoughts race around in his mind relating to Toraq: the Matoh he keeps as a companion never speaks and is much more animal than he; the fact he always seems to arrive at the right time and offers good solutions; how it was even possible for him to fend off such a formidable foe like Barel.

'Are you suggesting that you command the Synth as well?' questions Solus, finally putting the pieces together in his mind.

At that moment, he takes a step backward as he sees something marvellous occur – the tree springs into life with a rich display of leaves and flowering catkins. A once half-dead area of the garden suddenly becomes a spectacular focal point. Toraq removes his hand and looks at the emperor.

'I am a restorer, Solus,' he says.

'A restorer? I'm not quite sure I follow.'

'I can utilise the Synth but in the reverse of what most use it for. My skill is in the encouragement of life. I revive. Life is my work.'

This is the secret that all Ascended understand – to restore mortality and preserve it. The prize for winning the Tournament is the secret of life itself. In a surprising move, Toraq kneels down on one knee allowing him and Solus to be at near-equal face height.

'Solus, I wish for you to gaze into my eyes,' speaks Toraq, softly. Solus tries to speak a question about the meaning of this action, but Toraq is quick to hush his concerns.

'Just look.'

Not entirely sure what to expect, he focuses his attention onto the black, beady eyes of the furry character that kneels before him. Solus begins to stare into the eyes and as he starts to concentrate, something becomes apparent to him, and he has seen a characteristic to eyes like these before. Upon realising this, Solus takes a few steps back in horror.

'I take it from your reaction that you have seen,' states Toraq as he rises from his knee.

'I'm not sure what I have seen,' replies Solus. 'I don't know if I want to believe it. Your eyes — they are not what they seem. On first glance, the eyes look normal. No, I refuse to believe this!'

He looks again, peering upwards at Toraq's face and sees exactly what he saw before – the blackness of two vortexes swirling around inside each eye, but their overlapping is so subtle and one would have to know what to look for in order to see. Now over his initial shock, Solus changes his attitude to one that looks indifferent towards the Matoh that stands before him. He starts to question in his mind about the relationship between the pair: is Toraq the same as Barel? Could he suddenly explode into a frenzy of similar discourse?

'It is written all over your expression, Solus,' speaks Toraq. 'I can see how your perception of me may be changing. I came to see you immediately after leaving Barel because I feared our relationship could change in the future – it is time to be honest with you.'

Solus stands there with additional thoughts overpowering his mind. If Toraq has also not been fully honest with him, he isn't sure what to think now. He has flashbacks to before the time when Barel arrived: Ferlor and Rogaro lying to him, his mother lying to him and now his greatest diplomatic relation has revealed he has been lying to him as well. But amid the questions comes a sudden realisation. He is not upset about this revealed deception — instead he remains composed and seems ready to accept whatever Toraq is going to divulge. Solus looks towards Toraq with an enquiring expression on his face and asks a question with confidence – the confidence of a leader.

'Toraq, if you have revealed to me that you are not who you say you are... Who are you?'

'Your instinct is telling you to be enquiring,' Toraq states, trying to avoid the question.

'Damn right it is! What I have seen is that you appear to be one of them – the same swirling eyes that I saw in that of Ferlor back in the Temple. You are not from these lands; you are a Lightbearer as well!'

Solus still armed with his father's sword begins to unsheathe the weapon – such an action makes Toraq gasp and stand away. Upon hearing raised voices outside, Avornia rushes to the front door of the house and sees Toraq backing away from her son, with malice in his eyes looking ready to attack the seemingly defenceless Matoh.

'What are you doing, son?' asks his horrified mother, arriving.

'If this beast that stands before us is not who he says he is, then he is as responsible as Barel! How do we know he was not conspiring up on the hill, plotting our demise?'

'What has got into you?' Avornia shrieks.

He begins to wield the sword in front of Toraq who stands terrified from the threat before him.

'Please, Solus! It is not what you think! I am still Toraq. I have absolutely no malicious intent!'

'And why would that be so?'

'I stand here unarmed – I wish no harm upon anyone, especially you.'

Toraq turns his back to the both of them. This wasn't going how he thought it would – but it seems the emperor has flourished into a strong individual, much different than before. While he has demonstrated more than he planned, it would seem Solus has proved himself worthy of what is to come. He escapes out of the garden, leaving Solus and Avornia behind. She notices the rejuvenated tree, something that doesn't just happen immediately. The emperor begins to take chase with the Matoh, but Avornia grabs him by the arm before he can get away.

'What are you doing, mother?' he yells.

'Let him go,' she says softly. 'I can see what stirs in our furry friend. We should not fear him.'

She has a moment of clarity – her research back in the Temple of Ramor finally starts to bring in some understanding. The ancient texts were writing about strange events and unusual decisions but what she could never understand was why these occurred. It is known that Toraq has outlived several generations of Shaler, as he has revealed in the past, and she connects these passages to the causality of an outside influence.

'It is him, the unusual force that is spoken about in writings in the Temple and perhaps in the Book of the Daimons. He is the one responsible for the progress of our history.'

'What are you talking about, mother?' asks Solus, a degree of resentment in his voice.

'I see it clearly now. I am as sure as I have ever been.'

With Toraq returning to the Quadrangle, he quickly hurries Eko to prepare to leave. As their cart is all packed and ready to go from when Solus convinced him to stay, it takes no time at all as the gates to the east of the city are opened wide for the Matoh. For Toraq must travel to the Sulphur Deserts and make sure Barel arrives to see what happens with the Book of the Daimons.

* * * *

Storms are common in the Sulphur Deserts but it is not just meteorological occurrences that are responsible for them. Such a storm brews deep inside the Kaidis Stronghold, where King General Xarash is ready to unleash a metaphorical barrage of furious winds against what he sees as the traitorous Barel.

As the sunlight of Ramor falls near the horizon, but never entirely setting over the desolate plains, groups of the Second and Third Divisions patrol the Stronghold's courtyard and the outside in keen anticipation. They await the arrival of the new enemy under the orders of Xarash, but not to fight as the King wishes to hear the reasons behind the Lightbearer's apparent betrayal. Each group have eyes all over – some to the skies, waiting for the tornado-alike phenomenon that is associated with Barel; some to the distance, looking to see if a Knoria will arrive carrying their prized cargo.

Waiting deep inside the Stronghold is Xarash himself. Not known for his compassion and much more famous for his hatred of everything and a short temper, playing the waiting game is something he doesn't like but sees it as a necessary evil. Before becoming heir to the throne after his impatient father — Xarash III — was killed in battle, he realised that a good leader doesn't just rush in – one that waits, analyses and reacts is much more successful: this theory tested with assaults of the Shaler under his order. Even though they ultimately still result in failure, the failure isn't as extreme as before, improving time and time again.

One way Xarash deals with the eternal waiting is to keep battle-ready. In another area of the tunnelling Stronghold he and his assistant Doctor Samal are alone. This area is the King's private sparring arena – behind similar doors as to the entrance of the Royal Seat lies an enclosed cavern. With great lakes of magma funnelling itself around, above this is where the doors open into a small, raised platform of rock. Upon this stands a single object: a rudimentary mannequin, secured to the stone. The heat in this room would be life threatening if it wasn't for the high tolerance to their environment – to someone like Xarash, if you can't survive, you don't deserve to live.

It is here where Xarash spends his time to prepare for a fight or just to escape from the tedium, only this time he is not sure what he is preparing for. He stands in a battle stance with one foot ahead of the other, fully dressed in battle armour made from the best forged Luvolite. Equipped in both hands, he holds his father's axe – he swings from the left, then from the right and then from the middle to give a crushing blow to the rapidly deforming head of the mannequin. With every swing, every movement, he grunts or shouts to channel his aggression.

Samal stands at the edge of the platform with his back to the king and stares in a daydream at the magma as it flows past. He is concerned that Xarash will do something he will regret – when the Doctor attached to Barel's unit informed him of the apparent betrayal, the subsequent reporting to the king was not taken lightly. Samal was sure that the Lightbearer would be an essential asset in bringing down the Shaler, but the news becomes highly unexpected.

As the axe of his leader swipes and clatters with the mannequin, he thinks about the writings he has read that described a time when a different Lightbearer was called into Pri, despite Samal not realising this was the case until recently. These texts make out the Lightbearer to be a hero – if Samal's belief in Barel to do good for the Kaidis turned out to be a falsity, this makes him uneasy about ever trusting someone of immense power other than one of his own.

Back on ground level, something attracts the eye of one of the scouting warriors looking up into the sky. In amongst the orange glow, a blue haze surrounding a rapidly forming vortex stands out prominently. With a flash of electrical power, the vortex streams down to touch the barren ground not too far away from the entrance of the courtyard; almost as fast as it appeared it disperses leaving a small figure standing central to the point of touchdown.

The scouting party of Kaidis quickly move to intercept the disturbance and arrive to find Barel standing there, still in the same guise as the Doctor he possessed. Two warriors circle their target, like hyenas prizing a recent trophy. Barel doesn't expect anything less.

'Excellent,' he says, realising the situation. 'At least I do not have to negotiate with the front door again.'

'Silence, you traitorous filth,' shouts one of the warriors back.

'No need to raise your voice, I will come quietly.'

With that, the Kaidis grab him by each arm, lifting him off the ground and Barel does not protest. Since members of the Doctors Division are generally weaker and much lighter than their fighter counterparts, Barel is scooped up with ease and the party brings him towards the gates that cover the opening into the volcano. As they approach, grunts and muted cheers arise from the other warriors as they see that their target has been caught.

One of the gate operators with a fantastic display of brawn, growls with menace at the Lightbearer, spitting in his face – in his subdued state, Barel just has to accept it and makes no reaction. As they continue into the volcano and start to descend towards the confusing tunnelling system, the gate operator lets out a hearty cackle, which resonates around the cave-like opening. Clearly, the Kaidis are unanimously against their guest.

Barel's escorts know exactly where to take him as they dart through the tunnels. He becomes disorientated, not understanding where he is being taken, or indeed, how to get back outside. The arid air also starts to become a feature – even though Barel's host body is Kaidis, featuring the same yellow pigmentation and built up tolerance to the heat, it still becomes noticeable. In such a claustrophobic atmosphere and with limited knowledge of Kaidis life, Barel starts to wonder if this is a one-way trip.

With Barel becoming distracted as to thinking about an escape plan, he doesn't notice the distance that they have travelled in almost complete silence. He is only reminded of the current state of affairs when his escorts come to an abrupt halt; stopping outside a pair of doors that look similar to the ones going into the Royal Seat. However, one key feature that differs is the intense heat.

The two Kaidis that are carrying Barel start to pull back and let go, swinging him directly into the slightly ajar doors, to which he flies through with an almighty crash and lands face down on the floor of Xarash's personal arena. The fragility of the Doctor's body becoming a factor, where flesh meets rock is not the most comfortable of positions and the force of landing does not do Barel any favours. His pair of escorts walks in behind him and closes the doors.

Xarash still combating with the mannequin makes one final crushing blow to the side of it but suppresses his grunting – the sound of the axe impacting against the ripped padding makes a dull thud before a moment of near-silence, other than the rumbling and hissing of the magma churning around. The king takes a pause as he realises what has just entered to catch his breath, standing more upright and lowering the axe. Eventually he turns to see the squirming creature trying to pick himself up off the floor.

'I think you deserve to stay down there a little longer,' Xarash grumbles as he places a foot onto the back of Barel.

He applies almost back-breaking pressure, grinding his heavy armoured boot, smirking as he does so. Barel who usually suppresses any kind of pain from his host body genuinely starts to feel the hurt. Xarash removes his foot when he begins to wince.

'Get up, you fucking pathetic excuse,' he booms after he turns around and takes a few steps away.

Barel finds the strength in his host – who now has a boot imprint on his back from the heated armour – to stand up, even though still seeming to be in a degree of pain. When fully standing, he arches his chest out slightly causing his ribcage to emit a cracking sound, followed by a sigh of relief. He has a moment to observe where he has been thrown and sees the surrounding magma, the mannequin, the two guards waiting at the door and Samal standing at the back.

'I suppose—'

'Silence!' yells Xarash, spinning around to see Barel now standing upright. 'You do not deserve to speak to me until I say.'

He momentarily makes eye contact with the Lightbearer, looking directly down into the swirling eyes, narrowing his brow. In his empty hand, he clenches his fist and slowly turns his back, clearly angry. Barel stands there not really knowing what to expect and not coming up with any ideas for a plan of escape.

'I have not had an agreement with anyone outside of my kind,' says Xarash with slow speech. 'You are the first I have tried to reason with. I know see that doing so is a fatal mistake. I do not tolerate failure.'

He takes a moment to pause, as if trying to be reasonable. During this time, Doctor Samal turns around to face Barel and moves a few steps closer, away from the edge of the arena. Barel looks at Samal who in turn looks back, but nothing is said. Unexpectedly, Xarash lunges towards Barel and using his empty hand grabs him by the chest.

'Did you hear what I said? I do not tolerate failure! Yet, here you are – coming crawling back to my empire like a pathetic dog. What do you want – some fucking mercy?'

The anger and threatening tone of the king's voice is enough to subdue Barel's idea of trying to play this cool – making a sarcastic remark may not be welcome given the circumstance. It is clear that Xarash demands an answer and if Barel is to have one chance to explain his actions, this is it.

'Did you know that Toraq was defending the Shaler?'

Xarash raises an eyebrow and releases his grip on Barel who lands back on his feet. As Toraq is known as impartial it becomes a surprise to hear that he and the Shaler are working together.

'Is this some kind of pitiful attempt to reason with me?' growls the king back.

'I sense from the tone in your voice that you were unaware of his presence in Thoridon?'

Taking a couple of steps back from Barel, he sneers and turns towards Samal.

'Did your Doctor tell you of this, Samal?'

'Now that you mention it,' Samal replies, thinking about what he was told. 'He did say that there was a strange furry creature standing on a hill.'

'You casually forgot about this detail?' thunders Xarash.

'No, not at all! I just thought it was irrelevant – one of Barel's tricks, perhaps,' he says, pointing towards his opposer.

'Yes,' growls Xarash again, refocusing his attention on their guest. 'What proof do you have to back up this before I have a second thought about this whole meeting?'

Barel rummages around in the deep pockets of the clothes of his host body and finds the Book of the Daimons given to him by Toraq.

'This is the reason I came back,' he proudly announces, holding it aloft so the both of the Kaidis can see.

'A lowly book?' chuckles Xarash. 'How the fuck does a book prove anything?'

'But this is no ordinary book, my lord,' speaks Samal with delight, his eyes widened as to finding the hidden treasure. 'Is this the actual book? I don't believe it.'

'It is,' says Barel to Samal. 'I was hoping you could help me understand its secrets.'

'You need my help? Surely a being such as you is more than qualified to read this.'

'Not all of it is written in language I can fully recognise.'

'Explain yourselves,' yells Xarash, starting to lose his temper.

'This book – known as the Book of the Daimons – contains the secrets about our own existence. It contains all the knowledge there is to know about these lands and how it came to be,' explains Samal with confidence, convinced it is containing vital information.

'Why should I care about this?' says Xarash, not understanding its significance.

Samal pauses for a moment and moves to his leader. Making sure he is outside of earshot of Barel, he mumbles something to Xarash, explaining that it is the book of his ancient ancestor, who in turn smiles and chuckles. Barel becomes suspicious and isn't entirely sure what to make of the situation.

'Allow me to see if I can make some sense of this,' says Samal as he moves up to Barel, holding a hand out.

'You will help me understand the texts?'

'Absolutely, I think we can all benefit from knowing.'

Barel slowly gives the book to Samal, looking deep into the eyes of the Doctor. He has a feeling that this could be a bad decision, a decision that may be a defining error, but desperate to know what Samal knows, curiosity gets the better of him; he can trust them, since they trusted him before. Upon receiving the book, Samal smiles and thanks the Lightbearer. His eyes widen again as he opens the book marked "Do not read" and scans the pages, seeing the diagrams, pictures and differences in language fly past his eyes.

Xarash seems to have a change in mood and ushers Barel up near the mannequin in the centre of the arena, leaving Samal to leaf through the book.

'Come here,' says Xarash, beckoning to Barel. 'We need to talk while the good Doctor tries to understand this book.'

'Does this mean we are even now?'

'Just come here.'

Barel gingerly makes his way towards the mannequin where Xarash stands to its right, still holding his father's axe in one hand but resting it on the ground. The magma surrounding the entire arena seems to swell and churn more aggressively, bubbling slightly.

'You may think I am just an aggressive warrior, Barel. But you see – I lead my people for a reason. I am not as dumb as people think. My father was too blind to realise the importance of being a good fighter and a good thinker. We are built to survive, but to conquer we must go that extra distance. One thing I have learnt is that—'

He stops in mid-speech as an attempt to catch Barel entirely off guard. He is successful – with his impressive physique and a build-up of Bloodrage generated from practising on the mannequin, he is able to pull his axe into a two-handed grip with immense speed and swing the incredibly sharp blade around in a 270-degree arc – effortlessly slicing the neck of Barel's host body and hitting the head of the mannequin acting as a buffer. The body falls to the floor in a collapsed heap, blood oozing out onto the rock.

'—that surprise always fucks you over!' he says, concluding his speech, satisfied.

Xarash moves over to inspect the eyes on the corpse – closed, lifeless and absent of a swirling vortex. A feint puff of blue dust floats up from the head, forming a small cloud above it, before shimmering and disappearing from view as the Lightbearer's true form absorbs itself back to the Synthetic Domain. Confirming that Barel no longer exists – by poking the corpse with his axe – he moves over to Samal who holds the open book in his hands, but repelled by what the barbaric action has resulted in. Xarash drops his heavy axe onto the floor and then snatches the book from Samal.

'What are you doing?' shrieks the Doctor, as he sees his leader move towards the edge of the arena and dangles the book over the fiery magma.

'You said earlier that this book was responsible for bringing him here. We have seen that anyone like him cannot be trusted, whatever their powers are! It seems that they do not care for our concerns and would rather take us for fools. I do not care about its history — our history — as it is irrelevant. We are making that history now.'

'But, my lord! This book could contain vital information!'

Samal begins to plead with his leader.

'Look at yourself, Doctor. You are begging me for this. A miserable book that has damaged our honour! I cannot tolerate another deception by these outsiders!'

Convinced it is the right thing to do for the good of the Kaidis, Xarash lets go of the book and it falls down into the molten core of the volcano. Its black cover begins to incinerate from the intense heat and the pages fragment into ash before being fully absorbed into the magma. The secrets it contained within seemingly lost forever.

As Xarash turns around he sees the Doctor lunging straight for him, angry that such an important collection of documents is now destroyed. He catches Samal and restrains him before he does anything he'll regret.

'Calm down, Doctor. It is done.'

'The secrets of everything that we know and ourselves were in there,' Samal weeps.

'And what does that matter, you fucking idiot? It does not allow us to win against the cursed Shaler and we have properly defeated this enemy for the good of the Kaidis!'

He then ejects Samal from his grip.

'Stand up for yourself, pathetic Doctor. I sometimes wonder about you and your attachment to this wretched "information" that you prize so highly.'

Xarash picks up the torso that belonged to Barel and throws it into the magma with the cadaver immediately catching fire and descending downward. He stands there, watching as the flames lick up against the combustive carcass, the fire reflecting in his glassy eyes, illuminating his face – an expression of malice clearly written all over, wondering what to do next.

The Doctor storms out of the arena, almost tripping over the handle of the king's axe as he rushes to the door. An almighty crash reverberates as Samal slams the doors behind him. With the Book of the Daimons and its deepest secrets so close to being understood destroyed, Samal cannot believe the foolishness of his leader. In his mind, he sees his latest action as a fatal mistake for Xarash.

Bloodrage increasingly begins to run through Xarash's veins as he considers the options. Maybe it is time to strike the Shaler once and for all.

* * * *

At the outskirts of the Sulphur Deserts, Toraq arrives at Outpost Ora with Eko pulling the waggon that he sits atop. The Ascended Lightbearer is keen to make sure that Barel went to see Xarash with the Book of the Daimons, but is unaware of the tension that manifests at the Kaidis Stronghold.

Even though he has visited the lands of the Kaidis for many years, Toraq has never made it as far as the Stronghold itself – the hot environment is not something that is comfortable to him or his companion. Their thick, hairy coats provided by the body of the Matoh are more suited to the icy mountains of the north. As such, he and the Kaidis have had an uncomfortable relationship – the Kaidis have become suspicious of anyone outside of their circles, but the renowned and well-established impartiality of Toraq has given them no course of action. Until now, that is.

As Eko brings the cart carrying their depleted stocks of food and other assorted goods to a stop just inside the fortifications, Toraq dismounts and surveys the scene. The Kaidis rarely have need for change themselves as everything they do is carefully maintained through routine and discipline, and this outpost itself is a demonstration to that. Positioned between two massive piles of sand and collected material blown to the outskirts of the desert, it is not a large area with the base consisting of a single garrison, the large fortified gate covering the opening and to its right, a wind-shielded open area. It is enough to satisfy its purpose of being a gateway into Shaler territory.

Although the leader of the Kaidis is enthusiastic to meet with Toraq over recent revelations, none of the few idle members of the Second Division present at the outpost are aware of the situation, grunting their recognition of him as he walks past. The garrison building is not large when compared to somewhere like Wodar Drop, housing ten Kaidis and all the equipment necessary. Toraq nods at the single guard who stands outside its entrance as he steps inside.

The layout is open-plan with a resting area at the back. The walls of the wooden cabin emblazoned with banners and other cloths; standards bearing the volcanic symbol and racks adorned with various swords, axes and armour. A great fire roars central, providing more heat to the already warm environment, but making it more acclimatised to the Kaidis.

Behind a desk sits Captain Selak who oversees the day-to-day running of the outpost, surrounded with papers and documents. It seems he spends more time filing than seeing combat — a familiar theme that occurs the more senior one becomes inside the military machine — and he knows that as Toraq enters, it eventually means more paperwork.

'Greetings Selak,' says Toraq, trying to avoid the heat from the fire as much as possible.

'Oh, what do you want? Can't you see I'm busy?' the captain replies, not looking up from his papers.

'I was just wondering if Barel has been through here.'

Selak peers over the sheet of paper he is reading.

'How do you know about him?' Selak replies, curiously.

'What business of that is yours?'

The captain puts the papers he is holding down and looks directly at Toraq. He has been deployed to head up Ora for a long time and he knows everything that goes in and out. With Toraq being a frequent visitor over this period in his trader capacity, he and Selak have almost a friendship between them, but neither would admit to it. Selak tilts his head as he thinks about how to respond in silence. The fire behind him crackles as if to speak.

'I suppose nothing, much like the business of the Kaidis is of no interest to you,' he eventually says with a grin.

Toraq begins to laugh and Selak joins in, standing from his desk almost happy to see the Lightbearer. They exchange handshakes as the uncomfortable atmosphere before was merely artificial.

'No, haven't seen him since he went towards Thoridon, commanding some foolhardy members of the First and Second which Xarash no doubt assigned. A Doctor came wondering through, demanding with my men urgent transport to the Stronghold. He kept mentioning something about him, but I was too busy to be interested.'

'I see,' nods Toraq. 'I did not see anyone retreat.'

The captain bursts into laughter.

'Really? You were there?'

'Of course, Barel is dangerous,' Toraq replies, seriously. 'I had to make sure he did not do something untoward.'

'You mean destroy the Shaler? I understand now,' Selak chuckles, wise to know that if the Shaler were obliterated, life as a Kaidis would become very different.

The conversation changes to something more light-hearted, as the two catch up on each other's gossip. But it is these conversations that provide the tactical knowledge between them, even if it isn't explicit — Toraq learns what the Kaidis are involved with and Selak is kept abreast of what Toraq observes from the Shaler.

After a short while, Toraq returns outside allowing Selak to return to his duties. He stands looking south, deeper into Kaidis territory. The swirling sand dances across the barren landscape, with little sound other than various Kaidis warriors sparring or hammering fence posts into the sand. These wooden fences act as wind breakers, trying to redirect as much of the blown sand as possible out of the base. A sense of calmness prevails over the Ascended Lightbearer as he ponders over recent events.

Eko approaches his master and rubs a paw over Toraq's foot. Acknowledging his companion's presence by stroking him behind his small bear-like ears, Toraq continues to gaze out over the sands. In the distance is the omnipotent presence that dominates the horizon – Mount Sindre, home to the Kaidis Stronghold, with a bright orange halo broadcasting high into the sky above the bubbling and churning white-hot lava contained within its crown.

Toraq wonders what will happen next. He is surprised that everything seems so quiet, but with the Kaidis defeated at Thoridon and with their secret weapon effectively turning against them, he suspects that it is only the start of something.

* * * *

In the Kaidis volcano the mood is the complete reverse to the relative tranquillity of Outpost Ora. Doctor Samal — after storming out from Xarash's company when he destroyed the Book of the Daimons — has returned to the surface and to the external Doctors Division building. Slamming the doors behind him, he throws his cane down in anger, watching as it skitters across the wooden floor. Sighing sharply, he wipes some blown sand from his face and stands in silence for a moment.

Pushing his way past the big table, its contents scattered around in organised disorder, Samal increasingly becomes anxious and starts to continuously pace up and down between the various shelves to the rear. He begins to question in his mind about the capacity of Xarash and also whether his decision was emphatically incorrect.

He thinks about the various scenarios of what could happen next. Being strong warriors, more brawn than mettle, situations with the Kaidis often fly out of control. Samal can feel the mood in the air – the need to fight, the need to increase the war effort, the need to destroy. These thoughts are echoed outside — members of the First, Second and Third rally around the courtyard and there is a noticeable increase in the amount of preparation taking place. The Engineers Division has representatives scurrying around, carrying equipment and loading up several Knorias. Samal is unsure as to what is happening, but the amassing of forces suggests to him that there is going to be a large push against the Shaler.

And this would be against the advice that he had already given to Xarash. In his capacity as adviser to the king, he is privy to the overall details of the Kaidis' war against Thoridon. With the defensive wall breached, that alone is a tactical advantage, but Samal was keen to emphasise that it was simply that: an advantage. It is absolutely not definitive and does not increase the chances of success. His advice being that simply jumping on this is not the best strategy.

The Doctor doesn't want to be part of a rash decision and going by how Xarash is reacting it would seem that his opinion is no longer valued, if it ever was in the first place. He thinks about his own individual priorities. Noticing the synthesised Urtica plants on the table, he knows he is close to having a breakthrough with producing enhanced Urtica, but there is a definite missing piece to the botanical puzzle. With a snap to his fingers, he remembers a vital resource that could provide the answer — Toraq. Based on what was described by his colleague up on the hill outside Thoridon, Samal would be greatly interested to have an audience with this mysterious creature.

'I have to get out of here,' he explodes to himself, realising the situation could get out of control and convinced that Xarash won't listen to him.

But then, there is a noise from behind a shelf. The son of Xarash has been trying to quietly keep himself to himself, fearful of when Samal is in one of his thoughtful moods as he usually blurts out troubling nonsense as he thinks. Realising that he's been discovered, Rakos moves over to the Doctor.

'What do you mean by "get out of here"?' he asks.

A wave of shock is apparent on Samal's face as he remembers about the boy.

'I feel your father is about to do something stupid,' eventually replies Samal, as he moves over to the table and starts stuffing papers into a small shoulder bag.

'Is it something to do with the Shaler?'

'Yes, very much so.'

He pauses for a moment to think about the situation and turns to face the teenager.

'I know you don't generally do what I say, but, for the good of the Kingdom, you must remain here at the Stronghold. Do you understand?'

Rakos looks a little confused by what he suggests.

'I do have a lot more to read, Samal,' he says.

'Excellent. Keep reading, keep researching and keep thinking. It will reward you greatly in the end.'

Opening the doors, Samal takes his bag and turns around to look at the plants on the table one last time and then to Rakos.

'Now what do you mean by "in the end"?' shouts the boy, over the wind and strenuous shouting from outside, but his question goes unheard as the Third Division member guarding the doors closes them after Samal departs.

On the outside, Samal sees the great amounts of activity that are on-going. Looking out the northern entrance to the courtyard, he sees a Knoria inbound, presumably from Wodar Drop. An already mobile vehicle such as this would provide transport away from the Stronghold and the perfect opportunity to escape.

Eye-contact from various warriors and engineers is made with him as they see the Doctor; his panicking motions and urgent facial expression being noticeable attractions, even among the chaos. Taking his chances, the water-carrying Knoria approaches the edge of the courtyard and Samal makes his way towards it. As he meets its arrival, the vehicle glides to a stop and workers heave the barrels of water off. When the last of the barrels are removed, Samal climbs onto the back of the Knoria just as the engineers begin to push on the vehicle to give it a jump start out of the courtyard to return to the water collection facility.

'What do you think you're doing?' protests the driver from the cockpit above, who can't see into the back as the Knoria begins to gain momentum.

'Take me to Ora,' shouts back Samal.

'But I'm not going there.'

'I don't care!' shrieks the Doctor. 'Take me to Ora now or you will suffer the consequences!'

The driver peers down into the back of his vehicle and through the blowing sands sees the face of Samal. Realising who is ordering him around, he offers no further protest and steers the Knoria in the direction of the outpost. Samal slouches down in the back and looks as the Stronghold begins to ebb further away, and he wonders what will happen while he is gone and if he will return.

* * * *

From behind the closed doors of the Royal Seat, an enormous roar reverberates around the centre of the Kaidis. It is Xarash, who is becoming increasingly impatient with the situation. He has spent the last hour listening to representatives from all of the Divisions — except the Doctor's, for he does not care what they are up to — all discussing their current duties and assignments, reporting to the king about their progress and the potential for gains to be made from the assault on Thoridon.

But for Xarash, these meetings are far from progress. Every time he hears about some degree of success it is countered with a defeat or a problem. It is as if things go around in a circle, never actually coming up with a definitive solution. He hates these meetings, he hates everything and everyone associated with them. It is as if the Kaidis machine itself has become clogged with endless discussion and delay.

He stands with his heavily armoured back facing the officers who stand over a table with a large map of Shaler territory on top, each town meticulously detailed like blueprints with Thoridon central. Xarash's roar would have certainly been heard inside and outside the entire volcano – such a bellow causes the Division representatives to stand taken aback.

'What you are forgetting is the fact we are supposed to be fighting a fucking war here!' Xarash grumbles. 'I want to see Thoridon destroyed, those worthless Shaler wiped from existence. And what do I get in return? Just excuses, bad news and traitorous distractions!'

His last comment is in direct reference to Barel – the Lightbearer provided hope to the Kaidis' cause, yet was entirely detrimental instead: a waste of resources, time and effort – a distraction that provided zero worth. He turns around to look at the surprised delegates again.

'Do you not agree?' he asks, waiting for a reply.

His expectant brow narrows as no responses are forthcoming. He growls again – he needs a third-party to provide what seems to be excellent insight into what's really happening. He needs his adviser, but Samal is nowhere to be seen since their quarrel in the sparring arena. Realising that there is nothing of interest for him in the Royal Seat, he smiles as he removes his father's axe from the wall and attaches it to the back of his armour. Leaving the Division reps behind without saying anything, he bursts into the frontal double doors and proceeds to make his way to the surface. The marching Kaidis that he sees going past him all stop in awe as their leader is on the move. Xarash does not take to moving around the volcano and his doing so now is a rarity, hence the attention.

Arriving at the surface, he enters into the courtyard and sees the amassing armies. Nodding as soldiers and workers all realise that their leader is among them, Xarash is rallied by this recognition, but he is disheartened at the fact that their current assignments are likely for nothing. A near silence descends on the courtyard as his presence is felt, and he moves over to the headquarters for the Doctors Division. The Third Division solider standing outside gulps as Xarash approaches.

Opening the doors, he discovers the lab to be quiet. Where are all the Doctors? Where is Samal? Xarash casually strides over to the large table and is drawn to evidence that items appear to be unusually displaced or missing. Rakos realises who has entered and approaches the table from the rear. Xarash looks at the boy — as a father, he has disdain for his only son, not proud that he chooses to spend all of his time among these walls of paper, instead of fighting for the kingdom that he will once inherit.

'So, son,' Xarash says in a deep voice, desperately trying to hide his contempt. 'Do you know where Samal has gone?'

'Not really, father,' Rakos replies, not looking up from some papers he holds. 'He did leave in a hurry recently, though.'

'I see. He didn't say where he was going?'

Rakos sighs becoming agitated with his absent parent and turns away to return behind the shelves. Despite the disrespect, Xarash cannot be mad at his only son because he realises his own failings as a father — the fact he is never there and had no interest in his upbringing. Becoming angry with himself, he smashes a fist down onto the table with a loud crash as all the items on it jangle. Turning around, he exits out to the courtyard.

Any Kaidis that stand idle sharpen their stance on sight of him with eyes straight ahead.

'King in the courtyard, all hail our glorious leader!' shouts a member of the First Division.

'Hail Xarash!' sounds in a chorus, followed by an acknowledging grunt.

Smiling, he approaches a nearby engineer who is attending to a Knoria. The engineer takes a sharp inhalation of breath as he sees the leader approach. This doesn't happen very often.

'Tell me, have you seen Doctor Samal around here lately?'

'Sir, I have, sir,' he replies, almost shouting his reply, keen to eagerly respect the militaristic machine that stands before him. 'The Doctor was in a hurry, sir.'

'Hurry? Where was he going?'

'I do not know, sir, but he boarded a water Knoria, sir.'

'What?' bellows Xarash, making the engineer increasingly nervous.

'Yes, my lord. But the direction it took was not to the west, more to the north.'

As there are only two direct routes out of the Stronghold for Knorias – one to the west at Wodar Drop and one to the north to Outpost Ora — Xarash knows what this means.

'And none of you idiots tried to stop him?'

Entirely unimpressed with what has transpired, Xarash grunts his disapproval. It seems things are worse than he anticipated. Without anyone to query his judgement, it is time for decisive action. Enough of these pathetic excuses, too much has been wasted so far. Xarash begins to feel the adrenaline pump and the Bloodrage kick in.

He knows what he must do. It is his time.

Moving to a more central point in the courtyard, he beckons for the nearest to gather around him. They start shouting around so everyone further away can be aware that the king wishes to speak.

'Soldiers and warriors,' he booms in his bone-trembling commanding voice, making sure all can hear. 'The time for the Kaidis to strike is now! Our destiny has made itself clear to me. While that distraction from earlier has done little to our overall effort, it has given us a window of opportunity. For so long, I was blind to what my peers were failing to achieve. But now, we must achieve something. We – no, I – must lead a united assault, from all the Divisions, against the fucking Shaler. We must end their tyranny over us! It is their time to suffer!'

Applause, grunting, cheering and any kind of encouragement broadcasts itself around. His loyal fighters agree wholeheartedly with what he is proposing – a huge push against Thoridon, and he is keen to lead the offensive. Xarash rediscovers his power as king and general of the entire race of his people. It is invigorating, and he believes it will be a great battle, for glory, honour, respect. With the remaining ancient Bloodrage artefacts secured, the Doctors Division will be able to apply their extensive research into their affliction, produce great new methods and become an unstoppable force.

At least, that is the plan. But with Samal, the head of the Doctors Division gone rogue, more of a challenge awaits for Xarash and the Kaidis as a whole as he begins to order around the warriors in the courtyard, preparing to amass a formidable force to launch the assault.

# Chapter Thirteen

# Judgement

As twilight falls over Outpost Ora, Samal's hijacked Knoria rumbles in from the south. Curious as to why a water carrying vehicle — identified by its blue livery — would be arriving outside of the normal schedule, workers responsible for unloading its cargo approach.

Noticing them, the driver yells out to say that there is no delivery, other than a seemingly misguided representative of the Doctors Division. As he spins the vehicle around in a 180-degree arc, Samal is jolted off the back, sliding out of the cargo area and slams onto the soft sand which cushions his sudden ejection. With the Knoria now facing in the direction of the Stronghold, the workers give it an extra push and it trundles off back to resume its water deliveries. A shaken and disgruntled Samal, still holding onto his shoulder bag and gem-topped cane, groans as he lies on his back in the sand. Instead of coming to his aid, the workers return to their business and laugh at him as they do so.

From his upside-down view of the world, he notices what seems to be a welcoming sign – the cart of the Matoh, with Toraq's companion Eko snoozing alongside it. On his journey to the outpost, Samal was wondering what he was going to do when he arrived. He knew that he could just leave and disappear into Shaler territory, but by himself he simply is not built to walk around the countryside for days on end. He would need to recruit someone with a sympathetic ear and also realise what he intends to do. Toraq could be the owner of such an ear, despite his apparent anti-Kaidis actions as explained by Barel to Xarash earlier. Samal sympathises with him – maybe those actions were of good intention. He needs to know more.

His thoughts urge him to return to his feet. Pushing down with his thin, discoloured hands trying to elevate him, the soft sand gives way under his force and he begins to struggle. As he battles with the sand in regaining his balance, a white, furry paw-like hand outstretches itself into his view, and a tall, wide shadow casts a silhouette.

'Let me pull you up,' speaks the soft, soothing voice of Toraq.

Because Samal is much lighter compared to his brethren, the assistance provided to him by the Ascended Lightbearer quickly gets him back on his feet. With a considerable height difference between the pair, Samal stands dwarfed by the able and gentle beast. After collecting his bag and cane from the ground, he looks up at Toraq.

'Thank you, I suppose,' replies Samal, not entirely comfortable about giving gratification.

'You seem to be a little out of place,' says Toraq.

'Well,' says Samal, eyeing him up and down. 'So do you.'

Toraq smirks at this response. This is the first time he has come face to face with a member of the Doctors Division. Almost all engagements with the Kaidis in the past have been purely on informational basis, such as with Captain Selak at Ora. Toraq may or may not give them the information sought as his Lightbearer's role dictates; he rarely trades commodities with the Kaidis, so he does not see the non-military side of them, at least not as often as he would prefer. This meeting with Samal gives him an opportunity to do just that.

Likewise, Samal is taken aback by what he sees. Of course, being at the seat of power in the Kaidis kingdom, he hears all the stories about the Matoh. But actually seeing Toraq in the flesh — and fur — is a humbling experience. It is as if there is a certain radiance being broadcast by him.

An uncomfortable silence hangs over the engagement. Both are curious about each other, but there is also a degree of suspicion. Toraq knows that Samal is out of place, way out in the border between Shaler and Kaidis. Samal knows that Toraq may have quelled the Barel-led assault against the Shaler.

'What are you doing out here?' asks Toraq, breaking the tension.

'What are you doing out here?' counter-questions Samal, malice in his voice.

'Come now,' snaps Toraq. 'Are we fighting?'

'I don't know. You seem to be influencing things around here.'

'How do you mean?'

'Don't act like you don't know. You were there at Thoridon.'

'Oh, I see,' interjects Toraq, stroking his chin. 'Does this mean you are accusing me of something? If so, I ask again: what are you doing out here, by yourself?'

The added distinction to the original question makes Samal hesitate. He doesn't really know, but he cannot just admit that straight away – it would be a sign of weakness.

'Perhaps we've got off on the wrong foot,' suggests Samal. 'This is the first time we have finally met each other.'

'You already know who I am.'

'Indeed, allow me to introduce myself – Doctor Samal, Head of the Doctors Division of the Kaidis Kingdom.'

'Pleased to meet you, Samal,' replies Toraq genuinely.

'Since you are standing in my homeland, I think you should explain your presence here first.'

Despite the eventual welcome, Toraq doesn't feel especially comfortable talking about his actual reason for being at the outpost. A first meeting such as this is not warmed with confidence or a significant level of trust. After all, even though there is a definite facade being displayed by the Kaidis, it is Samal that is the weakened of the two.

Not entirely sure who could be listening, Toraq moves forward and out of the boundary of the outpost itself, into the barren desert, motioning for the Doctor to follow. A little apprehensive at first, Samal catches up to the Lightbearer.

'I do not know what you have been told,' Toraq starts. 'But I will admit I was present at Thoridon when the Kaidis attacked. For you see, there are much greater issues at stake. I will not let those come to pass.'

'That's a bit of a cryptic reason.'

'Well, you have not entirely demonstrated to me that you are able to listen. Besides, I would need to hear your side of the story before I can pass judgement.'

Samal narrows his brow and grunts. It would seem that the Matoh is more capable than he originally thought. He aggravatingly taps his cane in the sand and it kicks up puffs of darkened yellow fragments that carry on the warm breeze that blows across the exposed landscape.

'I have a proposition and I believe you are the only one who can assist me.'

He grumbles being troubled about what he has to reveal. There is still an air of antitrust between the two, but it is rapidly dawning on Samal that Toraq is his only way out of Kaidis territory.

'You want me to help you with something?'

'I never said "help"', grunts Samal, taking great offence to the word. 'But I believe there are "issues" as you say, although whether these are the same issues, I cannot say.'

'Go on.'

'Xarash is up to something,' Samal finally blurts out. 'And he is keeping me out of it. Despite what you might think, I want no part in what he is planning.'

He sighs.

'I see,' says Toraq. 'I am sure you are aware I try to remain as impartial as possible in political matters.'

'You "try",' Samal snorts. 'But it seems recent events have changed your mind! You are as much involved as anyone now.'

'You can keep your opinions to yourself, especially when you do not know the full facts.'

'We can argue semantics until the end of time,' says Samal, becoming impatient. 'What I need to do is get away from here as soon as possible.'

'Why should I assist you with that?' questions Toraq. 'You could go and ask the captain in the barracks.'

'Don't you understand? You saw how those workers mocked me. They won't assist me.'

Toraq considers the proposition. He doesn't really understand why someone so close to the leader of the Kaidis would suddenly just abandon him, but whatever the reason it is likely to be important. He looks down at the bag Samal clutches.

'What do you have in your bag?'

Samal grips tightly onto the bag and cowers slightly.

'Nothing but research I have been working on,' he replies meekly. 'I might tell you later, but now I need to know if you will assist me.'

'Tell me one thing,' speaks Toraq authoritatively. 'Have you seen Barel?'

'Seen him? I've seen him swimming around in the lava of the Stronghold, does that count?'

Based on the reaction of the Doctor, it would seem to be the truth to Toraq and he smiles about what he wanted to know. He turns around and begins to walk back into the outpost, once again motioning for Samal to follow.

* * * *

Being the superior military might that the Kaidis like to project themselves as, they have a duty to fulfil this. War is what they strive; war is what they believe in. Battle-readiness is constantly in mind, always prepared to enter into any fight that makes itself apparent. It is this preparedness that allows Xarash to control his vast armies with relative swiftness. No more than an hour passes since his call to arms and already legions of the Divisions have grouped, been given instruction, and armed with their appropriate weaponry and armours.

Each unit, regardless of Division allegiance, is dressed in the formidable armours of their designation. There is a definitive yellow tarnish to each of the heavily plated outfits and insignias of Mount Sindre adorn the chests. But it is not just the formidable troops that will be sending a clear message to the Shaler — as already demonstrated with the wind-powered Knoria vehicles and the impressive water collection facility at Wodar Drop, the Kaidis are excellent engineers. Supporting the armies are two siege engines named the Falla, wheeled out from storage inside the volcano. They feature powerful catapults, and at the rear, large bath-size containers, filled with fresh molten lava ready to launch a fiery rain onto the city of Thoridon.

Even the Doctors Division are preparing themselves without their chief — their primary role for the assault will be to supply the armies with food, water and whatever intelligence they can provide. It is a vast operation, but despite their timid approach to war, they have to support Xarash. They will look to take charge

241

of the remaining Bloodrage artefacts once recovered from the Shaler as well.

Xarash stands watching from the courtyard as he oversees the movement of the great devices, each one pushed along by twenty engineers. He smiles as he thinks that it is his time to win. With the legions, the Falla and the element of surprise all in favour of the Kaidis, the odds seem stacked against the Shaler.

As the last of the troops are prepared and the Falla are hooked up to a fleet of Knoria ready to take the army towards Outpost Ora and onward to Thoridon, the leader of the Kaidis does not need to say anything. He stands at the waiting royal Knoria, leading the fleet, and turns to look at the assembled. He gently nods to himself as he feels that this is his time to shine. Smiling, with bloodied-teeth showing, he raises a confident fist and emits a powerful roar that echoes down, right across the desert, carried by the winds.

In response, the armies grunt and shout back, a defining acceptance of what their leader seeks. Xarash boards his Knoria and it is shunted forward as the wind collects in its sails. The fleet of Knoria behind also begins to move and they all start to follow, in the direction of Ora.

As his royal Knoria rattles along, creaking under the strengths of the winds blowing into the sails, Xarash sits alone on a bench, with only his thoughts to occupy him. This will be his defining moment and he is fully aware of the fact.

Alongside him is the mighty axe that was wielded by his father, Xarash III, who died on the same battlefield that he is heading towards. However, this time the Kaidis have a tactical advantage; regardless of the opinion on Barel, he did provide a jump start. Xarash believes he cannot possibly fail this time and the Shaler will have to relinquish what is rightfully of the Kaidis and themselves.

What of Samal, the usually trustworthy adviser? Why would he suddenly just disappear? He has provided no tactical advice for this mission which slightly concerns Xarash for a brief moment. Yet, such doubt is quickly vanished — no, nothing can go wrong. They have the advantage, what more could they possibly need with such incredible power to make sure of success? Samal must know something else and has gone on ahead to inform the captain at Ora. Yes, that will be it, he concludes.

And also a brief image of his son appears in his mind. He is reminded that he does actually treasure his son greatly, but is troubled that he is not interested in leadership — as far as he is aware, anyway. With little conversation, Xarash simply doesn't know much about Rakos or what he reads and learns about in the Doctor's lab. Why doesn't he just pick up a sword and demonstrate what is in his blood? Perhaps he is too young to answer his calling as a Kaidis. Maybe he will realise one day.

Xarash's thoughts are interrupted as he hears an inspiring sound from the Knorias behind — rhythmic singing from the lower ranks. It is a stirring march, with lyrics enjoying glory and death equally, all in the honour of their affliction, the Bloodrage. As he hears the words, Xarash joins in by humming the tune to himself, smiling as he realises the armies are fully behind him.

All of this will be for Kaidis glory and the demise of the Shaler.

* * * *

Unaware of what is due to arrive, Samal and Toraq have been in deep discussion around a makeshift camp fire, close to the cart of the Matoh. On top of the fire sits a small pot and inside a thick soup bubbles over the heat. It is a green soup, made from a blend of various edible herbs that Samal keeps, making a nutritious but surprisingly odourless, rationed meal for the armies of the Kaidis.

Their discussions have been mostly on the subject of each other's business in Ora, but precise details have been not forthcoming, either due to slight but diminishing antitrust amongst the pair or concern about who could be listening — it is still Kaidis territory after all.

The atmosphere at the outpost is still calm. In the barracks, Selak still busies himself with various papers and endless filing, oblivious to the two guests and he would not care for their engagement anyway. Workers and soldiers surround the outskirts, adjusting screen defences to angle the wind and sand out of the base as much as possible. It is almost melancholy for such a fierce and militant people.

Almost uncharacteristically and shattering the calmness, laughter rises up from around the camp fire.

'Really? That is most amusing,' comments Toraq, surprised.

'Indeed, he can be such a hulk at times,' answers Samal, referring to his leader.

'And they have the cheek to refer to me as a beast,' jokes Toraq, pointing to himself as Samal laughs along.

As the laughter subdues, it seems that the air of antitrust has finally dispersed.

'I have a confession to make,' says Toraq, as he sips from a cup containing Samal's soup.

'I knew it, there had to be something!'

'You know I was there at Thoridon when Barel attacked, but what you do not know was that I gave him the book everyone seems keen on possessing.'

'The Book of the Daimons,' says Samal, his voice trailing off.

'Yes, I suppose. It is a curious moniker.'

Samal sits there staring into nothing, deep in thought as he is reminded to the words and diagrams he only glanced at while he had the book in his possession back at the Stronghold. He knew the book was incredibly important and would have spent many months studying it to learn its secrets; such secrets that could potentially benefit the Kaidis or himself directly.

'You seem to be driven by the existence of that book as well,' says Toraq, shattering Samal's train of thought.

'But you don't appear to be, judging by your tone,' replies Samal.

'Of course not, I already knew what it contained.'

'How is that possible?'

Just before Toraq has a chance to answer, his attention is diverted, looking past Samal and down towards the desert. He sees an unnatural wall of sand being kicked up and blown back to the south. In the relative peacefulness of the outpost, Toraq can hear what seems to be a low rumbling and can feel small vibrations in the ground upon he sits.

After seeing the surprise on the Lightbearer's face, Samal turns to look. As he does so, workers at the outpost flock to have a closer inspection out of their own curiosity. Samal knows what this is without needing to hear the reaction of the workers. They start shouting 'King inbound!' and the alarm call resonates around the outpost.

Captain Selak comes out from the barracks and observes from the door. He sees the red-coloured Knoria, Xarash's royal vehicle, leading the way. Starting to fret slightly, he looks around the barracks and quickly starts ordering soldiers to prepare for the leader's arrival. More shouts sound from the workers as they identify the legions following behind. Calls to fully open out the barricade leading into Shaler territory are raised.

'We have to get out of here!' says Samal to Toraq. 'They're opening the entire gate. This means something big.'

Workers begin to heave on the massive levers that control the barricade, a network of gears and pulleys start to spring into life as the full force of the enormous gate begins to split into two, revealing an extremely wide opening. It has been a long time since this has happened before — Xarash's father would have been in command.

The thunderous noise of the legions approaching gets louder. Toraq, usually composed, also becomes concerned as they move closer. With Xarash inbound, he is entirely unsure about how he would react to his presence. He starts to agree with Samal — it is time that they moved on, especially being significantly outnumbered.

Toraq turns his attention to Eko, who is also acutely aware of what is arriving. His master commands him to ready the cart for departure, but speaking in Ethereal. This makes Samal intrigued. It would be the first time that he has heard Toraq speak in the language of the Synth, as far as Samal is aware of its purpose.

'So, you will take me with you?' questions Samal, wanting some confirmation but not wanting to draw attention to what he has just witnessed.

'You will most likely need to hide in the back,' replies Toraq.

The sound of sand being kicked up makes itself localised as Xarash's royal Knoria rolls to a stop at the outpost and the king himself disembarks, holding his famous axe in his hand. The captain is there to greet his leader and is proud to give a well-rehearsed situation report.

But it is the scuffling near the gate that catches the ear and eye of Xarash. He sees the waggon of the Matoh. This alone is enough to immediately change his mood, and he pushes the captain out of the way, thundering towards the cart.

'You fucking disgrace!' roars Xarash as he runs forward.

Upon hearing the voice of the king, Toraq, now sitting on top of the cart, yells to hurry Eko to start moving. Just as the waggon starts to be propelled forward by Eko, Xarash throws his axe directly in the direction of Toraq, aiming precisely for his exposed white, furry back. As the axe flies through the air, rotating as it does so, it makes a vicious whooshing noise and its metals reflect the twilight.

The axe hits its target, straight into the back of Toraq. But, something entirely unexpected occurs — the axe, its blade sharper than a thousand blades, simply ricochets off the furry creature, not leaving a mark, not even disrupting a hair and lands on the sand, digging deep into the ground. As Eko accelerates, the cart carries the entirely unwounded Toraq through the gate and into Shaler territory, with Samal being completely surprised by what he has witnessed, looking up from the back of the cart and seeing his leader standing there open-mouthed.

'What just happened?' expresses Samal, looking at Toraq's scar-less back.

'Faster, Eko,' shouts Toraq in Ethereal ignoring Samal's obvious concern as they extend their distance from the outpost, heading towards the forests of Mistwood.

Xarash gives his axe a strong yank and retrieves it from the ground. He inspects the blade — not a drop of blood, just scratches from the sand.

'What the fuck just happened?' he yells, looking around at the workers for an answer. But none is forthcoming.

# Chapter Fourteen

# Druid

Empowered by Toraq's strong companion, the waggon also containing the unlikely passenger of Doctor Samal rumbles along the heavily stoned roadway leading northwest from Outpost Ora. Having left the armies of Xarash dumbfounded by the unexpected non-fatal attempt at the life of the Lightbearer, the moment has given them a head start in the escape.

Samal clings onto the sides of the cart as the speed at which they travel along the bumpy road makes it feel like the vehicle is going to splinter at any moment. He, too, is entirely surprised at what occurred. The lethal axe thrown at Toraq should have killed him, nothing more, and Samal would likely have been reprimanded and given eternal punishment for what would seem like collaboration.

But that is not the case. Somehow, they are running away.

As they follow the road, to the right-hand side is the tail end of the wide forest of Mistwood what both the Shaler and the Kaidis use primarily for forestry. However, it is extremely dense alongside the road, with tall oaks overhanging, occasionally blotting out the rising sunlight. Samal gazes into the woods, completely lost in thought, although still maintaining his grip on the bouncy cart. His thoughts try and piece together the latest events. Around the campfire back at Ora, he remembers the unusual admission that Toraq knows about the Book of the Daimons and supposedly down to what it contained. Samal himself only had the book in his grasp for moments, and from what he saw he found it extremely difficult to understand. Many concepts, diagrams and descriptions made no sense and would have taken years of study to at least learn some of its secrets.

He also considers what Toraq said before about "greater issues at stake". What could possibly be a greater issue than what the Kaidis desire?

'Just where are we going, you strange beast?' blurts out Samal, reverting to Kaidis instinct.

'I see,' shouts back Toraq, over the thunderous noise the cart makes. 'How quickly you have changed your attitude!'

As they continue down the road, the forest begins to thin and the vegetation generally becomes sparse once again with greener fields becoming the more normal landscape. They approach the Crossroads from the east and the makeshift cenotaph stands tall in the daylight. It is here where Toraq commands Eko to slow down and bring the waggon to a halt.

'Why are we stopping?' says Samal, even though he is slightly relieved that they have done so.

'You need to calm down, Samal.'

'Calm? How I can be possibly calm about what has transpired lately? You should be dead!'

Samal points to the memorial of fallen Kaidis and Shaler to illustrate his point.

'As I have said before,' Toraq reiterates. 'There is a great amount that you do not understand.'

'Perhaps you should start telling me then!'

'I do not think you will listen at the moment, judging by your tone.'

'My tone? I'm starting to wonder if everything you say is meaningless!'

Eko snorts as he hears the raised voices, clearly not seeing the point of the constant bickering. Not to be interrupted, Samal climbs off the cart and approaches the cenotaph. He picks up a reasonably heavy piece of weathered Kaidis chest armour which has been resting on the ground for many years.

'This once contained one of our brave warriors, but he is long gone. Dead. Yet you completely avoided injury to yourself from Xarash's powerful axe? Forgive an ageing Doctor, but I really do not see how that is possible.'

'You have made your point, Samal. I think the best way to describe is by action rather than words.'

In the heat of the moment, and Kaidis attitude taking control, Samal smirks, dropping the chest armour with a clatter and picking up a short sword from the pile. Even though he is not as strong as a warrior, the relative short distance between him and the Matoh allows him to execute a short throw of the sword. The aim is near perfect, yet the blunted sword seems to be effortlessly redirected, crashing to the ground by the side of the cart, leaving Toraq uninjured.

'That was not the sort of action I had in mind,' says Toraq.

'I really don't believe it!' shrieks Samal. 'Are you immortal?'

'Immortality is such a falsity, it is not possible.'

'Then how do you explain this?'

'Death is the absolute finite; do not concern yourself with that.'

Toraq hesitates.

'But its path can be altered.'

'What? How can you alter something that is the "absolute"?'

Before Toraq has a chance to respond, Eko makes a growling noise as he hears the sound of crashing metals making itself more apparent in the distance from the east. His master also starts to hear the same sound of Xarash's army moving towards their position and he quickly commands Eko to prepare to leave.

'You may want to climb back on, we do not have much time,' Toraq says to Samal.

'Perfect timing as usual,' he remarks sarcastically, slightly reluctant to climb back onto the waggon. 'I can't wait to see what the next surprise is. Where are we going then?'

'Into the forest,' Toraq replies, as Eko starts to pull on the cart once again, steering around the cenotaph and taking the northern road.

* * * *

Everything seems to be a series of new experiences for Samal, who has never had any serious reason to leave the confines of the Kaidis Stronghold, as the two Matoh catapult him over the winding and at times patchy road that leads into Mistwood. The roadway itself is not as stone-ridden as their escape from Ora, but it is significantly muddier, littered with potholes, splashing collected water as the wheels of the cart trundle over.

Continuously jolted around the back of where he tries to hold on, Samal grows increasingly curious about his surroundings. As they travel further along, the trees begin to form a tunnel as they overhang the constantly dwindling road. The morning sunlight is increasingly obscured the further away they travel from the Crossroads.

With the sound of clattering metal from the Kaidis warriors on the way towards Thoridon diminishing, a new sound is replaced — the gentle splashing of water, rippling over the stony riverbed of Still, starting off subtle, but the rushing noise grows with increasing ferocity as they move north and this new experience distracts Samal even further.

The overhanging trees begin to thin once again as they enter into a more barren part of the forest — an area used by the Shaler for logging and the river has swollen in size making itself a much more prominent feature. The river itself forks into two off the mountains in the far north, with one fork travelling through the middle of the forest and the other rushing past its western edge — where the cart travels past — eventually flowing into Wodar Drop.

Samal gazes at the shimmering sunlight reflected off the near clear water. It is a sight — once again — that he has never experienced.

'Stop at once!' he yells, overcome with intrigue.

Eko obliges, if a little reluctant, not really understanding why they should be stopping especially at the demand of someone like Samal. As the waggon comes to a halt, it slipping slightly on the muddy track, Toraq turns around to look at the Kaidis Doctor, a curious expression on his face trying to understand the demand.

He watches as Samal makes no attempt to explain his action, leaping off the back of the cart. He momentarily loses footing on the slippery ground — always damp from the moisture in the air and nearby. Regaining balance without falling over, he retrieves his gemmed cane from the back of the cart and walks down to the river's edge with a spring in his step not looking at Toraq.

The wet grass at the riverbank feels unusual to Samal underfoot. But not as unusual as seeing naturally flowing pure water, delivered directly from its source. No barrels of tainted water from the canyon; no vast effort required to secure it — it is just there, ripe for the taking. He sits down on the grass, cups his hands and lets the water flow over them. The sensation is overwhelming as he closes his eyes in almost a worshipping state. He brings the collected water in his hands up to his mouth and drinks. The purest of water tastes as refreshing as possible. He doesn't want this moment to end.

'What are you doing?' speaks the deep voice of Toraq, still sitting atop the waggon.

At first there is no response from the absorbed Samal, but eventually he slowly returns to his feet and turns to face Toraq.

'This is amazing,' he replies, slowly. 'I have not experienced water like this before.'

He picks his cane up from the ground and pokes the dulled gem into the water — the washing effect cleanses the gem, polishing it and restoring to its natural blue. As he pulls it back from the water, it glimmers in the sunlight with Samal looking at it impressed. Moving towards the cart, he looks at Toraq, with a raised eyebrow, his normal composure and inquisitiveness returning.

'What are we doing in this environment, anyway?'

'You wanted to know my secret,' Toraq replies.

'Indeed I do as your position is entirely questionable. Immortality? Nonsense! That is just impossible.'

Toraq disembarks from the cart and approaches Eko who stands catching his breath after the energetic escape from the Xarash-led horde. The Lightbearer talks in Ethereal to his companion, and Samal tries to understand what he says but is only able to make out the occasional word based on his own understanding.

'What are you talking to him about?'

'Oh, nothing of any importance,' Toraq responds with a degree of suspicion in his voice.

Samal strides up to the Matoh with an angry look on his face in complete contrast to moments ago.

'I have had enough of this!' he booms. 'It is deception after deception! Just tell me what is going on!'

'In time, you will understand,' Toraq retorts calmly.

Frustrated, Samal growls. He starts thinking about whether or not the Matoh is as trustworthy as he assumed him to be. Without any explanations forthcoming, he wonders if he is being taken for a ride, almost literally. But suddenly, something interrupts his train of thought. Behind a wide bush to the side of the cart he hears a noise and sees what seem to be the branches being disturbed.

'What was that?' he questions, the tone in his voice changing.

Toraq turns to look at where Samal points.

'There is nothing but a humble bush,' he replies.

As he does so, there is a definite movement behind. With adrenaline pumping, Samal moves towards the bush and peers around the side expecting to find something, but is disappointed as there is nothing.

'I was sure that we were not alone!'

'Maybe we are, maybe not,' Toraq says. 'Come, it is time we went inside the forest properly.'

'Why? What's in there? My patience for you is really running out now.'

'You will see.'

Toraq moves ahead, past the bush, and towards the deeper forest where the Shaler have yet to reach for forestry. He waves his hand like before at the outpost wanting Samal to follow. Grunting reluctantly, he gives the Matoh one last chance to explain himself and follows but still anxious about being watched by someone.

* * * *

Mistwood has a wide range of tree and vast mixtures of foliage. The ground is brown, littered with tree matter and very little sunlight reaches the floor in parts. Many exposed roots randomly dart around, making the pair's journey slightly more complicated, but with Toraq having a height advantage, he effortlessly traverses the undergrowth.

Winds blow over the treetops and the sound echoes around the entire forest, providing an eerie atmosphere in the already reduced light. Occasionally, what sounds like twigs snapping under foot reverberates around with no obvious reason — all of the unfamiliarity becomes overwhelming for Samal.

As he begins to develop a heightened sense of alertness; his attention diverts around to random areas of the forest and he doesn't see an exposed tree root, falling flat on his face as his foot trips over it, kicking up leaf and twig litter as he lands. The sound he makes breaks the tranquillity of the forest as a whole.

'That's enough!' he cries out, his voice sounding much louder than it should.

'We seem to have been in this situation before,' says Toraq, turning around to offer him assistance, familiar to the time they first met at Outpost Ora.

Just before he takes the furry hand of the Matoh, Samal notices some bright blue spheres at the foot of the tree. Returning to his feet, he bends down and picks one up — it is a solid crystal that has formed at the base of the tree, strikingly similar to the one attached to his cane. The brilliant blue that emanates from it sparkles as Samal rotates it around.

Toraq moves to snatch it from him.

'A nice find,' he says. 'You seem to have a talent for this.'

'And what do you plan to do with this unusual trinket?' Samal questions being slightly perturbed that Toraq didn't wait around to take it.

'You would be surprised what the Shaler will buy,' he smirks.

Their conversation seems to have disturbed something, however. Samal returns to his heightened sense of alertness after hearing a lot of rustling all around them, much more localised than the blowing treetops.

'We're not alone here,' Samal snaps. 'Why did you lead me into this trap?'

Before Toraq has a chance to explain himself, the blue crystal he holds is knocked out of his hand by a well-aimed arrow — its head made from sharpened stone. Immediately, they become ambushed by what appear to be ten Shaler, all naked, except entirely covered in a green and brown painted camouflage, armed with bows, arrows and stone catapults, all of which pointing directly at the Lightbearer and the Kaidis.

Toraq notices that Samal has an angry expression on his face and signals to him to not do anything. For indeed, if Samal were to start suddenly utilising the Synth, dense forest is not the best environment for anything fire-based.

'Come, Druka,' speaks Toraq. 'You must recognise who I am.'

'It is you that does not concern us,' replies a female voice.

'Oh, so it's my fault is it?' snarls Samal. 'I should have known that Toraq here was conspiring with the Shaler all along!'

'Shaler? We do not belong to them,' says the voice again. 'They are savages and destroy our home! How dare you accuse us of being them!'

An arrow is again launched, this time whizzing past the ear of Samal, narrowly averting a fatal injury — a definitive warning shot.

These are the people known as the Druka, formerly of Shaler society themselves. They were once living a prosperous life in Thoridon, enjoying the rich lifestyle that being a Shaler provides. Working as traders of exquisite items, either hand-made or otherwise, one of the sources for their trade was the forest that they now inhabit. Naturally rich in exotic crystals and valuable deposits of wild flora, the fruits provided by Mistwood made them wealthy and desirable merchants back home.

Despite this incredible luck, it was the forest itself that would have revenge upon them. In one venture, a thick mist descended over the trees, blown in from the river on a cool wind — a regular occurrence for which the forest gets its name. Consequently, the already premium light made navigation in the forest difficult with the Shaler ultimately becoming lost.

With food supplies dwindling and desperation taking hold, they struggled to traverse the seemingly endless mazes of trees, roots and bushes, going around in circles until the light entirely faded as nightfall took hold. As they were all traders with the People's Union, they never attended the Synth Institute and were unable to utilise the Synth to aid them.

After an uncertain night in the forest, the mist cleared by dawn. But the sense of isolation and adventure became attractive to these Shaler. They were alone, but it was as if the experience became a revelation — they didn't need to return to Thoridon. There were no customers, no stress and no financial requirements — they were free. Discovering that the forest itself was full of edible fruits and other resources, they adapted to the environment, reverting to an almost hunter-gatherer life and developing an ever-growing attachment to the forest itself, unofficially claiming it for themselves. Their self-given name, the Druka, literally meaning "one of the forest".

They also believe that they have a natural link to the forest — an awareness that allows them to "listen" to the plant life, being alert to any major disturbance throughout its vast area. It is this that provided them the opportunity to spring the ambush upon their unwelcome guests. And these guests, especially Samal, become increasingly twitchy about their predicament.

'What do you want from us?' he questions, tracking around the circling Druka.

'You have no reason to be in the forest,' speaks the leader who is only known as Kedar. 'Your trespass into our sacred land causes us great alarm.'

'I didn't want to be here anyway,' Samal protests. 'This lumbering beast brought me here.'

'This "beast" that you refer to has helped us to regrow the forest after the Shaler — and your kind — ravaged our home,' Kedar replies. 'You are in no position to be making accusations!'

'How do you mean "regrow"?'

Taking his cue, it would be a perfect time for Toraq to demonstrate his intentions plainly to Samal. He moves forward towards a decaying tree not too far away, its bark rotting from surplus moisture. As he moves, the Druka do not adjust their arrow aims which are firmly trained upon Samal. In a near replication of the act he performed on the tree outside the home of Solus, he places both hands upon its trunk, and softly chanting in Ethereal, he is able to encourage the bark to rejuvenate — its branches become restored. He takes a step back to admire his handiwork and then turns to Samal.

'This is what I have been trying to show you,' he says, in a calm, deep voice.

The Kaidis Doctor stands there, not really sure how to react and even though he has some understanding of the Synth, he has no idea what Toraq was chanting. On one hand, he is quietly amazed by what occurred — the strange beast was able to fix the tree! But on the other hand, it still doesn't explain to him how he has cheated death twice in his company.

In conclusion, his silence speaks volumes. The Druka lower their weapons seeing that their unwelcome guest appears to pose no further threat.

'I believe it is time to make our leave,' Toraq says. 'We have no further interest here.'

'Be at one with nature, Toraq,' Kedar replies, bowing to him.

She waves her hand in a circle to signal the others to leave and the ten Druka disappear into the overgrowth, out of sight.

Toraq smiles at the still shocked Doctor as he passes his side, returning to the direction that they came, making a point to step over the root that Samal originally tripped over. Samal walks up to the rejuvenated tree and touches it as a way to confirm that his eyes were not deceiving him.

Surprised to see that the tree is indeed recovering from its blight, he turns around and retreats to catch up with the lumbering beast.

✱ ✱ ✱ ✱

Their journey back to the cart is made in silence as Samal is left to constantly consider what is really going on. Numerous questions remain unanswered, and the shear possibility that what has occurred just seems entirely improbable. But he saw it for himself — the quick regrowth of the tree did seem to be controlled entirely by the Matoh, and inspecting his handiwork afterwards there was indeed a rejuvenation of sorts.

Samal spends the time considering what Toraq alluded to earlier about the possibility of altering the passage of death. It is true that death is the absolute finite, but changing its natural course? That is hard to believe.

As they arrive at the riverbed, Eko is sat down gazing out over the waters. His white, long-haired coat is damp as he has been washing the mud out of it, drying himself in the warm sunlight. Lost in thought about the current situation, he looks to the north and sees the mountains of Iskap, his native home; the ice and snow sparkling in the bright light. He doesn't realise the return of Toraq and Samal, and his master notices his snout direction pointing towards the mountain.

'We have returned,' Toraq speaks to him in Ethereal, with a raised but gentle voice. This reaction awakens Samal from his sleepwalking thoughts.

'What? Now what are you saying to him?' he questions frantically, immediately becoming agitated.

'I was just informing my friend that we are back,' Toraq replies, puzzled by the Doctor's reaction as Eko turns around and returns to his feet.

With the intention to continue up the road towards the eastern entrance of Thoridon, Toraq climbs back onto the cart and notices the shoulder bag belonging to the Doctor lying in the back.

'Tell me, Samal,' he says. 'What is in your bag?'

The Kaidis' eyes widen and he looks directly at Toraq, followed by a wry smile as he realises something. He retrieves the bag and rummages through its contents — various papers that he collected on his hasty escape from the Stronghold. Eventually finding what he was looking for, he pulls a sheet of paper from it covered in scribbles and diagrams.

'Why don't you take a look at this?' he says, the smile persisting on his face as he hands the paper to Toraq.

The Lightbearer looks at the paper, not really being able to understand what it says. The handwriting used is difficult to read and it is strewn with blotches and crossed out words as if there were constantly changing thoughts going into the composition.

'I cannot make any sense of this,' Toraq summarises, handing the paper back.

'This is the work I have been theorising on for some time,' Samal proudly announces. 'For years, I have been considering the possibility of providing permanent aid to our warriors on the battlefields — the ability to "repair" them, to keep them going for longer.'

His eyes widen again as he looks at Toraq.

'What you demonstrated with the tree has confirmed that my thinking was right all along! I hadn't realised it until now, being blinded by your infinitely vague responses. But you... You could provide the secret. Such a powerful secret. The ultimate weapon against the Shaler.'

Toraq doesn't really know what to think of the suggestion, but is actually impressed by Samal's initiative. In the eternal Tournament of the Lightbearers, Toraq feels that the time is nearly right to bring in the official player into the Arena of Pri. All along, he has been considering Samal to be a suitable host for the new player — the one known as Gadno, who was angry with Barel back in the Synthetic Domain. He realises that Samal may be starting to know too much, but he is also becoming further separated from his people with Toraq's temptation of occult knowledge that he is thirsty for. A loner such as Samal is the perfect candidate to becoming the host for a Lightbearer.

After a long pause, Toraq finally makes a response to the waiting Kaidis.

'Why should I reveal to you this secret, even if I knew?'

It was not the response that Samal wanted to hear. He roars with anger, because he cannot believe that Toraq will not answer, and also to the fact that his apparent immortality would prevent any kind of anger-based violence towards him.

'I cannot take this any longer!' Samal yells. 'You say one thing, then say another, but never actually say anything worthwhile! It is as if I am being played — a pawn in a bizarre game, one that you seem to be entirely in control. No matter what I say, no matter what I do, I cannot win.'

He spins around in a circle of frustration, raising his hands to the sky.

'You do not realise how true the words you speak are,' says Toraq.

'What do you mean? Are you trying to confuse me even more?'

'No, not at all. Perhaps you are ready to answer my question — what do you know of necromancy?'

The question merely stuns Samal. For him, it is a subject that has not been spoken about for a very long time. But Samal recalls the mentioning of necromancy from the much older papers contained back in his laboratory — the ones that relate to the time of the founding of the Kaidis, penned after they realised the Book of the Daimons written by Xarash I was commandeered by the Shaler.

There are also other memories from the past that come back to haunt him. The Doctors Division was not all as calm and supportive of the Kaidis as it is now. Prior to the reign of Xarash III — father of the current Xarash — the Doctors were involved in barbaric practises against their own kind.

Desperate to reveal all of the secrets of the Bloodrage, they adopted the use of reverse engineering, using at times violent and torturous methods to experiment on random members of the Divisions. The reasoning behind this was simple — to learn exactly what the cause of their affliction was. But instead of attempting to cure it, they wanted to know how to increase its potency, a continuing project to this day. It is this knowledge that the Kaidis seek, and one reason why Xarash is leading armies to assault Thoridon: to retrieve the remaining relics that the Shaler hold, rightfully belonging to the Kaidis as confiscated by Emperor Serenus. The theory being that having the material will help improve the Bloodrage further for future generations.

But to Samal, the reminder of necromancy is something that brings back horrific memories. As he is senior in his years, he was a junior Doctor in the Division when these very literal experiments were still being carried out. The cutting of flesh, the emitting blood, the smells of decay and the screams as these tests were performed on living subjects. But also the use of bizarre blood rituals, all in the name of the dead; attempts to attune the Doctor into being "at one" with the Bloodrage, to "see" about how it worked, all of it in vein and a practice now confined to history.

'I know enough about it to prefer to not know anything about it,' Samal says after a similarly long pause.

Toraq smirks at his response.

'What else do you have in your bag?'

Samal pulls out four more papers.

'All of these relate to Barel, and that Book of the Daimons. Notes that I scribbled down from what I could remember and based on what Barel was able to achieve. Although, I'm pretty sure they are meaningless to you.'

As the Lightbearer looks through the scribbles, one diagram is plainly recognised. It is a crudely drawn circle with an oblong inside and an outline of a skeleton. To Toraq, this represents the Necrocircle as it is in the same configuration used by Ferlor to call upon Barel.

'So I see you are aware of the necromantic,' he says, pointing at the diagram.

'Well, no. Maybe. I don't know what that represents.'

'This device is a ritual that has become to be known as the Necrocircle. It was what caused Barel to exist.'

Samal looks at Toraq, open-mouthed.

'How do you know this?'

'I devised it myself. I gave the instructions to the Shaler a long time ago and somehow it ended up in that book. Now — get back on the waggon. We need to intervene with what Xarash is going to do.'

Clearly shocked by what he has heard — and also by the strange fact that Toraq is actually answering his questions — he obliges, climbing back onto the cart without saying a word and stuffing his papers back into the bag. Eko pulls the cart forward and they speed off down the bumpy, muddy track which ultimately meets a rickety bridge over the river and toward Thoridon.

As they move along the road, instead of being in silent awe at the lush and unfamiliar environment, he constantly shouts questions back to Toraq, asking about the purpose of the book, how the Necrocircle works, and what the literal game is all about, with Toraq giving all the answers without hesitation. If Samal were to fully understand how the Necrocircle worked, Toraq knows that he will try it and he will become the host for Gadno.

# Chapter Fifteen

## Strike

Entirely on foot, the Divisions of Xarash's armies relentlessly march towards their intended destination — the home of the Shaler, the city of Thoridon. Despite being slightly encumbered with his heavy armour, King Xarash IV leads the progressing forces, his father's battle axe clipped to his back and a strong shield hangs from his left arm. Behind a merciless helmet, the eyes of the leader of the Kaidis are firmly fixated on his target as he trudges along the decaying road leading from the Crossroads into the Flatlands.

He knows that what waits is a defining moment in his leadership. Brought on by his own initiative, he is entirely in control of his people's future, with no advice or anyone brave or quick enough to challenge his prerogative. Perhaps in a bout of near stupidity, the Divisions that follow him do so without conviction — entirely loyal to his command they have no doubt that his word is the law.

For Xarash, his impending assault means two things — glory and respect from both his own people along with a vicious message to be sent to those that despise him, and also the reclaiming of what he believes is rightfully the ownership of the Kaidis: the artefacts and documents that detail the creation of their Bloodrage affliction, written by his distant relations. In owning these, he believes that with the Doctor's support, the information will enrich their affliction and make them a truly unstoppable force. Even if Samal is awry and that he also destroyed the Book of the Daimons.

But he knows that history is against him. His own father, Xarash III, led a similar assault with almost the same reasoning but with one key difference — the Kaidis were different then, the respect that his son requires was not guaranteed. The leadership was merely a figurehead, with no sense of direction or control over who it was supposed to be leading. Organisation was an ideal that was laughed at, with the Divisions making their own agendas, all of these ultimately failing. But Xarash III was keen to change this — his death on the battlefield outside Thoridon was symbolic; it changed opinion by demonstrating that it was possible to reach their goal and his son was able to bask in the new beginning for the Kaidis.

So how come history appears to be repeating itself? Xarash IV does not want to consider this question. He feels that his actions and the new unity behind him are what now define the Kaidis, and this will make them succeed where his father failed, all based on what his father achieved before.

The ground underneath his armoured feet becomes increasingly soft as they approach the Flatlands. Named so because of a combination between flooding caused by the river and the extensive deforestation by the Shaler, the land has become so flat and insignificant, the stagnant waters remain perpetually. While a road still exists, it is artificial, made from discarded tree matter and mud. With a consistently boggy atmosphere, it slows the overall progress towards the Shaler city, and this slowness begins to temper with the legions behind him.

The First Division are behind their King with a little distance between them; the trained and experienced warriors that will be either directing the fight or offering support when the lower ranks get into trouble. Seasoned on the battlefield from prior engagements, they think they know exactly what to expect. The Shaler are not known for their tactics and will generally always do the same as before, allowing these professionals to capitalise on their experience. But, an additional variable of the defected Levak was not present the last time such an army was raised and this may well test their capabilities.

Theoretically, they will fight alongside Xarash, following his every word to the letter and adapting to the situation with finesse. This is slightly in contrast to the Second Division which marches behind them, again with a small distance apart. These fighters are a lot less experienced, typically without any real combat knowledge and a few years younger than those in the First. There is more of a playful spirit among the lower ranks, joking with each other, much to the discord of their sergeants. But this attitude does not mean they are not committed to the cause. A little naive about what to expect, they are charged and ready to get their hands dirty — it is what they are born to do. Some may be slightly more reserved and have a degree of mettle — and these would eventually progress to the First — but they need to be tested in combat, for this is where the glory and recognition resides.

Despite all this, there is a level of doubt with at least one of the First. Proudly marching alongside his fellow colleagues, Legionnaire Volar has a reputation for being a bit of a thinker. Other warriors will turn to him when they need an opinion and he is more than happy to impart with his wisdom. Being intelligent doesn't make him less of a warrior however — he is a member of the First Division after all. His doubt is increased by history; following in the footsteps of Xarash's father may not necessarily be the best course of action. However, with increased numbers of warriors and the Falla catapults to provide covering fire, it does strengthen their chances, but the intelligent cannot always ignore scepticism.

With the legions traversing the bog successfully, Xarash approaches more stable ground as the ridge leading into the city becomes visible. It is here where he waits for the warriors behind to catch up, turning around to watch the armies move towards him. He gazes out over the Flatlands, not looking at anything specifically, but admiring the approaching horde in his peripheral. His thoughts are concentrated on the battle that waits. He feels the Bloodrage pulse through his veins as the adrenaline starts to pump.

Now is his time; now is the time for the Kaidis.

'The Kaidis are the supreme force!' he booms, standing below the lip of the ridge, his voice echoing over the Flatlands so all can hear. Cheers and clattering of weapons against armour begin to resound back. Xarash nods appreciatively. His fighters are ready as they wait for nightfall.

* * * *

Thoridon remains in a state of disrepair. Barel's initial strike against the city was devastating to the defensive perimeter that

263

surrounds it, ripping apart the thick stone wall, creating a hole wide enough to expose the Shaler for infiltration. But they are not stupid — under the order of Levak, an increased presence of Warlocks adorns the weakened defence and hastily erected wooden barricades are affixed as if to bandage the structure. Every other part of the wall remains intact and undamaged with lookouts continuously posted all around.

Despite the heightened security, they are entirely unaware of what awaits them over the ridge to the south. A relative form of tranquillity has returned to the city several days after the original Barel-led attack. Traders and common folk go about their normal business and the students have returned to the Institute, but their numbers are slightly reduced with Solus' call to arms as they are sided with the Warlocks, even though mostly inexperienced.

It is now late afternoon, the sunlight approaching the horizon and the more religious of the Shaler have gathered into the Temple of Ramor. A few traders remain in the Quadrangle packing up their stalls, the sound of low chanting filters down the white stone stairs. Inside, the priests of the Temple and various individuals that make up the congregation are stood in a wide circle inside the nave with the priests dressed in white cloaks with black sashes forming an inner arc.

At the Shrine of Ramor the sunlight beams down into the glassy receptacle which glistens intently. Emperor Solus stands in front, suited in ceremonial armour, with Emperor Vimlor's sword sheathed on his left side. He is silent, but the congregation that stands around him chant in a rhythmic prose — a prayer in recognition of Ramor and the energies that she represents. This is a complete turnaround for the leader of the Shaler. Before, he was questioning his own faith — now recent events have solidified his opinion, fully committing himself to the Temple and that of the all-empowering light of Ramor. He is born again.

With the last of the worshippers entering the Temple, the grand doors are closed and the wood booms in an echo around the large building as they are shut. After letting a few seconds pass to pause for dramatic effect, the chanting resumes.

It is the beginning of a ritual that is known as the Awaking of the Dark Light, a celebration of the arrival of the night that concludes the day, allowing the worshippers a chance to reflect on their service to Ramor. Within moments, the chanting of the priests intensifies with increased volume as the sunlight from outside begins to change direction during the sunset; the projected light by the Shrine beams onto Solus. Taking his cue, he reaches for his sword, pulling it out from its sheath; the sword making an extremely satisfying slicing noise as it is removed. The emperor moves to hold the sword horizontally above his head with both hands and stands directly into the beam.

Becoming bathed in its white light, his inherited radiance projects onto the white cloaked priests; the features on Solus' face seem to disappear as the whiteness becomes very strong. With the light at its brightest, the priests instantly stop their chanting and the nave is silent. Solus then lowers his arms, steps out of the light and grasps his sword with both hands, kneeing down. He whispers to himself in prayer, thinking of his desecrated father's grave and asking Ramor for protection against the Kaidis. As is believed with the ritual, anyone who stands in the projected light will have his wishes granted.

Unknown to the emperor, outside at the ridge, Xarash has decided that with all the troops now waiting for battle the time has come. He makes his way up the short path to the apex of the ridge, his heavy metal armour clanking as he does so. He stands tall at the tip, the setting sun behind him, broadcasting its light through him as he raises his arms to the sky, letting out a bloodcurdling roar.

On the walls of Thoridon, a lone lookout turns to the south upon hearing the unfamiliar noise. He narrows his eyes at the bright light being shone across the approaching road and field, he sees what seems to be a silhouette of a strange leviathan — its spiky armour and colossal size stirring caution in the Warlock. As he watches, he is repelled as the object moves down from the ridge, blinding him as the direct sunlight shines into his face. Taking a moment to readjust, he shields his eyes and looks again — smaller silhouettes begin to march over the ridge. It dawns on the lookout that this is highly irregular. He moves towards a tower in the wall and tells a colleague to look to the south and asks what he sees. His reaction says it all as he turns to the inner wall and yells the familiar cry: 'Kaidis inbound!'

As this alert is echoed to others all around the outer city, the First Division spills over the ridge, ready to direct what is about to happen. Next, the first of two long Falla pokes its frontal axle into view as it is carried along by a team of members from the Second Division. Being carried immediately behind it is a large metal box, sealed and containing rocks, formed from the now cooled Mount Sindre lava, making deadly ammunition for the catapults.

The lookouts atop the walls of Thoridon can only stand to watch as they see the mighty force of the Kaidis arrive at their doorstep. Each unit inside the Divisions lines up to cover the back of the battlefield, the army in its thousands standing in front of the Falla, all roaring in anticipation of what will happen next.

Xarash trots along the front line of his awaiting horde who cheer as he passes, with his axe held in his hand, clearly enjoying the recognition. They may have travelled many hours without rest but they are definitely ready for the battle. Orders begin to be shouted by the First Divisions, and sergeants in the Second issue terse instructions to each of their units. The Sindre rock is loaded up into the cradle at the back of one of the catapults. It seems everything is ready.

As the sunlight clips behind the horizon, the command to release the first payload from the Falla is given. The extremely hard, jagged and Luvolic material is launched into the sky, aiming into the city of Thoridon. The lookouts on the wall can only watch as it heads directly into their home.

✱ ✱ ✱ ✱

Emperor Solus was busy thanking the attendance of the congregation as they were leaving when the first rock struck the city. It landed on a humble home in the south. The random attack did not reach the intended target, the building and its contents reduced to rubble; if anything, it was certainly a clear message.

What the Falla was supposed to be aiming for was the weakened southern barricade; the hastily fixed wooden beams that would at least halt an assaulting army for a time, but entirely vulnerable to a heavy boulder falling from the sky. But to the Kaidis the missed target — while a slight setback — is still a victory in that it destroyed something Shaler.

Solus' attention is turned as the flattened building sends a shock wave around the entire city. The streets begin to fill with panicking residents, fearful that their homes could be targeted next, but ultimately putting themselves at greater risk. Solus descends the stairs of the Temple of Ramor towards the archway at the south of the Quadrangle. A row of Warlocks stand at the arch, preventing the troubled residents from entering as a method to protect the emperor. They constantly push them back and the residents shout back at them in desperation.

'What is going on?' Solus asks generally.

'We are under attack, Emperor,' screams back one of the residents. 'You have to do something!'

'Kaidis are attacking, sir,' qualifies one of the Warlocks.

'They're throwing rocks at us!' shouts another resident.

Surprised by what he hears and noticing the clear distress displayed by the people, he tries to calm down the amassed, saying that the defence plans put into place are suitable for a surprise attack. However, just as the crowd begins to subdue with the people being in complete trust of their leader, the negative atmosphere is recharged as another rock is fired from the second Falla and makes a devastating impact — this time hitting its target almost directly, destroying the wooden barricade opening up the southern breach.

As a triumphant howl carries over the wind from the Kaidis warriors, the Shaler people return to their panic. Shouts of 'Do something!' and 'Save us!' all resound and this changes Solus' attitude — his original plan did not foresee the use of an aerial assault. He decides to take matters into his own hands and turns around to other Warlocks that are positioned inside the Quadrangle.

'Follow me!' he calls to them, turning to the archway. His recruits begin to form a line in front of Solus as they march into the awaiting crowd.

'Clear the way!' they cry and the residents dutifully do so, forming a clear path leading towards the south, allowing for the emperor to inspect what is occurring.

As he travels along with some haste, getting further towards the southern wall, the roaring of the Kaidis becomes louder, this having a taunting effect. It is a sound that Solus has not heard before, but he doesn't realise the scale of numbers that wait to ransack his city. Within moments of approaching the breach, the full damage of what has transpired becomes fully aware to him. Scattered all around the immediate area are splinters of wood that once made the temporary barricade and pieces of cracked Luvolic rock are all over the place.

Aside from this environmental destruction, Shaler casualties are also apparent. Under the orders of Levak, the Warlocks assigned to guard the barricade — just in case there was a frontal assault — all lie dead, either suffering from multiple lacerations from shrapnel or crushed by the falling rock. It is a grim sight.

Before Solus and his small team have a chance to react, the roaring of Kaidis suddenly becomes a lot more localised. Thundering feet and clanking of metal make a quick approach from the other side of the wall, crashing against the stone. A single Kaidis unit stands behind the wall, armed to the teeth with devastating swords, axes and shields. There is a low grunt from the sergeant as he instructs the nearest to the gap to peak around the corner.

As the warrior does so, he catches a brief look at what seems to him to be nobody. He returns to his position and a nod at his sergeant as if to say the way is clear. Following this brisk assessment, the ten warriors turn the corner only to be greeted by Solus and his five Warlocks. They stop in their tracks as they look at the armoured emperor, still in his ceremonial gear and still with his sword at his side.

'Where do you think you are going?' he threatens, drawing his sword and relishing in the opportunity to use his combat skills.

The Warlocks alongside him begin to speak in Ethereal to conjure a wall of fire, each burning the warriors that dared to be in the presence of Solus. However, the sergeant and four others remain, and do not seem fussed, laughing off the sudden death of their colleagues.

'You are about to witness the full wrath of the Kaidis!' laughs the sergeant. 'You and all of your people are a fucking disgrace.'

As they turn the corner with a fierce roar, Solus rallies himself and charges the sergeant, striking him on the head with his sword. It doesn't pierce the plated helmet, but it does temporarily stun him, making him fall to his knees. In what transpires to be an excellent display of acrobatics, Solus drop kicks the sergeant in the face with an armoured boot, knocking him onto his back. It is now that Solus executes the final blow, driving down the sword into the chest, finally piercing the plate this time, delivering cold steel and an end to the sergeant's military campaign.

'Impressive,' comments one of the Warlocks, acknowledging his emperor who stands there catching his breath.

With the other four Kaidis seeing the displayed skill, they look at each other and retreat in cowardice. But, it is not long until another roar is heard and more rumbling approaches the breached wall. Solus pokes his head around the corner and sees a lot more than ten warriors coming straight for him — hundreds, much to his surprise.

'Retreat!' he commands, and they move back towards the Quadrangle leaving the wall undefended.

* * * *

Arriving at the eastern gate of Thoridon is the cart of the Matoh, with Samal still riding on the back. After successfully escaping the might of the Kaidis, it was time for Toraq to know what exactly they were up to. Their journey to the eastern side went unnoticed to the Kaidis that attack the city, as their efforts are much more concentrated elsewhere.

For Samal, it has been an incredibly enlightening experience, as the Ascended Lightbearer has been keen to explain great detail to him. The conversation also included one key piece of information that the Kaidis have been wanting to know for a very long time — precisely where the Shaler keep the lost artefacts relating to the Bloodrage affliction.

Why would Toraq tell Samal this? In fact, why would Toraq tell him anything?

Samal is someone who has an absolute thirst for knowledge, especially knowledge that no-one else is going to know. But he wouldn't communicate it to anyone: he is too power-crazed to weaken his own unique position to do that. He needs to know everything that everyone else doesn't know. The Lightbearer has recognised and capitalised on this fact. He knows this about Samal, so telling him what he wants to know allows him to play him — directly feeding him information about how to perform the Necrocircle and Toraq's revelation of his unique ability as a master of restoration: all of this will make Samal want to become ever more powerful, and by calling into the Synthetic Domain, Toraq is promising Samal that he will inherit ultimate power. Even if he neglects to reveal the fact that Samal will exist no more.

Eko brings the waggon to a stop at the closed eastern gate. Surprisingly, the gate is entirely undefended — there are no guards standing here. Toraq disembarks from the front of the cart and presses against the wood. Remarkably the gate opens as it was just pushed to. As the gates fully open, Eko pulls the cart just inside and Toraq closes them behind.

'So this is it,' says Samal, slightly in wonder as he steps off the cart, looking at the inside of Thoridon for the first time in his life. He tracks his eyes around the stone houses, mostly with flat roofs, some with front gardens with flowers and bushes growing.

'What a disgusting place!' he finally comments, despite the environment being relatively pleasant. It is more of a shock to him, being raised entirely in a hostile and volatile home. Toraq takes a moment to look at Samal, who uneasily narrows his brow towards the Matoh.

'What?'

'Do you know what you are going to do now?' questions Toraq.

'I take from your tone that this is the end of our journey?'

'It is time we went our separate ways, yes.'

'I don't really know what I should be doing, to be honest. I didn't have any plan to begin with, yet, here we are, at the Shaler capital which seems to be deserted and my leader is probably slicing them up personally as we speak.'

He pauses for a moment.

'Oh, and I suppose there's all that stuff you've told me, along with my rescue. Thank you.'

Samal grimaces after speaking those last two words.

'You should pursue what you now know,' says Toraq, not really warming to Samal's uncharacteristic gratitude. 'I have merely shown you the way, now you must traverse the path yourself.'

'I shall miss your cryptic way of talking, Toraq,' jokes Samal as he begins to move away, pointing in the direction that Toraq shows. This leads him in a westerly direction towards the Quadrangle and eventually out of sight with the sound of his cane tapping against the cobbled road fading away.

For the Lightbearer, the quietness is startling — there is no-one around and all the homes appear to be unoccupied. But it does seem to be safe from Xarash's forces for now, and therefore asks Eko to stand the ground and defend the cart should the need arise. He then moves down a southern street in an attempt to find some answers.

* * * *

It doesn't take long for Samal to discover why the streets and buildings are devoid of anyone. As he approaches the inner city, the roars and clattering of metal make themselves a lot more apparent, with the Doctor recognising some of the shouting issued by the Kaidis as they advance.

On the southern roads that lead to the Quadrangle, death and destruction has made its mark. Corpses of bludgeoned or skewered Shaler — either civilian or members of the Warlock Council — line the streets, but also piles of heavy armour and weaponry left behind by defeated Kaidis.

Lesser numbers of defenders stand around the city walls as resources on both sides of the fight diminish nearly an hour after the first rock fell. As darkness has taken hold, the Warlocks that remain take shifts to continue their assault with their Synthetic energies being less available. Not only because of the number of enemies, but with no Ramor in the sky to provide more of the Synth, this has reduced their effectiveness. No amount of training has prepared them for such an aggressive assault.

Despite this, the numbers of Kaidis are falling. The assault was led by sending in groups from the Second Division, effectively acting as cannon fodder. With the defences weakened, this allowed members of the First Division to lead a new charge. This element of surprise has allowed around twenty Kaidis to reach the prized inner city walls. Axes and swords fly, slicing through the weaker Shaler, most of which are not dressed in anything to soften the blows. It is a murderous rampage that takes no prisoners. With the Kaidis moving closer towards the Quadrangle, it seems success is in their sight.

Meanwhile, Samal is heading west towards the Quadrangle himself. Because he is not bulky or suited up like the Kaidis warriors, looking more like a feeble old man under the darkness, he doesn't draw any attention. Shaler run past him in the opposite direction fleeing from what they fear the most. But finally, as he approaches his target, he meets the assaulting team of Kaidis. While their numbers have shrunk by a few, it is the three First Division warriors that stop to look at Samal. They recognise who he is — as would anyone who knew about senior rank and file — and Samal sees them looking. Dodging some bodies on the ground, he approaches them.

'Where do you think you're going?' he asks, not speaking to anyone in particular.

'We had word that the fucking emperor was up here,' says one of the First Division. 'How the fuck are you here? The King wants your head!'

'Oh, does he now? Perhaps he won't, based on what I know.'

'What do you mean?'

'You idiot — the Bloodrage artefacts are inside there,' he says, pointing towards the Library at the Synth Institute.

'Are you calling me a fucking idiot?'

'Stand down,' speaks a deeper voice from one of the other First Division warriors. 'Do you forget who you are speaking to?'

'Fuck off, Volar,' protests the other. 'I've had enough of your commands.'

'Well, I have had enough of your insubordination!'

With that, Volar turns on his companion, rising up a twin-blade axe and bashes the head of his unnamed colleague, who in a similar fashion to Solus' attack earlier, falls to the floor dazed. Volar then reels back and strikes the neck with his axe.

Samal nods at Volar who stands there with blood dripping from his blades as the corpse sprays blood over the street. The other Kaidis that stand there back away from Volar and retreat south in fear that he has lost his mind.

'Cowards!' he yells to them as they disappear around a corner.

'It would seem it is just you and me, which is convenient, as I need someone to protect me,' suggests Samal.

'I had a feeling that would be the case,' says Volar, returning his axe to his back. 'What do you need to do?'

'We need to get inside the Library, and I plan to steal the artefacts. I need you to make sure nothing comes between me and that.'

'I will do my best — after all, regardless of what the other soldiers might think that is why we are here.'

Volar becomes all too aware that the two of them need to keep moving before they are singled out, so he starts moving towards the Quadrangle, ushering Samal to follow him.

'You are not like the other warriors I have had the "pleasure" of speaking to,' says Samal.

'I'm glad you noticed,' Volar replies as he readies his axe once again.

As they approach the archway leading into the Quadrangle, it is apparent that the defences which were there before have vanished. The rabble of Shaler residents pining to get inside have also disappeared. The doors leading to the Temple of Ramor are firmly shut; the Senate House similarly so. It would seem the Quadrangle is deserted.

Volar edges up to the archway with his back against the stone with Samal doing the same behind him, both lurking in the shadows. He peers around, trying to spot any sign of a threat, but there is nothing. It is heavily darkened and sounds of fighting still continue in the distance to the south.

The curious First Division soldier makes a move, disappearing around the corner and Samal pauses just in case something happens. But there is silence. He decides to take his chances and follows Volar, seeing for himself that the Quadrangle is empty.

'Where is the defence?' he whispers to Volar.

'I don't know. It is all very suspicious. Keep moving.'

They cross the largely unlit Quadrangle, traversing the entrance to the Institute and under the direction of Samal, reach the doors of the Library without issue and it is not apparent that they have alerted their presence to anyone. Following a nod from Volar, Samal pushes on the large door that leads to the Library's foyer and sees that it opens with a gentle creak. After looking around to make sure the squeaking hasn't drawn any attraction, they both slip into the building.

* * * *

Inside there is nothing out of the ordinary. The Hall of Legends is as it usually is — well-illuminated and all of the monuments to Shaler history are proudly displayed as normal.

Ferlor's memorial also remains but the display piece reserved for the Book of the Daimons has been replaced with a hand-written dedication from the emperor.

Naturally, it is the first time the two Kaidis have seen the various displays. As they enter, they see the staircase that leads up into the archives, and they both begin to look around at the various set pieces. They do so with caution, however — it is enemy territory after all.

Samal looks around with wonder. He had never dreamt that the Shaler would be so possessive about history. Looking at the artwork and other museum pieces, he is staggered by what he sees, either in the quality of the dedications or in simply what they depict.

Volar on the other hand is less than impressed. To him, all of this represents what is wrong with the Shaler, too hung up in the past and fearful of reality. Memories should be of glory, not what individuals achieve, and certainly not of anything to do with what he sees as the pointless Synth.

He notices Samal gazing at a painting — an illustration of the time when one particular student was able to create a wall of horizontal fire across the stone he majestically stands upon. Underneath is a bronzed placard with the text: "In dedication to Conjurer Jerel for his excellent theories".

'What are you staring at that for?' questions Volar, in a whisper.

'Can't you see the finesse and dignity that this picture represents?'

'No, all I see is a reason why we shouldn't be here.'

'I think this whole place is just incredible,' wonders Samal.

'I think you should do what you came here to do,' grunts Volar, getting increasingly edgy.

Samal turns to look at his protector and nods, remembering that there is a fierce battle going on outside. This is perhaps not the time to be enjoying himself. He turns to the staircase and recalls what Toraq told him about the location of the Bloodrage artefacts. The instructions were exact, and he goes behind the stairs and finds the door that leads down into the basement below. Volar stands at the door, just in case someone makes an appearance into the courtyard.

The Doctor looks at the door and sees the keyhole and shrieks a little.

'Come here,' whispers Samal, but loud enough for Volar to hear. Annoyed that he has to leave his tactical position, he approaches. Samal points at the door's lock, and not having a key, needs some force to be able to get inside. Using the head of his axe, Volar rams the handle repeatedly — making significant noise in the process. It eventually gives way.

'You could have done that a little quieter,' grumbles Samal as he pushes on the door. Smiling to himself he proceeds inside, down the dusty and haphazard steps, leading into the prized refuge of Bloodrage artefacts. The light is quick to fade as he descends and he is soon enveloped in darkness.

'Hurry up!' comes a shrill whisper from Volar above, becoming increasingly anxious as he is left alone.

The final instruction that Toraq gave him was to conjure fire to light up the underground basement. Therefore, cupping his hands and speaking in the Ethereal that he was taught by the Lightbearer, a small flicker of flame appears before him and he pushes it towards the wall, catching a torch on fire and illuminating the vault, mirroring the behaviour of Ferlor before.

It is all laid out before him — all the documentation, the idols and the other strange objects responsible for the synthesis of the Bloodrage affliction. He takes a moment to absorb all that he sees. Such a cache was never confirmed to exist, only rumours and theories. All those Kaidis losses are now entirely justified. Xarash and his father before him were right all along.

'What are you doing down there?'

Volar's threating question brings home the required urgency. Samal starts immediately scrabbling around, rummaging through the shelves and containers trying to find something that might be the clues he is looking for. With his shoulder bag, he begins stuffing papers into it, not really looking at what they contain — it could all be useful or it could all be junk. But then, he stumbles across a dust-covered urn — opening the lid, inside are vast quantities of Urtica seeds used to grow the poisonous plant that acts as the main ingredient to creating the Bloodrage affliction.

He closes the lid and picks up the entire container — such a find is what he was really looking for as the Urtica plant hasn't grown in the wild for many years. Extinguishing the torch, he rushes up the stairs, carrying the urn as it is too large to fit in his paper-filled bag.

'What is that?' asks Volar.

'This contains the basis for developing the Bloodrage,' Samal explains. 'I wouldn't expect a warrior to understand, but it is vitally important this urn and its contents make it back to the Stronghold.'

'You had better hold on to it,' Volar suggests. 'Besides, it would just get in the way of my blades.'

The two return to the front of the stairs leading to the archives and head for the exit, but are met with a strange occurrence.

'Why is this door shut?' asks Volar. 'Be ready.'

'Did I tell you that I'm not very agile, by the way?' informs Samal.

'I noticed,' the warrior replies, sternly.

Volar casually pulls the door open and it creaks gently as it did before. From the crack, he cannot clearly see what lies in wait for them outside. With nowhere else to go, he pulls the door open further, grabbing Samal by the arm and the two launch themselves out of the Library. To the relief of Volar, there is no-one waiting and they hurry across the Quadrangle to the southern archway.

But, just before they can do so, a deep, commanding voice makes itself heard from behind.

'Stop right there!' threatens Solus with Levak at his side, emerging from the darkness. Samal turns to look at the emperor, and Solus sees that he is clutching the stolen urn. Solus is not aware of what the urn contains but he does recognise it as an old artefact.

'Run!' grunts Volar who stands at the archway, ready to get away. But Samal in his stubbornness does no such thing and instead looks at the emperor. He has never seen him before and his inquisitiveness gets the better of him.

'You must be—'

'Don't say another word,' interrupts Solus, his voice turning increasingly hostile and begins to unsheathe his sword. Samal sees what he does and freezes, not really sure what to do next.

'Doctor Samal,' speaks Levak. 'It would appear the Division has been weakened significantly if you are here on a personal errand.'

Samal turns his attention to the former Kaidis Doctor.

'I know you,' he says, recognising the voice. 'What is...?'

Before he can finish his question, acting as a guardian Volar rushes up from behind, scooping him up with a fierce yell, directed at the emperor. All in a matter of seconds, he retreats to the archway.

'They have an artefact! Stop them!' yells Solus at the top of his voice in an effort to attract attention of any defenders nearby.

But Volar and Samal disappear around the corner, running as fast as the First Division warrior can. Realising that there are hardly any Shaler around to answer his plea, Solus decides to pursue them himself.

# Chapter Sixteen

## Deliverance

Charging ahead, the two Kaidis make impressive ground against the Shaler emperor as they attempt to escape from Thoridon. With the Bloodrage enhancing his abilities, Volar of the First Division has much more stamina available to him than Solus allowing the warrior to speed ahead. The journey is fraught with obstacles — ransacked buildings and burning wreckage; corpses and armour litter the ground. A few Warlocks still try to counter their escape, but Volar is able to avoid them, either by taking a side path or running through cover.

Doctor Samal is being carried in a fireman's lift, but he is carefully positioned not to skewer himself on Volar's studded armour. It may not be the most comfortable ride of his life — not only the position but also carrying the urn containing the Urtica seeds — but at least he is still alive. With Volar ducking into a passageway, Samal is nearly flung off his carrier. To say the ride was bouncy would be an understatement, and the warrior's grip on his legs can be firm to loose.

'I'm not sure if you're trying to throw me,' Samal says with broken speech as each step Volar takes jolts him.

'I have thought about it!' Volar shouts back, ducking around another corner and returning to the main road leading south in the direction of the breached wall.

'You must take me to Xarash,' says Samal, not entirely impressed with the response, but now is not the time to criticise.

'Are you sure that's a good idea?'

'He doesn't scare me!'

Volar laughs — for a weak Doctor, he certainly has a lot of courage.

At the southern breach of Thoridon's wall, the front line of Kaidis has moved up directly near it, but the total number of warriors are less than a quarter of what they started with. The Falla stand inactive as the stocks of hard Luvolic stone have been depleted. The remaining fighters are tense as the odds seem to be increasingly stacked against them.

However, Xarash remains determined, and as long as he is, his warriors will be as well. Encircled by a small pocket of First Division fighters, he looks to the sky and listens. The thunderous sounds of raging Kaidis has mostly diminished, but there is a gentle burning sound as fire crackles around the heavily damaged city. He breathes in deeply, smelling the air which has a tinge of burnt flesh and blood on it. His senses are satisfied and that alone is worth all of the effort. But he is still concerned that the mission has not been completed — there is no word of anything to do with the Bloodrage artefacts or a resounding victory against the Shaler.

'Why don't we just finish them off?' asks an impatient First Division soldier. 'We could charge in and put an end to their misery.'

Xarash turns to face him and smashes him around the face with the back of his armoured hand.

'Foolish maggot!' he retorts. 'This battle is far from over — and there is plenty of time left to go.'

He starts to pace up and down.

'Time is on our side. We shall strike when they don't expect.'

He pumps a fist into his other hand to emphasis his point. The others nod in approval, but one doubt still lingers in their mind — when that will be. But this does not concern the king. He doesn't want a repeat performance of what his father did and storm the city. He has learnt that timing is what wins battles and he is all too keen to wait for the right moment.

Even though he has it all planned in his mind, he does not anticipate what happens next. From behind the breached wall, disturbing the relative calmness, footsteps thunder with clanking of metal causing Xarash to turn to the breach and makes a hand gesture to command his troops to ready themselves. They draw swords and axes and move into a defensive stance.

'Who approaches?' yells Xarash in a threatening voice, not really expecting anyone to come rushing towards the breach. The crashing footsteps suddenly come to a stop.

'Stand down!' shouts the softer voice of Samal.

This takes Xarash a little by surprise, definitely not ready to hear the slightly unwelcoming sound of his right-hand adviser. As Samal and an out-of-breath Volar turn the corner, Xarash signals to the warriors behind to relax and they all look questionably at the Doctor.

'Well, that wasn't the greeting I had hoped for,' Samal says, being lowered to the ground.

'Quiet you worm!' Xarash barks. 'What the fuck are you doing here? I should cut you down right now for going off with that furry beast!'

'If you did that, then you wouldn't have what I have in my hands.'

He proudly displays the stolen urn containing the seeds. Xarash rips his axe from his back, unimpressed.

'Some fucking pot? Is this your reason for disobeying me?'

'Calm down before you make a complete idiot of yourself,' Samal says, confidently.

'Have you forgotten who you are fucking talking to?' roars Xarash.

'Enough!' interjects Volar. Xarash raises an eyebrow to the First Division warrior.

'This urn contains a vital ingredient to creating the Bloodrage,' continues Samal. 'We stole it from inside the Shaler's Library.'

Xarash lowers his axe and begins to laugh. Samal and Volar look at each other, surprised by this reaction.

'You don't believe me, I take it,' says Samal. He passes the urn to Volar and then rummages around in his shoulder bag, taking out some of the papers he also stole from the Library.

'Look,' he says pointing at the papers. 'We also stole these — instructions, theories and other information about the Bloodrage.'

Xarash leans forward and snatches one with his free hand. After casually looking at the paper, something upon it catches his eye and it makes him look at it in more detail. As he reads, he becomes increasingly convinced that Samal tells the truth. He takes his eye off the paper and looks at the Doctor. After a pause, he hands the paper back.

'How the fuck did you manage to do this?' Xarash eventually asks.

'I will have to explain later,' Samal says, taking the urn from Volar and walking forward towards the front line. He motions for his protector to follow.

'Why?' grunts Xarash.

'Because there is one little surprise due to arrive at any moment,' Samal responds, motioning for Volar to pick him up again. 'We're going back to the Stronghold so I can start on my work!'

The warriors in the front line clear a way for Volar to resume his running and they head for the ridge leading towards the Flatlands, leaving an astounded Xarash behind.

'Incoming!' sounds a shrill alert from one of the warriors on the front line, as more footsteps approach from behind the wall.

'I guess this is the surprise,' says Xarash to himself, readying his axe.

*** * * ***

'What are you waiting for?' barks Xarash as the footsteps from behind the wall stop just before the breach. 'My axe thirsts!'

It is Solus who waits at the wall, with Levak at his side. A roar rises from the First Division warriors that support Xarash much to the surprise of the emperor. He was expecting to see Samal and the lone soldier protecting him, not an army waiting around the corner.

This would be the first time that the two leaders have met. They are both aware of each other's actions and would know a lot about what they have done in the past, but do not know themselves in person. But the situation that they stand in now is unique — purely in the way that Xarash announced himself and the supportive roar that proceeded. Only one person could have that kind of allegiance.

'General Xarash,' Solus speaks from behind the wall, authoritatively. This makes the leader of the Kaidis loosen his stance.

'Who is this that speaks?'

Solus calmly walks around the corner without his sword drawn and Levak waits out of sight. He stands in full view of the awaiting horde with Xarash standing in the front. It is a tense moment as he looks along the front line — thirty heavily geared warriors with faces of anger, all with swords and axes held ready to charge. The dull steel of their Luvolic-forged armour in the darkness of night refracts minimal torchlight and provides an extremely menacing backdrop.

But Solus has developed into a strong character, despite his desperate pleas with High Priest Rogaro only a few weeks ago. This sort of display would normally instil terror in his mind, but his perception of everything has changed and is entirely unperturbed by what stands in front of him.

He takes a moment to observe the hulking Xarash. The jagged armour with incredibly sharp and long spikes that rise up from his broad shoulders; his head entirely covered in a helmet that seems to mirror in appearance the very gates at the entrance of the Stronghold; his two-bladed battle axe with strong two-handed grip that could rip through anything in a single swing.

Xarash stands relaxed, as he also is observing the lone emperor that waits at the wall's breach. Still dressed in ceremonial armour used during the Awaking of the Dark Light ritual, it provides a full chain mail suit sparkling in the reduced torchlight. He does not wear a helmet, but his sword is sheathed at his side; its long blade and decorative bird-like hilt making an eye-catching impression to Xarash.

'I am Emperor Solus of the Shaler and you have committed the most punishing crime that these lands have known in recent memory.'

'We do not bow to your fucking law,' laughs Xarash. 'We have come to take what is rightfully ours! Yet you hide it away from us, like the pathetic worms you are.'

'What do you seek then, general? I fear it is much more than trinkets and treasures.'

Xarash scoffs, but then hesitates. He remembers that there is much more at stake than the Bloodrage artefacts, and it seems Samal has already managed to secure something of that anyway. This is his chance to take an opportunity with the enemy. He turns to the bloodthirsty horde and signals them to stand down — he wants this encounter all to himself.

'Perhaps it is more. For years, you have tormented my people in this exile. It is you that is ultimately responsible for the destruction of your own kind. You have caused all of this.'

'Are you suggesting that I am destroying my city? Through your own actions? You are mocking me, surely.'

'I can mock you even more if you want,' Xarash threatens, and he moves closer to Solus who does not flinch. He looks Solus right in the eyes from behind his massive helmet.

'You have the same fucking eyes as your father.'

What a curious statement, thinks Solus. How does he know about his father's eyes?

'What do you mean?'

'Are you too fucking stupid to realise that I have to spell it out for you?'

He gives a short, sharp sigh.

'I was the one that killed Emperor Vimlor,' Xarash speaks through gritted teeth. 'I looked him right in the eyes before I ploughed my Luvolic dagger deep into his side. He tried to cry out to me, but there was no breath. Fucking pathetic, just like you.'

Smiling behind the helmet, he backs off from a wide-eyed Solus. It was a young Xarash IV that slipped away from Solus' residence all those years ago. This single action proved his worthiness of Kaidis leadership. It is this that precedes his reputation as a bloodthirsty and cutthroat warrior earning him the utmost respect from his kind.

Solus experiences a wide range of emotions. Thoughts race through his mind trying to recall his father's assassination. He drifts into fantasy as he was only an infant. Desperation and despair drives these thoughts and he gets increasingly wound up and annoyed with himself that he is unable to recall what happened. As his self-inflicted mental beating reaches a deafening crescendo, a moment of silence follows in his mind. He refocuses his attention on the vile, disgusting and absolute abomination that stands in front of him, which snickers to himself with a horde of thugs waiting in anticipation of the next move.

There is nothing in Solus' mind that suggests anything other than the urge to destroy Xarash. He needs no further justification. Only pure unadulterated hatred is boiling up inside him. Solus unsheathes his sword in an instant, teeth showing as his sneers at the reason for years of pain and suffering. He roars and charges his absolute enemy, with Xarash readying his two-handed axe as he does so. The sword crashes into the handle of the axe as Xarash parries the attack — a spark flies when the metals collide. The general swings around on his axe forcing the two weapons to come apart and knocking back Solus in the process.

As the emperor regains his balance, Xarash gives a hearty laugh.

'Come on then, you fucking maggot!'

It is Xarash's turn to strike; giving a fierce yell, with his axe held high above his head he dashes forward — the assembled horde behind him booming an encouraging grunt. Solus moves to the side as he thinks he cannot counter such a powerful surge, with Xarash annoyed that he does, stopping himself and lowering the axe before he crashes into the wall. Unperturbed, the two leaders encircle each other, both looking deeply into each other's eyes, only seeing complete hatred, with shouts of abuse rising up from the pack behind.

From the eastern road behind the wall, Toraq makes himself known to Levak that waits. The Lightbearer can hear the jeers and clattering of weapons on the other side and he makes a hand gesture to ask what is going on. Levak shrugs his shoulders, not really wanting to get involved with melee combat and is also in conflict with himself about what allegiance he has. Toraq peers around the corner without making himself seen, observes what is transpiring and reels back with no reaction.

With the fight now in full swing, with a rally of successful parries and misses, to the on looking horde it is an entertaining match. Xarash is also enjoying himself — he has nothing to lose. But to Solus, it is a fight for his life, his people and his father.

Eventually, something gives. Solus is able to make a strike against Xarash as his sword crashes into the large helmet. The force is so great that it reverberates and becomes loose, with Xarash dazed for a moment staggering back. As he moves, his head is jolted backward and the loosened helmet falls from his head to the floor with a clatter. Xarash's face is now entirely exposed, showing his sweat-drenched, yellow-pigmented skin and a head lacking hair. Shaking himself down in a moment of recovery, he smirks at Solus.

'Is that all you've got?'

The Bloodrage of Xarash reaches a point of ecstasy and with another fierce roar; he swings his axe horizontally towards Solus. A dull thud as the axe's blade hits the right-hand side of his chest, just below his ribcage. The chain mail armour provides only a little protection from the lethal blade and Xarash gives a wicked smile as it lands. This causes the younger Shaler leader to fall to the floor, much to the delight of the crowd. He is in much pain: the axe has pierced his side; blood begins to seep into his armour. It suddenly feels very cold to the emperor. However, for Xarash, this is a moment of victory.

'Do not fuck with the Kaidis!' he yells, turning to face his warriors. He then roars in defiance, thrusting his axe above his head with both hands, clearly in a state of great euphoria. Cheers and grunts supporting their leader reach deafening levels. He rallies up and down the front line and they slap his armour in a sign of gratitude.

But the mood swiftly changes as the warriors see the white bear-like beast emerge from behind the wall. Xarash turns around with a narrowed brow as Toraq approaches Solus who lies on the increasingly blood-soaked ground. The general scoffs when Toraq kneels down beside the fallen emperor.

Gasping for air and having mild convulsive shocks, Solus looks intently at the Lightbearer. He cannot speak, the pain is too great, but with blood gushing from the wound he knows there is little time for him. But for Toraq, having the leader of the Shaler die — the most powerful people and most easily influenced — is simply unacceptable.

Toraq never really anticipated that the Kaidis and Shaler would have such an epic battle. For all the years he had been manipulating both sides, he was trying to strike a balance that would never really result in a devastating blow to any side. Tempers would flair and situations would be complicated, but he never planned on it to have an ending. Such an ending also ends the playground for other Lightbearers to partake in. This Arena needs two polarising leaders — Solus cannot die. It is not currently part of the plan.

'What the fuck are you doing?' booms Xarash, as he sees Toraq place both of his white hands over Solus' wound. Speaking in Ethereal, just like he has done to the tree in Mistwood or the garden at Solus' home, his restorative incantation begins to heal the wound.

'Get away from him! He is mine!'

Xarash begins to fear that his victory has been vanquished. Grabbing a dagger from one of the warriors on the front line, he throws it at Toraq in desperation, only to watch as it bounces off him just like before and landing on the ground. An untroubled Toraq stands as he completes his healing and holds a hand out for

Solus. His near-fatal axe wound has been completely sealed. Still a little woozy from the blood loss, he takes the furry hand of the Matoh and is pulled up to his feet.

'No! What have you done?' bellows Xarash. 'He should be dead! Dead to my hand!'

'It would seem now isn't my time,' speaks Solus, slightly slurred but gathering strength all the while.

Xarash and the rest of his minions stand in silence as they watch Solus bend down to the ground and retrieve his father's sword. He breathes deeply, his nostrils flair, and his brow narrows as the eyes of the emperor look menacingly at the general. Adrenaline pumps. Toraq steps back and retreats behind the wall, smiling as he sees that the situation is returning to normal.

'Now for my retribution,' speaks Solus in a threatening voice, his focus entirely upon his mortal enemy.

Still in shock about what has transpired Xarash is caught entirely off-guard as Solus roars with fierce energy and charges the leader of the Kaidis with sword readied. In what seems like a microsecond for the stunned invaders, with perfect execution, the blade of his sword swings with one hand in a horizontal slice, aiming directly for the exposed head of the general. With an air-breaking slice, metal strikes its target, the strong and sharp blade piercing the skin of Xarash's neck, sluicing through the muscle, the spinal cord, and out the other side — completing a clean decapitation of King General Xarash IV. The head flies up into the air and the blood-spurting body crashes to the ground under the weight of the armour.

His head is caught by a member of the First Division, much to the warrior's surprise. He isn't prepared to make an assessment of the situation as he stands there with the head of his desired leader in his hands. Panic instils into the warriors, perhaps uncharacteristically, but more of a natural reaction. Years of military training forgotten in an instant as their world crashes down upon them.

'Retreat! Fall back!'

Solus drops his sword to the ground, panting furiously and eventually collapses as he watches the remaining Kaidis flee south towards the Flatlands; the one that caught the head of Xarash leading the charge. Levak comes to the aid of his adopted leader, picking him up with his Kaidis-born strength and carrying Solus back into the city.

Toraq peers from around the wall after seeing what Solus was able to achieve — his interception to give Solus a second chance is absolutely interference and is against the rules of the Tournament, as it has led to a direct result of the death of Xarash. He cannot believe that Solus performed such an act in a weakened state, and decides he should retreat back to his cart.

As the battlefield empties, the headless body of Xarash lies chest down on the ground. All the respect and honour that the former King General earned in his forty years as leader draining away into the mud.

* * * *

Overlooking the city of Thoridon is the wide mountain ranges of Iskap. It features many spectacular peaks, jagged rocks formed by distant volcanoes and other earth formations a very long time ago. This most northern part of the world is the single source of water, where the snow and ice that dominate the landscape constantly melt over time, only to be replenished by blizzards and powerful snowstorms at regular intervals.

Iskap is in complete contrast to the Sulphur Deserts to the south — the temperature is opposite, the landscape much more difficult to traverse. But Mount Sindre is the only partially active volcano left as the ranges of Iskap are long dormant. However, the arctic conditions are not entirely hostile to life. Ancient caves and tunnels persist throughout, offering plenty of shelter from the elements. Inside these, ice is in abundance with caverns lower down offering a slightly warmer atmosphere where water exists and limited plant life grows — the native homeland for the Matoh.

It is now mid-afternoon following the events of the night. Toraq and Eko fled from Thoridon, leaving their waggon behind at the eastern gate and heading in the direction of Iskap. With the healing of Solus leading to a direct intervention of affairs between the Shaler and the Kaidis, he thought it would be best to lie low and avoid any kind of unwanted attention. Using the superior speed empowered to the both of them, they are able to reach the foothills of Iskap in quick time.

The huge river of Still itself starts in these foothills and is massively broad with long waterfalls that deliver vast quantities of fresh, pure water direct from its source and flowing south. To the untrained eye, these foothills do not provide any access to the peaks — without any kind of climbing ability this would be the case, but the Matoh are natural terrain negotiators. Toraq is able to utilise this by propelling over the rugged ground climbing higher and higher with relative ease.

Progressively cooler air and increasing winds make themselves more prevalent as the two Matoh ascend further. Toraq knows exactly where he is going as the alpine trees begin to disappear. Eventually, the snow makes itself known, it being increasingly piled high to the point that they are truly in the mountains.

Upon reaching a plateau, Toraq turns around as snow is danced around behind him by the variable icy winds. The sunlight of Ramor beams over the entire landscape and he can see the partially destroyed city of Thoridon, the forests of Mistwood, the Flatlands, the distant canyons of Wodar Drop, and a silhouette of Mount Sindre providing a backdrop. It is a breath-taking vista which also provides the perfect vantage point to observe from: for this is Toraq's current agenda, to watch and wait for something to happen. He knows exactly what to wait for, however — the calling of a Lightbearer, confident that Samal will eventually perform the ritual with the ever-inquisitive nature of the Doctor a guarantee of that assurance.

To the left of the plateau on which he stands is an entrance to one of the many caves that adorn the mountainous landscape. As Toraq looks out over the world, Eko takes the opportunity to explore the cave. Families of Matoh will typically stay close to a particular cave which they would call home — meaning many of the caverns remain uninhabited or unexplored.

This cave provides a personal refuge for the Lightbearer and his companion allowing them to call it their home, even though Toraq's true home is the Synthetic Domain. But as Toraq has been on the Arena of Pri for considerable time now, that home seems so distant and he has developed a great deal of sentiment for the world and the people within it, regardless of what side they are on.

His homely cave does not offer much. There are no comforts and the variable wind whistles past the cave entrance, but there are a few things that can be attributed to Toraq's exploits. A little bit of a hoarder, there are a few trinkets and oddities that Toraq has collected. A small wooden box is positioned in a darkened corner of the cave — it contains writing implements, ink and parchment. These tools, obtained by him over time from Shaler traders were used to create the anonymous document handed to Ferlor – what he thought to be part of the Shaler's Twilight Compendium, and many more pieces of influential information fed to them.

There are also seeds dotted around the cave, prevented from growing in the harsh climate, but are the same as the ones required for the synthesis of the Bloodrage as Toraq indirectly influenced its formulation through Kaidan.

Perhaps the most surprising objects are some dated white robes — these are as old as Toraq's original host body, belonging to the curious Shaler student that called Toraq into the Arena all those years ago, a feat plotted by Uriro before him.

Toraq eventually returns to the cave as well after gazing out over the landscape in quiet contemplation with snowflakes blown into his fur while he stood. All he can do now is watch and wait for the inevitable.

* * * *

'Enough of this idiocy!' pants Volar of the First Division, still carrying a visibly shaken Samal over his shoulder. They have crossed the Flatlands from the south of Thoridon and the warrior is becoming tired, losing his stamina and needing a break.

He comes to a stop just as the roadway rises up a small embankment that leads to the Crossroads, lowering his shoulder and Samal pushes himself off to stand on his own feet. As he does, Volar just continues falling and collapses on the ground with a satisfied grunt to lie on his chest — as much as his uncomfortable armour will allow him to, anyway. Sighing happily, he revels in the moment that he can take a short rest.

'Get up, you brute,' says Samal unimpressed, still clutching onto the urn containing the Urtica seeds. He gives a small kick to the heap on the ground to emphasise his dismay. Volar just grunts again and bats away in the air in the general direction of Samal, suggesting he wants to be left alone for a short while.

'We have to keep moving, this will not wait!'

No matter how much he protests, the warrior is refusing to move. Samal sighs in contempt and turns around. If this delay was not enough for him, he realises that the urn he carries has become very heavy, especially for someone who is not as strong as his other kin. He tries carrying it with one arm, and then the other, but its weight seems to double as he does that.

His dilemma is that he doesn't want to ditch the urn because it contains thousands of seeds. Then it dawns on him — he doesn't need the urn, but he does need its contents, and also the fact he doesn't need all the seeds since he simply wants to experiment first and learn how the synthesis works. A smile lights up on his face as he sees the cenotaph central to the Crossroads.

Being slightly tired from all that bouncing around on the shoulder of his carrier, he strains a little as he approaches the decaying tower. The amount of rusted armour and weaponry that stands here all piled up has persisted for many years. Even if it is war, there is still respect for the dead — no-one removes anything from the memorial and the amount of metal that rests here is perpetual.

To Samal, the monument provides an excellent opportunity to hide something. If nobody knew, nobody would know to look. He places the urn on the ground and notices a dock leaf plant nearby. Taking a handful of seeds from the urn, he wraps them up inside a large leaf creating a small package and places it in his bag, along with the other documents stolen from the Shaler's Library. Carefully, he slides the urn across the ground into a small opening underneath the rusting armour, pushing it far enough so it couldn't be seen without someone knowing what to look for.

He dusts his hands off with a job well done and hears a clattering of metal from behind him. It is Volar who has picked himself off the ground and regained enough strength to continue heading towards the Stronghold. Samal turns to see him approach.

'Did you enjoy your time on the ground?' smiles Samal.

'I heard shouting carried by the wind across the Flatlands,' Volar replies, concern showing on his expression.

'What sort of shouting?'

'I couldn't hear anything specific but it was definitely Kaidis.'

'Are you sure? But it seemed Xarash had everything under control.'

Samal looks around the warrior in the direction of the Flatlands. Under the afternoon sunlight, the entire landscape is brilliantly illuminated and the visibility is good enough to see Thoridon's walls in the distance. Reflected in the light, however, Samal can make out something that seems to shine and appears to be moving in their direction.

'Is that armour?' he asks, pointing, with Volar turning to look for himself.

'It would seem so.'

'Well, whatever happened, I don't want those brutes getting in the way of my research. We should head to Wodar Drop to see if we can secure faster transport to the Stronghold.'

'I agree. What happened to the urn?' he asks, glancing around the immediate area.

'Never mind that,' Samal replies, as he retrieves his cane from his bag. 'Let us continue south.'

'But what about the seeds?'

'They're in my bag. Come on, let's go,' he says, as he starts to walk off to the southern path, leading to the canyon.

'Wait,' Volar grunts.

Samal stops in his tracks, sighing, but doesn't turn to face Volar. Slightly overcome, the warrior undoes a series of chains and straps around his chest, loosening part of his armoured plating. He pulls on the top of his armour, removing it, exposing his bare, yellow-pigmented shoulders. In a moment of sentiment, he places the armour on top of other pieces of armour that make up the cenotaph. Taking a step back, he bows his head.

'For my fallen brothers,' he says, under his breath.

Interested in the clattering of metal, Samal turns to see what all the fuss is about. He sees Volar standing there at the memorial and is surprised by the emotion from a brutish warrior. Perhaps he is not as much as a brute than he originally assumed.

'Are you done?' questions Samal impatiently, but not sounding as abrasive as he could.

'Yes, yes,' shrugs Volar, moving to overtake Samal in the direction of Wodar Drop.

They start to walk down the path that leads alongside the river. As they leave the area of the Crossroads, the greener pastures of Shaler territory make themselves known. With the river itself varying in width and depth as they amble along, it is a serene and idyllic atmosphere. This is a complete change to what Kaidis life in the Stronghold is like. The rolling blue skies, the green fields, flowers around the river, fresh water running freely alongside them — for two emotionally charged Kaidis it gives them time to consider their predicament.

'Can we drop this ridiculous silence we seem to have imposed on ourselves?' asks Samal as they walk along, his cane tapping on the stony ground.

'I suppose,' replies Volar. 'Not that there's much to talk about.'

'Oh, but I think there is, and you saying that just proves it further.'

'What do you mean?'

'Come on! You are in the First Division. A highly talented warrior! You should be hurling abuse at me — a member of the Doctors Division — threatening me with your sword.'

'You don't pose any threat to me.'

Samal raises a fist to the sky in frustration.

'That is just my point — why don't I? The rest of your rabble wouldn't hesitate to yell something obscene at me, thinking I was a Shaler. But here you are, actually willing to assist me.'

'Yeah, but I'm not like them. I have my reasons.'

'Don't keep me in suspense!'

Volar sighs, not really wanting to surrender all of his secrets. No-one has actually cared to ask him before — he is a little unprepared.

'I don't know where to begin,' he says, looking at Samal whose expression suggests he really does want to know. 'Why do you care so much that I might be... different?'

'I am simply intrigued into why you haven't run me through yet, after all we've been through.'

'Have you ever wondered if there is more to this... all of this?' Volar questions, pointing around randomly.

Samal isn't really too sure what he means. After some hesitation, Volar can see that he doesn't understand and sighs in frustration.

'You're just like the rest of them,' he says.

'No, hold on,' protests Samal. 'What do you mean by "this"?'

'I don't know — everything, I guess. It seems like there is more to our existence — more than constantly fighting the Shaler. You must have seen something?'

The Doctor narrows his brow as he begins to understand what he is talking about. He supposes that it could be possible for at least one warrior in the fighting divisions to have ideas anything other than what they are born to do. A warrior capable of independent thought — he'd never have dreamt to see one in the flesh.

With Samal's recently acquired knowledge about the Lightbearers and the instructions required to perform the Necrocircle ritual, he is completely aware of an "extra" to their existence — what Volar seems to be alluding toward. Volar looks at the Doctor and can see it written all over his face.

'There is something, isn't there?' Volar asks. 'Have you seen it?'

'I can't tell you anything,' says Samal, defending what he knows.

'Curious — can't or won't?'

'All will be revealed soon enough.'

'Now you are the one talking in riddles,' grunts Volar.

'It is a skill I have recently picked up,' says Samal, chuckling to himself, remembering how Toraq spoke to him on the waggon.

Volar becomes annoyed by this denial, but has developed a degree of trust for the Doctor. He can understand that he does know something, but for whatever reason — be it for his own good, or simply pulling rank — he has to appreciate that he doesn't want to reveal the whole story.

'Whatever,' he sighs. 'I guess you have this all figured out.'

They continue down the road for a short while with the landscape beginning to change and the river quickening its pace. As the air turns much warmer, the large barricade and tall gates that lead into the barracks of Wodar Drop make themselves apparent. Bright fires light the entrance with the gates firmly closed and no signs of any patrols around the parameter.

Volar marches up to the gate and bangs on it and eventually a guard opens an eye slit, sees who stands there and opens the gate, allowing the two inside. They make their way across the courtyard and into the administration building seeking someone to authorise their need for a speedy journey to the Stronghold.

# Chapter Seventeen

## Revelation

Awoken to the sound of birdsong from a window, Solus opens his eyes. He lays upon his luxurious bed inside the emperor's house, draped in white sheets, his head resting on soft pillows. The scene is in complete contrast to his last memory from a few hours ago. He remembers a fight, outside of the city, severely outnumbered against what he presumes where Kaidis warriors, but has no absolute memory of what happened. The emperor's eyes take a moment to adjust to his surroundings and he gently moves underneath the bed covers.

His movement draws the attention of Avornia who sits at the side of his bed, busying herself with some embroidery. She is a little startled to see her son awaken so quickly after what appears to her as an incredible ordeal. She stands up from her wooden chair and places her textile working on a side table, looking at Solus with an expression of sympathy. Placing a warming hand on his forehead to make herself aware to him, she smiles as he looks at her.

But he doesn't return the gesture. Instead, he looks coldly at her as if his eyes were to look through her. He then closes his eyes and tries to think about what happened previously, knowing that something is not right: the mind of the emperor goes around in circles, desperately trying to understand the situation. The thoughts flow for what seems like hours but only a few seconds pass as Avornia removes her hand and Solus' eyes open wide as she does so.

In the hours that have past, Levak rescued him after his fight with Xarash. Solus passed out overcome with exhaustion and the leader of the Warlock Council carried him through the battered streets of Thoridon, weaving over the bodies and armour that litter them, through the Quadrangle and up to the residence of the emperor. Avornia was in the house, hiding from the chance of a Kaidis invasion. Shocked to find her only son being carried inside by the burly outsider, Levak took him to the bedroom under her worried insistence.

Still unconscious, Solus was gently laid down upon the bed and Avornia removed the damaged ceremonial armour from his chest, a hole ripped right through its side from Xarash's fatal axe blow. They paused for a moment to look at their emperor, lost in a dream. The Warlock told Avornia what happened, how he was the one that saved the city from total destruction and delivered the crushing defeat to the leader of the Kaidis. She doesn't believe the story at first, but as Levak reveals that Toraq seemed to revive him, she remembers what the Lightbearer did in the garden. With this sketchy detail in mind, she sat down on the chair and waited for him to recover, fully believing that he would do so if Toraq was involved.

With his reopened eyes looking at her face, she sees that this is the case and he is making a recovery. He begins to push himself up to sit in the bed, straining slightly as his body is still battered and weary, even if the damage caused by Xarash's mighty axe has miraculously healed, leaving only a bite-shaped scar on his skin.

He turns his head to look directly in front of him, still without saying a word. More questions race through his head as he begins to recall some detail. Noticing his damaged armour on the sideboard, he wonders if it is true. To his mother's surprise, he pulls on the sheets covering him, revealing his bare, hairless chest. He places a hand on his side and feels below his ribs — there is nothing, no wound. How can this be?

'I died out there,' he flatly remarks, turning to his mother.

Avornia moves to sit down beside him on the bed, taking his hand from his side.

'But you are not. You are right here, with me — the saviour of the Shaler.'

He looks at her with cold eyes once again.

'"Saviour" you say? No, there is no salvation. I did not win. There is no victory. Only remorse.'

'You defeated Xarash with your own sword,' she says. 'How is that not a victory?'

It all comes back to him. The way Xarash looked at him as he drove his axe deep into his side. The smile on his face; the piercing dark eyes; the absolute hatred.

'I remember now. He said I was pathetic,' Solus replies. 'Pathetic, just like father. Why was I so blind?'

'I'm not sure I understand.'

'I do — I can see everything so clearly.'

After realising there are voices in the bedroom, Levak enters to see Solus sitting up in bed. This is an unusual situation for the defected Kaidis to be in — on the one hand, he is supposed to despise the leader of the Shaler, but on the other, even if who he truly is has yet to be revealed to anyone, he acknowledges that the Shaler have at least given him a chance. From the shadowy visage of his disguised facial features, a wry smile makes itself shown. Watching him enter, Solus also remembers another detail of recent history — one that was easily overlooked in the heat of the moment, but such a memory screams out to the emperor.

'You are awake,' recognises Levak in a thankful manner.

'That may be the case,' replies Solus. 'But you, Levak, are dead to me. I remember our problem at the Library. That Kaidis Doctor who was stealing artefacts — he knew who you were.'

To the accusation, the Warlock pauses for a moment. He, too, remembers when Samal seemed to recognise his voice — an attribute, which no matter how much the visible appearance is covered, cannot be hidden. Avornia isn't really too sure what to make of the situation between the two men, and her surprised expression switches between them, waiting for the next move. A bird tweets outside the window, piercing the awkward silence.

'Perhaps it is time to be honest, Solus,' sighs Levak.

He realises that such a difficult and harsh appearance would be next to impossible to keep up forever, believing that recent engagements and his sweeping success of introducing defence to the Shaler should be enough to allow him to reveal his true self to the emperor. Hiding for so long is not only becoming tiresome, but it is wholly dishonest to himself, let alone the others that trust in him.

But there is that twinge — he is still through-and-through Kaidis. His education and indoctrination as a child and younger Doctor are hard for him to entirely ignore. The Shaler are still the enemy to him, but ever since Ferlor was happy to take him in as his mentor, that perception has been rapidly changing while he has been in their company.

Removing a scarf and eventually a long cowl covering his head, his Kaidis face is revealed to Solus and Avornia. He is a similar age to Doctor Samal — the two would have been in the Third Division at the same time — but his Bloodrage affliction is much more developed allowing him more strength, despite still being a Doctor. As the yellow-spotted face and bald head become recognisable features of the Kaidis to Solus, he becomes alarmed.

'You are Kaidis? In my home?' he yells.

'Please, Solus, calm down,' protests Levak.

'Don't tell me to calm down! Your kind killed my father in the same room that you stand!'

Avornia's emotions also begin to run wild as she has flashbacks to the time when a young Xarash IV plunged a dagger into her husband. Anger flows over her as she doesn't want the same to happen to her recovering son, she reaches for the nearest crafted pot and lunges to smash it over Levak's head. As it cracks down on his cranium, he stumbles momentarily before the Bloodrage starts to pump in his veins from the aggravation.

'You murderous bastard!' she shrieks.

'I am not here to fight you,' Levak cries, this time avoiding another attack. 'I am not working for the Kaidis any longer! Ferlor listened to me, at least give me a chance!'

'I never trusted Ferlor either,' responds Solus. 'How do I know that you two were not plotting my downfall?'

'If that was the case, why did I not leave you to die?'

'Perhaps I am more valuable to you alive!'

'But you don't understand,' protests Levak. 'I wanted to leave the Kaidis. I have defected from the Doctors Division. They wouldn't give me a chance to prove myself.'

Solus stands from the bed, although he staggers slightly, still weak from the blood loss. The stress becomes too much for him, even though he is determined to skewer the Kaidis on the end of his father's sword, he doesn't have the physical capacity to do so and instead collapses on the floor in a daze. Levak jumps to his aid while Avornia weeps, traumatised by the revelation.

'Get away from me!' mutters Solus, groggily.

'I am here because I want to help the Shaler,' says Levak as he collects a disabled Solus from the floor, returning him to the bed. 'If it wasn't for Ferlor or the Warlocks that I have personally overseen, none of us would be here.'

'But why? The Kaidis are always defeating us,' sighs Solus.

'Victory and defeat are relative, Solus. There is so much more than these devastating quarrels. I could not explain this to my own kind, but Ferlor understood this. Despite what he may have done in the past, I believe his intentions were beyond what he could communicate himself. He wanted to end the wars between our peoples. It is hard to remember that you and I were once one.'

Solus mutters as he begins to pass out again, but he thinks there is a degree of weight to what Levak says, even though he is unable to articulate his feelings. Avornia dries her face after hearing what was said, and as he steps away from her son, she can see that Levak has no intent to cause harm to the family.

'Maybe we do share a common ground,' she says. 'We, as a people, do not want these wars, yet your kind insists.'

'Believe me, Avornia,' nods Levak. 'I do not want to play these games. Our affliction is an unfortunate accident; we can do much more if we were to work together.'

She apologises for her overhand reaction, but Levak realised it was going to happen. They retire to the front of the house, deciding to give time for Solus to recover, as Avornia is interested in hearing more of what the Warlock has to suggest. What may have been an uncomfortable relationship initially begins to bloom from the ideals the unlikely pairing increasingly share.

❋ ❋ ❋ ❋

A single Knoria arrives at the Stronghold with its sail being lowered in order to decrease its speed. The vehicle not only carries a small shipment of water barrels, but also Doctor Samal with his sympathetic protector Volar of the First Division. It took some convincing, what with the stunt Barel pulled before, but they managed to persuade Karzol at Wodar Drop that their reasoning was a matter of utmost importance for the supremacy of the Kaidis. It is not every day an opportunity comes along to develop the Bloodrage.

However, their arrival is not greeted with a warm welcome. Even though Doctor Samal is high up in the chain of command, being right-hand to Xarash, his avoidance of him before didn't leave the best of impressions. As the pair disembarks from the Knoria as it comes to a stop in the courtyard, workers from the Engineers Division see who it is and sneer or mutter under their breath making disparaging comments. Samal is entirely oblivious to this. There is only one thing on his mind: the research and possible development into the Bloodrage, the first time since it was originally created.

Despite the events that transpired at Thoridon, the Stronghold is yet to receive the news that their king is dead, and the numbers of Kaidis have been reduced significantly following his assault upon the city. Because of this, the courtyard is a lot more quiet than usual. There is an unusual atmosphere as the ones that remain are acutely aware that the leader and over three-quarters of the armies are away on a mission, under his command. Workers still operate the forges, the water deliveries still arrive — the day-to-day hasn't changed. But without the marching lines and busyness of the Divisions, everything seems more insignificant.

Immediately as his feet and his cane touch the well-trodden hard-packed sands that make up the courtyard, Samal heads in the direction of his laboratory, clutching his shoulder bag with his other hand. He has never been so determined to try and make sense of the Bloodrage — the Urtica seeds and pilfered manuscripts from the Shaler's Library should provide great food for thought. But it is not just these artefacts which drive him — his deep and incredibly insightful conversations with Toraq are also clear in his mind.

Feeling uncomfortable, Volar moves to catch up with the Doctor. He can feel the eyes of others watching him. With large numbers of the fighting forces away from the Stronghold, he is one of the few First Division on site. Volar is not a warrior that prefers to lead, despite his seniority, so he sides up with Samal as if to give the impression he is busy. Grunts of disapproval make themselves known from the lower ranks as they see him do so.

With no Third Division grunt standing outside the Doctors Division laboratory, Samal bursts the two sturdy doors open, with dust from the sand blown against them falling to the ground as they project forward. To his relief it would appear that anyone who shouldn't be inside hasn't taken the opportunity to poke around.

Samal insists that someone stands outside as he doesn't trust anyone outside his organisation in fear that they would simply trash the place. Too much work and history resides inside for that to happen. With him and Volar safely inside, he closes the doors — Samal does not want any unnecessary disturbance.

He takes a moment to look around; making sure everything is as it was. Silence descends.

'Good,' Samal says to himself.

'What is?' asks Volar, not realising he wasn't being spoken to.

As such, Samal doesn't really hear the question. With a smile on his face, he moves over to his large table, central in the front of the lab. As its contents become visible to him, he is reminded of all his previous work — all these new ideas introduced by Toraq makes him consider that his prior research into Bloodrage advancement becomes a lot more trivial. Despite the desk being covered in papers, books, bottles and other equipment, he manages to find a spot to place his bag down and gently opens it.

Placing the Urtica seeds still wrapped up in a withered leaf gently down on the desk, he then lifts up the bag and begins to shake out the papers inside. Sitting down on his small stool, he begins to read each one very carefully, completely absorbing himself and making absolutely no reaction to Volar who still stands at the door, not entirely sure what to do with himself.

Volar is appreciative for what the Doctor is trying to do, but he didn't risk life and limb for the opportunity to watch someone read. He uncomfortably moves from the door, feeling like a spare part, towards the side wall on his left. Attached to it is a makeshift noticeboard, with notes and scribbles affixed to it, all hastily written and unlikely to make any sense to anyone other than their author, although going by the fading on some of the parchments, perhaps the author himself would fail to recall their purpose as well.

Turning away from the wall, he sees Samal still intently studying the stolen documents. The expression on his face is one that shows great interest in what he is reading. Just as Volar is about to speak, he is immediately interrupted as Samal jolts himself up from the stool, knocking it back slightly, making a short scraping noise as it does, shattering the silence. This sudden frenzy of activity takes Volar completely by surprise, breaking his train of thought.

In contrast to Volar's boredom, Samal is full of energy and he steps around his desk looking for a mortar and pestle, knocking over empty bottles and small piles of paper. Eventually finding his tools, he quickly returns to his stool. Opening the leaf containing the Urtica seeds, he pours them into the bowl. With Volar watching closely, the Doctor begins grinding down the seeds. As they have been in storage for years, the shells have become quite hard and Samal is frustrated that his weak efforts prove futile.

Slumping in his stool with a sigh, he realises that he is not as young as he used to be. Then he looks up and sees the strong warrior standing there.

'Make yourself useful,' he suggests to Volar.

'What are you trying to do?' he replies, moving over to Samal.

'I want you to crush these seeds as hard as you can.'

'Why?'

'Just do it!'

Feeling a little demoralised to be tasked with something so mundane — not really the work of a warrior — he grudgingly takes the mortar from the Doctor, holding the pestle in his other hand. He starts to stab the pestle into the container, much to the alarm of Samal.

'No, stop, you'll break everything!'

Volar looks up at Samal, who snatches the device from him and places the bowl on the table.

'Keep this on the desk and grind the seeds; roll the pestle over them. You're not trying to kill someone,' advises the Doctor.

The warrior grunts, and taking the advice, applies a gentle but firm rolling to the seeds. He gets encouragements from Samal as he does so, making him speed up and apply more pressure, but still rolling, working to a rhythm. Eventually, the hardened shells crack and Samal smiles with glee. His smiles are reduced as Volar grinds because the expected results are not forthcoming.

'Stop!' he commands, slightly angrily.

Taking the mortar away from Volar — who gives him an uncomfortable look — Samal looks more closely at the crushed seeds. They are supposed to explode into a liquefied poison, but there is no liquid — only a greenish powder and a pungent smell.

'No, this can't be,' exclaims Samal.

He stands up from his stool in a panic and looks around for a container of water. Finding some, he pours it over the dried powder in a hope that it will become liquid, but his dismay turns to anger as the water refuses to combine with the substance.

'What is wrong with you?' questions Volar.

'The seeds have dried up! They are completely useless!'

The intense heat of the Sulphur Deserts is not a natural environment for the organisms. Even though they were in storage at the Synth Institute for many years, this was actually a perfect location to preserve them, being cold, dark and untouched. The transition to the hostile lands of the Kaidis has seen them perish.

'So what?' grunts the warrior. 'All that effort to get them was wasted? I helped you for nothing?'

'Well, not entirely for nothing,' Samal considers. 'Merely a setback.'

'I should fucking kill you now!' shouts Volar.

'But you won't. You know what that will do to you.'

The warrior of the First Division roars angrily and strides across to the doors, almost bashing them down as he returns outside to the courtyard in a rage. Samal shrugs at the reaction, as it is clear to him that Volar fails to realise that their breach into Thoridon was not entirely fruitless — the urn containing the seeds would still be hidden at the Crossroads, but instead of bringing them back to the Stronghold, a different tactic will be needed.

'Rakos, come here,' yells Samal, knowing that the boy of Xarash would be lurking at the back. His assumption is realised as the heir to the throne makes his appearance.

'What is it?' he asks.

'Despite this upset, I can still perform additional research based on what I now know. But to do this, I need your strength since it seems the First Division has deserted me.'

He stands up from his stool, moves to close the doors left open by Volar and turns around, pointing to his table.

'I need you to push my table over towards the nearest wall,' Samal instructs, the smile returning to his face and motioning to the blank eastern wall.

'You expect me, son of the king, to do physical labour for you?'

'Don't pull rank with me, boy; after all you have been privileged to. My work is for the good of the Kingdom — surely out of everyone you would be the one to understand that.'

With a growl, Rakos begins to push on the edge of the desk, sliding it across the floor towards the wall. As it moves, its contents bounce up and down, rattling and making general clattering noises, but Samal is unperturbed — he is too much in thought about what he plans to do next. The desk comes to a stop as Rakos decides it cannot be moved any further and also that he can't take any more of the noise. Samal casually picks up his stool and moves it himself, nodding his head as he begins to make conclusions, sitting down at the desk and picking up more papers, this time with ideas he has written in the past.

As his hearing begins to return to Rakos, he notices a roaring sound coming from outside over the winds, with Samal blissfully unaware. Intrigued, he opens the doors and stands outside, turning in the direction of the northern track that leads to Outpost Ora. In the distance, he can see sand being kicked up as two Knorias approach, travelling at considerable speed. As they move closer, Rakos can see the royal insignia on their sides — the king's personal vehicle is returning.

'Father is inbound!' he shouts back into the laboratory, trying to get the attention of Samal who looks up briefly to nod and then returns to his reading, not really bothered. Deciding to leave the Doctor to his work, he pulls the doors closed and moves to greet the incoming, entirely unaware of the situation.

* * * *

As the leading royal vehicle comes to a stop just inside the courtyard outside the Stronghold, a sense of pride waves over the workers that tend to their duties — each one interrupting themselves and turning to face the Knoria with its easily identifiable insignia on its bow. But the door on its side — which would normally be opened as soon as the vehicle had arrived — remains closed, and this delay in the arrival of who everyone expects is unexpected.

Leading the curious is Volar who approaches the Knoria. He looks up to the driver that sits above who just shakes his head back at him without making comment. Narrowing his brow, Volar becomes slightly concerned, moving to the side door. Pulling on its handle, it slides open and he peers inside wondering why the Divisions aren't supporting their king with the unnecessary delay.

Sitting on the bench inside is a single warrior from the First Division, one that is unfamiliar to Volar at first glance. As he looks at him, initially about to hurl abuse at the impostor, his attitude rapidly changes as he sees the warrior gazing into nothing with tears in his eyes. A highly uncharacteristic state for one Kaidis to be in, and this alone is what shocks Volar.

Tracking his vision down, he sees that the light armour of Captain Selak is slightly covered in dried blood and eventually noticing the severed head of Xarash IV resting in his lap. How Selak, captain of Ora, came into possession of the head is attributed to the original warrior that caught the head of their leader as it flew through the air. After their subsequent retreat from the front of Thoridon, this lone warrior knew what he had to do. In a panic, fuelled by incredible emotion towards the devotion of his leader, he simply ran from the battlefield through the Flatlands, past the Crossroads and down to Outpost Ora.

It was here that Selak was introduced to the proof of his highly desired leader's demise. At first, raging questions were thrown towards the bearer of grizzly news. Details that Emperor Solus himself was the most responsible for delivering the final blow were first dismissed by an emotional Selak. But his attitude quickly changed as it was revealed that Toraq was also involved and instrumental in the downfall of Xarash. With this, Selak's face fell at the revelation — his friend for so many years now officially turned against his own kind, all the trust and companionship shared seemingly for nothing and becoming meaningless. Deciding it was his duty to take the responsibility of delivering the news to the Stronghold, Selak took the head and ordered the king's Knoria to take him to meet with the orphaned son. And this is where he sits, staring at the side of the vehicle, Xarash's head in his hands and a dumbfounded Volar looking straight at him.

'I sometimes wonder what all the point of this is,' says Selak. 'Why do we do what we do? Why do we have to fight against what we call the enemy? When, in the end, all we are doing is destroying ourselves.'

Volar shuffles in his stance, slightly uncomfortable about the words the captain speaks. It wasn't what he wanted to hear; far more interested in what actually happened to Xarash, but the words strike a chord in the mind of the First Division.

'I believe it is what we're born to do,' he responds. 'We are here to fight, because that is what we are told to do, whatever the consequences.'

'But there is no end. It will never end. Defeat after defeat. It is as if everything is against us. And this is the result!'

He holds up the head of Xarash, it now rapidly drying and decaying under the heat from the deserts and giving off a morbid smell. The entire colour has drained from his face — a frozen expression of blankness being quite the memorable image, one that Volar was not ready to accept so plainly. He steps out from the Knoria, trying not to vomit from both the physical death and also the mental stress brought on by the situation.

The second Knoria arrives from behind — this time the door on the side is flung wide open immediately as expected, and the warriors that were at the side of Xarash after his execution disembark. They arrive to a surreal scene in the courtyard, where the engineers and others stand around wondering why Xarash has yet to make a celebratory appearance.

Rakos moves closer to the vehicles and approaches Volar who stands at the side, collecting his thoughts. Volar prevents the teenager from going any further, holding him back. He begins to struggle, but eventually relents as the stronger warrior is clearly not going to let him past.

'Where is my father?' he queries.

Volar takes a sharp inhalation before responding.

'He has been defeated, Rakos.'

This time, without contest from Volar, he moves inside the Knoria and sees for himself the proof. Selak looks directly at him.

'Cherish this moment, young Kaidis,' says Selak as he hands the head of Xarash to him. 'From now on, everything is your responsibility.'

Slightly reluctant at first to take the severed head, Rakos rapidly changes his approach to the situation as he realises what Selak is saying. With the death of his father and being heir to the throne, everything that belongs to the Kaidis is now his. In a moment, he makes a very conscience decision — with the head in hand and displaying no visible emotion, he steps outside and holds it above his own so all in the courtyard can see. Grunts of surprise resound, but Rakos is quick to dismiss them.

'My father has fallen on the battlefield,' he shouts across the courtyard, his voice not having the same deepness as Xarash, but still proves to be an affective orator. 'Let it be known that I fully intend to replace his leadership. I declare myself as King Rakos, and assume command of the Divisions.'

His decree is met with silence. For the son of Xarash has never made himself public, choosing to spend most of his time buried in the writings kept by the Doctors Division. Xarash has also publicly acknowledged in conversation of his own disdain for his son to members of the Divisions, never proud that he hasn't displayed any enthusiasm for following in his militaristic footsteps. And this fact has passed around as gossip, with most in the courtyard aware of this detail, making it difficult for them to accept Rakos as their leader, doubting whether or not he would continue Xarash's direction.

The new king is surprised of the lack of reaction and not aware of the reasons. Before he has a chance to consider the situation, the warriors from the second Knoria lunge their way towards Rakos, the Bloodrage obviously taking control. One of them picks up the slightly immature rightful leader of the Kaidis with one hand and holds his face toward his own.

'You are not my fucking king,' the Second Division grunt yells. 'You are worthless. You hold the head of our greatest leader with disrespect. How dare you make these suggestions?'

'That's enough!' commands Volar, intervening and punches the grunt back, forcing him to drop Rakos who lands on his feet while the grunt crashes to the ground. The new king retreats back to the Doctor's laboratory, dropping the head on the floor almost in fear. Volar collects it and passes it to a nearby engineer who stands near a forge and tells him to dispose of the head.

As Rakos approaches the doors of the lab, Samal also moves to them, agitated at them being left open by Rakos before, and also at the distinctive shouting which is disturbing his concentration. With the new king dashing past him, Samal looks out into the courtyard and is alarmed to see the group of warriors charging the doors, heading straight for him, roaring at the tops of their voices.

All he can do is stand there, watching as they approach — ferocity in their eyes, their weapons drawn and blood is what they seek. What is going on, he questions to himself. It dawns on him that they are looking directly at him: is it he that they wish to murder? What could he possibly have done? But Samal is approaching his senior years — he has achieved a lot, but not achieved what he desired. There is still so much work to do. He doesn't realise that the approaching horde see him as the instigator for the death of Xarash — if it wasn't for him, he wouldn't have led Solus to the front line outside Thoridon. They would have had more time to prepare for the arrival of the emperor, and perhaps done something about Toraq's intervention. Samal is the excuse they need.

While Samal is dumbstruck about the situation, Rakos turns to see the frozen Doctor who is lost in thought as the horde approach. Echoing his silent decisions from earlier, he thinks it is time to prove himself. He does place considerable value in what Samal knows and practises — in contrast to Xarash — and cannot afford for him to perish to the sword of a disrespectful rabble.

Moving to the doors, the young king is not one for physical combat. But based on his fascination of the Synth and what the Doctors Division is able to achieve, he holds his arms out and starts to talk in Ethereal. Even though he has not had much practice or opportunity to try his tireless research, his enunciation is natural — in front of his arms the local time and space becomes distorted, collecting the heat from the hot environment, forming rapid combustion. With one final utterance, fire blows directly across the courtyard, fuelled by the winds, and hits the warrior that picked him up. The intense heat is enough to burn through his Bloodrage fire resistance, and he screams in pain as he falls to the floor as a burnt carcass.

Rakos smiles at his use of the Synth and the remains of the charging horde cease their advance and fall back in fear that it could happen to them. Samal snaps out of his trance realising that his attackers have been repelled by an unlikely champion.

'What are you doing?' asks a surprised Samal.

'I cannot have you die just yet,' quips Rakos, mischievously. 'I have plans for you.'

'And what do you mean by that?'

Laughing, Rakos retreats inside. Shaking off the disbelief, Samal realises the smouldering corpse in the courtyard. An excellent opportunity, he considers, retrieving a container and a brush from his table. Moving to the body, he scrapes off the burnt flesh.

'You Doctors do some strange things,' comments Volar as he watches.

'Oh, the best is yet to come,' replies Samal, with a sheepish grin. Collecting enough of the remains, he returns to the lab and closes the doors behind him.

* * * *

Samal returns to the stool behind his long table and pauses for a moment, placing down the glass bottle containing the burnt matter from the warrior outside. He is visibly shaken and oblivious to the reasons behind why his own kind would suddenly charge for him. Because Xarash didn't like the Doctors, this sentiment would have filtered down among the fighting ranks in addition to what his actions led to at Thoridon.

'Are you alright?' questions Rakos, showing a degree of compassion for his fellow man, not necessarily fitting with the Kaidis way of life.

'Of course,' Samal sighs after a short delay, before bursting into energy. 'There is much to do. I suppose you would be king now?'

'Indeed. It is a little humbling.'

'Nonsense!' exclaims Samal, a smile returning to his face. 'I'm sure you have plenty to get on with, running the Stronghold. You do know how to do that, I assume?'

Rakos looks at the Doctor — he really has no idea. In a moment, the realisation of what being King of the Kaidis means suddenly hits home. It isn't just about having a fierce fighting force or clever Doctor's at his side — he has to make decisions and choices about things he has yet to understand. Most of his time has been spent learning from the archive that is in the laboratory that he stands; none of it is an actual real world experience.

This point was made clear to him outside — while he proudly declared his leadership, he had no idea what the reaction would be. The fact that no-one actually knows who he is, aside from being son of Xarash, and the hostility shown against him proved that it wasn't as easy as saying he was king. As he is only a teenager, opportunities to prove himself and make him worthy of the kingdom haven't been forthcoming, especially locking himself up with writings and papers of Kaidis Doctor's been and gone.

'Actually, no.'

'I see,' says Samal, stroking his chin. 'With that rabble, you wouldn't stand a chance.'

'I think I am beginning to realise that,' laments Rakos. 'I am not a warrior; I can't wield an axe like my father.'

He sighs, and the descent makes Samal consider his position. Since Toraq revealed to him many secrets, as he looks at the much younger king, his recent brush with death also brings realisation to him. Even with the great knowledge, he knows his natural time is short. He can't possibly make use of all the occult teachings, and indeed, he has already forgotten parts of what he was told. But there remains one key set of instructions as clear as if Toraq had just told him.

'It seems the odds are stacked against you,' Samal grins. 'But perhaps I can assist you this time.'

Rising from his stool, he takes the glass bottle and moves to the cleared area on the opposite wall. Samal's intention is to utilise this recovered space as the location for the Necrocircle ritual. The amount of corpse dust that he was able to collect doesn't amount to much, but there is enough to construct a smaller circle, and as he trickles the fragments over the floor, the circle becomes defined.

'What are you doing?' questions Rakos.

'Do you remember that stranger coming from Wodar Drop? The one that looked like a sergeant from one of the Divisions, but clearly had no idea what he was doing?'

'Not really, you know I'm hardly away from here.'

'A good point,' smiles Samal. 'But surely you must have heard or seen something outside in the courtyard?'

He narrows his brow as Rakos shakes his head, not following him at all.

'It would seem that you really don't stand a chance the moment you step outside of this lab.'

'What is your point?'

Samal begins to reveal the details behind Barel — his cyclonic demonstration inside the Royal Seat, the assault on Thoridon and his subsequent change of priorities. The Doctor is not really bothered about Barel's deceit; far more interested in the power that he was able to control. His manipulation of the Synth was a considerable eye-opener to Samal, and this alone is enough for him to admire the Lightbearer.

'Your reaction earlier was enough to convince me that you have great potential,' Samal concludes. 'Perhaps you would be interested in knowing more about how to control such power for yourself?'

As he proposes the question, some boisterous shouting becomes closer towards the closed doors of the lab. Samal turns to the table, taking a blank piece of paper and starts scribbling down some words on the page. Rakos stands at the door wondering what is going on outside, but the muffled voices are not clear.

'What do you say?' asks Samal, becoming slightly more urgent.

'You make it sound like I have no other option!' replies Rakos, moving away from the door.

Just as he does so, with a backdrop of some hearty laughter a series of loud knocks reverberate around the wooden doors. Samal makes the decision for the king and hands him his hastily written — but nonetheless clear — note. It is the phrase, in Ethereal, that he must communicate both vocally and in his mind to invoke the Necrocircle ritual. Although, when Toraq quoted him the phrase, there are differences from Ferlor's attempt.

'Stand in the circle and concentrate your control of the Synth,' Samal commands. 'Read the note as I have instructed and keep doing so, regardless of what happens.'

Rakos looks at him as if to question what he is suggesting.

'Do it now, boy!' yells Samal at him, now starting to get angry.

With the banging on the doors becoming more ferocious, the wood starts to splinter from the force of the weapons bashed against them. Not taking another moment to think about the situation, he steps into the circle and looks at the paper. He reads the words over a couple of times but it isn't immediately clear to him what they actually represent.

'Call them out!' shouts the Doctor as he sees Rakos trying to think. A portion of the doors breaks from the blunt force of an axe handle. Closing his eyes, the young king can see the words from the page in his mind and begins to recite the ritual.

"Through celestial transcendence; Into the Ethereal; I call to Gadno; Mother is honoured; Calling Gadno to me; Into the Ethereal; And out to Arena; For time awaits!"

As he repeats the Ethereal words over and over, the doors of the lab finally give way and a horde of Divisional warriors charge in, led by the same ones that came from Ora. They survey the scene, seeing Samal behind his desk watching and waiting for them to do something, but their attention is diverted towards Rakos.

'Fucking stop him!' yells the leader of the mob, and they begin to charge the king, rallying with their weapons.

But, with Rakos' excellent delivery and imagining of the Ethereal knowledge, he begins to experience the electricity that Ferlor realised over the grave of Emperor Vimlor. Jolts fire up and down his spine and he is transfixed by the curious sensations becoming more prominent. As he is finally paralysed from the arrival of the Lightbearer, only a few seconds have passed — the immediate area contained inside the circle of corpse dust explodes into light, with the merging of the Synthetic and the mortal complete.

The Kaidis warriors are blown back from the blast, right across the width of the laboratory, crashing into each other or the far wall with weapons scattered around. As they stumble in their armour to regain posture, Rakos' clothes have been ripped away and the now former Kaidis heir to the throne stands there naked — the eyes replaced with cyclonic voids with a dark green colouration. Coughing slightly as he adjusts to the possession, Gadno turns to look across at the Kaidis that clamber around.

Smiling, he cackles at the result.

'Finally! My time has now come, it would seem.'

Samal returns to his feet after hiding underneath the table and slightly relieved that he didn't perform the Necrocircle ritual for himself, but dismayed at the holes ripped into the wall and ceiling by the explosion.

'Rakos?' he queries, but immediately shakes his head in denial as he sees the eyes. 'No, you must be Gadno.'

'What the fuck is going on?' barks the leader of the horde. 'The boy still stands! Get him!'

Gadno scoffs as he realises that they refer to him. Placing his hands out as if to touch an invisible wall, he speaks in Ethereal, but there is no visible effect. Lowering his hands, Gadno smiles as he sees the warriors running towards him. They run through the invisible wall and immediately start to slow their pace and drop their weapons to the ground. They stop and turn to look at each other, confused by what they were doing moments before. No words are spoken, no gestures are made — they have no idea who they are or what they were doing, standing there making no reaction.

'Excellent, the first test has successfully passed,' he says to himself and walks forward, before stopping to see Samal looking at him from behind the table.

'Fascinating!' Samal enthuses. 'Tell me, what have you done?'

'Oh, this? Their memories have been suspended. They might start to remember things in a few hours. Or, they might not. And you are who?'

'Doctor Samal, leader of the—'

'I did not ask for your life story,' interrupts Gadno, walking around the group of confused warriors. 'Doctor, eh? That sounds important, but I am not sure. Oh, and I suppose I had better find some replacement clothing. I am starting to remember how this works.'

As he makes his way to the back of the laboratory, he finds a cloak similar to what Samal wears and places it over himself.

'Where is Toraq?' he questions.

'I don't know,' replies Samal. 'I haven't seen him since I escaped from Thoridon.'

'Ah, Thoridon. I remember that name. But curious — "escaped"? You mean we are not there right now?'

He tuts. In a similar situation to Barel, the emergence of the Kaidis is unfamiliar to him, but such details don't concern him. All he wants to do is get started with his chance at being deemed successful at this Arena, and he would prefer it was done properly — unlike Barel's accidental arrival — meaning he would need to seek Toraq.

Conscious of the appearance of Gadno, Samal rushes over to him as he looks out into the desert courtyard and nodding slightly for no discernible reason. Samal tries to speak to say that he probably shouldn't stand at the door but before he can breathe the first word, Gadno turns to him quickly with an expression of silence on his face.

'I am sure we will see each other in the near time,' the Lightbearer says with haste.

As Samal makes eye contact with Gadno the Illusionist, with a smile on his face he begins to fade into the air — to disappear and become entirely invisible. Completely surprised, Samal stands with open mouth in awe of the power that such a conjurer was able to utilise. He waves his hands in front of him over the area where Gadno stood to try and believe what happened. Turning to his left he sees the confused warriors standing there vacantly, entranced and entirely unsure of their existence. Samal is lost for words.

Not really sure what to do, especially with the Kaidis leadership now worryingly expelled, it would seem things have completely turned upside-down. There is no king and no heir. As he steps outside with his cane, he sees Volar talking to a few from the Engineers Division. Perhaps he will bring some order to the chaos, Samal considers, approaching the Legionnaire. Stopping and listening, attempting to make sense of the conversation, the Kaidis Doctor is bemused about how recent events have unfolded.

Volar turns to look at the Doctor with a questioning expression. The shock is obvious to Volar, but he is not aware of Gadno or his sudden disappearance. He simply has one conclusion about the situation: the Kaidis are crippled and no strong leader is around to bring order. His belief is that someone has to take charge sooner rather than later.

'What do you think, Samal? Is it time to move on?'

The Doctor sighs and turns to look out across the desert, becoming hypnotised by the swirling sands. He has no answer and no question. There seems to be no point in continuing.

'Everything is out of our control,' he eventually says. 'We cannot make our own decisions. There are much larger things at stake. I just don't understand.'

Volar shakes his head and returns his attention to the engineers, resuming his mutinous conversation. Samal refers to what Gadno will choose to do in the future. He knows that by having first-hand experience with the Lightbearers, change — or fate — is not anyone's choice.

# To be continued...

# Part III: Appendix

# Around the Cosmos

Ramor, as the powerful sentient sun in the centre of her own planetary system, is not always interested in what her children — the Lightbearers — are doing. She has much greater goals, experimenting and cultivating the worlds she created.

Pri was her first experiment into the creation of species, and the birth of life. The extreme differences in hot and cold, north to south, and its very orbit, were all engineered by Ramor in this test of ability. While she is pleased with the results, even if the behaviour of the life that exists is a little objectionable, her priorities have moved on.

In mortal space itself, Ramor keeps the Piecestorm near. This swirling and dense cluster of rock, minerals and other matter is a belt that surrounds her, albeit at a distance. It is this material that becomes the building blocks for Ramor's experiments with the creation of worlds.

But Pri is not her only experiment. Also following a constant orbital path around her is another world. Named in Ethereal as Tagom, it is a vastly different world compared to Pri; highly volcanic, for instance. Because life is what Ramor finds the most fascinating, the population that exists there is more advanced and able than the Shaler and the Kaidis, even if their world is not as accommodating.

Through the creation of these grand playgrounds, the Lightbearers have plenty to keep them entertained. Also, the known populations are usually under threat from each other or outside influences, even if they are unaware.

But what is Ramor's ultimate reasoning? How does one question the ability of a creator of worlds? The purpose to it all remains unknown.

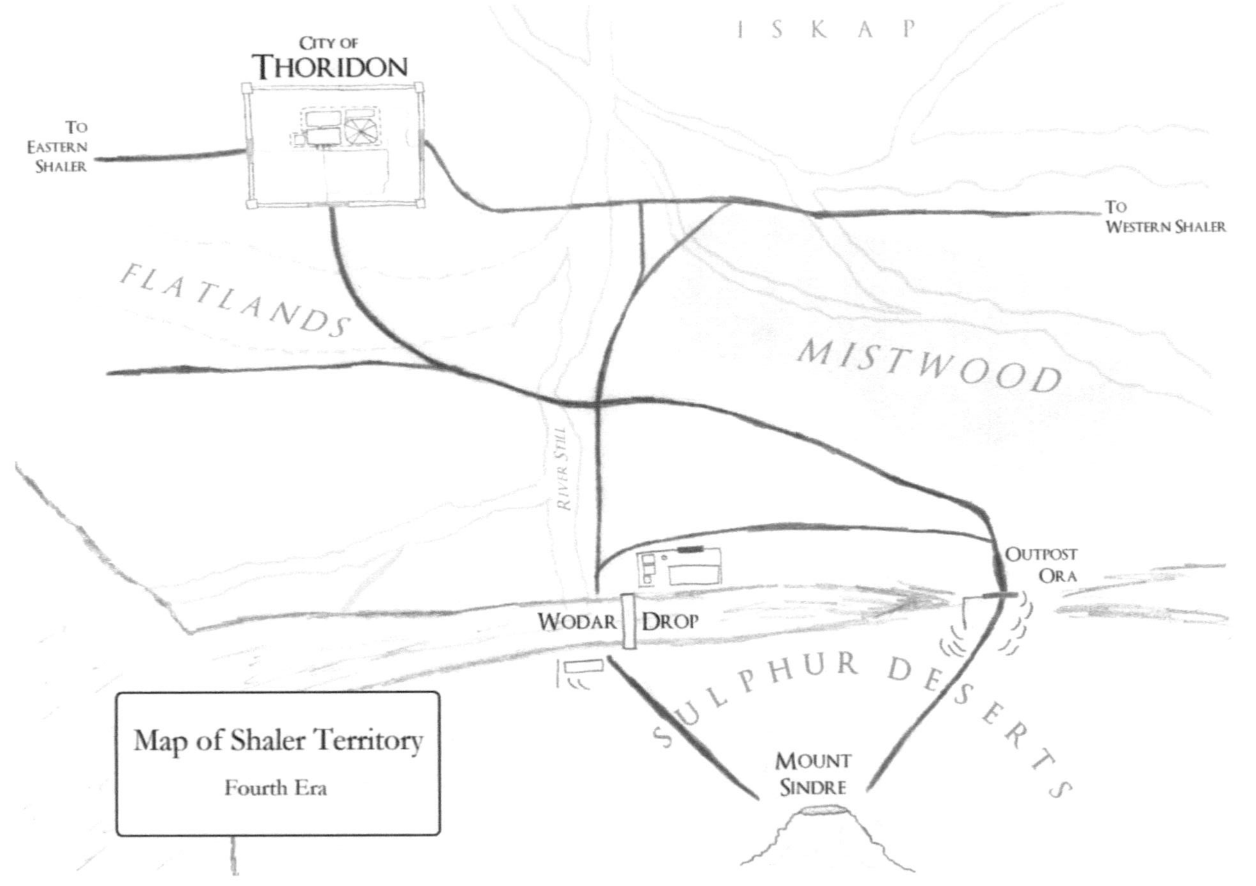
ISKAP
CITY OF THORIDON
TO EASTERN SHALER
TO WESTERN SHALER
FLATLANDS
MISTWOOD
RIVER STILL
OUTPOST ORA
WODAR DROP
SULPHUR DESERTS
MOUNT SINDRE
Map of Shaler Territory
Fourth Era

# About the Author

Derived from a small family of avid readers and electronic excellence, Bart has always had a passion for the written and spoken word. His inspiration for English came to light in his mid-teens in Scotland.

Always having a passion for music, he learnt to play the drums. Quickly becoming interested in rock music, Bart's tastes became more diverse over the years, enjoying the complexity and finesse found in underground doom and death metal.

Taking an acute interest in minor religions, this mixture of culture and fascination with ideals portrayed in music and religion planted the seeds that formed the concepts behind Changeable Worlds.

When he's not dreaming about fictional worlds, Bart can be found writing computer software for a variety of platforms and now lives in the south of England.